P9-CCV-907

"This brilliant historical fiction brings to life the events that preceded Culloden and gives the audience a taste of how the Highlanders felt going into the war."
—*Midwest Book Review*

"[*Sword of the White Rose*] will surely please fans of the genre . . . It's impossible not to compare this series to Diana Gabaldon's darker Scottish epic, with its similar setting and conflicts, and fans of one will definitely enjoy the other."
—*Romantic Times Bookclub*

PRAISE FOR J. ARDIAN LEE'S PREVIOUS NOVELS

SWORD OF KING JAMES

"Cross Sharon Kay Penman with Mercedes Lackey and Judith Tarr and readers will understand that *Sword of King James* is historical romantic fantasy at its very best. J. Ardian Lee has created something wondrous with this haunting novel."
—*Midwest Book Review*

"Fans of Diana Gabaldon's Outlander series will enjoy this story of adventure and romance in a magical time and place . . . Re-creates a colorful chapter in Scottish history, bringing to life a period of fierce warriors and fairie magic."
—*Library Journal*

"[A] welcome entry in the author's time-travel series."
—*Publishers Weekly*

"An intelligently written time-travel romance novel."
—*Chronicle*

continued . . .

OUTLAW SWORD

SON OF THE SWORD

"[An] earnest mix of history and romance . . . those interested in things Scottish will appreciate the background,
while most readers will empathize with the likable Dylan."
—*Publishers Weekly*

"From Highland Games to highland hills, Lee takes us on
an entertaining—and ultimately Scottish—journey as witnesses to the making of a legend."
—Jennifer Roberson, national
bestselling author of *Lady of the Glen*

"A good historical fantasy." —*Science Fiction Chronicle*

"A veritable *Braveheart* buffet for the Scottish fan. The
plot pace is energetic and the characters likable. The details of everyday life are excellent." —*Kliatt*

"A stand-out novel." —*The Historical Novels Review*

SWORD
OF THE
WHITE ROSE

J. ARDIAN LEE

ACE BOOKS, NEW YORK

THE BERKLEY PUBLISHING GROUP
Published by the Penguin Group
Penguin Group (USA) Inc.
375 Hudson Street, New York, New York 10014, USA
Penguin Group (Canada), 10 Alcorn Avenue, Toronto, Ontario M4V 3B2, Canada
(a division of Pearson Penguin Canada Inc.)
Penguin Books Ltd., 80 Strand, London WC2R 0RL, England
Penguin Group Ireland, 25 St. Stephen's Green, Dublin 2, Ireland (a division of Penguin Books Ltd.)
Penguin Group (Australia), 250 Camberwell Road, Camberwell, Victoria 3124, Australia
(a division of Pearson Australia Group Pty. Ltd.)
Penguin Books India Pvt. Ltd., 11 Community Centre, Panchsheel Park, New Delhi—110 017, India
Penguin Group (NZ), Cnr. Airborne and Rosedale Roads, Albany, Auckland 1310, New Zealand
(a division of Pearson New Zealand Ltd.)
Penguin Books (South Africa) (Pty.) Ltd., 24 Sturdee Avenue, Rosebank, Johannesburg 2196,
South Africa

Penguin Books Ltd., Registered Offices: 80 Strand, London WC2R 0RL, England

This is a work of fiction. Names, characters, places, and incidents either are the product of the author's imagination or are used fictitiously, and any resemblance to actual persons, living or dead, business establishments, events, or locales is entirely coincidental.

SWORD OF THE WHITE ROSE

An Ace Book / published by arrangement with the author

PRINTING HISTORY
Ace trade paperback edition / July 2004
Ace mass market edition / May 2005

Copyright © 2004 by Julianne Lee.
Cover art by Tristen Ellwell.
Cover design by Lesley Worrell.

ISBN: 0-441-01223-X

ACE
Ace Books are published by The Berkley Publishing Group,
a division of Penguin Group (USA) Inc.,
375 Hudson Street, New York, New York 10014.
ACE and the "A" design are trademarks belonging to Penguin Group (USA) Inc.

PRINTED IN THE UNITED STATES OF AMERICA

10 9 8 7 6 5 4 3 2 1

*In memory of
Alan Ross Bedford, Jr.,
my little brother
who has finally found peace*

ACKNOWLEDGMENTS

The following have my heartfelt gratitude for their generous help: my agent, Russell Galen; swordmaster F. Braun McAsh; Ron Cameron of Na Caraidean, Tucson, Arizona; drop-spinners Jean Krevor and Harriet Culver; Ernie O'Dell and The Green River Writers of Louisville, Kentucky; Gaelic language instructor John Ross; the kind and generous ladies at the Nairn Museum, Nairn, Scotland; native guides Gail Montrose and Duncan Mac-Farlane of Glenfinnan, Scotland; Teri McLaren; Trisha Mundy; Diana Diaz; Betsy Vera; Lynn Calvin; Rev. HyeonSik Hong; and always, Ginjer Buchanan.

AUTHOR'S NOTE

Though this story is based on historical fact, the fictional characters are not actual people, and any resemblance to historical or contemporary persons is coincidental. Glen Ciorram and its people are imaginary, and no fictional character is meant to represent a historical member of Clan Matheson.

However, the nonfiction characters and events are as true as possible to what is known about them.

On spelling: In the early eighteenth century, spelling was a dodgy affair any way one looks at it. Standardized spelling in English didn't come along for another century at least, and for Gaelic it didn't happen until the latter part of the twentieth century. The spellings for Gaelic words in this book are from *MacLennan's Dictonary,* which tends to the archaic and therefore lends itself to the period. All other words are either English or dialect words used by English-speaking Scots, and for the sake of internal consistency are spelled according to American usage.

E-mail J. Ardian Lee at *ardian@sff.net,* or visit *http://www. sff.net/people/ardian/.*

CHAPTER 1

The laird stood naked before the mirror and considered his form.
No paunch. Nae bad, particularly as old as he was feeling today.

The sun rose, gold and pink among the morning clouds, over
the steep granite to the southeast of Glen Ciorram. Slowly, a
benevolent patch of warmth crept through the castle gatehouse
and over the bare ground of the bailey at Tigh a' Mhadaidh
Bhàin. Pleasant weather had arrived, the Summer King victori-
ous over the Beira, the Winter Hag. The heady smell of thawed
earth and new growth made Ciaran smile as he drew deep breaths
of crisp air. He and his father proceeded with their warm-up before the morning workout.

Beltane had come and gone the week before, festive and hopeful in its celebration of new life, and now yellow and white May
flowers were bursting out all over the Scottish Highlands. Even
happier than the fine weather, news from the Continent of late
was of a fresh chance to rid Scotland of the English blight of redcoat soldiers. The son of exiled King James sought French support for an uprising, and there was every reason to believe he
would get it. Ciaran's heart soared at the thought as he stretched

muscles that were yet winter-stiff, and he could fairly feel the blood in his veins.

Ready now for the formal exercise, they each bowed, then settled into the horse stance, feet at shoulder width, knees slightly bent, body relaxed. They began, slow and easy, in perfect synchronization.

"Do you think Prince Charles will come, then?" Ciaran couldn't help the smile on his face and the excitement in his voice, though his father was ever subdued on the subject of the Stuarts.

"Aye, he'll come." His voice was the low, rough rumble of age. "You can bet your bottom dollar on that." Having been born in America, Da had a way of speaking that was a bit odd, whether in Gaelic or English. Sometimes it drew criticism from clansmen, but Ciaran paid it no mind. He'd always figured the strangeness was part of what made Da a great man. Often he repeated his father's alien figures of speech, though he'd never had the slightest notion why one should be invited to wager German money, or how a cow or even a "moley" might become holy. Whatever a "moley" was.

However odd his colonialisms might sound in Gaelic, though, Da did have a way of being dead right about things political. If he said Prince Teàrlach was coming, it was a certainty one could bet even one's last farthing on it, and so Ciaran was absolutely certain the prince was coming. The day was joyous, and his heart lifted in spite of Da's misgivings.

Ciaran's father groaned, and his eyes narrowed as his left leg took extra weight in a low stance. He muttered to himself in English, "Don't be a candy-ass, Matheson." In addition to his Colonial accent, his diction was much the worse for several missing teeth. Though Dylan Dubh retained more teeth than most men at the rare, advanced age of sixty-two, he was missing nearly half and spoke with a bit of sibilance. In addition, he had an odd habit of sucking on the single remaining tooth on the left side, a canine that seemed long and narrow in its isolation.

Ciaran looked over as he followed his father's lead in the form. It was tai chi today, as it had been for months—a "yin" form that would not be too much strain on the laird's aging body. Every day of Ciaran's life, his father had risen early of a morning to train his body for fighting, and over the years there had been few concessions to his age. He no longer kicked above his waist, and it had been more than a decade since he'd made a leap of any kind. But he'd seemed fit and strong until only a year or two ago and had always seemed extraordinarily young for his age. Many still called him Dylan Dubh—Black Dylan—though his hair had not been black for years, and his prowess with a sword was still fabled, though he hadn't touched one in a very long time.

The two men moved together with harmony possible only after years of practice. *Step, block, hold the ball, push, step back, push.* It was relaxing but not particularly challenging, and so Ciaran would perform the more strenuous training of his day later. For now, he enjoyed his father's company.

Recent years had brought the laird sensitivity to cold, so beneath his kilt and his sark he wore the odd garment of costly cotton he called "longjohns." Many years before, he'd taught his wife to make them, declaring they were "a sight warmer and more comfortable than those damned, itchy trews." God knew why, but the laird had insisted the longjohns be dyed red; they were now faded to salmon pink. Ciaran heard tell they had a trapdoor in the seat, held up by buttons, but he'd never actually seen it.

Once again in a low stance, Da refrained from tossing back the hair that dropped into his eyes. His was a bit shorter than most men hereabouts, and so he was able to perform exercises without covering his face entirely with loose hair. Ciaran preferred his own hair long, but had long ago discovered the value of tying it back as the English soldiers did. As much as he hated anything English, the physical discipline Da had taught him was all the more difficult if his hair was forever sticking to the sweat of his face. Given a choice between cutting it short and tying it back, he tied it.

"So we're to join the prince when he lands, and rise against the usurper?" *Crane, step back, push....*

Da frowned. He took a glance over to the side, which was his habit when thinking. Then he said, "No."

Ciaran groaned at his father's bullheadedness. He quit the form and stood straight. "And when King James comes to take his rightful place, where will we be then?"

Da also paused in the form, struggling some for breath, but retained his stance, weight on his right foot to the rear and hands ready to push again. Without looking over at his son, he said with strained patience, "Ciaran Dubhach, I've said it before, we must stay neutral."

"We cannae. We're either for James or for George. Neutrality would do naught but put us on the bad side of both."

Da closed his eyes for a moment, then whispered to nobody as if in prayer, "Yes, I know he's right." This was also his habit. Some said it was the wee folk he addressed, but others said it truly was prayer. Ciaran held the opinion it must be God with whom the laird had such intimate and informal conversations. Da resumed his exercise and said between heavy breaths, "We can't follow Bonnie Prince Charlie. We're going to sit tight until this is over, then we're going to ride out the aftermath and hope they don't wipe us out."

"Father . . ." Ciaran's heart was sore to see his father shrink from the cause. "Da, we're nae cowards."

Now the laird gave up his stance and heaved himself up to stand straight. He looked his son in the eye, and said with a voice that was papery with age but held a noble conviction that made Ciaran ashamed of himself, "No, we are not cowards. *Never* cowards. I fought in two risings against the English. I did my level best to keep this clan safe from the depredations of English opportunists, Protestant bigots, and red-coated murderers. I fought on behalf of what I knew even then was a lost cause." Anger rose, and his voice tensed. His Colonial accent thickened as well. "I done paid my dues to the Jacobites, boy, and now I decline to sacrifice my sons to a king I know for a dead certainty will never again set foot on Scottish soil. We will not . . ."

With a groan, the laird sank to his knees.

"Da!" Ciaran dove and caught him before he could collapse entirely to the ground. He was so thin! It was almost nothing to hold him up anymore.

For a moment, Da knelt and gasped. His gnarled hand clutched Ciaran's shoulder. "O God," he whispered in English, "not now. Please, not yet. One more year. Please, God, one more year."

Gradually the pain faded enough for him to stand again. He gripped his son's arm as he struggled for air.

"Are ye well now, Da?"

Ciaran's father shook his head no, and continued to lean on the arm. "Help me inside."

Three black-and-white collies scattered from the hearth as Ciaran took his father into the Great Hall and eased him into the massive armchair by the hearth. It was a worn, old chair, but the wood was solid, and it had been the laird's seat as far back as anyone could remember.

By the time Da settled in front of the fire, his color had returned. Ciaran's sister, Sìle, hurried to see what was the matter, and the laird managed a smile for his favorite child. There were six sons and daughters still living—eight if one included Mother Sarah's sons from her first husband—but Sìle was Ciaran's only full sibling, and the only one who showed the least resemblance to their mother. The laird doted on her for that resemblance. It was well known that after nearly thirty years, he still pined for his murdered first wife, Caitrionagh. He had hung her wedding ring on the same silver chain around his neck on which hung his crucifix, and had not been without them a day since her death.

Sìle knelt by her father's knee to take his hands in hers. "Da, have ye had another episode?" She gazed up at him, searching his eyes for the truth he might or might not speak.

Ciaran murmured to a member of the kitchen staff to fetch the laird a quaiche of ale, and the servant hurried to comply.

"I'm fine. I just overdid it, I think." He touched his fingertips to some of the curls framing her face, then laid a crooked, trembling finger aside a purple swelling of her lower lip. Anger brightened his eyes, and he looked over at Ciaran. His son read the glance easily. *Do something about Aodán,* it said.

Ciaran had known a confrontation with his brother-in-law was coming, and that as his father's firstborn son it was his job to protect his younger sister. He gave a barely perceptible nod.

But suddenly the laird paled to a greenish color and his eyelids drooped with extreme pain. He leaned forward in his chair, gasping and whispering in English again, "O God . . . O God . . ." Sweat popped out on his forehead and he struggled for breath again.

The kitchen maid came with the ale, but the laird waved it away. "Whiskey. Bring whiskey. Fill the cup."

A full quaiche of whiskey was brought, and Dylan Dubh took a long draught from it. When he could breathe again, he took another. His lips pressed together and his eyes glazed, he sat hunched over and breathed as deeply as he could. It was several minutes before he turned to Ciaran and spoke again though he didn't seem to see his son.

"Take me to my bed. And send for Robbie."

Ciaran's stomach flopped over. He wanted to shake his head

and refuse, denying his father's condition, but he obeyed and bent to pick up Da from the laird's chair and carry him to the top of the West Tower. In a voice almost too weak to hear, his father begged to not be bled. Ciaran nodded and promised, knowing well Da's morbid fear of physicians. Halfway up the stairs, his father fell unconscious, head dropped back and his mouth open.

Servants hurried to ready the laird's bed. Ciaran laid him in it, then stood back. The chambermaid relieved Da of his outer clothing, then tucked him in under the heavy linen sheet and bearskin coverlet.

A gillie came to the door. *"Och,"* he said, wide-eyed at the sight of the collapsed laird. The roses of his young cheeks diminished, and his mouth worked though there were no words. His eyes glistened.

Ciaran turned to him, irritated at the gawking. "Summon Lady Matheson."

The boy obeyed immediately, at a run.

More servants came for a glimpse, then hurried on their way. It seemed everyone understood the thing Ciaran wished to deny: that, barring a miracle, this would be the laird's deathbed. Ciaran took a seat at a table where his father kept quills and paper, and began a letter to his youngest brother, fifteen-year-old Robert Dilean, who was at university in Glasgow.

Presently Mother Sarah came, her skirts in her fists and her face pale with terror. A smear of dark earth on her chin betrayed she'd been in the garden with her herbs and flowers, and against it her skin had the pallor of death. At the sight of her unconscious husband half buried in the bed, she murmured a plea to the Virgin Mary and hurried to his side. The chambermaid brought a short stool from the hearth for her to sit by the bed.

Sarah took Da's hand and patted it, urging him to awaken. His eyelids fluttered, then opened. An immense sigh escaped her, and a trembling smile lit her tear-filled eyes. Even through his pain he conjured a smile for her, and lifted her hand to his lips to kiss it. "Robbie," he said. "Summon Robbie."

"Aye, Da," Ciaran assured him. "He'll be here."

Mother Sarah whispered, "Ye must hang on, my love. Stay with us for his sake." She cut a glance at Ciaran. At top speed, for a messenger to return with Robbie from Glasgow would take more than a week.

* * *

Fort William was by far the most repulsive, ungodly place Leah Hadley had ever seen. But even so, she hated to leave it, for she knew where she was going must be far worse. Her carriage rocked and jolted abominably along the road that led even farther into the wilderness, surrounded by mountains that rose all about—steep, desolate, forbidding, and unforgiving. *Brown,* for pity's sake! She longed for the lush, rolling countryside of England. Even more, she longed for the polite society of her English friends. This place was more remote from civilization than she'd thought was even possible within the kingdom. Far from belonging to Britain, it was plain to her Scotland was the Devil's own garden, made entirely of stone and peopled by strange creatures with no more sense than to walk around barefoot everywhere.

Her father rode behind the carriage with his dragoons, oblivious to her as always. With this relocation of troops, Captain Roger Hadley had too much else on his mind to be concerned with her welfare, not that her comfort was ever topmost in his consideration. She could hear him ordering his men to and fro, paying not the least attention to her suffering. The abandonment choked her with grief. She leaned her head against the frame of the carriage window and gazed dully at the evil landscape.

Oh, how she wished her mother were here! Mother had always managed to put a good light on things and jollied her out of any bad mood. Mother had been the strength of their small family. Oh, to God that she had lived!

But now, jouncing along this forsaken Scottish road leading to nowhere, attended by nobody but the disagreeable—and barefoot—Scottish maid hired in Glasgow, Leah missed her father as well as her mother. She was as good as orphaned, it seemed. Worse, she was an invisible orphan, for she was surrounded by Father's raw, untrained, uncouth soldiers who scratched their private parts, picked their noses, and stank sharply of last week's camp followers. None of the dozens of uneducated and otherwise unemployable red-coated men would dare talk to their captain's unmarried only daughter. Not even her father's lieutenants, who might have been interesting were they not so cowardly in the face of their captain's ire. Regardless of what Ciorram might be like, she was certain to be bored to tears there and lonely unto death.

She rode in silence, trapped in the musty and filthy carriage, struggling to hold down the nausea that rose as a result of the bouncing on this rough and primitive road. Her eyes closed against it.

A rush of hoofbeats from the rear caught her attention. There was a shout of alarm and warning from the lieutenant riding behind, and she poked her head out the window to see. A rider, low in his saddle and urging his horse onward, rushed past in a dark blur. She looked after to find a boy in his teens, pursued by a soldier not yet up to speed. For a moment it seemed as if the boy might outdistance his pursuer, but he was quickly overtaken, his reins seized, and brought to a halt just ahead of the carriage.

It rumbled onward, and as it drew near, Leah took a good look at the boy. He was attempting to explain himself, more than annoyed at having been stopped. He spoke quickly, with an edge of desperation to his voice he tried to disguise with a still, proud posture. He surely knew he was in trouble. Jacobite sentiment here in the North being what it was, hardly anyone went anywhere without permission from the army. Anyone hurrying toward or away from a soldier was certainly suspect and subject to questioning. The boy should have known better than to race past a column of dragoons like that, as if his mission were so important as to supersede the need of His Majesty's representatives to control traffic. This boy stood a good chance of arrest if he couldn't give good cause for being in such a suspicious hurry.

As the carriage passed, Leah heard him say in a thick Highland brogue, "I may be too late." Tears stood in his eyes, but it was plain he was struggling to not let them fall to his cheeks. Dark brown hair slipped into his face, and he shook it away. Even as her heart went to him for his plight—for it was apparent the poor boy was in some straits—it struck her he looked the soldier directly in the face as he spoke. His eyes were the deep brown of a doe's and his cheeks glowed pink with health and exertion, not the splotchy red of shame or anger.

His effrontery was astonishing. After all, his dress was that of the wild Highlander. The boy's rank couldn't possibly have warranted such composure in the face of arrest. He wore the skirtlike garment they called a "kilt," and the checkered material was further draped around his plain woolen coat. Somewhat like a Roman toga, she thought. His head was bare, and his long, windblown hair fell about his face in thick, wavy locks. Bare knees over stockings of more checkered wool further demonstrated his lack of breeding and taste, though it was hardly at question.

The soldier continued to detain him as Leah's carriage moved onward and she sat back once more in her seat.

Several minutes later, however, the rider approached again, alone this time, hurrying along on his way. A tiny smile on her face, Leah watched the boy race past and on up the road, then sat back again and returned to dwelling on her own desperate plight.

Oh, how she longed to return to civilization! These Highlanders were the worst sort of rabble. The ones she'd encountered between Glasgow and Fort William were a surly crowd, dirty and ragged. Like the boy, most had an awful habit of behaving above their station, and they all were known for quick, evil tempers coupled with a propensity for settling disagreements at knifepoint. Her father frequently declared them all to be liars and thieves, and she was surprised the dragoon had let that one go. Racing away like that, the boy surely must have stolen something. The horse, perhaps. Surely no Highlander would own a horse so fine as that one. Not legitimately, in any case. He must have stolen it.

She would have to ask her father about the incident when she saw him next. That dragoon would need to explain why he'd let the boy go. Perhaps Father would be pleased she'd taken note, and then finally take notice of her.

During the next days, Ciaran came and went often from his father's bedchamber. There were times the laird was entirely lucid. The pain, which he'd held at bay for many years, overtook him and receded like the tide. Copious amounts of whiskey and willow bark tea seemed to dull it, and during those times when it abated, he was able to speak to those who attended him. Mother Sarah never left his side except to eat and tend to her own necessities. She slept sitting, her head on the mattress beside her husband. The twins Kirstie and Mary hovered over their father almost as relentlessly, and Sìle came often with her small daughters. The women fed him soup and mulled wine, and if he vomited it, they cleaned him up and fed him again. Each day, all day, they kept a lookout for Robbie.

Ciaran's other half brother, Calum, who was older than the teenage twins by nearly eight years but younger than Sìle by three, came and went fretfully. On the surface, he appeared unconcerned about his father's condition, joking and shrugging it off as if it were nothing, but Ciaran knew it was his way and nothing more. Calum had always had a smiling, jocular demeanor, and their father's illness did nothing to alter the facade.

If anything, Calum became more filled with nervous energy. He often paced in the alcove outside Da's bedchamber, then hurried away to visit in the village for a time, usually to take comfort with Deirdre MacGregor, the daughter of the merchant Seumas Glas. Tiring of that, Calum would return to look in on Da for a moment. But just for a moment. Agitated and irritated by long faces and solemn spirits, he would again flee to the village, or to the peat bog, or someplace else.

Nearly a week after the collapse, Da rallied and was able to sit up in bed. Hope for recovery fluttered in the hearts of his family. At the news, folks came from the glen to pay respects, and the laird received his kinsmen in small groups so as not to tire him.

Donnchadh Matheson the blacksmith; Keith Rómach Campbell, who had fought with Da in the '19; Ailis Hewitt, who was mother to Aodán Hewitt and sister to Donnchadh; and Seumas Glas MacGregor, with his two sons Alasdair and Seumas Og, were among the first to come and the longest to stay. The well-wishers seemed relieved to see Dylan Dubh, and there was warmth in their voices that belied the fear in their eyes. It was plain everyone in the village knew this would be their last chance to see the laird alive.

Some MacKenzie cousins arrived, shocked to find the laird of Ciorram so ill. They'd come to trade with Seumas Glas and stayed to visit. The elderly Alasdair Og had brought his sons: William, who was Ciaran's age, and Alasdair Crùbach, who was a year younger and nicknamed for his clubfoot. It was good to see these MacKenzies, first cousins of his mother's who had once lived in Killilan only a day's ride away, for since their return to the MacKenzie lands to the east he'd visited with them not more than twice in ten years.

The opportunity to catch up on family news and low gossip was welcome relief from the morbid waiting. They drank ale together by the hearth in the Great Hall, yellow firelight flickering over them, warming and drawing them in a familial embrace as the night wore on. Ciaran could barely remember his mother, and he loved his cousins as a part of her he would otherwise never have known.

Two days later the laird declined again. He began inquiring again after Robbie, disappointed each time he was told the boy was on his way but had not yet arrived.

More days passed, and still the laird clung to life. The entire glen waited quietly, breathlessly, for news. A dark expectation settled on them, and especially on the Tigh. Ciaran tried to shake off the tension, having been taught by his father that tension, either physical or mental, left one vulnerable. But soon even he began to feel the irritation, like a hair shirt, always there and ever distracting, making inroads on his mind. He began to wish it were all over, and was appalled at himself for it.

Given his frame of mind, he couldn't help but burst forth with rage the morning Sìle came to breakfast with a freshly split lip and a black eye she couldn't quite hide by ducking her head. Ciaran looked up from his bowl of parritch, and the sight of his injured sister galvanized him. His better sense quite left him.

"I'll kill him!" Ciaran Matheson rose from the table in the Great Hall and set out to do so, tossing his spoon down on the table with a loud, wooden clatter.

"No! Ye cannac!" Sìle followed him.

"Where is he?!"

"Ciaran!" Reaching for his sleeve, she caught the plaid draped over his shoulder instead and it slipped.

"I can, and I will! Where is he?!" A shrug of his shoulder adjusted his plaid as a gillie carrying an armful of dried peats for the hearth held open the entrance door for him to pass. Ciaran bellowed to the castle at large, "Where's Aodán Hewitt?" Everyone in the bailey turned.

The boy's gaze flicked toward the open door of the stable across the way. There Ciaran saw his sister's worthless husband lounging on the chopping block where he'd moved it to lean against the door frame, chatting with a member of the castle guard.

"*Aodán!*"

Hewitt blanched at Ciaran's approach and climbed to his feet as the guardsman faded into the darkness of the stable. Chin up and challenging, he replied, "Aye." He was not much younger than Ciaran, but had an insolence about him that denied his years. Aodán was a boy in a man's body, and not a particularly bright one.

"I told you the last time ye hit my sister it would *be* the last, or I was likely to see ye dead!" Ciaran shouted as he strode across the wide dirt bailey. A raven picking at a bit of refuse was startled into flight. "Did you think I was only joking?" Too many times he'd found Sìle slinking around in the shadows of the castle, trying to hide the bruises and cut lips. Ciaran was fresh out of patience and in no mood to tolerate any more injury to his family.

"She's my wife. I cannae let her go undisciplined, particularly as spoiled as she is." He looked around the bailey for witnesses as Ciaran bore down on him at a brisk walk. Aodán was thinner than most, and his blue Matheson eyes were large in his long, narrow face. But thin though he was, Aodán was not weak, and he had the blinding speed of a whip. His dirk was kept sharp, and he wasn't afraid to use it. "And you ken well she's a stubborn woman. 'Tis my right—"

Ciaran's fist shot out to clout Aodán in the mouth the instant he was within reach. His brother-in-law went reeling, and Ciaran took a fight stance, his weight balanced and fists ready at his sides. "You forget, Hewitt, she's my sister. Even more important, she's the laird's daughter, and your rights are exercised at my pleasure and his, for as long as she and her children live in this castle she is under the protection of myself and my father. Your rights be damned, and if you think he will have aught else to say about it, you're daft and should be put down for a criminal lunatic in any case."

Hewitt glowered, and rage suffused his face. Muttering a few epithets as he recovered himself, he reached for the dirk at his belt. Ciaran took a step back, likewise pulling his *sgian dubh* from inside his sark. The small dirk had been a gift from his father—its blade from Toledo and its handle carved by the laird himself from the antler of the first buck Ciaran had killed as a lad. He flexed his fingers, and the dirk settled into its accustomed place in his hand.

The two men squared off, and Aodán attempted a slash at his opponent. Ciaran dodged, then returned the attack, pressing for space and crowding Aodán into the stable doorway. "Good," said Ciaran, a cold grin on his face, "make me kill ye."

"Ciaran! Stop it!" There were tears in Sìle's voice now, but Ciaran ignored her. Aodán had gone too far this time and needed to be taught a lesson. Sìle stood to the side, one hand over her mouth and the other over her injured eye.

Aodán made another attack, to force Ciaran away from the door, but Ciaran was too quick and countered, so Aodán was forced farther into the musty darkness. Horses inside stamped and fidgeted at the disturbance. Dust rose and floated in the air. Aodán stumbled against a stool, but recovered himself without dropping his guard as the stool toppled. Rage seethed in Ciaran, and he was quite ready to make Aodán bleed for the assault on Sìle.

But Eóin's voice came from across the bailey. "Ciaran! You'll want to lay off fighting for a time. Mother says Himself is asking after you!"

All interest in killing fled in an instant, and both Ciaran and Aodán stood down. The edge in Eóin's voice clenched Ciaran's heart as he turned to see the wide eyes and pale face of his older stepbrother in the middle of the bailey.

Oh, no. Asking after him, not Robbie? Ciaran wasn't ready for this. No matter what he knew in his mind, his heart refused to believe. He took a step toward Eóin, then back toward the stable door to the West Tower, then back toward Eóin again. "*Och,*" he said softly. "Get Calum," he called to Eóin. "Is there word yet from Robbie?" Eóin shook his head. "*Och,*" Ciaran repeated, and took another uncertain step backward.

The *sgian dubh* went back into its scabbard. Ciaran's eyes narrowed as he hurried past Aodán into the stable. Under the wooden stairs that led to the tack room above, and into the short, stone passage to the West Tower, then up the spiral steps five flights. Behind him, Sìle called to her wee daughters, and they all followed.

The laird's chamber was at the top of the tower. His closest friend and *fear-còmhnaidh*, Robin Innis, stood outside the door in a vigil he'd kept for days without respite, sleeping wrapped in his plaid on a straw mattress in the alcove outside the door. Calum was with him, and they were speaking in low tones out of respect for the dying laird. Robin's faded eyes were set deep in a weatherworn face, and the fear in them was terrible. A chill skittered through Ciaran.

"Where are Kirstie and Mary?" he asked.

Robin nodded toward the door to indicate Ciaran's half sisters were already inside, with their father. There was movement in the stairwell, and Ciaran turned to see who else was coming. The three MacKenzies approached, wary of being in the way but at hand in case they might be needed. Ciaran addressed Robin again.

"Has there been nae news of Robbie?"

Robin shrugged but Calum said, "He'll be coming as quick as he can. He'll make it here before the messenger could, sure."

Ciaran had never been particularly close to Calum—he'd felt much closer kinship to Robbie—but now his heart softened. He understood Calum was protective of little Robbie, the baby of them all. He nodded. Even with the fine English road built for the benefit of His Majesty's minions—which would take him only as far as the Great Glen regardless—at top speed Robbie couldn't be expected to arrive before tomorrow.

As he passed into his father's bedchamber, Ciaran prayed they hadn't left it too late to send for their littlest brother.

The fire in the hearth was high, and the room close. But even with the lively wood fire on the hearth and the morning sun warming the dozens of glazed panes, the bed was well stacked with blankets. Kirstie and Mary sat on a trunk by the southern window, their eyes wide and their hands twined tightly in each other's.

Mother Sarah sat on a high-backed chair next to the head of the bed, gently holding one of her husband's hands, stroking and petting the gnarled and scarred knuckles as if to make certain he knew she was there. Though one tendril of hair dangled from her kerchief, she was otherwise properly dressed and held together. The strain of these past days showed in her eyes, in their redness and the black circles beneath them.

Ciaran stepped close to the bed and leaned down to take the other hand. Gently, for it was covered with splotchy purple bruises that lately seemed to appear for no reason. Someone brought a stool, and he sat. He looked into his father's pale, still face and feared it might be too late.

Dylan Robert Matheson of Ciorram was barely alive. His chest rose and fell so slowly it took a moment to be certain of it. For several seconds at a time it would stop, then start again. His tanned skin had turned papery gray beneath his silver hair and beard, and his already scant flesh now sagged on a bony frame. Since the night before, another bruise had blossomed at his temple. Ciaran's heart ached for the vital, healthy father he'd known in his childhood, and knew the frail old man would soon be gone.

Kirstie and Mary came to perch on the foot of the bed. Kirstie laid a hand on the bearskin over her father's feet. Sìle set her small, blonde daughters, aged four and five, near the bed and shushed them—unnecessarily, since the girls seemed to grasp the solemnity of the gathering and were silent as little rabbits. They gazed at their grandfather with wide eyes. Calum stood behind Sìle. Robin stayed near the door, his job to make himself available to the family, and the MacKenzies gathered behind him.

Eóin and Gregor Matheson, Mother Sarah's sons by her first husband, entered quietly and stood near Robin.

"Da," said Ciaran.

The laird's eyelids fluttered. There was an ugly, wet sound from low inside his chest. His eyelids fluttered again, and opened.

"Da, I'm here."

The dry lips parted. "Ciaran."

"Aye." The thin hand squeezed his, and Ciaran was alarmed at how terribly weak it was. His father's eyes found his, and there was a glimpse of the man inside the failing body.

The laird seemed to gather his strength, breathing more deeply for a moment. Then he said, "Son, remember all I told you." He sighed, then summoned his breath again. "Lead as you were taught." Ciaran's heart clenched, and he wished there were something he could give—anything—that would keep the lairdship, and life, for his father.

Another difficult breath, and Da continued. "Mind the *Sidhe*."

The *Sidhe?* Ciaran frowned. His father's affinity for the wee folk was well known, but nobody had ever taken it seriously. Mind the *Sidhe?* What could that mean? Nevertheless, he promised. "Aye, Da."

His father's eyes closed again as the struggle to breathe continued, and there was a pause between sentences so long as to make Ciaran wonder whether he'd fallen unconscious. But finally the eyes opened and found Ciaran again. Da said, "Above all, son, remember where your home is"—Ciaran's lips moved along with the rest, for he'd heard it many times before—"and remember who your people are."

"Aye, Da." Ciaran held his father's hand in both of his.

The eyes drooped closed again, and silence fell in the room. The family was still, waiting for him to speak again, but a minute passed. Then two. Several minutes went by, and it was apparent the laird had lost consciousness. Calum sagged against a bedpost, hugging himself, his chin pressed against one shoulder. Mother Sarah continued to stroke her husband's hand. The twins sniffled and wiped their eyes. Ciaran watched the erratic rising and falling of his father's chest, the struggle punctuated by long moments of stillness. Each breath seemed a victory.

Just when he began to wonder whether Da might hang on for another day, there was a long sigh. Seconds passed, but the next breath didn't come. The twins began to whimper. Mary laid both hands over her mouth and began rocking back and forth. Kirstie whispered over and over, begging him to take another breath, "Please, Da, please, Da, please, Da . . ."

But the seconds became minutes. Two minutes, then three. Da was gone.

Sharp terror filled Ciaran, and he struggled to appear calm. The twins began to weep pitiably, causing Sìle's daughters to join them in crying. Sìle knelt by the bed and pressed her face against the coverlet to sob, her hand resting on her father's knee. Calum hugged himself harder and hunched his shoulders tight as tears came to his eyes. Mother Sarah held the hand to her cheek and wept softly. Ciaran stood, and refused to cry. He gazed at his father's body, holding at bay the feeling of being a little boy again, needing his da. For a moment he remembered the childhood horror of realizing his mother was dead, and tears tried to come. He fought them back, drawing deep breaths and clenching his fists over and over.

He was the laird now, and he was required to appear much stronger than he felt.

Then a new voice joined the grieving family, a heartbroken sobbing. Ciaran looked around, but Robin's tears were silent and Calum's were still contained. Besides, this unfamiliar voice was female. A young girl, perhaps, or a small woman. And, even more strange, it was coming from . . .

Ciaran looked up. There, sitting at the corner of the curtain rail at the foot of the bed, was a tiny faerie, about the size of Sìle's oldest daughter. Her dress shimmered white, and her white wings drooped like petals from a dead rose. Pointed ears poked through her short, white hair, and her blue eyes were rimmed with red. She hugged herself and rocked back and forth in her grief. The tip of her nose was bright red with weeping.

He'd seen this creature before—in a dream, he'd thought. It had been years since the dream had even come to mind, but now the memories came clear. He remembered this faerie.

"Sinann?"

CHAPTER 2

The sark was silk, and lace at the front, buttoned with ivory except for one pearl at the short collar. The fabric fell over his hips, just covering his behind.

Ciaran couldn't let himself be seen staring at the faerie. He looked at his father's corpse instead, lying there, the stillness horrible. For one crazed moment, he wished to shake the body and beseech him to wake up. Then he took a deep breath and returned to himself.

To the others he said, "Come. Sìle, Kirstie, Mary, all of you. Let's allow Mother Sarah some privacy for the moment."

They obeyed, leaving Sarah to continue holding the hand of her departed husband, whispering to him of her love and her grief. Ciaran was the last one from the room, and as he closed the door behind him he thought of how devoted she'd been to his father. As far back as Ciaran could remember, even before they'd married, Sarah had looked upon Da as the center of her world. He knew her heart must be breaking now, and it added to his own responsibility.

A servant stood by to attend to the remains of Dylan Dubh. She would disrobe the body and clean it, then sew it into a linen winding sheet for burial. After laying it out in the Great Hall, they would keep watch tonight. The funeral would be in the morning. A crier was sent to spread the news to the clansmen scattered throughout Glen Ciorram.

The family went to the Great Hall, and Ciaran said to Robin, his voice low, "There were stones, I recall . . ."

His father's friend nodded. "Aye. They're kept in the stable, covered with a horse blanket. Already carved."

A shudder took Ciaran. There were many things he'd never understood about his father, and readying his own headstone—and his wife's—many years before his death was one of them. But he said only, *"Och."*

Robin, however, understood. "Perhaps it was the expense he wished to save his heir."

"Perhaps." But it wasn't a usual expense, for only the very rich required a monument to themselves. What Ciaran didn't understand was why the stones had been thought necessary to begin with.

He looked around for that faerie, but she had disappeared. Perhaps the vision had been nothing more than his imagination gone wild in his distress, but there was a horrible feeling in his gut that she could be real.

The children and grandchildren of Dylan Matheson settled among the chairs and benches near the hearth in the Great Hall, the women gently weeping and the men in stunned silence. A servant girl came to Ciaran and folded something into his hand. His heart clenched to look at it, but he opened his hand to see. The sturdy silver chain slipped and dangled on his fingers. In his palm, strung on the chain, were the small ebony crucifix bearing a silver corpus, and the gold wedding ring that had been his mother's.

Sìle, staring at the hearth, sighed. "Poor Robbie."

Ciaran hung the chain around his neck and nodded. Aye, poor Robbie. Away at school in Glasgow, he'd not returned quickly enough to see his father a last time. It was a common enough thing to happen, but they'd all hoped for him to have been there, for it had been a final request.

The day was long, and the night even longer. The entire clan attended the wake in the Great Hall of the Tigh, and the kitchen stepped lively to feed them all. A cow and several sheep were slaughtered and roasted, loaves of oat bread baked and eaten, gallons of ale were drunk, and an entire cask of *uisge beatha* from the laird's own illicit still was consumed.

The whiskey was the most appreciated by the folks of the village, especially the poorer farmers, for the product of Glen Ciorram was known for its smoothness and flavor and when sold to neighboring clans brought a fair quantity of cash to the glen. There was a secret for the making of it, which only the laird's sons knew, and neither of the other stills in Ciorram could match the quality of whiskey from the Tigh.

Though Ciaran was not one to drink to excess, tonight he held the pain at bay with enough ale and whiskey to put a spin on the room. Neither did he eat much. Talking to folks was an exercise in concentration, for his mind kept slipping sideways into morose memories of his childhood, and that caused him to take another drink. Very quickly his thoughts were awash in alcohol and the pain dim enough to control.

The ale, as always, went straight through him, and when his bladder demanded attention, he carefully made his way from the Great Hall, reaching out occasionally to touch a wall beside him to orient himself vertically. Up the stairs of the North Tower he went, and to the garderobe on the north curtain. He didn't bother to close the rickety door as he relieved himself, for it was dark and the facility was nothing more than a hole overlooking the vegetable garden. Humming a maudlin tune a fraction behind the pipes in the bailey and focused on the task at hand, he was quite taken by surprise by a hand at his inner thigh beneath his kilt just as he finished. Startled, he sprinkled the seat.

"Whoa." He shook himself off and dropped the front of his kilt, then sidled away and turned to find Deirdre MacGregor, daughter of Seumas Glas MacGregor. He leaned against the stone at the side of the narrow room. She stood and leaned into him. A large-boned lass, she was a handful when her interest was piqued.

"May I offer some comfort this evening, Ciaran?" She groped at the overlap at the front of his kilt, but he intercepted her hand. Tonight he was in no mood for the sort of distraction she offered.

"Thank you, no, Deirdre. I wouldnae wish to intrude on the rights of your betrothed."

There was a small, petulant sound in the back of her throat, and she stood close enough to make him wish she weren't promised to that blacksmith in Glasgow. Her reddish-blonde hair shone in the scant starlight through the doorway. Her hand slipped into his sark. "It wouldnae be anywhere you've nae intruded already."

"Before you were promised."

"I dinnae want the marriage." Her finger found his nipple, and his resolve wavered as goose bumps rose all over.

He placed his hand over hers to make it still. "I believe ye need it." This one would need a constant guard if her husband would not be cuckolded.

"I'd rather stay in Ciorram." She bent to kiss the hand over hers. What she meant was she'd rather marry him than the blacksmith. But the entire glen knew she was also banging Ciaran's brother, with no indication she would ever stop as long as she lived in Ciorram, and that made her a poor candidate for the next Lady Matheson. Indeed, it would have made her a poor wife for anyone in the glen. Ciaran was certain her true goal was to live at the Tigh, and never mind who she would carry on with once she arrived.

"Nevertheless, ye cannae."

She kissed his chin, then his mouth. Her lips were wide, full, and soft. The warm wetness brought to mind other places he knew her to be wet and soft. The whiskey all seemed to rush to his head, and the world spun faster. Her hips pressed against his, and for a moment he thought of how easy it would be to lift her skirts, turn her back to the wall, and nail her to it.

But then he reminded himself of his desire this woman not take a bairn of his to her marriage. He'd not touched her since the betrothal. If she wanted she could take Calum's bastard to Glasgow, but not his.

He retrieved his mouth from hers and said, "No. I've drunk far too much whiskey and dinnae believe I'm up to the task in any case."

A disappointed whimper came from her, and she reached between his legs to prove him a liar, but he intercepted her hand. "No, I said. Now, go."

"Ciaran—"

"No."

There was a long silence, then she let go of him and left the garderobe.

With a sigh, he slid down the wall to sit on his heels, leaning against the stones behind. His body was a collection of aches now, and he knew by morning there would be more of them.

The entire night Mother Sarah sat by the body of her husband, which lay on a trestle table, one hand on the winding sheet and her other filled with rosary beads. Pipes wailed in mournful voice, echoing from the castle towers and curtains in the bailey. All through the dark hours many poignant tunes were heard, and many genuine tears were shed by even the poorest and most distantly related clansmen, for Dilean Dubh nan Chlaidheimh had been well loved by his clan. An achievement for any clan leader, but all the greater for him, for though he was a Matheson he had not been born in Scotland. Dylan Robert Matheson may have been a Colonial from Virginia, but nobody doubted that in his heart he was as Scottish as anyone.

Sometime during the wee hours, Ciaran fell asleep from too much ale and whiskey and too little food.

He awoke with a start to a wail of grief, and found himself lying on the stone floor amid dried reeds and sleeping bodies. His head was like a balloon filled to bursting with pain, and his stomach lurched as he rose. Other clansmen were stirring, looking around in confusion. Ciaran was covered in a sour, alcohol-sodden sweat, now joined by a cold sweat of alarm. *No more pain. Please, no more.*

The hearth was bright with a wood fire in the hall lit with low and guttering candles. Ciaran drew his *sgian dubh* and looked around, his heart racing and his gut churning, and saw Mary near the trestle table that bore the body. A freshly lit candelabra was in her hand, but her attention was not on it. The candles tilted as her arm sagged, and one candle dropped to the floor. She continued to scream and weep, sobbing something about "Mother." Ciaran ran to her, vaulting benches, trestle tables, and stirring clansmen to see what was the matter.

When he saw, he had to turn away. Lying on the table, one arm laid across her husband's corpse, was the lifeless body of Mother Sarah.

Ciaran stomped on the candle burning on the floor lest it catch the dried reeds there, then paced, frantic to do something but knowing there was nothing to be done. There was nobody to hit. There was nothing to rail at. Men and women came to gather around the two bodies. Ciaran restored his dirk to its scabbard under his arm, left the Great Hall, and went across the bailey to the stable.

There he picked up a wooden pitchfork and swung it against

the wall with all his strength. The shock of the blow jolted his arm to his shoulder, but he swung again. The building shook, and bits of straw and motes of dust floated around in the morning sunlight streaming through the doorway. The horses snorted and stamped. Ciaran emitted a long, bestial roar of frustration and grief, then swung the pitchfork again, sending the animals into more frenzy of terror.

Furious, he went to the corner where the two marble head-stones were stored, and yanked the heavy wool horse blanket from them. His father's name carved on the top one sent him into paroxysms of anger. He swung again and broke one tine of the pitchfork on it. "Why?!" he bellowed. "WHY?!" He turned and uttered another inarticulate roar. His head throbbed with hang-over till he thought his eyes would bleed. He stood, panting, and wishing for something else to destroy. In a whisper, he repeated, "Why?"

"She loved him too much to live on after him." It was the voice of the white faerie.

Ciaran turned and shouted to the thin air, "You! You did this!"

"I did naught." She appeared, perched on the wooden stairs that led to the tack room, and hugged her knees as she gazed at him, her long, thin toes curled over the edge of the step. Her eyes were still red and teary, though her nose had recovered from her weeping. " 'Twas his time. And hers as well. Just as Cuchulain was joined in death by Emer."

"What could you know about it?"

"*Och*, first it's my doing, and now I must be ignorant of it. I ken more than you might imagine, laddie, and would that your Yahweh had blessed me with the sort of understanding yer father had. The coming year would be a great deal easier on us all, had he lived."

"What are you talking about, faerie?" His father's words *Mind the Sidhe* echoed in the back of his mind, and that was all that kept him listening.

" 'Tis the spring of 1745. According to yer da, the Stuart heir will be landing soon on the west coast, and shortly thereafter will gather the clans for another rising."

Ciaran blinked. It was no news that King James VIII was fo-menting rebellion from his sanctuary in Rome, and had been for some decades. Neither was it news that his son Charles was so-liciting assistance for such a rebellion from King Louis of

France. Every Jacobite in Europe knew that, and not a few Hanoverians. "You're suggesting my father helped plan an uprising that is expected to happen this year?"

The faerie shook her head. "Nae. I'm saying he *remembers* an uprising that will happen this year. He read about it in a history book when he was young."

"*Och.*" Ciaran was not in the mood for faerie tricks. "Dinnae try to fool me, faerie. I understand your kind, and willnae be taken in."

She frowned and flew to hover before him, arms crossed over her thin chest. "The name is Sinann, if ye please, and 'tis true what I'm saying. I'm trying to tell you something very important about your da, and listening might save you some grief. I spent many a year doubting him. I fought him and denied what he would tell me, until I found everything he said was true. You cannae make the same mistake I did, not if you wish to save your people and yourself.

"Laddie, what I'm telling ye is that yer father was born in the future. He came to this time when he was your age, and so kens what will happen because he read about it. In books. To him, the coming rising is a story of the past just as the ghost of the white hound is to us."

" 'Tis madness." Ciaran started for the door.

Sinann flew to block his way. " 'Tis truth."

"Let me by."

"I willnae, until ye've come to your senses." She pointed to the white gravestone with his father's name on it. "See that? What does it say on it?"

Ciaran replied without looking, "Dylan Robert Matheson."

"And what else?"

"Naught. It says nothing else."

"Look at it, will ye?"

His eyes narrowed, but he grudgingly turned to look at the white marble that threw hundreds of tiny refractions. Below his father's name was a thistle carved on the stone, and below that were the words "Hi, Mom." He frowned, puzzled. "What does it mean? I dinnae ken what those words mean. What language are they?"

" 'Tis English of the future. It means, 'Hello, Mother.' 'Tis a message to his mother, who he thought might come a-looking for his grave someday."

"His mother . . ." Now Ciaran was confused. His paternal grandparents were supposedly buried across the sea, in Virginia.

"You must understand what I'm saying is true, for you're the laird now and you must lead your people through the times ahead. And you must do it as your father wanted. The way he would have done, had he lived. You must abide the wishes of your father."

That touched Ciaran in his most tender spot. *Mind the Sidhe.* So he stood back from the faerie, hipshot and arms crossed, and frowned at her. "Very well, then. Tell me these things about my father he could never tell me himself."

Sinann settled atop the marble headstone and sat cross-legged. "Have a seat." She gestured to the dirt floor, and Ciaran sat with his back to a stall post. She began, "Yer father was—or will be—born in the year 1970. He was thirty years old, as you are now, when he laid hands on an enchanted sword. . . ."

"I expect I ken who did the enchanting."

The faerie's voice took on a defensive tone. "I wished to save our people from extinction by the English! And would you not have done the same, had ye the power?" Ciaran had no reply to that, and the faerie continued. "So the sword brought him to me, and that was in 1713. I must say that at first he was none too willing to help."

"Ye lic. My father loved us. Naught mattered to him but his people."

The faerie held out her palms, pleading for understanding. "Your father loved *you.* And your mother. 'Twas after you were born he came to truly love his life here. And as he did so, he came to love the clan and to appreciate his responsibility to them. 'Tis true what I'm telling you. He was from the future, and he used his knowledge of history to help his people. Why do you think he began putting folks to work spinning and weaving wool and linen, and making whiskey, instead of dividing the land between more and more people for them to farm? Why did he so encourage giving land over to sheep rather than cattle and oats? Why did he subsidize and otherwise encourage the production and trade of excess goods rather than let each man make only what he could use?"

Ciaran shrugged. " 'Tis a mystery. We're nae more prosperous for it, for a certainty, and old Seumas Glas will attest there are years when trade is nae good."

"But, you see, that is proof what I say is true. Your father understood what was to be, and what is *yet* to be. 'Tis nac finished, and you must carry on. You must help your people keep the land. You must help them even when the English take away your entitlement to rule."

"Nae." Ciaran decided he understood nothing of what she was saying, and didn't wish to understand. He rose from the floor. "Now you're talking true nonsense." He left the stable, headed for the Great Hall, but stopped dead and stood in the middle of the bailey when he realized he didn't want to return to that room, where death held sway.

The faerie hovered nearby, saying, "Aye. They can, and they will. They'll take away your jurisdiction and your responsibility to the people, and leave you with the land. Your sons and your grandsons will come to believe as the English do, that their worth is only in their personal wealth, and the people living on that land will cease to matter to them."

"Leave me be, faerie."

"My name is *Sinann!* And you must heed me! You must teach your children what your father would have them learn, but first *ye must not die at Culloden!*"

Ciaran frowned at her and opened his mouth to speak, but Eóin came from the Great Hall. The conversation was ended, and Ciaran went to tend to even more unpleasant business.

The funeral to bury Dylan Dubh and his wife was the largest procession the glen had seen in years. Even the tacksman Dùghlas Matheson was there, and his tenants from the Southeast. They must have walked all night to have arrived so quickly. Tenants gathered in the village near the drawbridge that crossed from castle Tigh a' Mhadaidh Bhàin, and crowded around the stone pedestal at the center of the village square.

In recent decades the village had grown to a group of cottages built closer together than most Highland farms, in which those who were not allotted enough land for a good living worked at home rather than in the fields. Some cottars worked the wool taken from the laird's flocks, some tended the still he kept hidden in the woods. Donnchadh Matheson made a fair living as the village blacksmith and had taken in an apprentice for lack of a son to teach, but unlike his predecessors, he did no farming. The land the previous blacksmith had once tilled was now a separate tenancy given over to Keith Rómach Campbell and his family. Old Seumas Glas kept a shop of sorts on the village square. It was little more than an ordinary peat house, but

Seumas Glas had built into it a booth window from which he sold his wares the same as if Ciorram were a real town. He and his sons traveled to bring goods from cities such as Inverness, Glasgow, and even Edinburgh, trading the wool, linen, and iron goods produced in Ciorram for things the village couldn't produce for itself.

Ciaran, as he walked along the track down the center of Ciorram, adjusted the weight of his father's corpse on his shoulder and gazed about at the changes Dylan Dubh had achieved during his life. It was a strange system, and not entirely pleasing to those without land, but the laird had been careful to encourage it slowly, allowing the people of Ciorram to adjust over the years, and in allocating tenancies he'd adhered to accepted rules of primogeniture.

The Ciorram holdings being not large compared to the great clans of Fraser, MacDonald, MacKenzie, Cameron, and others, there was but a single tacksman. Dùghlas, also a pallbearer for the laird's body, managed the outlying farms to the southeast. He collected rents, which were then sent on to the laird minus his own tribute. Unlike most tacksmen, he did not manage with a completely free hand but was charged by Dylan Dubh to not divide tenancies beyond a certain point. Over the past two decades, younger sons in the Southeast coming of age who did not inherit tenancies came to the glen to find work. If they would not work, they were encouraged to move on—to Glasgow, Inverness, or Edinburgh. Some went, some stayed, and the laird had always made it clear he esteemed the ones who stayed to work as the better men. For them, he'd found or created jobs. He'd kept the wheels of commerce carefully greased, and so far nobody had gone hungry, despite the sharp rise in population after the last uprising.

The Ciorram Mathesons who gathered in the village square to accompany their laird to his final resting place were grief-stricken to have lost such a strong leader. As Ciaran looked around at them, he realized some gave him sideways glances of doubt. It was clear they wondered whether he was capable of carrying on in his father's place, and the more he thought about it, the more he wondered the same thing himself.

Mathesons followed the pallbearers from the village and along the track that led up the glen to the church. Pipes raised keening music to the hills, and tardy farmers brought their families to join the procession along the way. The ancient Catholic church, Our

Lady of the Lake, stood at the dogleg that was the narrow entrance to the glen, across from the Queen Anne Garrison.

Though the walled garrison where His Majesty's red-coated minions were housed was within sight of the church, no trouble was expected today. The current complement of dragoons was small, consisting of naught but one independent company. Though Catholicism had been outlawed for a century, there would be no harassment from the soldiers, for there had been no priest in Glen Ciorram for nearly thirty years.

The Mathesons of this tiny glen were staunchly Catholic in their hearts, but in ceremony were reduced to irregular measures. Marriages were conducted by hand-fasting, baptisms performed by midwives, and funerals—even this one—were absent of church sanction. Private Catholic prayers were spoken in low voices, and the soldiers across the way pretended not to see folks crossing themselves. Religion was always expressed furtively, and Ciaran burned with anger at the shame of it.

Nestled against a wooded hill, the church was surrounded by graves, most of them unmarked. Before today, only one stone had ever been erected—that of Ciaran and Sìle's mother, Caitrionagh. Now there would be three, all of white marble. Today the clan buried Dylan Dubh next to his first wife, and his second wife was laid to rest at his other side. Once the prayers were said by Robin Innis, the graves filled in, and the stones placed, the clan dispersed quietly. Each returned home to overcome his or her own grief, for everyone in the glen had lost a beloved kinsman and a trusted leader.

On his way from the churchyard, after nearly everyone had gone, Ciaran paused at the top of the slope and gazed across at the garrison.

One red-coated sentry stood at the gate, watching. Revulsion gathered in Ciaran's gut at sight of the English uniform. At an early age he'd learned to despise the English. All his life he'd hidden from soldiers who had been free to search his home with muskets fixed with bayonets whenever the mood struck. He'd been taught to never challenge them or look them in the eye. He'd heard stories of torture, and had seen the flogging scars covering his father's back in great, white knots. Every day, along with his rosary, he prayed for the day there would be no more Englishmen in his country.

The sentry noticed him staring and shifted his weight. The

musket in his hands came to the ready, and he stared back at Ciaran just as steadily. Ciaran stood there for a moment to convey his lack of fear. *"Sasunnach neòghlan,"* he muttered, then spat on the ground for good measure before moving away with the others. Filthy Englishman.

For the rest of the day, Ciaran was at a loss for what to do with himself. A numbness set in, and concentration was impossible. Everything he saw was a reminder of his father, and that he would never see Da again. Servants were hard at work shifting belongings between bedchambers so the twins could move to Ciaran's from the room they had shared with Sìle's daughters. Personal items belonging to the laird and his wife would be taken from their bedchamber and given to those who would either use them or have them for keepsakes. Clothing would be distributed to the poorer clansmen. Most of Da's things would be kept by Ciaran, whose belongings would be moved from his own chamber to the laird's chamber on the top floor of the West Tower.

Ciaran wandered through the castle, restless. He had no wish to witness the packing of his father's belongings. At heart, he had no wish to take his father's place in anything. Da should still be there.

He went to the laird's office, on the ground floor of the North Tower. Though nothing here had been touched, and little would be, the room seemed appallingly empty. Ciaran had no sense of his ascension to the lairdship, though his father had prepared him carefully to assume the role. It simply wasn't real.

He stared at the bookcase across the room. No longer was there any living soul other than himself who knew of the passage behind the office bookcase that led to the track near the old broch. Though Da had never told him the purpose of this passage, it had been easy enough to guess, for the secret was never known to anyone but the laird of the Tigh and his designated successor. Anyone attempting to displace the rightful heir was vulnerable to sneak attack through the passage and easily removed by assassination. The purpose of the secrecy was to assure the succession.

He was familiar with the account books his father had kept for thirty years, leatherbound and heavy, filled with tightly written figures and dates. There were older ledgers predating the time of Dylan Dubh, but the books kept by all the lairds who had gone before took less space than the accounts of Ciaran's father. There were also the christening, marriage, and death records Da had rescued from the church in 1722. Such things were now recorded by the laird, ever since the arrest and transportation of Father Turnbull in 1719.

Ciaran sat at the heavy oak desk and looked around, thinking and remembering, sorting through what he would need to do in his new role.

All things considered, he'd been well prepared. He knew all there was to know about the making of the whiskey and its distribution, and knew the history and the current status of his father's unsuccessful attempts at legitimizing his still. Da had felt strongly the whiskey would be the future of the glen, and Ciaran had always figured he was right.

Glen Ciorram whiskey was as fine a drink as any French wine, and over the years the demand outside the glen had risen. He knew demand and revenue from the sale of the whiskey would rise even more if the Mathesons were given the freedom to produce their whiskey in the open and distribute it more widely, because of the secret that Ciaran shared with nobody but his true brothers.

Theirs was the only whiskey in the world that was aged more than a few weeks. Each cask was hidden for three years or more, then brought out to sell as if it were the current year's production. Only Ciaran, Calum, and Robbie knew the secret and where the casks were stored while they aged, for as much as Dylan Dubh had loved his daughters, he would never let the secret go to a son-in-law. Or even a respected stepson.

The office had been kept tidy and organized. The ledger books on their shelves were lined up like English soldiers, the box of quill pens sat next to the well-tended ink pot, and the candelabra on the desk was filled with brightly burning candles. Mounted on the wall behind the desk were the crossed blades of the silver-hilted dirk his father had called Brigid and the silver-hilted sword that had been a gift from King James I and VI to one of Ciaran's distant ancestors. Across from the desk hung the tapestry depicting his mother's paternal grandfather, Donnchadh Matheson, who was also a great-uncle on his father's side. The large, red-haired laird was shown riding through a forest on a unicorn, followed by a white faerie in flight. Now Ciaran recognized that faerie as the one in his father's bedchamber. The one he wished he'd only dreamed as a boy. Ciaran took a nervous glance around the room, wondering where that creature had gone off to.

A tap came on the heavy office door, and Robin's gray and brown head showed itself as he shoved the massive oak inward. "May I inquire after the mental state of the laird?"

For an instant, Ciaran's thought was to remind the old man that the laird was dead and therefore could have no mental state, but then he realized it was himself Robin meant. "Come in. Sit yourself down. Tell me what's on your mind."

Robin walked slowly and carefully across the room to the red-upholstered chair before the desk, then eased his unsteady frame onto it. Nobody was quite certain how old Robin was, but the best guess was he was nearly as old as Dylan Dubh. He also had fought in the last rising, and carried a scar on his chin from it. One of the many acts of heroism attributed to Ciaran's father, told often at *céilidhean,* was the saving of Robin's life in a river crossing during a *creach* of cattle from the MacDonells. Ciaran had heard it many times at clan gatherings of an evening. Robin, while guiding MacDonell cattle toward Matheson land, had slipped in the current of a swollen stream. He would have been carried away and drowned but for the quick thinking of Dylan Dubh, who had grabbed Robin's collar and held on. Both might have died, but Dylan never let go until Robin found his feet and made it to the opposite bank.

Robin settled into the chair and arranged his limbs to affect the least discomfort before speaking.

"I expect the *Sasunnaich* will give ye a day or so before they begin testing you."

Ciaran nodded. "They'll be after me, sure enough, nervous as they are."

"Will ye give them aught to be nervous about, Ciaran Dubh-ach?"

An excellent question. Much depended on choosing the right side in these times of unrest. A deep sigh escaped Ciaran, and his gaze wandered to one of the shelves behind him. A wedge-shaped piece of wood caught his eye, and he reached for it. Dim memory stirred. He recognized a toy he'd had as a small child, a bizarre carved bird of some sort, with wings stiff and straight, its tail divided in three parts. And there was no telling where the head might be distinguished from the body. It had no eyes and no feet. The soft wood bore tiny marks of his own baby teeth.

He gazed at it as he said, "They hate us, and the sentiment is returned. I cannae abide their presence. Their interference."

"They're more powerful than we are."

Ciaran looked hard at Robin. "They fight like women."

"You dinnae ken how they fight." Robin shifted in his seat with agitation, but he kept his voice even. "You've never been in battle. How can you claim knowledge of what it is? All you've heard is stories told at a *céilidh*."

Ciaran glowered silently.

Robin continued, "And what of your father's still? You ken full well what his hopes were for that. His failure to gain license for it caused him great anguish. You would do well to forget your hatred and do your best to continue the effort to accomplish your father's dream and legitimize the still."

Calum's voice came from the doorway. "The clan willnae have peace with the Protestant king." The two men looked up, startled.

He was right. It had long been plain the Ciorram clansmen, to a man, were eager to join the next Stuart to set foot on Scottish soil. Calum shrugged, his eyes hooded and his attitude matter-of-fact. "Peace is an impossibility."

"Your father never wanted war."

"Father was a great man," said Calum, nearly laughing as he spoke, "but he had a blindness concerning the English. He never kent the lengths they would go to destroy us."

"*Och,* but he did. He hated them more than the two of you combined could ever. He understood things even I dinnae. He fought them and yet did his best to make peace with them when he could."

Ciaran thought of what the faerie had said about Da coming from the future and knowing what would happen, but shook it from his head. It must be a faerie trick. Impossible. It couldn't be the truth.

Robin continued, "He fought because he understood the need at the time. But he never caused a conflict or fed their disdain of us. Once he became laird, he acted toward the English and their army as he would toward a sleeping dog. Leave them alone, and they willnae tear off yer leg."

It made sense. And it was certainly true over the years Da had tried to ease the anger of his people. In spite of his own hatred, Ciaran began to see the value of the argument.

But Calum's voice rose and took on an angry edge as he said,

"And it hasnae worked, has it? The still is as illegal as ever, and subject to confiscation and fines to the clan should the *Sasunnaich* find it. Which is how they like it, aye? With ourselves at their mercy, and that will never change so long as we remain Catholic." He came into the room and approached the desk.

"We leave that sleeping dog lie, and it will one day rise and turn on us. Then it will tear off all our legs and rip our throats and leave us bleeding into the sod! The English hate us as Catholics, and as Scots, and no appeasement will change their minds. So long as we are who we are, they will hate us and kill us, and they will continue killing us until we are all dead."

He leaned on the desk, speaking directly into Ciaran's face. "And let me warn ye, brother, should you go against the wishes of the clan, they will follow a laird who believes as they believe."

Alarm caused Ciaran's pulse to skip a beat. Had he a treasonous brother on his hands? In a tone of offended authority, he called that brother by the English of his name because Ciaran knew it was hated: "Malcolm . . ."

But Calum shoved off from the desk, turned, and left the room.

Ciaran sighed and muttered to himself in English as his father might have, "I'm too old for this shit."

Robin chuckled to himself.

It was just at the last orange light of sunset that hoofbeats came pounding across the drawbridge to the castle. Ciaran was in the bailey, giving orders to the sergeant of his guard, as the solitary rider rushed past the gatehouse, pulled up his mount, and leapt immediately from it. Ciaran's heart clenched when he saw who it was.

"Robbie!" He ran to intercept his little brother near the entry of the Great Hall. "Robbie, no!" He grabbed the lad's thin arm, and they both skidded to a halt in the dust.

Robbie's face was slack with surprise. Then he looked stricken as he realized Ciaran's meaning. At fifteen, he'd nearly achieved his full height, and his lanky, awkward frame held the promise of a strong man, but for a moment he seemed a child. The high color in his cheeks fled, and his adolescent voice was little more than a squeak. "Da?"

Ciaran said, "Yesterday."

Robbie took a deep breath and a brave set came to his jaw,

though his eyes swam with tears. "I came as fast as I could without killing the horse. I couldnae run him most of the way in any case, for the terrain."

"I understand, Rob. There's—"

"Where's Mother?" Robbie looked around. "I must see her. She'll need—"

Ciaran gripped the arm again. "No, Robbie. I'm sorry."

Now the lad was truly puzzled. He frowned, and stared at Ciaran for a moment. Then understanding crept in. His lip began to quiver. "Mother? No. Nae Mother."

"She passed on this morning. She joined Da in the churchyard today."

The brave face crumpled. The tears of a little boy suddenly orphaned spilled onto Robbie's cheeks. Ciaran laid his hand on his brother's shoulder. Robbie looked around, as if hoping for someone to come tell him it was a lie, but though Sìle and the twins did come from the Great Hall, they only hugged him and let him cry. Ciaran watched the girls take him inside to the hearth, where they would feed him and talk it all out until well into the night. A second wake for their parents.

Ciaran gestured to the stable gillie that he should see to the exhausted horse, then went to be with his family.

CHAPTER 3

His kilt was in the red, formal tartan, buckled at the right side with black leather and silver.

The road into the Highlands quit well short of the Hadleys' destination, and Leah's carriage could accompany the dragoons no farther. At first she was appalled, having never conceived of the possibility of living where there were no roads. It was as if she'd crossed the River Styx, to a place where she would never again see those of her own disposition. But the change in mode of transportation turned out to be a blessing in disguise despite the wear of the sidesaddle on her thighs. Her first day on horseback, breathing fresh air and being more or less in control of her mount, banished the nausea brought on by the relentlessly bumping and swaying carriage. Her spirits picked up a bit.

She rode at the head of the dragoon column, aside her father. The maid, that drudge of a Scots woman, rode far behind, with the baggage train. That in itself was a relief, for Leah much preferred the company of her father.

Leah said to him, "I expect I shan't ever like this wretched place."

The captain sat his mount with grace, a proper officer, and

barely glanced at his daughter as he replied, "You're not expected to like it, daughter. You are, however, expected to tolerate it with good cheer."

She glanced over at him, then away. It was difficult to speak with him when his men were around. He was a handsome man, with kind eyes and a gentle demeanor, but when near his men his command presence was like heat that came from him in waves. She was intimidated in any case. So she looked around at the harsh landscape and said, "You needn't have brought me. I would much rather have stayed in London with Uncle Henry." Anything, to have stayed at home amid the familiar. Among memories of her mother, where sometimes a presence could be felt and she knew her mother's spirit must be nearby. She could never speak of it to her father, whose acquaintance with the spiritual never went beyond remembering the name of his company chaplain.

"I did, indeed, need to bring you. You're my daughter, and I won't have you raised by my irredeemably dissolute brother."

Her voice steeled to keep out the quaver. "Raised? Even still? I'm quite grown up now, Father. I do wish you would at least admit it."

Her father reddened at the ears and neck, harrumphed for a moment, then said, "Indeed. Quite a bit too grown up to be let anywhere near my brother under any circumstances."

Another deep breath and she continued, "So you have brought me near your men, who are not nearly so civilized as Uncle Henry?"

The captain's voice turned hard, and he cut her a sharp glance. "Have any of the men shown you disrespect?"

She glanced over at him, alarmed now there might be repercussions over something that hadn't even happened. His eyes were aflame, and she shivered. "No, sir. Not at all. Nobody has so much as spoken to me." As much as she disliked the soldiers, she didn't wish anyone falsely accused of impropriety on her account.

Father nodded, satisfied, and returned his attention to the trail they followed as his anger calmed and his color returned to normal.

Her face flushed to realize he didn't care whether anyone ever spoke to her, so long as there was no disrespect. "Nevertheless, I don't see why I couldn't have stayed with Uncle Henry. I might have found a husband in London and been happy there."

A sharp laugh broke from the captain and he muttered, "Not

bloody likely." She wasn't certain whether he meant it was unlikely she would have stayed with Henry, or unlikely she would have found a husband, or unlikely she would have been happy. Neither did she want to know what he'd meant, so she let it pass. She began to wonder if he intended her to marry one of his lieutenants, but on second thought knew it couldn't be so. More likely, Father simply couldn't imagine her marrying anyone. Oddly, she found that even more frightening.

There was a long silence in which she fiddled with the coarse horse's mane aside her upper knee. Idly, she braided a few strands, then picked out the braid, merely to do it all again. Only the dull thud of hoofbeats and the random squeak of leather could be heard. The tension between them grew, and she let it. She could sense his discomfort.

Finally he gave in and spoke. "You'll be pleased to learn we'll be living in a castle," he said brightly, and the corners of her mouth turned up in a suppressed smile. It was the tone he used to jolly her out of a pique.

It worked somewhat. Leah thought castles were grand, though she had her doubts about anything he would say just then. "A genuine castle? Really? I shouldn't think they would need them out here, where there are no roads and so few people."

The captain shrugged. "I'm told it isn't a large one, and it's lost its outer curtain. Breached in a siege centuries ago, I believe, then dismantled over the years for building materials. But the keep is intact, and by all accounts quite comfortable. It stands on an island at the edge of a lake. Strangely enough, it was named after a ghost dog, if you can believe that. The name of it is in that Irish language they speak hereabouts. Quite unpronounceable, and translates to English as House of the White Hound. Most people call it simply the Tigh."

Leah chuckled. "A ghost dog?" This promised to be an amusing tale, and a shiver skittered up her spine.

"Indeed. Some deceased hound who allegedly avenged his master's defeat in battle by single-handedly murdering the entire opposing war party as they made their way home. There are those who claim to have seen the ghost, and local legend has it the apparition is an omen of bad fortune."

She shivered again. "What strange people to actually name their castle for an apparition! Particularly one they see as bad luck."

Her father made a disparaging face. "In my opinion, it seems a complete waste of a perfectly good castle to have it filled with Scots. Not only are they Highlanders, but they're papists as well. Though by all accounts the current laird is sympathetic to the Crown, we shouldn't hope for much civilized behavior from any of them."

Leah's eyes widened, and her pulse picked up. "Catholics? Indeed? Won't you arrest them, then?" She'd never known anyone who dared to openly practice Catholicism. Images of hairy, half-dressed men worshiping graven idols came to mind. She pictured her father and his men taking them all away in chains.

But Father shook his head. "No, I'm afraid I must tread lightly on that issue in this case, as much as I would like to rid Britain of all the superstitious lot." His words were clipped. "These people are ripening for rebellion, and it behooves me to not spark one off precipitously by too confining a policy. So long as they have no priest, there's little damage they can do in any case. It's the priests who disseminate their error. If I see their beads I'll confiscate them, but I can do little else."

Leah fell silent, entertained for a time by exotic images of crucifixes and holy water and savage men in skirts crossing themselves and praying in Latin to saints whose names she could only guess.

That night the company rested in tents at the foot of a steep, rocky peak, for there was no convenient lodging to be found. The cot was hard and the night cold. Leah shivered miserably in her blankets, longing for a real bed.

The following day they crossed the most forbidding part of their trek. Slowly, carefully, the horses traversed treacherous expanses of solid stone, above a long and steep slope that ended in a sudden drop only God knew how far down. Occasionally the shod hooves slipped and skittered. A fall would have killed both rider and horse. Beyond that were boggy areas, over which the company was forced to go in single file, hoping not to lose the lead horse to deceptive ground.

Finally they came to a solid, visible track that seemed to begin nowhere but slowly came into being as paths of travelers coming from many directions converged on this spot. It led through a narrow gap between two very steep mountains. Here the crags crowded in on Leah so forcefully, she felt as if she couldn't breathe as she passed among the great rises of solid rock. Her mind boggled there were people who actually lived in this wilderness. With relief she glimpsed the garrison ahead. But there was no other structure in sight.

"Father, I thought you said there was a castle."

He declined to reply, but gestured to his lieutenant to come for orders. Leah listened, an ignored fly on the wall. The bulk of the men were to present themselves to the garrison commander, with the message he would be relieved in the morning by Captain Hadley. The first lieutenant, several privates, and the captain's personal servants with his baggage horses were to accompany him onward to obtain billeting for himself and his daughter. The lieutenant executed a crisp salute and turned his horse to obey. Then the captain turned to Leah and said, "Now I'll take you to our new home."

Her heart sank. For a time she'd forgotten they were coming to stay, and now hated to be reminded how long it would be until she would see England again. She felt trapped by the mountains, high, granite walls impassable and unsympathetic to her desire for familiar country.

Just past the garrison stood an ancient church—plainly a Catholic church, by the architecture and carvings everywhere about. Angels nestled in crevices, and more than one gargoyle peeked from the eaves. She stared, fascinated.

"Father, how is it this church yet stands?"

He also stared, a dull look of disgust in his eyes, his square face hard and set. "This glen has been something of a stronghold for papists. Far away from civilizing influences, the population has resisted reformation. Even the zealot Covenanters never penetrated this far."

As they passed, Leah's mind turned with images of Catholics burning people at the stake. Hard to believe there were people left in Britain who followed the barbarous religion.

The valley that opened up before them was long and narrow. Low hovels dotted the landscape. The people she glimpsed hurried away from the English uniforms, small though the party was, and ahead in the village ragged people standing in the road melted into the surrounding houses. As Leah and the soldiers passed through the village square, the place appeared empty but for one small boy who stared at them through a low window. His eyes were wide with terror, and when Leah waved to him he ducked into the darkness of his earthen house.

The Tigh, as her father called it, was an ancient gray monstrosity that looked like a block of moldy, badly nibbled cheese. Two crenelated towers rose from its far corners, and at the near corner its gatehouse was an ungraceful set of angles without so much as a curved arch to relieve its severity. They rode through it, and inside the bailey Leah and her father finally encountered some Scots who did not run away. But even these seemed apprehensive, poised to flee. Her lips pressed together. Fierce people, indeed!

Those standing in the barren enclosure, staring as if they'd never seen an Englishman before, were appalling. Dirty men, wearing those kilt garments, came from a wooden building she took for a stable. Slatternly women in ragged dresses stood about, gossiping, in a filthy animal pen tucked into a corner. Some pigs grunted at the excitement of the people around them, and seemed the more intelligent for at least they were not slack-jawed. More women and men emerged from the large doors that would most likely have led to the Great Hall. Some were less dirty than others, but all were dressed in ragged linen shirts and underdresses overlaid with that gaudy checkered wool they all seemed so fond of. Leah could hardly distinguish one from another. Many men wore no stockings, and the women and children were all completely barefoot.

As her horse stamped and shifted beneath her, she searched the clusters of people for their "laird." Surely he would be more presentable than these, who must be servants. *Please, God, let these be the servants!*

One of her father's private soldiers came to assist her in dismounting, and grasped her around the waist. She smiled, hoping for a reaction, but his face was impassive. He carefully set her upon the ground while her father asked after the laird of Ciorram.

Laird. What a strange title! Like a mispronunciation of "lord." She straightened her cloak as she inched her way from behind the dragoon who guarded her, hoping for a better view of what was going on. Soldiers and Scots milling about were too numerous for her to see much. Then she looked up to see a tall man in one of those kilts approach her father.

"What is it ye want?" His accent was pronounced but understandable, and the tone was brusque. Leah blinked and peered at this unutterably rude man.

The Scot was even taller than her father, who was himself

large and powerful. Nobody here seemed to know of the existence of wigs, and this fellow was no exception. His long, smooth hair was nearly black, and though it was tied at the back in a half-hearted attempt at civilized appearance, a single short lock had fallen free of the black ribbon he wore and dangled aside his face. Fortunately he was clean-shaven, or she might have fainted straight away at the sight. His complexion was also dark—tanned but not leathery as would be a peasant in the fields. On the contrary, his skin was as smooth as his hair, and his cheeks showed a ruddiness that, given his tone of voice, might have been from wrath as easily as from health. The more she looked upon him, the more she realized how remarkable he was. His blue eyes were the deep color of a lake in summer, but at this moment threw stormy anger.

Her father replied with perfect composure, though his eyes were also beginning to spark with annoyance at the rude reception, "I wish to see Dylan Matheson, if you please. Or his representative, as I'm given to understand he may be indisposed."

The man snorted, and his cheeks flushed even more so the redness crept down his neck. "Indisposed. You might say that. My father has recently passed on. It's myself you need to speak to now."

"And you are . . . ?"

"Ciaran Robert Matheson of Ciorram." No smile, no offer of his hand. Leah frowned, embarrassed for her father to receive this treatment.

Still her father was unruffled, maintaining personal calm in spite of it. "Well, then, Ciorram, I'm Captain Roger Hadley, here with an independent company of dragoons to relieve the garrison in this valley. I require billeting for myself and my daughter. Posthaste, if you please, for Leah has come a long way and she is quite exhausted. She'll want supper immediately, as well."

The dark blue eyes flashed with even more anger, and without a glance at her the laird saïd, "Ye'll get . . ." But the man stopped himself in midsentence. His eyes went unfocused for a long moment and his gaze drifted to Father's boots. Then he looked up again and said to the captain, grudgingly as if his mind had suddenly been changed against his will, "I'll have a chambermaid prepare rooms for the two of you." Still no offer of goodwill, but at least his tone was no longer quite so hostile.

Ciorram raised his chin and looked Leah's father in the eye, just as that boy had done three days before, and now she saw the resemblance between them. Perhaps they were brothers? This fellow didn't appear old enough to be the boy's father. Leah couldn't help but stare. No man had ever stood up to her father this way. She was accustomed to men saluting him and speaking in tones of respect. Even Father's superiors never used as rude a tone as this Matheson, with his bare knees and rough shirt and unkempt hair.

Without another word, the young laird spun on his heel and returned to his Great Hall, leaving his guests in the gathering gloom of the castle bailey. Leah watched him go, appalled. And fascinated.

C iaran's head buzzed with rage as he returned to the Great Hall, leaving Eóin to delegate the tasks involved with arranging rooms for the intruders. Muttering under his breath, Ciaran disparaged the *Sasunnaich* with every Gaelic vulgarism he knew, and a few in Colonial English as well. Sinann followed at a flutter over his shoulder. Planked down hard in front of the fire, sprawled in his father's chair, he stared into the flames though he saw nothing. His entire being was focused on his hatred of the English and how much he did not want them lurking about the Tigh. Soon Eóin came to sit with him and rested his hand on Ciaran's shoulder. The rest of the castle was agog with the rapidly spreading news there would be a redcoat officer and an Englishwoman billeted there, and workers came from the kitchen to gawk.

Sinann told him, " 'Tis a blessing."

He turned toward her, his eyes wide. " 'Tis not!"

Eóin said, " 'Tis not what?"

Ciaran ignored him, but kept enough presence of mind to at least look toward the fire instead of the faerie, whom Eóin saw only as thin air. Ciaran muttered, "I'd rather kill them all than to let them befoul my home with their English stench."

Eóin said softly, "You cannae kill them." Sarah's eldest son was seven years older than Ciaran and by blood was only a third cousin, but there had never been a time when Eóin hadn't seemed like a real brother. Ciaran took him seriously.

In reply, his voice was equally quiet, lest someone in a red coat with any amount of Gaelic overhear. "How can you bear it? They murdered your father. You said ye remember seeing it."

"And if you dinnae bow to them, cousin, they'll murder you."

Sinann said, "He's telling the truth, lad." Ciaran shot the faerie an angry glance, but she continued, "There's more you dinnac ken, laddie. Are you aware of the tapestry in the laird's office? *Your* office? The one bearing the likenesses of myself and your great-grandfather Donnchadh Matheson?"

He shut his eyes briefly in lieu of a nod.

"Well, there's a secret to that tapestry. Long ago, at the turn of this century, I made your great-grandfather a gift of it. One day it appeared on the wall of his office. He tried to remove it, but the next day it was back. He removed it again, but it simply wouldnae stay away. So he left it there, and each laird since has left it there. It willnae be moved, for 'tis enchanted."

Her voice lowered, and tensed as she continued, "What nae man but yer father kent, and now you will, is its true enchantment is that I, who put it there, can look into the room through it." That perked Ciaran's attention, and he looked at the faerie. "Aye," she said. "Whenever I wish to look, I can see and hear whatever happens in that room, from wherever I may be. Were I hundreds of miles away, I could have knowledge of the business of whoever uses that room, did I have a mind to."

Ciaran sat up a bit straighter in his chair.

The dragoon captain and his daughter entered the Great Hall, accompanied by a number of castle servants bearing trunks and such.

There was some hesitation among the servants, who seemed as reluctant as Ciaran to accept the intruders. Ciaran, having quickly decided what he must do, stood and approached them at a long stride.

"Captain!"

Hadley and his daughter paused, and Ciaran noticed her for the first time. Her oval face struck him as beautiful, her coloring pale yet her hair a rich chestnut color, and her build slight and graceful despite her unusual height for a woman. Such a frail flower of English womanhood was she, he knew she must wilt at the least cause. The weakness of the English character was well known, and it was the thing he hated most about them.

He watched her as she continued on her way, following the

gillie with her trunk. Her fine riding habit was possibly the most costly dress Ciaran had ever seen, accented with lace and velvet. Even Mother Sarah had never worn a dress so fine.

His attention returned to her father and the issue at hand. "Captain."

Hadley tendered his attention and raised steel-gray eyebrows in query. His face was square, with lines so clean as to be described as sharp. The white wig was expensive, though plainly coiffed in neat rows of tight curls. In spite of his weariness, having come a long and treacherous way, his eyes were clear and betrayed only a slight redness at the lower lid. In fact, at this moment they were somewhat bright with challenge.

For a brief moment Ciaran had a nearly overwhelming urge to rid himself of this unwanted burden, but instead he chose diplomacy and said, "It occurs to me you will need space for your work, convenient to your quarters. Allow me to offer my own office for the duration of your stay."

The captain blinked with surprise at the sudden change of heart, though his expression did not soften. He said, "We're to be here indefinitely."

It was Ciaran's turn to blink. This was extremely bad news. But he continued, "Quite all right. Allow me to move some things, and the space will be yours."

Hadley smiled, and finally appeared to accept the change of heart.

A smile crept to Ciaran's face. His hatred of the English was pure, well nurtured his entire life by dangerous and unruly redcoated soldiers, and he was certain he would see Hadley dead in this castle one day soon.

Leah, on her way to the far end of the Great Hall, paused to listen to the Ciorram laird, surprised at what she was now hearing. His voice no longer held the rough tone of before. In fact, his brogue nearly disappeared in his sudden gentleness. Now she looked at him more closely, wondering how a savage, kilted Highlander could become a gentleman with such ease. It struck her he must have learned it by rote somewhere, like a dog that has learned to bark on command. He couldn't possibly understand what it meant to actually be a gentleman.

Even so, she continued to peer at him. He was terribly well

made for a Scot. Straight of limb and back, he held himself proudly, though his body was relaxed. For a brief moment she wondered whether he might be the bastard of an English nobleman. The thought amused her, and it would explain quite a bit were it true.

Once all was settled between Father and the young laird, a maid came to lead the way to their chambers, through a narrow corridor. Spiral stairs in one of the towers took them first to the second floor, where her father was installed in a bedchamber, then to the third-floor room where she herself would stay.

It was quite large enough, but there were no windows, only shuttered arrow loops. While the servants hurried to unpack her things and ready the bed, she sighed and went to pull one of the wooden shutters out by its iron handle and set it on the floor. The night air was chilly, and the wind blew against her face. This opening looked out over the lake to the west, and the sky was still purpling with the sunset. The surface of the lake was still and clear as a mirror, reflecting the surrounding mountains in perfect detail.

It was all too much for her. So very . . . ungentle. She felt trapped in a wild world she couldn't begin to comprehend. If only she could fly away, over those mountains, and south, to where meadows were green and unbroken by great crags and expanses of stone. Where forests were well managed and traversed by carefully tended roads. Where men treated each other with respect, and anger was an ugly emotion to be concealed in the interest of polite manners.

When the unpacking was finished, she replaced the shutter and turned to dismiss all the servants save her maid. The heavy, carved door closed behind them with a soft, wooden thud. The maid removed her own cloak and laid it on the low servant's bed near the hearth. It was nothing more than a straw mattress in a long, narrow box, covered with linen sheets and a single woolen blanket.

The mattress on the large oak bed was feathered, and though the sheets were not silken, the coverlet was of fur. Bearskin, it appeared, as she ran her fingers through the thick brown hair. The room had a dark, musty smell. Like wood smoke, but not as sharp. She sniffed it, and found it disagreeable.

The maid came behind her and attempted to help her off with her cloak, but Leah waved her away. "It's cold in here."

"Shall I put more wood on the fire?"

Leah nodded, and the maid moved to comply. Then she straightened to address her mistress again. "Shall I be off to the kitchen to fetch a bite to eat, miss?"

Leah wasn't the least bit hungry, but she was certain the maid was, so she said, "Very well . . . ah . . . Ida." She had the devil of a time remembering that woman's name.

The maid left the room.

Leah waited at the door until her steps faded down the spiral stairs, then lifted the latch and slipped out to the alcove. Candles in sconces lit the way, and she clutched her skirts to hurry up those same stairs.

The entry alcove immediately above was dark and the door to the chamber beyond closed. She proceeded upward, her slippers nearly inaudible on the stone, and on the fifth floor of the tower she found a lit alcove. The door was fully open and candelabra inside threw light, so she paused in the shadows of the stairwell for a moment. Her pulse hastened at her adventure. God knew what these strange, rough people would do if they found her lurking. Goose bumps rose, and a fluttering grew in her belly that was a nearly unbearable combination of terror and excitement.

In utter silence, she approached the door, and her ears detected a low murmur. It was a man's voice—an old man, from the quality of it. Slowly she peeked around the frame of the door, and her eyes went wide at what she saw.

A carved mahogany kneeler stood before several tall windows. A man knelt at it, elbows resting, wearing only a linen shirt that draped slightly over the backs of his bent knees. His graying brown hair was wet, slicked back as if he'd combed it, and his beard was neatly arranged against his face. In his fingers was a chain of beads. A rosary, with a crucifix dangling from it. His murmuring was in Latin. He was praying the papist rosary.

Leah was shocked to her toes. Of course, there were people even in England who were stubbornly Catholic in defiance of the law, but she'd never seen one before. Fascinated, she listened, though she didn't understand any of the words beyond "Maria" and *"Patri."* She decided it was a pretty language, particularly the way this man spoke it. The words tripped quickly from his tongue, but though he executed the prayers efficiently, he also spoke them sincerely. His voice rose and fell with the meaning of what he was saying, and she could hear the love in his voice for those he addressed. A smile touched her lips as she listened to the music of it and the beads slipped through the man's fingers one by one.

Then he said, "Amen."

Oons! There was another word she knew, and it meant he was finished! She ducked away and fled before he could rise from his stiff and unwilling knees. In an instant she found herself continuing up the stairwell, and it was too late to turn back and remain undetected. So she hurried onward to see where this might take her.

A door at the top opened onto the thickening darkness and the chill of the spring night. Wind from the lake buffeted at this height, and found every tiny opening her clothing offered. She pulled her cloak close around her and looked about. The crenellated battlement of the castle seemed much larger than it had from the bailey below. The stones were cold and worn, the edges rounded and crumbling in spots. By now only the moonlight suggested her path along them. At the place where the tower was joined by the curtain wall was a garderobe hunched over the edge of the wall. Good. Now she knew where to go when she would need to relieve herself. For a certainty, chamber pots were too much to expect in this wilderness.

She continued along the top of the curtain, her fingers brushing the rough stone beside her, gazing up at the starry sky. It astonished her to realize these were the same stars that rose over London, for Glen Ciorram was an entirely alien place. The very sky seemed untamed and at odds with the jagged, lofty horizon. Too cold. Too stark. Too hard. Homesickness choked her, and tears stung her eyes. Oh, how she wished to return to England!

A cry from the bailey below caught her attention, and she halted in her walk. Torches had been lit, and she could see two dragoons standing on guard by the gatehouse, a welcome brightness of red in this gloomy place. Then she observed a man in a kilt in the middle of the dirt expanse of the bailey performing some sort of dance. But without music. An occasional grunt drifted up to her, and she thought it might be a madman having a fit, but the dragoons took no alarm and only watched the performance. Soon she saw there was a purposefulness to the movements, and began to wonder if this might be the Highland sword dance she'd heard about. But no, there was no sword. Nor even a dagger. Only the man, punching the air and kicking it with his feet. She'd never seen, or even heard of, such a thing.

He turned toward her, and she saw it was Ciorram. That Ciaran Matheson fellow. She was certain of it, for he was the only man she'd seen here with his hair drawn back in a queue. Also, the line of jaw was his, and the severe, dark brow was curved in concentration. Enthralled, she watched. There was a beauty to this dance, and a visceral meaning to the actions she nearly understood but didn't quite. The grace and strength of his body were captivating. It was impossible to take her eyes from him.

But finally he bowed to nobody there and began shaking out his arms and legs as if he'd run a long distance. Then he walked back toward the Great Hall.

Leah hurried to the tower whence she'd come, and slipped into the stairwell. All the alcoves were empty as she passed, and even the chamber of the praying man was now closed. She slipped into her bedchamber to find Ida there, sitting on a stool next to the fire. The maid stood, and gestured to a tray on a small table near one of the arrow loops.

"Yer supper, miss."

Leah loosened the clasp on her cloak so Ida could take it from her, then sat at the table. Ida hung the garment in the armoire, then stood by while her mistress ate. A wooden plate held a single slab of meat, which appeared to be mutton, and a round, flat sort of bread. A tumbler made of horn stood by, and she sniffed it.

"Ale? Is there no wine?"

"I'm sorry, miss, no wine was available."

Leah frowned. "How could anyone not have wine?"

"Nae, miss, I said there was none *available*. From what I've gathered, ye might have been offered illegal whiskey rather more readily. I brought ale instead, for the other choice was water."

"Well . . ." Leah sipped the ale. She could tolerate the drink, though she didn't particularly like it. Then she reached for the knife and fork. "Ida, you've neglected to bring a fork." A wooden spoon sat on the tray, and an iron knife with a wooden handle, but there was no fork.

"Begging yer pardon, miss, but there was nae fork to be had within miles of here."

"You can't be serious. They don't use forks here? What, do they eat with their fingers, then?"

"Aye, for the most part. There are spoons for soup and stew."

Leah groaned and shut her eyes, disgusted once again with this barbaric place and wishing she were home. Then she sighed and picked up the bread. With quick, efficient fingers, she tore it open and laid the piece of meat inside, then took a bite of the assembly.

It was dry, so she washed it down with some of the ale. Some cheese would have made it not so dull, but she supposed the laird's cheese must be as unavailable as his wine. Famished as she was, she ate the food as nothing more than flavorless nourishment, and struggled not to wish for the fine cuisine she'd known all her life in London.

Losing herself in her thoughts as she chewed, her mind wandered away from the poor food to dwell on the laird's dance. So strange, and yet so pleasing. And, as that thought crossed her mind, another accompanied. Wouldn't Father be mortified to think she could be pleased by a redshanks Highlander! She smiled to herself as she took another bite of supper and chewed on it.

Once finished eating, she allowed Ida to undress her, and she slipped into a silk nightgown. She then slid beneath the covers of the bed, grateful for the heavy fur against the insidious cold, and burrowed deep into the mattress. Ida readied herself for bed, then blew out the many candles alight around the room.

In the darkness, Leah dwelt upon the image of the young laird until she slept.

C iaran's patience with that faerie was wearing thin by the time he prepared for bed at the washstand in what had once been his father's bedchamber. She perched in her accustomed spot atop the corner of the bed curtain frame and harassed him from there as he unbuckled his belt and unwound his kilt from around himself. The faint chill of the room raised a few goose bumps, but they didn't stay long.

"You ought to have seen your father when he first came to this century. Modest as a virgin, he was, embarrassed even to bare his chest in your mother's presence to have his sark laundered."

Ciaran grunted, not caring much for this topic, as he untied his leggings and removed his shoes and stockings. But she continued.

"Nae telling what sort of life he had in the future, running around ashamed of his body like that. But he was cured of it soon enough, and was performing his meditations and such skyclad before a fire."

"Why are you telling me this?" Ciaran pulled his sark over his head and tossed it on top of the kilt he'd draped over the back of his chair. Then he pulled the ribbon from his hair and turned to the washbowl. Early on as a child he'd been taught to wash every night before bed, and since his ascension to the lairdship he now enjoyed the luxury of having his wash water heated. Overly fussy cleanliness was one of the things that had always set his father apart from most other folks, but it never occurred to Ciaran to let go of the habit.

Sinann said, "Nae reason. Except there are many things you dinnae ken about your da, and I think it would be well for you to be told."

Another grunt as Ciaran scrubbed himself with a wet linen towel.

"You ken how your father loved your mother."

"Aye." His fingers lightly touched the gold ring and the crucifix he wore around his neck. Then he ran wet fingers through his hair.

"He loved her on sight, you understand. The very first moment he laid eyes on her. I saw it in his face."

Ciaran shut his eyes and conjured the image he'd always treasured of his mother, his only visual memory of her face laughing. He couldn't recall when or where it had been, but her smile had been bright and her blue eyes shining. She was the most beautiful woman who had ever lived. "Of course he did."

"There was a time, when he was injured so horribly it would have been a blessing for him to slip into death, she was his reason for clinging to life."

He nodded as he continued his wash on down to scrub his privates. He'd heard the story of the arrest and imprisonment at Fort William, where his father had been flogged nearly to death.

Then the faerie took a sideways tack and said, "Have ye had a good look at the captain's daughter this evening?"

Ciaran stood straight and peered up at her, in the dimness above the bed. He shivered as water ran down the backs of his legs and said, "She's a ninny, that one."

"What makes you think that, you knowing her so well as ye do?"

He returned to his ablution to finish up with his feet, then run a dry towel over himself. "They all are. Every Englishwoman. They're silly, vain, no-account ninnies."

"And you having met so many of them, you would know."

That made him frown, for she had a point, and he hated to admit it. He'd met very few women from England and had never known one well. But he shrugged and reached for the rosary on the table by the window. "Now if you'll excuse me, faerie, I wish to pray." He knelt by his bed and leaned his elbows on the edge of his mattress. The beads, made of ivory, were smooth and familiar in his hands, for he'd held them like this every day since he was nine. He took a deep breath to focus his mind, then whispered softly, crossing himself, *"In nomine Patri, et Filii, et Spiritus Sancti."*

"You might be interested to learn, laddie, the young woman was watching you this evening from the battlement."

Ciaran blinked and looked up at her. "Watching me? When?"

"During the exercises. She couldnae tear her gaze from you."

That brought a light snort of laughter and a deprecating smirk. *"Och,* aye."

"Aye, indeed."

The faerie left it at that and was silent. But as Ciaran prayed, the image of the very English Leah Hadley crept into his mind unbidden and unwanted.

CHAPTER 4

He threaded the black leather belt through the loops in his kilt.
The buckle was silver, in an intricate Celtic knot design of thistles.

L eah dressed quickly in the morning, eager to breakfast in the Great Hall.

"Please, miss, allow me to fetch breakfast for you." Ida protested all the while she helped her mistress with her clothing. "It cannot be good for ye to eat with them downstairs."

"Nonsense, Ida. I should go mad to stay here in the tower, like a Rapunzel, waiting only for someone to come talk to me. This place is quite stultifying enough, without limiting myself to one bedchamber." She smoothed her skirt over the hooped petticoat beneath. "So we'll have no more talk of taking meals alone as if we were prisoners."

"Aye, miss."

Downstairs, the Great Hall was alive with castle residents at breakfast. Since the night before, a long row of trestle tables had been erected down the middle of the room, with one table athwart the end nearest the hearth. Many fell silent at sight of her, though they all seemed to be speaking that gibberish language Gaelic and she couldn't have understood a word had they shouted in her ear. Eyes turned toward her as quiet descended.

The laird sat at the table near the hearth, and also was silent. He leaned back on an arm of his chair, nearly lounging, one hand resting on the opposite chair arm, and watched her, his face betraying no gentleness, no concern for her comfort. It was plain he looked on her as an intruder. She turned away, reddening.

A kitchen maid stood nearby, and Leah addressed her. "Where shall I sit?"

The girl's eyes went wide, and she said something in that alien language. She shook her head, then pointed to it, giving Leah to assume she didn't speak English. Or else she was admitting to madness or stupidity, which seemed doubtful. Leah glanced about at the tables to see if there might be an unclaimed seat.

A young man caught her eye, and she saw it was the very boy she'd seen riding so hard out of Fort William. He pointed with his chin to a spot across from himself, then returned to his breakfast, head down. Though she knew he spoke English, he apparently didn't care to speak to her.

Leah sat, and the wait was short before a bowl of mush was set before her. A wooden spoon stuck out of it, and she found herself grateful to not have to eat this with her fingers. She picked up the spoon, touched her tongue to the mush, and found it without flavor of any kind. But then she put the spoon into her mouth. A larger taste revealed a toasty quality.

A small, earthenware bowl of salt sat on the table before her. She sprinkled a pinch of it on the mush and tasted again. Better. She guessed the stuff was of oats, for this certainly wasn't wheat or barley. It was soft and bland, and went down smoothly, but it left her wishing for meat. There should be meat at breakfast, but she looked around and found everyone eating this mush. Boiled horse feed. Surely even these people should be better off than this.

Though the boy across from her had kind eyes and smiled at her frequently, nobody spoke to her the entire time she was in the Great Hall. When she finished eating she returned to her chamber.

C iaran didn't eat much at breakfast. His mind was elsewhere, thinking about the issues he would need to address among the clan this morning. Today would be the first test of his new authority among his kinsmen. Today was the day set aside for the hearing of disputes and judgment of accused clansmen.

After everyone had finished eating, villagers began to arrive. The floor in the Great Hall was cleared for court, the tables moved to the side. Soon the entire village was gathered to sit on chairs, benches, and stools about the floor, looking expectantly to Ciaran for his answers to their questions.

Ciaran wasn't ready for this. His father had been wise but he was not, and he felt the immense pressure in Calum's cold, smiling gaze. It was clear his brother thought he was taking power he didn't deserve—judging people he had no right to judge. At the heart of it, Ciaran might have agreed, but he had no choice in the matter.

The oppressive red presence of Hadley's dragoon guards in the room didn't help matters.

Robin, continuing his service as *fear-còmhnaidh,* supported himself with his staff beside the laird in his seat by the hearth. When all was ready, Robin called for silence. The room quieted. Ciaran watched his kinsmen lean forward in their seats. Nobody spoke above a whisper, and every eye without exception was on him. He could see the doubt. Could feel the tension as they waited for him to speak. They looked to Ciaran for something he wasn't yet certain was his to give.

His belly fluttered, but his face betrayed nothing. Sitting in his father's chair before the hearth . . . no, *his* chair. It was his own chair. As he realized that, a warm certainty stole over him. It was his own chair now. He was the laird, this was his chair, and it was his place to keep the peace. There could be no accord in the glen without this court and his authority. Far from privilege, this was duty. His people needed him. His father had taught him that.

So he heard the first case with no more flutters in his gut. His eye was steady and his thoughts clear, for his presence in this room today was not a display of self. It was confirmation of continuity and assurance that all was right in the glen.

Robin leaned down to whisper in Ciaran's ear the particulars of the first case to be called, and Ciaran tilted his head to listen. Anna Campbell Matheson, daughter of Keith Rómach, granddaughter of Owen Brodie the carpenter, and wife of Gregor Matheson, had been accused of stealing. Ciaran had heard the uproar surrounding the incident, folks gossiping here and there about the Tigh, and also knew Anna had been accused of this before. She was probably guilty, but he patiently requested the accuser state her case.

The seamstress, Iseabail Matheson, daughter of Colin Matheson, stood, red of face and appearing ready to assault Anna there before the laird. Iseabail said, "She took a great length of cloth from me and never paid for it!"

"I did! I did pay!" Anna sat with her arms crossed and a scowl on her face.

"Ye dinnae!"

"I left the money for you there, on your table."

"I dinnae see any money. Nae silver, nor even copper!"

" 'Twas right there, in plain sight!"

The seamstress leaned toward her, fists on hips, and repeated, slowly as if talking to an idiot, "I dinnae see any money!" A burble of laughter moved among the onlookers.

"Quiet!"

The room fell silent and turned their attention to Ciaran. He continued, "Anna, how much money was there?"

"Five English shillings!"

That brought a murmur from the gathering and raised Ciaran's eyebrows. He leaned forward with interest. "Five of them, you say. And where did you get so much money?"

"I had to have it." Anna pointed with her chin to the seamstress. "She willnae give me the cloth without silver. 'Tis robbery!"

"The eggs you brought me—"

"Iseabail!" Everyone fell silent again to hear the laird. "Anna, you havenae answered my question. How is it you found yourself in possession of all that silver?"

Gregor's wife faltered for a moment, looking around the room. It was plain whatever would leave her mouth next would be a lie. She said, "I saved it up."

"From what?" He clasped his hands together before him, his elbows on the chair arms to either side.

There was another pause, then Anna said, "I needed the cloth!"

"But you dinnae pay for it."

Tears rose in her eyes. "She wouldnae give it to me."

An angry edge crept into his voice at her childishness. "Of course, she wouldnae. She needed to sell it. You're guilty of stealing."

"Ciaran!"

The laird frowned. "Anna!" She ducked her head. He leaned back and continued, "Can you give back the cloth?"

She shook her head. "I've made clothing with it."

"Have you any of the silver?"

She shook her head again.

He grunted and scratched an itch at the end of his nose. After a moment of thought he said, "Then you must do two things. First, I want all the eggs your chickens produce to go toward the debt until it's paid. And in the meantime ye'll stand in the stocks for three days."

"No!" Anna wailed and stamped her feet, her fists striking hard the air before her.

"Aye, and nae argument from you! Another word, and you'll stand in them for four days!"

Anna clamped her mouth shut so hard a white line appeared around her lips. Her fists pressed against her hips. Then she sat back against the wall behind her and glared at the seamstress.

Ciaran felt something loosen in his gut as the next case was called. Breath came easier, and the tension fled his shoulders. Next up was Alasdair MacGregor, son of Seumas Glas and cousin to the legendary Rob Roy, who was accused of sexual congress with a cow.

Ciaran had not heard of this incident, and peered at Robin to know whether he'd heard right. Robin nodded.

"A cow?" Ciaran shifted in his seat, suddenly uncomfortable.

Robin nodded again.

Ciaran was forced to take a moment to digest this, and shifted again. The crime, were Alasdair found guilty, would call for hanging. Perversions such as this were not taken lightly. "Who is the accuser?"

"Aodán."

"Och." It still made no sense. He rubbed his chin as if it would help him think.

Robin called Alasdair forward. Though the accused tried to keep his head up, his face and neck were mottled red with shame. This went against him, for it seemed he must be guilty to be so ashamed. But Ciaran forced himself to keep an unprejudiced mind. He knew Alasdair well, and this simply made no sense. Aodán was called to state his case.

"Ye say you witnessed an unnatural coupling?" A slight cough was necessary to clear his tightening throat.

Aodán's eyes flashed with anger. "Aye. There was a hole in the wall of the MacGregor byre, and I was passing by. I heard the sounds of a man in ecstasy, and leaned in for a peek."

"Because you thought he had a woman in there? His wife, perhaps? Thought you'd have yourself a bit of a gawk, then?"

The gathering erupted in laughter, and Aodán's face reddened. But he continued, one arm tucked behind him holding his other elbow. "It was nae woman he was with. 'Twas his milk cow. He was at the back of her, a-pushing and a-groaning."

A light titter of embarrassment skittered through the crowd.

"And you're certain he wasnae simply trying to move her off his foot? Expert that you are at telling the sounds of ecstasy from those of a man in pain."

That brought another good laugh.

Aodán's voice rose. "He was a-banging her! And you might be a bit more concerned, Ciar . . . sir, for he and his father trade milk from that cow to others in the glen."

Ciaran blanched as he recalled the milk he'd drunk with supper the night before, which could very well have come from a cow tainted with a man's seed. But he shook off the queer feeling, ran a thumb and finger over the corners of his mouth, and turned to Alasdair. "What have you to say in your defense?"

Alasdair ducked his head but said, "I dinnae do it."

There was a long silence. Then Ciaran said, "Is that all you've to say? Have you any idea why Aodán would say such a thing if it isnae true?"

Alasdair glanced sideways at Aodán, then sighed and said, "I voiced a desire for his wife."

A soft muttering rose in the room. Ciaran frowned. "His wife? You told him you wanted to bull his wife?" He blinked, then added, "My sister? Are ye mad, then, lad?" He found himself adjusting his seat again.

"I dinnae say it to him. I dinnae ken he was near enough to hear." He looked up and quickly added, "Also, I wouldnae ever attempt such a thing. I would never approach your sister. I swear it, Ciaran!"

The laird sat back in his chair. "I'm certain your own wife must be pleased to hear that."

Everyone in the room turned to look at Alasdair's wife, who was staring at the floor, her chin hard to her chest and her arms crossed before her. Her belly was quite large with their fourth child, more than likely a son like all the other grandchildren of Seumas Glas.

Then Ciaran said to Aodán, "Was there anyone else to witness this event?"

A scowl came to Aodán's face. "No."

"Is there anyone to tell of cow's shern besmirching Alasdair's clothing?" He hesitated before adding, "Or aught else belonging to Alasdair?"

Nobody offered testimony to that effect, though Ciaran waited a good, long moment for someone to speak up. When nobody did, he said, "Right, then. 'Tis Aodán's word against Alasdair's. Since it makes nae sense for a married man to carry on with a cow, but it does make sense for a man to find a woman not his wife desirable"—a snicker rippled through the room, and his voice took on an edge—"sister of mine though she might be, I find Alasdair's story the more credible." He leaned forward in his chair and said to Aodán, "And, laddie, the next time you bring a case before me as absurd as this one, I'll have you in the stocks."

There was another snicker in the room. Aodán and Alasdair reclaimed their seats, glaring at each other.

The cases proceeded, and Ciaran could feel the mood in the room ease. Those who had been leaning forward now sat back, resting against the walls or trestle tables behind them. A low conversation toward the rear of the room was silenced by his glance. He felt even stronger now. He was the laird, in both name and deed.

It wasn't until afterward the full realization of what he'd done that day came over him. Leaving the Great Hall, his skin went cold as he realized the punishments he'd commanded were at that moment being carried out. He headed for his bedchamber, and as he climbed the stairs of the West Tower he found his hands shaking. As the weight of his judgments began to make themselves realized, he began to understand the power he now wielded. In his room, he knelt by his bed, his forehead pressed to his clasped hands. His heart clenched, and he trembled for missing his father as his kinsmen could not.

"Where would ye like me to put this, sir?"

Ciaran looked up, startled, and climbed to his feet. One of the

Tigh guardsmen had been recruited by the head chambermaid to haul crates from the laird's office, and now he stood at Ciaran's chamber door with a sour look on his face. The castle guard were hired swords—honored warriors paid to protect the glen from rival clans—and didn't take kindly to menial tasks. His mouth was a hard line and his eyes had a dull, hooded look of insolence. Ciaran ignored it.

He gathered himself and nodded to the table beneath the eastern windows. There were already several crates stacked on it, filled with ledgers, papers, books of poetry, and bottles of wine. He picked up the birdlike toy that had been brought up from his father's office and turned it over in his hands. Brigid and the king's sword rested temporarily atop his bed, nestled in the thick fur of bearskin. The moving had taken most of the morning and would be finished soon. Ciaran looked around and wondered where he was going to put all this detritus.

The guardsman set his box on the floor, was dismissed, and left the room. Ciaran set down the wooden toy to dig through the boxes, and shifted them around to arrange a less obstructive organization in his bedchamber. The large room had become a maze where narrow paths led here and there among the boxes.

"There's an empty room in the North Tower." Calum at the door again, and Ciaran looked up. "In my opinion, ye should have installed the *Sasunnach* there rather than in Da's office."

" 'Tis my office, little brother." Ciaran was in no mood for his brother today. The five years between their ages had always been an unbridgeable chasm. Calum was the charming one, the one who smiled through everything and seemed to care about nothing. Calum was the one always pushing and teasing, always laughing at whatever he would discredit to his own ends, and he never seemed to stop moving. Even now he couldn't stand still, but was wandering around the room, picking things up to look at them, then putting them down to pick up something else.

Ciaran had always tolerated the challenges thrown down by his little brother, the annoyance like a bad smell one ceases to notice after a while. Da had loved all his sons, so Ciaran tried to love Calum as Da had, for his smiling demeanor and his easy laughter, his personal energy, and his loyalty to the clan. Ciaran continued to browse his father's things, and picked up a *sgian dubh* that sat atop an old, cracked leather baldric rolled up in a wad.

"Even better," said Calum, "ye could have packed him and his demon seed into a single chamber and let them make do. For all that, she may not even be his daughter and they would have preferred it that way. But ye've gone all soft on the English, I can see."

That stung, and Ciaran retaliated. "I have my reasons, *Malcolm*." A sideways glance told him he'd struck home again. His brother was reddening. So sad for the lad to be so vulnerable over his own name.

Ciaran looked again at the dirk in his hand, wondering what to do with it, then turned to his armoire and opened one of the drawers. It was filled with sarks and woolen stockings, but in the left corner were some odds and ends that had nowhere else to go. He put the *sgian dubh* there, among the pretty rocks, old iron shoe buckles, and found musket balls of his childhood.

But as the items shifted, Ciaran saw the talisman brooch he'd had as far back as he could remember. He hadn't seen it in years, and had completely forgotten about it. He picked it up from the drawer and looked at it, brushing a small wad of lint from it.

The thing was a steel brooch about three inches in diameter, in the shape of a belt made into a circle. It surrounded a crown, from which emerged a hand wielding a sword. Long ago he'd been told it was a clan badge, though he'd never seen anything like it before or since. To him, a clan badge was a plant or feather one wore in one's cap. Around the edge of this, on the belt, was inscribed the words *Fac et spera*. Do and hope. The clan motto, Da had said. Aye, good words to live by.

Sinann, perched on the bedframe above, said, "Recall the uses for the talisman."

He looked up at her, not daring to speak to her in Calum's presence, but he didn't need to. He did remember why Da had given him this. It was a talisman that made the wearer invisible when still. He'd carried it as a boy, and it had saved himself and Sìle from the Redcoats more than once. Turning it over in his fingers, he remembered the terror of those times he'd needed it, sitting with his sister as they watched armed soldiers search with their bayonets and swords, poking shadows under beds and behind furniture. But the years his father had been laird had been relatively peaceful, punctuated by only an occasional arrest or search. It had been a long time since he'd needed this magic. He rubbed the brooch with his thumb, then set it on the table by the window.

Calum strolled over to the stacks of boxes and looked in. "What all have ye found?"

"Naught but old papers. Da was a believer in writing things down, for a certainty. Back when I was a wee lad, he showed me how to enter names in the church book when folks are married and die and are christened."

Arms crossed over his deep chest, Calum said casually, "Have you entered Mother and Father's names, then?"

Ciaran stopped paging through papers and looked at his brother. The tips of his ears begin to burn. Without reply, he picked up the church record book and opened it. "Hand me that ink pot over there, and a quill." He sat on the edge of his bed with the book on his knees, and with the quill and ink carefully inscribed his father's and Sarah's full names and the dates of their deaths. His heavy heart yearned for a priest, who should be doing this instead of himself.

As Ciaran blotted the ink and closed the book, Calum reached into one of the boxes he was browsing and pulled out an old, stiff packet of oilcloth. As carefully as he opened it, though, the packet nevertheless cracked and fell to pieces, leaving some dark, yellowed papers in his hands. "What's this?"

Ciaran had no idea, and set the church book aside to come look over Calum's shoulder. The paper was also stiff, but held together as it was unfolded.

The first sheet was bottom-heavy, affixed with the royal seal of King George I. It was a full pardon, absolving their father of guilt for his participation in an uprising. The disturbance of 1715, from the date on the pardon. This wasn't news to either of them; they'd often heard the stories of the battle at Sheriffmuir, and had always understood their father had been pardoned during a time when pardons were easily had.

But the second sheet in the packet was one neither had seen nor heard of. As Ciaran read, the world went sideways and the floor seemed to drop from under him.

It was an adoption, in which one Ciaran Robert Ramsay, the son of Caitrionagh Silas Matheson, had been taken as son by her husband, Dylan Robert Matheson. The paper was dated November 1716, when Ciaran had been twenty-two months old.

"*Och.*" Calum's eyes were wide. His weight shifted with excitement as the realization sank in. "*Och,*" he said again, his voice soft with awe at what he'd discovered. "You're nae a Matheson."

There was a moment of stunned silence, then an explosion of motion as Ciaran grabbed for the paper and missed, and Calum dashed for the door with it.

"Bring that back here, ye queer prancer!" Ciaran reached for his *sgian dubh*, but quickly changed his mind and snatched the larger dirk, Brigid, from his bed before running after Calum. As he hurried down the stairs of the tower, his head spun with the horror of what he'd just learned, and the implications of it. The succession of the lairdship was absolutely determined by blood and along the male line. Regardless of what might be the letter of the law, an adopted son could never inherit if there were blood sons living. The clan would never accept him, regardless of who his maternal grandfather was.

Ciaran burst from the stairwell at the bottom of the West Tower and ran to haul open the door to the corridor of the servants' quarters. Calum was not there. Ciaran ran back into the West Tower and through to the stable. No Calum. Up the stairs to the tack room, and there was nobody there.

He slammed through the rickety door at the opposite side of the room and strode through the barracks, his footsteps thudding on the thin wooden floor, where sleeping guardsmen snored and those who weren't sleeping lurched to their feet in the presence of their laird. Ciaran barely noticed them and hurried out the other door and down the stairs at the side of the building.

He stood in the middle of the bailey, turning and searching for his little brother. His heart sank to his shoes as the full realization of truth landed and he felt suddenly hollow.

I'm not my father's son.

His chest tightened and he was unable to breathe. He turned his face toward the stable wall and coughed. A couple of hard swallows enabled him to take a good breath, and he straightened to look around at who might have seen anything untoward. Nobody in the bailey seemed to notice his distress. Though colors, for him, had gone to dun and the air had thickened enough to suffocate, the rest of the clan went about their business as if the world hadn't turned entirely to dust.

Not his father's son. The thing that had defined his entire life had never been true. It was as if his very body were a lie.

He headed toward the Great Hall, but hesitated when he noticed that Hadley girl staring at him from the open doorway. Something in her eyes alarmed him. There was too much knowing there. He turned and went into the stable instead, through to the West Tower, and returned to his chamber.

L eah was gazing out at the bailey, wondering if her father's guard would stop her should she try to wander out to the village. What if he told Father? Might she then be restricted to her tower room? The thought was abhorrent. She was about to turn and retreat into the Great Hall when the laird came running from behind the corner of the stable across the way.

He was an alarming sight, panting and red of face, in a terrible sweat over something. He stood in the bailey, looking about, in search of something or someone. Whatever it was, he wasn't finding it, and that seemed to make his situation even worse. In one fist he held a long dagger and appeared quite ready to kill someone with it. She burned to know what had upset him so. Somewhat it was curiosity, but also she wished to know how to ease his pain. Perhaps then she could become less of an outsider here.

One step toward her, and her heart leapt. But then he saw her and hesitated. She prayed he would come this way, but instead he turned and fled into the stable. Her heart sank, and she watched him go.

F or the rest of the day, and for days thereafter, Ciaran paged through his father's papers, reading carefully. Though he told himself he was only organizing them, his real wish was to discover something to disprove the adoption. A diary, perhaps, explaining a falsified adoption paper. Or an entry in a ledger or record book suggesting he'd been born a Matheson after all. *Any-thing*.

But there was no diary, and his baptismal record was in Edinburgh, where he'd been born in January of 1715. He'd always assumed his parents had lived away from Ciorram because of the unrest that year. Nobody in the clan had ever spoken about his mother being married to anyone other than his father.

Ramsay. Who was Ramsay? There were no clues in Da's papers, though Ciaran searched for three days.

Neither was there any sign of Calum. Nobody else thought it significant, for Calum was wont to hunt if the weather was fair.

And often even if the weather was foul. His disappearance on a hunting expedition in spring raised no eyebrows, and only Ciaran knew his brother must be hiding nearby, raising support for a challenge to Ciaran's succession.

Each day with no news was reassurance, for it was taking Calum longer than a day to bring together men and arms. Ciaran waited as time spun out. A mishap for Calum would be luck for Ciaran. Perhaps the lad would never return.

Meanwhile, Captain Hadley tended to his business in the laird's office, and there was a steady stream of Redcoats in and out of the North Tower, traipsing through the Great Hall and across the bailey. Sinann looked in on conversations minor and major, relaying details of the Redcoats' activities to Ciaran. Forewarned was forearmed, and the laird of Ciorram wished to know what his enemy was up to at all times. He knew the troop strength, patrol frequency, training status, and health of the men, and he tucked that information away in his head.

Fortunately, the illicit whiskey production was finished for the year and this year's casks were already hidden safely away, for the unusually close proximity of soldiers would have brought it to a halt. Though they still resided in a cave in the forests beyond the peat bog to the south, explaining daily traffic to and from that cave would have been difficult. And then there was the issue of the annual secret swap of aged barrels for new.

The casks from this winter's production had already been moved to the space inside a destroyed cistern over the Tigh kitchen, and there they would wait out their years of aging. The three-year-old casks and one five-year-old awaiting their turn had been brought to the cave in the forest. For many years there had been one five-year-old cask a year, and that whiskey was held out as special, aside from the younger casks. Beginning next year, there would also be a cask of the astonishing age of twenty-one. Dylan Dubh had begun to save out such casks each year when the harvest allowed for it, and there was a store of casks designated to be opened at twenty-one, representing most years since 1725.

Once Hadley was on the premises there would have been no chance of continuing production or moving the whiskey. The secret of aging was far too important to Ciorram's future to risk it being learned by anyone else at all, let alone the English.

One day Sinann sat atop the curtain frame on Ciaran's bed when a Redcoat messenger rode into the bailey below. Ciaran stood to look out the window and observed the dragoon hurry into the Great Hall.

"Something important, Sinann. See what it is." They waited. Sinann concentrated on looking through the tapestry at the other side of the Tigh. Soon she spoke, relaying the information as it was relayed to Hadley in the other tower.

"A dispatch from General Wade. The king's spies in Paris have learned Charles plans to land in Scotland on July fifth, and he's expected to attempt one of the western islands. They believe the prince is counting on gaining a toehold, which will encourage the French and perhaps Spain to send money, men, and arms." The faerie's face lit up with joy as she spoke. "Aye! Prince Teàrlach is coming!" Her wings fluttered, lifting her from the bed for a moment.

Ciaran's heart also lifted, but then cold sweat broke out and he had to remind Sinann, "He's coming, and the English are aware of his plans." He sat back down in his chair and pressed a thumb to the middle of his brow to ease the tension there. Tension made one vulnerable. Now was not a time to be vulnerable.

But Sinann leaned over the bedframe and said, "Yer father told us the prince would come. This year. It's plain Teàrlach will succeed for a time before he fails."

Ciaran grunted. "I dinnae believe it, faerie. If he comes, and succeeds in landing, he will also succeed in restoring the Stuarts. 'Tis naught but a matter of him coming."

The faerie crossed her arms over her thin chest. "Ye call yer father a liar?"

He frowned up at her. "I call you mistaken."

The faerie made a guttural sound of disgust and narrowed her eyes at him.

But he ignored her. "I must discuss this with Robin and Eóin." He rose from his chair and headed for the door.

"And should they ask where you received this information?"

That gave Ciaran pause. He stood hipshot, sighed, and said, "I'll speak to Robin. In general terms. My father trusted him." There was a pang as Ciaran wondered who his father really was, who Ramsay was, but he shrugged it off. The paper had to be a lie. Aught else was unthinkable. "Robin kens how to not ask too many questions." With that, Ciaran left the room and climbed the stairs to the battlement.

Quickly he crossed the north curtain and entered the dimness of the North Tower stairwell. But halfway to Robin's chamber on the top floor he heard footsteps and paused. The rustling of many skirts and a whiff of French perfume told him who was down there, and he stood by the wall for her to pass.

Leah Hadley appeared below, climbing the steps with her skirts in her fists. Though her hoops were not as wide today as he'd seen them, they took up most of the width of stairs. When she saw him, she also paused, looking up at him with large, curious eyes. The candles in sconces along the curved wall flickered and lit those dark eyes like the sparkle of stars. For a moment her dainty beauty almost made him smile. But he caught himself and only stared.

She climbed the steps toward him slowly, her face coming level with his feet, then his knees, then his belt, his chest, staring up at him all the while as she came. Her hoops were pressed together, collapsed for lack of space in the stairwell, and she came quite close. When her eyes were even with his, inches away, a tiny smile lifted the corners of her mouth. She looked straight into his eyes, and he felt it to his toes. There was a mad urge to reach out and press his thumb to the slight indentation in her chin that wasn't quite a cleft, but he restrained himself. She was a silly Englishwoman, and he would have nothing to do with her.

Then she returned her gaze to the stairs and continued on her way. Ciaran watched her go, half hoping for a glimpse of underskirt, or possibly even bare ankle, as she went. But she rounded the curve of the stairwell without showing him so much as a slipper. He sighed and continued to Robin's chamber, for a conference he knew would be nothing more than vague speculation about an unknowable future.

S itting in the garderobe, her skirts gathered under her arms and the breeze along the north curtain playing through the hole at her bare bottom, Leah took this private moment to close her eyes and see the image of Ciaran Matheson in her mind. It was a most pleasurable visage, the way his brow curved as it lifted, and the depth of his eyes was as fascinating as a deep, labyrinthine palace. God knew what savagery lay within that man, hidden by a complex pretense of civilization. It made her shiver.

On the way back to her room, she slowed as she passed the

chamber belonging to the praying man. Robin, his name was. The door, which had been open when she'd passed by here before, was now shut. Muffled voices came from inside, and she longed to hear what they were saying. Her heart pounding, she leaned close, but still it was unintelligible. It took her a moment to realize they were speaking in that Gaelic tongue, and she blushed at her own stupidity. She hurried away, frustrated and irritated. England had been good enough to take on Scotland to share in her wealth—the least these Scots could do would be to learn English.

In her bedchamber, Ida was tidying up, though there was nothing to tidy. She plumped already plump pillows, then went to straighten the clothing in the armoire. Curtains had been hung on the bedframe, for the sake of a modicum of privacy from the maid, and Ida rearranged those as well. They were nothing more than linen drapes, but she insisted on trying to make them hang like sheer silk. Hopeless and fruitless. After a while she gave up and returned to plumping the pillows.

Leah sat at the table by an arrow loop and gazed out on the small patch of the castle bailey she could see below. Nothing moved down there, other than a boy walking toward the stable. Then he disappeared inside and there was nothing at all.

She said, "Ida, tell me what you know about these Highlanders." Ida paused in her work, and Leah sensed a reluctance to answer. "Come. Speak to me."

Ida thought for a moment, then said, " 'Tis wise to fear them." Leah blinked. "Indeed? Fear?" It surprised her to learn even a Scotswoman could be afraid of her fellow countrymen. "Why?"

The maid held the post at the foot of Leah's bed, her eyes wide and her voice filled with palpable fear. "They're the most bloodthirsty folk ye'll meet, miss. Were a body to glance at one of them slantways, they would take it wrong and kill ye on the spot." Leah remembered the sight of the young Ciorram laird with anger in his bearing and a dagger in his fist. Ida continued, "They're each as mad as the devil. They take what they like, even from each other, and 'tis nae safe to travel anywhere in the Highlands."

"We weren't bothered on our journey here."

Ida rolled her eyes. "Aye. And we were traveling with an entire company of dragoons, were we not? I'd shudder to think what would certainly have happened to us, were we to have been without such well-armed escort."

Leah raised her eyebrows in acknowledgment of Ida's point. Another brief image crossed Leah's mind, this time an imaginary one, of their host the laird sweeping down upon her, taking her at a run, and throwing her across his saddle to carry her off. But she shook the image away. It was a silly, childish thought, and she was an adult now. She said, "So, were we to leave this glen without benefit of my father's men, we might be assaulted, then?"

"Aye, indeed. Or worse. Ye see, they're nae human. They've nae sense of right nor wrong. They even say a man from the Highlands is immune to cold. When he is traveling through the mountains, even in the dead of winter, he makes himself comfortable of a night by wetting his plaid in a stream then winding himself in it. Wrapped all in wet wool, he then lies down in the snow and considers himself quite snug."

Now Leah was boggled. Did Ida truly believe this ridiculous tale? But the maid crept closer and continued in a low whisper.

"They're animals, at home in caves and under the sky the same as an animal. And"—Ida lowered her voice even more—"they believe some of themselves are seals."

That made Leah laugh. "Seals? With flippers and a tail, you mean?"

"Aye." Ida's eyes were wide, and she seemed quite serious as she nodded affirmation. "There are tales of selkies who come to marry amongst them. These seal creatures take human form, and live as humans. Sometimes they take folk back with them to the sea."

She glanced at the door as if in fear of eavesdroppers, then leaned in to speak in a low voice, "There is a story of a brother and sister, and the brother was lost at sea. His death broke their parents' hearts. But years later, the sister had a visit from her brother. He told her he'd not died but had been taken by the seal folk. He told her of his life with them and how much he loved being one of them. It was where he'd truly belonged all along. And though she begged him to return to the land, he wouldnae come back. He lived out his days in the sea, swimming with his true people."

Leah was speechless.

Ida nodded solemnly. "Aye. There's them as loves the sea too much and they go to live in it. It's the truth I'm telling you. They're nae human." She nodded as if to affirm again the truth of her story.

Leah considered that for a moment, then said thoughtfully, "Bloodthirsty seals."

Ida fell silent, then went on tidying the already neat room. "With all due respect, miss, I've lived near the Highland line all my life. I know about these people. They're treacherous, and will betray you as soon as look at you. They have no loyalty, save to their laird, and even then they're quick enough to put one down in favor of another. It's a dangerous place we've come, Miss Hadley."

Leah looked out at the castle bailey and thought of how silly Ida sounded. Seals, indeed.

O n the third morning after Calum's departure, at breakfast Ciaran looked up to find Sìle with yet another swollen lip.

Rage filled him, and he took her by the arm as she passed on her way to sit with her husband and children. "He's hit you again."

Sìle looked over at Aodán, and whispered, "Dinnae fight him." A lisp betrayed a newly missing tooth at the front, and Ciaran blinked, shocked.

"And why? So he can clout all the teeth from yer head, until you can eat naught but this parritch?" Good teeth were hard enough to come by, without knocking them out for no reason.

" 'Tis nae worth the trouble." She held a hand over her mouth to keep him from seeing, but the sibilance in her speech enraged him even more. "Better I should take a punch now and again, than for you to be injured. Maybe killed. He hates ye, Ciaran, and will kill you if he can."

Ciaran looked down the length of the table at Aodán, who ate as if nothing were wrong. The rest of the castle residents were there, including the Redcoat captain and his daughter. It seemed they preferred to eat their food hot in the Great Hall rather than cold in their chambers whenever the kitchen staff would finally allow their servants to take it to them. Hadley and his daughter sat at the foot of the long row of tables, attended by their own servants.

Now was not the best time to press this, but to leave it until later would be to suggest Aodán's offense was not serious or that he himself was weak. Ciaran could allow neither. He reached down to the scabbard strapped to the legging around his right shin, where he'd taken to wearing Brigid after the manner of Dylan Dubh. He drew the dirk and stood, stepping away from the end of the table and to the clear space of floor near the bailey entrance.

"Aodán Hewitt!" he called to the middle of the line of tables. "I'm about to make ye quit hurting my sister, one way or another."

Hewitt looked up, chewing a cheekful of bread. Understanding was immediate. He glanced at Sìle, then stood and stepped over and away from his bench seat to face off. "I've told ye before, Ciaran, she's my wife." His tone was of strained patience, as if he wearied of explaining. He swallowed his mouthful. "Ciaran Dubhach, ye'll have nae say as to how I discipline my wife." He drew a dirk from his belt.

Ciaran glanced at his sister, who stared at the floor. Aodán was asking for a fight, and it was plain she no longer wished to defend him.

"That's it." Ciaran ran at Hewitt with Brigid cocked, then hesitated just before reaching him. Hewitt swung and missed. Ciaran attacked, and Hewitt parried. The two men then circled, each trying for an advantageous position, but the quarters alongside the trestle tables were close. Those sitting nearby rose to flee the flashing knives, making a wide circle around the combatants. Sìle herded her daughters away from the fighters, and a maid took them to the kitchen, out of sight.

From the corner of his eye, Ciaran saw two dragoons enter the Great Hall with muskets ready at the disturbance. Hadley rose from his seat. Ciaran shouted to him in English while keeping his eye on Hewitt, "Keep them off, Hadley! Keep them off, or ye'll have to fight your way out of here through clansmen!" Dirks all over the room were drawn in confirmation. Hadley flushed red as he looked around and assessed his position.

The dragoons were ordered to stand down, but the captain remained on his feet to observe the fight.

Ciaran made an attack on Hewitt, and had his forearm slashed for his trouble. Angrier now for his own carelessness, he came on with a roar and stabbed hard, taking his opponent aback. Hewitt stumbled as he parried. Ciaran pressed as Hewitt landed on his back. Ciaran dropped to his knees, and Brigid found the throat.

"Yield!" Hewitt's voice cracked with terror. "I yield! Spare me!"

Ciaran dug Brigid's point into the soft skin of Aodán's neck. His own arm was throbbing and dripping blood, and it seemed unfair to just let him go without getting even. However, a glance at his sister's wide, reddened eyes and tear-stained face softened his heart. As much as he wished to make Aodán bleed, he refrained. Instead, he leaned into Aodán's face and shouted so all could hear and his brother-in-law blinked.

"Very well then, Aodán. I'll spare you this once. But know this: should I ever see my sister with a mark of any kind, anywhere on her person, regardless of how it got there, I will have you hung. Therefore, Aodán, you would be well advised to make your life over to keeping my sister comfortable and safe, and above all unbruised. I'll expect to see you following her around, to make certain she doesnae trip and fall, nor cut herself in the kitchen, nor prick her finger with a needle. Are ye understanding me, Aodán?"

The man on the floor nodded. Ciaran regained his feet, turned, and walked away, returning Brigid to her scabbard as he went.

Behind him, Hadley said, "Take him."

The dragoons grabbed Ciaran's arms, and one of them pressed the muzzle of a pistol to his throat just under his jaw.

CHAPTER 5

Drawing on the white silk hose, carefully, to his knees, he picked a bit of dark lint from one of them. Careless maid. He would need to speak to her.

Leah watched the fight with wide eyes and a pounding heart. There was a scuffle with knives, the laird of Ciorram was stabbed by that other man, and suddenly it was over. The laird had his knife at the throat of the other man, who was nodding and whimpering. Scottish justice. She could hardly breathe. She laid a hand over her mouth, wondering what it had been about, for most of the shouting had been in Gaelic.

And Father was enraged. It was plain he was appalled this scene had been played out in front of his daughter. Now Ciorram was arrested for fighting that man, and the soldiers had a gun to his throat. Leah put her hands over her eyes, but peeked through her fingers, terrified the gun might go off. Ciorram held himself very still, his head tilted as far away from the muzzle as it would go. His eyes glistened with rage, and his gaze bore into her father. She found herself terrified more for Ciorram's life than for her own sensibilities, and she whispered into her hands, "Please don't hurt him. . . . Please don't hurt him. . . ."

But the laird's voice was calm as he said in English, "I've jurisdiction here, Hadley."

Father replied, "Laird or not, I can't allow you to carry on in this manner."

"Don't be absurd." Ciorram's voice was utterly reasonable and nearly free of brogue, though tendons stood out in his neck and the muzzle of the gun pressed into his flesh. "You'd be a fool to put your nose in my business. Gordon and Argyll, as well as every other Whig laird at His Majesty's beck, would have your hide, if for no other reason than to protect their own rights under the law." Leah's hands lowered from her face, and she looked at her father. He was listening, carefully considering Ciorram's words. She realized this "wild" man was manipulating her father by his accent. Her jaw dropped at the look on Father's face as he thought it over. It was working. Ciorram continued, still calm as the pistol dug into his throat. "Not the most advisable of political moves, to be sure."

There was a very long pause as the two men gazed at each other blandly. Finally Father said, "Very well. You take it upon yourself to assure me I won't be required to disperse another brawl when he takes revenge on you. I warn you, any deaths will cause me to pack you off to Inverness for trial."

Without so much as blinking, Ciorram replied, "I will assure nothing. As I said, any attempt to take me anywhere will be met by strenuous resistance, from within and from without."

Father took several long moments to think this over as his face darkened horribly. Leah knew he was backed against a wall, for the fight had not been serious enough to press the issue. But he'd made the mistake of attempting control he had no power to exert. Even she, who knew very little of politics and power, could see he had no choice but to back down. Finally, Father ordered his guard to release the laird. There was nothing else for it. The gun came away from Ciorram's throat, and tension in the room eased.

Dirks were scabbarded all over the room in a scattering of metal on metal. The elder of the laird's sisters, who seemed to be the defeated man's wife, went to her brother to tend the cut on his arm, while some Mathesons hurried from the room and others returned to their breakfast.

Father leaned over her where Leah sat, and spoke, but she didn't quite hear what he was saying. She was watching one of the kitchen maids tend to the laird with a needle and thread, wet-

ting the end of the thread with her mouth to put it through the
needle. Ciorram spoke sharply to her and waved it away, and it
appeared he didn't wish for his wound to be sewn. But then the
maid took the needle to the hearth and placed it in a small pot,
which she then filled with water and set on the fire. It seemed she
was boiling the needle and thread. Ciorram watched with a disparaging look that said she should have done that to begin with.

"Boil it?" Leah murmured.

"Are you listening, girl?"

Leah started to attention and looked up at him. "I apologize,
Father. What did you say?"

"I said, I wish you to stay in your room today, with Ida. No
sense in letting yourself in for whatever nonsense these Mathesons will be up to after a fight like that one. Let Ida bring you
your meals for a while, and keep away from trouble."

"Certainly, Father." Leah smiled and nodded, though she had
no intention of obeying. If he would force her to leave England,
she nevertheless would resist being imprisoned. When she returned to her room it was to await her chance to leave it. Where
she might go, there was no telling. But she would certainly go, if
only to prove to herself she could.

It was in the afternoon that she was able to elude Ida and her
father both. Since she couldn't show her face in the Great Hall for
a while, she now needed to go farther afield to entertain herself.
She went in search of a discreet route out of the castle.

On the pretext of a trip to the garderobe at the battlement,
were she to encounter anyone, she simply continued walking past
it and hurried across the north curtain to the other tower. Then
she went down the spiral stairs, hooped skirts in fists and as
quickly as she could. At the first bedchamber she came to,
through the open door she glimpsed stacks of ledger books and
knew this must be the laird's chamber. Bright afternoon sunlight
flooded the room through glazed windows, so she knew for a certainty it couldn't be anyone's room but the most important man in
the castle.

She continued on her way.

At the bottom of the stairs she found herself in a short, curved
corridor. Through one of the doors was a long corridor lined with
many doors placed close together. These would be the servants'
quarters, with rooms so small, and this corridor would only lead
her back to the other tower. She shut that door and tried another,

this time finding herself in the stable. Inside, wooden steps rose to her left, and she passed them. The sharp, warm smell of horses and manure stung her nose. There was dust everywhere, and motes floating in the air. But beyond the stalls was a wide-open door, and she could see the bailey outside. She picked up her skirts and went toward it in hopes of discovering a way from the castle.

"Disobedient lassies are frowned upon in these parts."

Leah jumped, and sidled behind a stall post. It was a man's voice. She couldn't tell where it was coming from, and looked around as he continued, "I wonder what your father might say were he to find you wandering about in dark corners like a perfect wanton." The brogue was thick now, but she recognized the voice. Then she saw him, sitting on a rickety wooden chair leaned against the front wall of the stable. Ciaran Robert Matheson of Ciorram.

Straightening, she gathered her composure and said, "It would seem, disobedient *lassies* are likely to have their teeth knocked out in these parts."

A disgusted look crossed his face, and he grunted. "Aodán willnae be hitting my sister again, or he'll find himself dead." Leah noticed the laird had changed his clothes and his hair was wet, slicked back, and tied, but still with that stubborn lock that drooped into his face. The blood had been cleaned from him, all but a string of three dots along the sleeve of the arm that had been cut.

He hung the other arm over a slat of a horse stall next to him and said, "Would there be aught I can help ye with, miss? Any other part of my home you would care to take for yourself? Is it my horses ye're wanting now?" He pointed with his chin toward the stalls across from him, where four Thoroughbreds drowsed or snorted according to their equine inclination. Ordinarily her father's horses were sheltered here as well, but they were not present just then.

Leah blinked at the criticism, but maintained a properly polite demeanor. She looked over the laird's four and had to concede, "They're very fine animals. You should be pleased with them."

"I should be arrested for them. And could be at any time, should your father deem it to his advantage."

That puzzled her for a moment, then she remembered. "Oh. Because you're Catholic? The law says you can't have horses worth more than five pounds."

He snorted and eyed her up and down. "And they say the English are idiots."

Finally irritation overcame her breeding. Her eyes narrowed at him. "I didn't come here to be insulted."

"I dinnae ask you to come here at all."

That felt exactly like a slap, and she jerked her head back in reflex. "Trust me, Ciorram, I would leave if I could." Tears rose, and she held her breath for a moment in an effort to control them. Then she continued, "My father brought me here, though I pleaded with him and begged him to leave me in England with my uncle. I miss my home, and I miss my friends. I was taken from the life I had been born to, and now I'm forced to live among people who despise me. More than anything, I wish I could go home."

The tears rose again, and won this time. She ducked her head so he wouldn't see them, and picked up her skirts to make a dash for the large door to the outside.

He heaved away from the wall and leapt to his feet to catch her by the arm. "Wait."

She waited, but looking up at him wasn't possible. She kept her head down and stared at the dirt floor covered with straw. Tears fell from her eyes and made marks on her skirt.

But he continued, "I apologize. I shouldnae blame you for the actions of your king. Or of your father." His voice had gone soft, nearly sweet in contrast to the anger.

There was a long silence, and he continued to hold her arm gently while she refused to look up. His hand on her was firm but not nearly as rough as she would have expected. The pressure was just enough to let her know he could detain her by force if he wished, but for the moment he preferred her to stay by her own volition.

Finally he said, "Here's another seat. Rest yourself and let the redness in your nose die down before you rush into the bailey for all to see your distress."

Leah touched her nose and found it tender. Sniffling as gently as she could, she turned and found the other chair near the one Ciorram had been using. It was no more than a stool, but wide and stable enough as she lowered herself onto it. Ciorram returned to his chair and tilted it against the wall again. His feet, encased in soft leather shoes and sheepskin leggings, dangled above the floor. With his knees splayed, she was glad for the copious folds of his kilt that lay on the chair between them. She might have been tempted to stare.

Instead, she examined his face. The blue eyes were nearly limpid, now that the anger was gone from them. But even in the dimness of the stable, they shone with an intelligence she considered decidedly un-Scottish.

After a long silence, she spoke. "Why do you speak the way you do?"

There was a flutter of blinking, and a puzzled smile came over his face. "Begging yer pardon?"

"Why do you speak with an accent? I've heard you speak without it, so why do you ever have the brogue if you know how to rid yourself of it?"

A chuckle rose from his chest as he glanced at the floor for a moment. Then he said, "Why should I wish to 'rid myself of it,' as ye say?"

"If one wishes to be civilized—"

"*Civilized.*" He spat the word. A glimmer of the anger returned to his eyes. "I speak as I do because I speak as I do. You may find, were you to pay genuine attention, that even my brogue is a mite different from others in the glen. My father spoke English and Gaelic both with an American accent. I grew up with the knowledge there were many ways of speaking, and I was never pigheaded enough to think one was better than another."

"But since you do know how to speak English properly—"

"I use it to my own advantage when it pleases me. I use it against those of narrow sight who think manner of speaking is the same as function of mind. I turn the stupidity and bigotry of men like your father against them."

"You fool people."

He shrugged. "If they are too blind to look past the manner of speech and dinnae attend to the words themselves, then they are at fault if they are more easily convinced for it. They are already fools, and I am nae the one to make them so. Dinnae mistake I might give a damn what such men think of me. I am who I am, and Captain Hadley can like it or dislike it. I care not which."

Leah found her mouth dropped open, and she closed it in a hurry. She'd never seen a man prepossessed enough to not care what her father thought. And it was apparent Ciorram truly was unconcerned. It was not the sort of bluff she'd seen in him the past several days; it was honest courage and dead seriousness. She said, "Ciorram—"

"Call me Ciaran. Nobody in the glen says 'Ciorram' but the Redcoats, and I'm hoping ye're one to never hold a weapon to my neck."

"Very well. Ciaran." Then she found the thing she'd intended to say had been quite replaced by the memory of the pistol at his throat. So she thought a moment and said, "I wish to extend condolences for the loss of your father. Please accept my apology for having intruded on your household at such a sensitive time."

He grunted, and turned to picking slivers from the slat on which his arm rested. "Thank you." And that was all he said.

She studied his face in the silence, watching the muscles on his jaw work. Her heart softened for him, and she wished she could ease his pain.

But then he said, "Perhaps 'tis time for you to return to where you belong." He glanced about the stable to indicate they were alone. "I wouldnae wish to find myself arrested for rape, now."

The word struck her between the eyes, for though she'd heard it before, it had never been said to her in anything more forceful than a whisper. She blushed furiously, nodded, and fled. Forgetting her original intention of sneaking from the castle, she hurried across the bailey, into the Great Hall, and from there returned to her room.

Ciaran didn't watch her go. He focused on the splinters he pulled from the wood slat under his hand until she was gone. Then he heaved a great sigh and knew he was an idiot. A cruel one, with no more grace than to offend a young girl who had meant him no harm. He stood, intending to go after her, but knew it would be unwise to be seen following the captain's daughter across the bailey. God knew where she'd got off to, and asking after her would be even more foolhardy.

So he sat once more and leaned his head against the wall behind him. If only it had been the captain himself who had happened by instead of the daughter.

As Leah readied for bed that night, she thought hard about what Ciorram had said to her earlier. Not so much *what* he'd said, but the *way* he'd spoken. Forceful, and straight across to her rather than condescending. The words had been deeply offensive, but at least he'd not spoken to her as if she were a child. His rudeness carried an underlying assumption she could stand up to it.

But she hadn't stood up to it at all. She'd fled exactly like the weak, stupid child she wished not to be. As Ida combed out her hair, Leah's cheeks warmed at what Ciorram must think of her now. How he must have sneered at her when she'd run away. He couldn't think of her as a real woman after that display.

Mother had never been like that. Not that Leah could remember, in any case. Mother had always held her own, even with Father. Never backed down. Never appeared less than brilliant and perfect. Not a hair out of place, not a wrinkle in her dress, and always in control, even when she was allowing Father to think he was the one in charge. Mother had always been the one to make the three of them a family, in spite of Father's long absences and the terrible danger of his position. She'd always been there to speak to him in a language he could understand. One that had always eluded Leah.

But now the bridge was gone. For more than a year Father had been impossible to convince of anything. And he never spoke to her of her mother, as if she'd never lived at all. Pretending there was no gaping hole in their lives, he went on as ever before, ignoring the changes in her. How she wished he would listen to her when she spoke!

Resolve stole over her. She dismissed Ida from her task, drew her dressing gown on over her nightdress, gathered its folds around her tightly against the cold, and slipped from her room to her father's bedchamber below.

At first there was no reply to her knock on the massive oak door. Her fine-boned hand made hardly a sound even the second time she knocked, but there was an inquiry from inside. "Who is there?"

Her voice was soft, and she struggled to keep it steady. "It is I, Father. May I speak to you?"

There was no immediate reply, but she could hear movement inside. Presently the door opened. "Leah?" Father wore a heavy blue silk brocade robe trimmed in velvet. The day's stockings still adorned his feet, looking very much the worse for wear on this straw-covered stone with their tops sagging horribly and the toes dangling inches beyond his own. His wig, of course, was on its stand, his own steel-gray hair revealed to be short and unruly. There was no receding hairline to cause him to wear a wig; it was only the strictures of fashion that made him cover his hair. The thick gray mass stood out in every direction, making him appear much younger than the wig allowed. In this state he seemed an ordinary man, and she drew courage.

It struck her yet again how handsome he was. His narrowed eyes were intense, his jaw square and strong. There was a solidity about him she'd always admired, even when she feared him. "Father, may I speak?"

"Whatever about, child?"

She lowered her eyes and hoped the light by the door was dim enough that he couldn't see the furious redness of her face. "May I come in? For the sake of privacy . . ."

Father stepped away from the door to allow her entry. The room was much like her own room, for these Scots had little in the way of furnishings and even less in the way of taste. The bed was large and oaken, the armoire painted in the Dutch fashion of the previous century, and the desk nothing more than a small table and chair of rough pine. She sat in that chair and raised her chin to speak to her father.

"It would seem a good thing the laird has given you his office downstairs for your work."

Father grunted as he looked around the room. "In a way, I suppose that's true. Though there are times I think I'd as soon make the ride to the garrison for every bit of business. The office downstairs has a decidedly Scottish nature, very rough and otherworldly. Indeed, there are times when I would almost swear that faerie in the tapestry across from the desk is staring at me."

The smile that tried to come was very hard to stifle. "Father, perhaps you run the risk of becoming Scottish yourself if you spend too much time here. You once laughed at those who believe in such children's tales."

His chin raised with offense, and from his voice she knew she'd made an error in teasing him. "Never mind what I believe or don't believe, child. Tell me what brings you here. Spit it out, and then off with you. I've a long day ahead of me tomorrow, and I must rest."

Now Leah was at a loss for what to say. To "spit out" the thing on her mind would be impossible, and in any case she was more interested in what he would tell her in response, if he would say anything at all worth hearing. She struggled for a moment to form a thought, then finally said, "I miss Mother."

His eyes went blank for a moment; then he looked away before she could glimpse anything in them. His voice was hard. "Is that all you came to say?"

"Is it not enough?"

"So you think this is a revelation of some sort?" Still he looked away.

"We've never spoken of it before."

"Some things need not be said."

"Neither should they be hidden. You never speak of her. It's as if you're happy she's gone."

Now he turned on her, his narrowed eyes aflame. "How dare you." He pointed toward the door. "Leave me. Return to your room. Immediately."

Leah, terrified, leapt to her feet and hurried for the door. But she paused as he spoke again.

"And know this, daughter: I wish to God your mother were still alive, so you would still be in London with her and I would be spared your childish puling."

At that, Leah fled as she had done earlier.

For several days Leah avoided her father. It was appallingly easy. Also during that time, she never so much as laid eyes on Ciaran. Whether he was avoiding her or not, she couldn't know. But it did seem odd.

One morning she heard an uproar in the bailey. Shouting men and a scuffle below brought her to an arrow loop in her bedchamber to see. But she emitted a small noise of frustration when she saw the disturbance was too near the Great Hall for her to see more than a cluster of castle servants staring at someone shouting in Gaelic. Oh, how she wished they would speak English!

"Stay here, Ida," she said, and hurried from the room over the maid's protests.

Down the spiral stairs with her skirts in her fists she hurried, through the corridor to the Great Hall, and out to the bailey. But by the time she reached the castle courtyard there was nothing to see. A stableboy across the way stared at her with dull blue eyes, and the pigs in the kitchen pens grunted at her in hopes of being fed, but there was nobody about who might be likely to tell her what had happened. Even her father's guard at the gate was absent.

"Leah."

She turned to find Father coming from the Great Hall, squinting in the morning sun.

"Father, what happened here?"

He was donning his gloves, and his gaze flitted over her. "Nothing to concern you."

She raised her chin as frustration grew. "Why shouldn't it concern me? I live here, do I not?"

He peered at her, and his jaw set. Then he looked up as his guard came from the stable with horses. Father said, "It was only a disgruntled villager."

"He seemed very upset."

"I expect he was. Nevertheless, it's not a matter to even interest a fine young girl." He prepared to mount one of the horses.

"Father, I wish to know what happened." She set her hands on her hips and frowned up at him.

He sighed, and a frown creased his own brow. "Very well, then. A farmer came to protest the killing of his dog."

"Why? Who killed his dog?"

"One of my men. Apparently the dog snapped at a private. It was plain the animal was vicious, so it was put down."

"What was the private doing to the dog when it snapped?"

An edge of impatience came into his voice. "I don't know that it matters, daughter."

"Of course it does. Any animal will snap if sufficiently provoked. What did the private do that made the dog snap at him?"

"Nothing at all." Father's lips were a thin, white line, and that meant it would behoove her to not press the issue further. So, quickly, she stepped toward him and said, "Father, may I accompany you to the garrison today?"

That seemed to take him quite aback, and his eyes widened. "Whatever for?"

"I've never seen it. I think I should like to see where you spend so much time away from me."

That touched him, she could tell by the shift in his countenance and the sudden roses in his cheeks. He gave it some thought for a moment, to not seem too easily swayed, then addressed his lieutenant to order another horse saddled for her.

The sun came and went among heavy clouds, but as yet there was no threat of rain. Great puffs of white and gray left wide shadows on the fields and pastures across the glen as Leah rode with her father and his guard to the garrison.

As they passed the church at the crook in the glen, she couldn't help but stare at the weathered old hulk of stone. She'd never been inside a Catholic church. She wondered what sorts of statues they worshiped in there. What sorts of prayers were said to the saints.

Inside the wooden battlement of the garrison, her father dismounted, and a soldier came to help her from her horse.

"Lieutenant, I'm charging you with the safety of my daughter for the day. Show her the garrison, and see she gets whatever she may need." Leah's heart fell.

The dragoon beside her replied, "Yes, sir."

With that, her father executed a crisp about-face and hurried into one of the buildings.

Leah watched him go and felt deserted. She'd hoped to spend the day with him, but it was plain he didn't want her to disturb his work. So she looked up at the lieutenant.

He was a nice-looking fellow. Earnest and rosy-cheeked. He ventured a polite smile, the first one she'd ever received from any of her father's men. She asked him his name.

"Lieutenant Jones, miss."

"Have you a first name, Lieutenant?"

"Kenneth, Miss Hadley." Utterly polite and obedient. Completely dull and boring.

"Well, then, Kenneth, my father has ordered we tour the premises. Let us proceed, lest he have us both demoted."

"Yes, miss." It pleased her to see his smile broaden into a real one.

It was a short, uninteresting tour, and Leah learned nothing more than that all garrisons were alike. This one was built a bit more roughly, perhaps, than Fort William, the ramparts of wood rather than stone. The buildings, however, were stone, of the same type as the castle and the church, but quite naturally were less worn. This garrison had been built during the reign of Queen Anne, not half a century before, and most of the buildings had been added even more recently than that.

There were several small office buildings and a wooden stable that opened onto the narrow bailey, but towering over the lot was a barracks several stories high. It appeared to be the oldest structure, its roof showing its age. The front, quite near the portcullis, faced toward the church across the way rather than the bailey inside the fortification.

Before the barracks, soldiers in various states of disarray went about their duties, cleaning weapons, repairing saddles and such. One very young private, perched on the side of his cot, was attempting to sew up a hole in his breeches while still wearing them, all the while cursing under his breath each time he stuck himself with the needle. A card game being played on a barrelhead was briefly interrupted by her passing, the players apparently wishing she would hurry along. The soldiers in shirtsleeves ducked their heads to go unnoticed. Nobody wanted to be engaged in conversation by the captain's daughter.

She engaged them regardless. All the young men she addressed were polite to her, speaking only when spoken to, and some were obsequious to the point of absurdity. Kenneth was unfailingly proper. The only moment of interest to be had this day was when she overheard two soldiers joking to each other about the target practice on a farmer's dog the evening before. Apparently the dog hadn't been close enough to the soldiers to have even thought of biting any, for the marksman bragged about how far away his target had been. Leah's cheeks warmed for the lie her father had told.

Once the tour was accomplished and there didn't seem to be anything else to do, she began to regret coming. If there was little to distract her at the castle, there was nothing at all here. Not even earnest and rosy-cheeked Kenneth was much amusement.

At midafternoon she decided she'd had enough of watching men groom horses and drill with weapons. She told Kenneth she wished to relieve herself, and walked away. It occurred to her that were it not for the privacy afforded her for body functions, she should never have a moment of freedom.

Quite naturally she did not go to pee, but instead slipped behind the barracks, picked up her skirts, and headed along the fortification to the front gate. Darting to it, she slipped through quickly and paused just out of sight of those inside the garrison.

For a moment she stared across the way at the church. It fascinated her. It wasn't supposed to be there. That it stood intact, in defiance of law, touched her in a way that made her burn to go in. What evil lay inside it, that had moved her ancestors to destroy these places in the past? She stepped past the guard at the gate to see.

"Ah . . . Miss Hadley?"

"Yes?" She turned to address the sentry.

"Shouldn't you have an escort outside the gate?"

A light laugh rose, as if that were the silliest thing she'd ever heard. "Nonsense. I'm only going across to see those wonderful roses in the graveyard. So many of them, and so white. I should like to have some. I'll be perfectly safe, with you standing right here all the while."

The guard thought that over for a moment, and she could almost hear the gears clanking slowly inside his head.

She added, "Lieutenant Jones said it was permissible. He knows where I'm going."

He nodded and stepped back to his post. She went on her way.

For the sake of form, she did stop by the graveyard to pluck one of the roses blooming among the bracken near the hillside behind. Then she glanced back at the sentry across the way to be certain his attention was elsewhere, and slipped around and into the church vestibule. The heavy wooden door creaked as it opened, and she quickly closed it behind her.

Inside, the large room of the sanctuary appeared stripped. There were no chairs lined up on the stone floors, as there would have been in a living church. Also, there was no altar, but a gigantic crucifix stood below the stained glass rose window. Clouded daylight made the room glow softly in deep reds, blues, and greens.

She went to the crucifix for a close look. A painted wooden carving of Jesus hung on the cross, his face showing the agony of his death. Every rib was represented; the wounds; the blood. As she gazed on it, she thought about that day so long ago and what this one man had suffered. It was hard to look upon. She'd never seen a statue quite like this before. Tears began to rise.

She shook them off, took a deep breath, and looked around. To one side was a single kneeler and a table where some candles stood. A confessional at the back gaped open without its curtain. She shivered at the emptiness of the room.

Then the door to the vestibule opened, and she turned in expectation of a soldier come to retrieve her to the garrison. Instead she found the young laird.

He stopped dead when he saw her, expressionless as he stared. She said nothing. Neither did she move, though her first impulse was to run away from this place as an intruder. She certainly didn't belong here and he couldn't possibly have wished her presence. But instead of running, she waited for him to speak.

Without a word, he turned and went to the kneeler, crossed himself, then lowered himself to it. After a moment of silence, he pulled a pitch-soaked rush light from a small stack on the table, struck a flint to light it, then touched it to one of the candles. Then he blew out the rush light and bent his head in prayer.

There were no seats, so she stood in silence, certain now that it would be rude to leave before he was finished. She turned to gaze at the rose window, following with her eye the intricate design, such a delicate thing in this harsh land.

When he raised his head, the laird rose from the kneeler and stood for a moment, shaking out soreness from the unnatural pressure on his knees. Then he extinguished the candle and headed for the door. For a moment it seemed he would simply leave, but then he stopped and turned toward her. His demeanor changed as if he'd decided something, and he sauntered across the floor toward her.

"I've an apology to make." He stood as if at attention, formal and penitent. "I was rude to you, last we spoke. I regret it."

She smiled. "I accept your apology. I don't believe my sensibilities were damaged in any permanent manner."

A sigh escaped him rather than the laugh she'd expected, and he nodded. There was a stiff silence; then he glanced at the crucifix and said, "I dinnae expect you've come to convert."

She shook her head, though she knew he was not serious. "I've come to have a look at this beautiful window." One hand gestured to the stained glass above.

" 'Tis a miracle it's survived."

"Indeed."

He shrugged and shifted his weight into an insouciant, hipshot stance. His head tilted toward hers as if in conspiracy. "Just as well you dinnae wish to convert. There being nae priest here, and all. At least with your company chaplain across the way there's someone to pray over you once in a while."

"Have you never had spiritual guidance? I certainly hope you've been baptized."

Now he stood straight. "Aye, but in Edinburgh, where I was born."

"In Edinburgh? By a Roman Catholic priest?"

That brought a frown. "*Och*, I cannae be certain, for I was too young to remember. But many folks hereabouts were baptized only by a midwife, for there's been nae priest here for near thirty years. Being baptized by a minister isnae so terrible as that."

"But you still pray as Catholic?"

"Of course we do." Now he seemed agitated and angry, his arms crossed over his chest, and she was sorry, for it had not been her intent to upset him. He continued, "Why should we change our beliefs for the sake of expedience? And would that nae be exactly what you Protestants want? For us to turn to your ministers?" His face flushed red. He set his fists on his hips and leaned toward her so she took a step back. "Is that nae why you arrested Father Turnbull to begin with?"

Quavering inside now, she nevertheless stood up to him. "My dear Ciaran, I hope you don't blame me personally for the loss of your priest. Thirty years ago, I assure you, I could have had nothing to do with it. I don't believe my parents had even met by then."

He gazed at her for a moment, taking deep, slow breaths, and she watched the fire in his eyes die down. Then he said, his voice calm, "I've never made confession. I dinnac even understand what it might be like to confess. Or even take communion."

"Then how can you miss it?"

He shrugged. "I do. That's all I can say. I do miss it, and when I hear of how the older folks in the glen wish for a priest, I feel it as well."

"And you blame me."

"I blame the king. And your father who does his dirty work."

"Ciaran—"

"Nae"—he raised a hand to stop her—"dinnae say it. There's naught you can do or say to change it."

She raised her chin. "Well, then perhaps I can listen. If your sins weigh on you so heavily, tell them to me."

His mouth opened as if to reply, but he seemed at a loss for words, as if he wasn't certain whether she was joking. She continued, "After all, such a fine, upstanding fellow as yourself shouldn't have so very much to tell in the confessional. I'm certain you must be pure as the driven snow."

A slow smile came to his face, and he chuckled. "If you only knew." He had an enchanting smile, of white teeth and ruddy face. It made her heart lift to see it, and she realized this was the first genuine smile she'd seen from him. He continued, "There is much for which I need forgiveness."

At that moment a cloud blocking the sun moved past. A wide, multicolored ray shone through the rose window and down on them both, lighting them where they stood and leaving the rest of the sanctuary dim. The warmth of it filled her, and she turned her face toward it.

Ciaran looked up at the window, still smiling, and sighed. "Aye, He hears me, even if His priests do not."

Leah gazed up at the bright window and had to agree.

That night after supper there was much excited talking and joking, smiles and laughter among the Mathesons. Leah wondered what was afoot, and she saw an exodus of people from the castle. Quickly she went to the portcullis to look over the village. Across the valley in the gathering dusk, straggling groups here and there were on their way upward and into the wooded hills to the north. Whatever was about to happen, Leah did not wish to miss it. She hurried to her father in his office.

"Please, may I go?"

"Go where?" He looked up from the book in his lap.

"Up"—she had no idea where—"into . . . the gathering. The entire clan is gathering." Somewhere.

"Why on earth—"

"They're *gathering,* Father. Don't you want to know what they're up to? Would it not be wise of you to monitor their activities under the premise of allowing your daughter to socialize?"

That last brought a smirk. "Socialize?"

Leah nearly groaned. "After a fashion, at least. Father, it would be so entertaining to see what the excitement is about, and you must need to make an appearance."

"I make appearances every day for meals, thanks to you—"

"Father!" There was a long moment while he considered, and she added softly, "Please."

Then he sighed and put his book aside. "Very well. Put on your cloak."

Leah nearly laughed with surprise and joy.

Though Ida fussed at her, the maid followed along for the short walk up the wooded hill to a large clearing. A bonfire had been built and was now being lit, heaps of wood that crackled as it caught. A jug was being passed. The mood was light, despite the presence of the English.

Leah settled onto a large stone near the edge of the clearing, while her father stood by the entry with his guard. In the gathering night, the temperature was nearly unbearable, and she huddled into her cloak. If only she'd brought a blanket as well. Clansmen stood casually about, some older folk sat on stools, some perched among the rocks or on rotting logs. A set of bagpipes was warming up, slowly coming to life. Conversation was lively, but entirely in Gaelic.

Children ran everywhere, laughing and playing, and rarely chastised for the shrieking. Leah noticed discipline, scant though it was, was imparted by whoever was nearby, whether parent or not. One little boy toddled past, who looked at her and spoke in what may have been language or merely baby gibberish. She smiled at him, wishing for the courage to reach out to him, but she knew such a gesture would not be taken well by the boy's many relatives nearby. So she merely continued smiling at him and watched as he made his unsteady way across the clearing.

Soon there was music. Of sorts. A man sat on a three-legged stool in the center of the clearing with a violin, playing some lively and unsophisticated tunes. It sounded like a cat being murdered by slow degrees, and Leah wondered whether the man was damaging the instrument. Soon she began to regret her decision to stay.

Unwilling to admit she was bored, however, she entertained herself by watching the women who sat near her. Some whispered together, and all had their spinning with them, using a little gadget she'd never seen before. Women in England used spinning wheels, not that Leah would have any experience with those either. These spindles were nothing more than a thin wooden dowel stuck through a small wooden wheel no bigger around than an apple.

She watched the work closely, fascinated by the quick flip of the finger, executed with insouciant skill. The women barely attended to their hands as they chatted amongst themselves. The spindles whirled, and the raw wool slung over one arm was drawn bit by bit and fed into the thread with expert fingers. Every minute or so the spinning was stopped to wind the completed thread around the spindle rod; then with another flick of a finger the thing was set to spinning again, dangling nearly to the ground and twisting the thread. All done unconsciously while the women listened to the music and talked.

For the first time in her life, Leah found herself envious of women working. This didn't seem like work at all—it seemed more like the sort of socializing her mother had enjoyed in London. Friends visiting, telling the news, filling the time . . . that had been her life with Mother. This didn't seem so different. Watching them made her long for her mother and her home.

She returned her attention to the music and took deep breaths to keep the tears away. Then she caught sight of the laird, he and his close friends well lit by the fire. His hair was freed from its queue and hung about his face in thick, black locks that touched his shoulders. He laughed at something he'd just heard, and his white smile reflected the fire across the clearing to her. He shone like a beacon.

Ciaran stood near the fire that night, basking in the heat and taking quick glances across the clearing at the captain's daughter. She sat with her father just beyond the pale of the fire, so staring was out of the question. That girl was a puzzle. The more he saw of her, the less he understood. And he so terribly wanted to stare.

The fiddler was entertaining tonight, though Leah seemed bored and was drawing deep sighs. It wasn't until Kirstie got up to dance for the gathering that Leah's interest perked. The captain didn't seem enchanted with the dancing, but his daughter's toe began tapping lively enough. With bright eyes she watched Ciaran's sister and appeared to want to try it herself. He could only guess what a disaster that would be, the *Sasunnach* ninny stumbling all about the place.

A chill skittered up Ciaran's back, but he shook it off. A second later, the bonfire blazed high, and once again that creepy feeling stole over him. Again he shook it off. It reminded him the world was filled with things unseen, spirits of dead folk, and such. For a moment he wondered if perhaps his parents were present, but rejected the idea. There had been nothing benign about this. Not at all. He gazed up at the surrounding trees, their branches whispering in the night, and wondered of the comings and goings of those not quite of this world.

Then, at a break in the music, Leah called out, "May I ask, what is this sword dance I've heard of? Can someone here do the sword dance?"

Silence fell. There was no sound but the crackling of flames.

She looked around as if oblivious and said, "May I see it?"

Then she turned to her father. "Oh, do please ask them to do the sword dance." Ciaran wanted to shake his head, to warn her away from what she was asking, but a perverse urge made him wait to see what the captain's reply might be.

He was not pleased. "Leah, I doubt—"

"Oh, but Father, I'm awfully curious. I've never seen it and I wish to see it. Just this once, then I won't ask again. Please, Father."

Ciaran spoke up. "We seem short of swords for such a dance." Damned if he was going to send anyone for the weapons in the castle in the presence of the captain and his guard, for they would be confiscated. Never mind that the dance was traditionally performed on the eve of battle and in any case completely inappropriate for the amusement of an occupying enemy.

But Leah persisted, "Oh, but we have sabers right here! She gestured to her father and his guard, then addressed Ciaran. "Please, sir, won't you do the dance for me?"

Oh, now it was Ciaran himself she wanted to perform the dance. And over the swords of her father's men. The idea amused him. "Very well, then, bring out the pipes." He started for the soldiers to relieve them of their swords, but old Keith Rómach called to him.

"I've a Matheson sword here, Ciaran."

Ciaran turned and frowned. "A real one?"

"Aye. This here." Keith drew an old broadsword from a scabbard at his belt. " 'Tis one your father gave me after the last"—he threw a glance at the Redcoats—"when he no longer needed it. It served me well until the tang loosened." He handed it over. It was a pierced steel basket hilt at least a hundred years old. The blade being loose from the hilt and wobbly, the sword was useless in battle, but for the purpose of the dance would do as a Matheson weapon. It had once belonged to his father, and Ciaran liked the idea very much. He took the broadsword from Keith Rómach.

Then he accepted the captain's saber and went to bow before Leah. "I'll perform the dance for you, miss, if you wish, though I confess the curved saber will make it a mite more difficult than the usual."

As he cleared space amid the onlookers and stood in the center of it to lay the swords down, Leah clapped her hands with delight like a little girl. His father's old sword was crossed over the English saber, as the dance had been performed originally, in exultation over a vanquished foe.

He glanced around the silent gathering, and the corner of his mouth twitched as he saw stifled smiles everywhere. Standing at the base of the cross, chin up, hands on hips, he nodded for the piper.

The dance began slowly. Chin up, eyes forward. Stepping between the swords. One quadrant, step, leap to the next, step back, on and on. Gradually the pipes sped up. Hands in the air now, Ciaran danced on, turning, stepping, and jumping, hair flying, not looking down and not touching either sword, for touching a sword would mean defeat in battle. The pipes skirled faster. Back and forth Ciaran leapt over the swords. Never looking down. Never touching the weapons. Round and round, faster and faster, turning, turning, turning.

Then done, hands in the air and chest heaving, tendrils of hair stuck to his face. He hadn't touched them. Victory.

The Mathesons erupted in cheering. Face impassive, Ciaran stood for a moment, hauling in deep breaths, and looked Hadley in the eye. He saw a gleam of anger there. The captain knew. His daughter may have been ignorant, but the captain knew the meaning of this dance.

Good.

CHAPTER 6

*His garters were traditional and in the same sett as the kilt, tied
and tucked, with fairly long ends dangling at his calves.*

Ciaran lived through another week of waiting, and there was
no murmur of what Calum might be up to with the paper
he'd found. He began to wonder if his brother was having diffi-
culty finding supporters he could trust, or if he was having such
success he was busy consolidating power and would return to the
Tigh with his goal of overthrow a fait accompli. Ciaran took
heart in hearing no rumors, yet feared what he might eventually
learn. He wished to hear. Anything. The waiting was torture.

It didn't help that in every quiet moment Sinann took the opportunity to remind him of his duty to his father's memory and
that he should keep the Mathesons out of the coming conflict. He
wondered whether the duty truly existed and whether he would
be laird long enough to fulfill it even if it did.

Even worse, her other favorite topic seemed to be Leah.

"Have ye seen the lass today?" She sat atop the frame of his
bedcurtain, arms and legs akimbo.

"No."

"She's lovely, is she not?"

"Aye, she is." It would be absurd to claim she wasn't, and he didn't wish a lecture on the myriad virtues of the captain's daughter in any case. He reached into a crate by the bed for an aged, leatherbound volume of poetry, opened it as he flopped onto the bearskin on his bed, then pretended to read, though his mind wouldn't focus on the words. Of course it was in English, and he wasn't in the mood for anything English just then.

"Why do you not seek her company, then?"

"Because she's the daughter of a man with many guns aimed straight at my head and the heads of my people." *Duh,* as his father would have said.

"All the more reason to win her over, I say."

He laid the book on his chest and peered up at her. "Is that what this is about? You think if I can make Leah love me I'll be safe from the Redcoats?"

Her face brightened, as if he were finally getting her point. "That, among other things, aye."

He snorted. "Then why should I bother seducing her? Why should ye nae simply put a love spell on her and leave it at that?"

A heavy sigh and a groan came from the curtain frame above, and Sinann's wings drooped. All this surprised Ciaran. Regret from the wee folk? He hadn't thought it possible. She replied, "I learned a hard lesson about love spells, lad. Trust me, ye dinnae wish that for her."

He grunted as he leafed through the poetry book some more. "We cannae have her mooning over me the way Sarah did my father, aye?"

The faerie's wings drooped even more. "You saw it, then."

"There were murmurings. Some folks blamed Da for it, him and his consorting with faeries." He glanced up at her. "It would appear they were right. Though I myself cannae say 'twas such a bad thing after all. Sarah was good to us all, and did not seem to suffer much for loving Da."

"So you see, then, why you must—"

"No. I willnae."

She crossed her arms over her thin chest and made a disgusted noise in the back of her throat. "You're exactly like your father."

That struck him sideways. He tossed the book into its box and blurted in anger, "Then one day I'll marry a woman I'll love as much as he loved my mother. And until then, I wish to be left alone about it." Shame flushed his face, and he leapt from the bed to throw on his coat and leave the room.

He headed up the tower stairs to walk the battlement for some peace and quiet. The faerie didn't like the wind on her, for it made flying an effort, and wouldn't follow him there.

Rather than peace or quiet, what he found on the battlement was Leah. She sat in a crenellation, in a spot that was low for some stones missing from the ancient wall, bundled in a cloak and her legs tucked under her. By the time he saw her, it was too late to pretend he hadn't. He slowed as he approached.

"Hello," he said.

"Good evening, Ciaran." Her smile seemed genuine, and that brought an equally genuine smile to his own face. Whatever else might be said about Englishwomen, this one was undeniably pretty. There were roses in her cheeks, a bright sparkle in her eyes, and that spot in her chin almost begged for his thumb.

He was about to pass her on his way when she reached out to touch the sleeve of his coat and he stopped.

"May I ask you something?"

"You may ask, but I reserve judgment as to whether I might answer."

She blinked at that, but her smile remained. "Very well, then. I wonder . . . why is it that a part of your hair is shorter than the rest and won't tuck into your ribbon? Surely you don't cut it that way deliberately."

He couldn't help laughing. "Well, to be perfectly literal, I did." He fiddled with the stubborn lock of hair that dangled before his face.

"There's a story, then." She folded her hands on her lap and sat back against the stone, appearing hopeful to hear it.

"Aye, a story. 'Twas a number of years ago, when I was in the shielings with the younger folk and the kine."

"Kine . . . cattle, you mean?"

"Aye." It lightened his heart when she smiled, pleased with herself she'd understood his meaning correctly. He continued, "There was a *creach*—"

"And that would be . . .?"

"A . . . raid. Some MacDonells came to steal our ki . . . cattle from the high pastures. We awoke in the night to discover them in the act. They outnumbered us, but we were angrier by far. I had my *sgian dubh*—"

"*Sgian dubh?*"

"Small, hidden dirk. Knife." Absently he touched the one strapped under his left arm. "I attacked in the darkness and wounded one of them. I'm certain of it, for there was blood on my hand after. However, I dinnae think I killed him, for he turned and seized me by the forelock. I never wore a queue then, and so my hair was easy enough to grab, all loose and like that. Though I struggled, he would have slit my throat had I not reached up with my own dirk and cut off my hair. I then dropped to the ground and scurried away. Having lost his hold and with nae way to find me in the dark, he then fled, along with the rest of his thieving kinsmen. No cattle were lost that night."

"Only a lock of your hair was lost."

He made a disparaging noise in the back of his throat. "A small price to pay for the welfare of the clan. Not to mention my life." He shrugged and smiled, and looked around as his voice lowered, "Though I assure you, thereafter I wasnae found outside my bedchamber without a woolen bonnet for quite some time."

Leah giggled, and that amused him, so he continued and touched the front of his hairline. "I had just a wee bit of hair, sticking straight up, for nearly a year. I can tell ye, I was never so glad of anything when it grew long enough to drop over."

She said, "And now it's grown long enough to hang in your face, but not long enough to tie back?"

"Aye." Again, he fiddled with the stray lock and brushed it back over his head, though it immediately flopped alongside his face again.

"And you never thought of wearing a wig over it?"

Ciaran lost his smile, and he looked out over the loch as he said softly, "Lowland foppery."

"English, you mean."

He looked at her. "Aye. English." For several seconds he refused to look away as she seemed to struggle with what to say next.

Then, "Why do you hate us so much?" She looked him straight in the eye.

His jaw nearly dropped with surprise at that. He'd expected her to tell him not to feel as he did, that he was wrong in his thinking. Instead, she accepted his anger and wanted to know the reason for it.

He replied, "Ye cannae understand."

"I wish to try. There is something terrible in your eyes."

He gazed out over the lake again and tried to shake off the chill that came over him. Did he dare tell her? Would she understand? Could she comprehend? For a long moment he weighed the possibilities of how she might respond. When he spoke it was an effort to make the words leave his throat.

"All my life, I've been told to beware of the English. Your soldiers come into our homes, take our kinsmen away or kill them outright, they eat our food and give back only laws that mean naught to ourselves."

"The soldiers—"

"Allow me to finish." His eyes found hers. "You asked, and I'm answering." She nodded, and he continued. " 'Tis far more than a simple wish to be free of the soldiers' threatening presence. My stepbrother Eóin, who is cousin and friend as well, when he was six years old witnessed a musket ball blow out the back of his father's head. The musket was fired by a dragoon who was helping evict the family at the time. Another time, my father witnessed the beheading of an idiot boy who had done no harm to anyone in his life. The sword was wielded by a dragoon who did it for sport. Before I was born, my father himself was tortured. Flogged, nearly to death. The whip was wielded by a dragoon who wished him to betray the clan."

Leah opened her mouth to speak, but he raised his voice and overrode her.

"I myself"—she closed her mouth and stared at him with wide eyes—"I myself, when I was but three years old"—a shiver took him and his jaw clenched—"was grabbed at back of my sark by the major of a dragoon regiment. He then pressed the edge of his saber to my throat and held my life hostage before my horrified father." His voice began to waver, and he cleared his throat before continuing. "It is one of my earliest memories, and it is as vivid as yourself standing here before me now. I can still feel the cold steel against my throat, and recall how I was convinced I was already cut and bleeding and about to die. How my heart raced, and thudded in my ears with a terror I'd never known before and have not since."

His throat closed, and his voice lowered to a growl. *"At three years of age,* I was taught the true meaning of mortality and to ken the danger presented by men in red coats. That is why I hate the English."

Tears glistened in Leah's eyes. Her lips opened to speak, but she said nothing.

"Ye asked."

"I'm sorry."

Whether she was sorry for what had happened, or sorry she'd asked, he didn't know. Neither did he inquire, but instead he simply nodded, then turned to go back to his bedchamber.

But she stood and took his sleeve before he could leave. He turned to look back at her. "No, Ciaran. I am sorry. Truly. I hope that officer was punished."

"Oh, aye, he was. He died by my father's blade."

She blinked, shocked. He in turn was surprised she was shocked. It was astonishing she could have believed the major would ever have been punished by English legal process.

But then Leah looked out over the loch for a moment and said, "I'm glad."

He stared at her, beginning to see her now with new eyes. With a nod of acknowledgment, he then returned to the West Tower.

During these weeks Ciaran continued to practice his form regularly, as he had with his father. At first the pain of Da's absence made it difficult to continue, but with each passing day the heartache grew less. He hated to become accustomed to doing it alone, but not as much as he would have hated stopping entirely.

Captain Hadley often paused to stare at him while on his way out of the Tigh when there was business at the garrison. Ciaran pointedly ignored him, making every effort to demonstrate he didn't give a damn what the *Sasunnach* thought he was up to. Concentrating on his breathing and control of his body, he looked straight through the red-coated figure.

But one morning the captain spoke to him. "Ciorram, what is that you're doing?" His tone made it clear he thought it was silly, whatever it might be.

Ciaran preferred not to answer, but thought better of his initial impulse to ignore the question and stood to reply. "My father called it kung fu. He learned it in the Colonies, but said it came from the Orient."

The captain made a dismissive gesture. "Is there a purpose to it, then? You appear to be engaging in an imaginary fight of some sort." He raised his chin to look down his nose, and Ciaran noticed the same cleft as graced Leah's. He thought it far prettier on her.

"*Och.*" Ciaran wasn't given to lying, but plundered his brain for a half-truth. " 'Tis exercise for health. To keep the blood pumping well. It . . . it balances the humors. Too much black bile, and it will rid you of it. Too much yellow, and this will remedy the situation." His eyes narrowed. "But it must be done correctly."

Hadley's eyes also narrowed. "Seems a waste of effort, then, if the same end might be gained by the ministrations of a physician. To keep the blood flowing only requires a bit of fencing, and one has the advantage of a useful skill learned at the same time."

"It is against the law for me to own a viable sword, Captain." Never mind that he owned several of them, his words were the truth.

"Oh, surely you know how to fence for sport. A wooden practice sword, perhaps? Or a foiled smallsword?"

"Aye. My father taught me with sticks." Also true.

A tiny smile came to the captain's face. "Of course." Then his face brightened, as if he'd just thought of something. "Here! Let's have a match! Take the lieutenant's sword over there, and see what it's like to wield a real sword."

Ciaran's eyelids drooped, and the muscles in his jaw worked. He quite knew how to wield a real sword, for there were weapons of every type secreted about the Tigh, that had been hidden since the Disarming Act of 1716. It was only since this dragoon had installed himself in the castle that Ciaran had been forced to put the sword aside and practice unarmed.

The lieutenant's eyes were wide with surprise when the captain ordered him to hand over his saber, but he obeyed. Ciaran took the sword and switched it back and forth a few times to learn the feel of it. The wirebound grip was smaller than he was accustomed to, and he didn't care much for the single quillon, but the knuckleguard was solid, and weight and balance were good. The sword that had threatened his life as a child had been like this one. He glanced over at the captain and thought it might be good to teach this *Sasunnach* something of Highland skill with edged weapons.

Hadley drew his own saber and saluted with it. Ciaran executed a salute in response, and they both went to *en garde*. The hairs stood up on Ciaran's arms and neck as he found himself faced off against a Redcoat with a saber in his hand. His pulse surged and a smile tried to come, but he forced his concentration into focus, and his face remained blank. Relaxed and centered as his father had taught him, he made a foray to test his opponent's defense. Swords clanged once, Ciaran parried the reply with another clang, and they both returned to cautious *en garde*.

Unbidden, the fantasy of accidentally-on-purpose killing the Englishman gamboled in his head. These sword edges were not foiled with leather covers, as they would ordinarily have been in practice. They both knew injury was likely in this risky circumstance, and an accidental death entirely possible. But he shook off the thought as ultimately a bad idea. As likely as such an accident might be, these dragoons were not reasonable men, and he would surely die for any serious injury to the captain.

So he attacked with care, almost lazily harrying the captain's vulnerable lower left quarter. The *Sasunnach* held his weapon too high for such a tall man. Hadley looked to be as tall, or taller than, Ciaran's father, who had stood six feet. Had they been engaged in a real fight Ciaran would have drawn blood already, and quite a bit of it, from a hit to that thigh.

Hadley attacked with a flourish, and Ciaran defended with insouciant ease. Each movement was with almost no thought, for his father had taught him well. The Redcoat frowned and tried to circle, but Ciaran liked having his back to the Great Hall rather than to the lieutenant standing before the stable, so he sidled and prevented Hadley from moving him. Another attack, and Ciaran was backed against the stone wall. They locked hilts, and Ciaran kneed his opponent's gut, then moved to his own left as Hadley bent to catch his breath.

Anger rose now, and Ciaran drew deep breaths to keep it down. Hadley attacked wildly, and Ciaran defended in a flurry of steel. The Redcoat pressed, and forced Ciaran back toward the animal pens. In a moment he would be toppled over the low fence to lie with the pigs.

But Hadley was still attacking high. In a burst of force, Ciaran parried hard, forcing his opponent's sword even higher, then stepped forward to deliver a hard side kick. Hadley reeled and, unable to retain his balance, fell to the dirt on his ass. Then Ciaran hurried to hold the edge of his sword near the captain's neck. Far enough away not to cut accidentally, but near enough to make it clear he was the victor.

The captain scowled. "Yield!"

Ciaran lifted his sword and stepped back. Hadley then called for his lieutenant. "Jones!" The dragoon hurried to help up his commander, then retrieved his saber. Irritated, Hadley brushed dirt from his uniform, saying, "For good health only, you say? Indeed. A man could stay healthy a long time knowing these tricks. It makes one glad to be armed with a pistol."

Ciaran was silent, and his gut churned as he watched his Redcoat guest mount the horse readied for him, and Hadley said nothing further before riding from the bailey. The *Sasunnach*'s stormy demeanor made Ciaran wonder if he'd made a mistake by letting him live.

A month passed, and more. July brought high summer. Ciaran began to hope something terrible had happened to Calum and that evil paper had been destroyed. The thought brought a modicum of ease, though he couldn't depend on it. Sinann's eavesdropping on the captain produced troop strengths and movements, but little information regarding Prince Charles other than that the Hanoverian government was not much in fear of Charles Stuart or his father. Because Louis of France didn't appear inclined to provide men or matériel for a venture he was certain couldn't win, King George didn't consider the Stuarts a threat worth his own men and money. It appeared there would be no mobilization of troops to meet the Jacobite threat.

Nowadays, Ciaran found himself oddly pleased by the sight of Leah about the Tigh. If he entered a room and she was there, it was all he could do to not stare. Sheltered though she was, and overly concerned about her clothes and hair, he now saw her as more than the vapid ninny he'd assumed her to be. To be English, yet neither evil nor stupid, made her a fascinating anomaly.

One day in the bailey where few could hear, catching up to Sìle on her way to the village, he asked whether she, Kirstie, and Mary might offer a bit of friendliness to Leah.

Sìle made a disgusted sound in the back of her throat and shifted the empty basket she carried to her other hip. "The silly *Sasunnach* deserves only to be chased away from here. She has no manners and is completely without skills."

Ciaran walked beside her. "Aye. She's a stranger, and unaccustomed to us. Perhaps, though, it would not be amiss were you to offer to teach her something." He glanced around to be certain nobody could hear. This might not be a good idea, for it would cause him trouble if word got around he was soft toward the English.

Sìle frowned at the silly idea an Englishwoman might be taught anything worthwhile. "Such as?"

Ciaran shrugged. "I imagine she might have an idea of how to thread a needle. Even in England, women must do something with their time. You could invite her to do the embroidery with you."

It was Sìle's turn to shrug, and she continued on her way to the castle gate. Ciaran accompanied her, struggling not to look as if he were tagging along. She said, "And if she answers my offer with hatred? For you ken they cannae abide us. She's as likely to be offended by the suggestion as she might be were I to suggest she kiss a goose."

He thought about that for a moment, about the loneliness Leah had expressed, then said, "I think she willnae. Try her and see. If she refuses you, then dinnae ask her again. That's simple enough, aye?"

There was a long consideration of that. Then Sìle said, "Aye. I suppose."

"Good girl." Ciaran patted his sister's shoulder. He fell back to return to the Tigh, but paused when Sìle turned and spoke again.

"Ciaran, and what is this sudden interest ye've got in the welfare of our unwelcome guest?"

The light of amusement in her eyes made him compose his face into an expression of derision. "Naught, sister, beyond keeping her father's goodwill enough so his men willnae kill us."

That seemed to satisfy her, and she nodded. But Ciaran had to admit to himself that he wouldn't give a damn about Leah for only her father's goodwill. The Redcoat sonofabitch meant nothing to him.

Leah was quite taken aback when Ciaran's oldest sister spoke to her in English one morning in July. She hadn't known the girl even was able to speak the language, for only the servants ever addressed Leah, and always in Gaelic accompanied by frustrated and confusing gestures. Communication for Leah, aside from her brief chats with the laird, was always a tedious process of pantomime.

But here, suddenly, was Ciaran's black-haired sister, sitting with her at breakfast and chatting as familiarly as if they were children in a nursery, introducing herself as "Sìle." It was at once disconcerting and a relief. It shamed Leah to be so grateful for the company of a rough Highland woman, but there was no denying she was lonely and eager for any sort of companionship.

"Come with us to sit under the willow trees this morning," Sìle was saying. "My sisters and I like to take our sewing down by the water when the weather is fair, and today appears as sunny as any we're likely to have."

Leah hesitated. Her first thought was to wonder whether Sìle had an ulterior motive, but then she decided she was being foolish. And it would be nice to sit out in the air with people of her own sex who were not in her father's employ, chatting and sewing. She smiled and said, "I'd love to."

Surprise flickered across Sìle's face, but then it disappeared and she smiled in return. "Wonderful."

Leah wondered what answer had been expected, and why she'd been asked to begin with.

The weather was, as Sìle had said, quite fair. The shade of the willow trees by the edge of the island was dappled by a myriad of tiny leaves that fluttered in a slight breeze. Long, lithe branches swished overhead like a drape. Sìle, Kirstie, and Mary sat with Leah in a spot on the island where the remains of the ruined outer castle curtain made a rocky ledge just above the lapping water of Loch Sgàthan. The long, tight whalebone stays of her bodice made sitting on the ground difficult, so Leah claimed a large stone of the ruins on which to perch. The fresh air filled her head, and for a time she didn't even mind the rugged landscape all around. The sun warmed her brow, and the company eased her soul.

Sìle was embroidering an unbleached linen shirt with bleached white thread. The pattern was intricate, and Leah asked to see it up close. What was finished so far showed a line of dogs, it seemed, around the cuffs, their legs and necks impossibly lengthened and interwoven, accompanied by branches and leaves likewise entwined. All in white on nearly white. As strange as the design was, she had to admit the stitches were immaculately precise. In fact, it made her own work seem amateurish.

"For Aodán," said Sìle. "Dogs are lucky for him, so I always put a dog somewhere on his sarks."

Leah smiled. "Would even the white hound be lucky for him?"

The twins giggled, and Sìle gave a theatrical shudder. "*Och,* we would never care to put that to the test. Nobody wishes to see the white hound, not even Aodán."

"Have you?"

All three girls shook their heads. Sìle said, "It's been decades since anyone has. To the best of my knowledge, our father was the last to see it, shortly before being arrested by the murdering Red—" A quick glance sideways at Leah, and a blush rose to her face. She finished, ". . . shortly before he was arrested mistakenly."

Leah blushed as well. She was certain anyone who was arrested by the army must have deserved it, but thought it unwise to press the issue here. Instead, she said, "So the ghost was unlucky for him."

The three sisters nodded.

In an attempt to shift the talk away from "murdering Redcoats," Leah said, "Have you ever seen a selkie?"

Kirstie giggled and Mary said, "Our father was one."

Leah blinked stupidly. "Indeed?" Now she was certain they were having her on, and wondered whether she should pretend to go along with it or challenge the girls and see how far they would insist.

But they seemed quite sincere. "Aye," said Kirstie, eager to tell the story. "You see, his father had been taken by the seal people as a young man and never returned. They say he married one, who then gave birth to our father. Then when Da returned to his people, all dark-haired and overly fond of the water, everyone could tell his mother must be one of the seal folk."

Sìle had a smile on her face, but she remained silent.

A tiny frown creased Leah's brow. "But I thought your father was born in America."

Kirstie's eyes were wide, and she was completely in earnest as she insisted, wiggling up and down where she sat, "*Och,* but that doesnae explain how he swam so well and why he bathed so often."

"Often?" Leah was skeptical on this point, having seen many truly filthy people in the glen.

"Aye. He washed every night before bed. Even if he'd washed earlier in the day, he'd scrub again at the washbowl at night. And in summer he sometimes stood under the falls below the high glen, or he would take the lye soap and scrub all over in the burn. As often as he could. He taught us the habit as well."

That was a surprise. Even in England, Leah had never known anyone who bathed *every* night. Often, for her, was twice a week. "It's a wonder you don't all catch your deaths of cold!"

Sìle shook her head, and Kirstie said, "Da was never ill a day in his life."

"Unless he had a bad tooth to be taken out," Mary added.

"Oh, aye." Kirstie allowed as that was true. "He was mighty sick and irritable whenever that happened. But aside from that, he was never sick. He was the strongest man in the glen."

Mary added, "And the handsomest."

"Oh, aye, he was," Kirstie allowed. " 'Tis a pity I'll never marry a man so handsome as he, for there are none. Aye, Da was handsome."

"Until he died." Sìle's head was bowed over her work, and her voice was tender and soft. The other two girls fell silent, and focused again on their work.

Leah said, "But he didn't die of a cold."

The girls all shook their heads. There was a long silence as they worked, and Leah burned to ask whether their father was as handsome as Ciaran, but dared not. She wished they would talk further. As silly as was the selkie story, it was fascinating nevertheless. She plundered her brain for a way to broach the subject of Ciaran without appearing obvious, and finally said, "I've heard your brother called 'Ciaran Dubhach.' Is that to indicate his relationship with Dylan Dubh?"

Sìle twisted up her mouth as she struggled with that question. "Well, perhaps a wee bit, yes. But not entirely. 'Tis a bit of a play on Father's name, aye, but while Da was named for the color of his hair, Ciaran is called Dubhach for his dark demeanor. It means sad, or melancholy. Ye may have noticed he rarely smiles. 'Tis always been that way with our brother."

"I see." And Leah did, for she could imagine how Ciaran's childhood could have quelled any impulse to smile.

Another silence fell, and she cast about for a safe subject this time that would not bring the image of "murdering Redcoats." She said, "Your frocks appear very comfortable."

The three sisters erupted in chatter about their soft, wool dresses, and how could she stand to be so bound up in stays, and wouldn't she like to have a nice Highland dress to wear, and there was a piece of wool among Sìle's things at the castle that would so complement Leah's hair and skin.

Leah nodded, pleased to have broken through at least some of the ice. It was a certainty she couldn't let her father see her in a Highland frock, but making the dress would occupy her for a time. There were things far worse she might do to entertain herself here than wearing an unsuitable garment. Father should be pleased she was making the best of things. Perhaps if he learned of it, she could ease his disapproval by pointing that out. Meanwhile, she sewed with Ciaran's sisters and discussed the piece of wool that would certainly be checkered and impossible, but she would wear it for the sake of smooth relations with the castle and its laird.

C iaran's waiting ended in July. Calum finally made his move. It was late one afternoon when a tenant near the village came running to the castle from his fields and breathlessly reported to his laird of a contingent of armed men making their way up the glen. The farmer had counted but ten of them, a relief to Ciaran. Ten would not be enough for a violent coup. Calum would need to talk first and draw steel later, resorting to a fight only as an escape measure.

Unwilling to risk confiscation of the king's sword, he left it in his chamber. With Brigid strapped to his legging, Ciaran went calmly to the bailey to meet his guardsmen, who did wear swords in spite of the law against them. He led the men to face Calum and his equally well-armed men. Eóin strode at his right hand, and the rest of the clan gathered around and behind the heavily armed guardsmen. Robin, hobbling along with the help of his staff, lagged behind, but began to catch up when the guardsmen stopped at the village square. Ciaran chose his ground so that if the meeting turned violent Calum would be required to fight his way through the press of loyal clansmen where they lived.

The summer sun was bright, and glinted from the swords and dirks wielded by the Mathesons who approached from up the glen. At this distance Ciaran could see now that Calum had brought Dùghlas Matheson and his tenants from the southeast. Calum's plan clicked into place in Ciaran's mind. No wonder there had been no word of the plotting, for Dùghlas had not been an overly close ally of Dylan Dubh. Control of the southeastern tenancies had been given as appeasement during the early years of Dylan Dubh's tenure, for Dùghlas's allegiance had been elsewhere when Ciaran's father had succeeded to the lairdship. More than likely, Calum had promised more land and more autonomy in exchange for his loyalty, and expected Dùghlas's endorsement to sway the rest of the clan.

Also with them was Gregor Matheson. Ciaran peered at him, wondering how and why his stepbrother was involved. Then he frowned at Gregor's brother, but Eóin stared ahead at the approaching party. Only his reddening ears indicated his reaction to Gregor's betrayal.

As expected, farmers and villagers hurried from all around when they saw something was going on. Some brought dirks; others brought only their pitchforks and sickles. When Calum and his ten entered the square, Ciaran called out, "What is the meaning of this?"

Calum halted, and his followers ranged themselves across the width of the square. He said, "You're nae the son of Dylan Dubh." Audible reaction came from the gathered clan and he continued over the murmur, "As his eldest son I mean to take my rightful place as laird."

Shock, surprise, disbelief all were voiced, and there was low muttering all through the crowd. Readied weapons drooped, some lowered entirely, and Calum had the attention of every clansman in the glen.

Ciaran responded, "That's an absurd lie."

"You're a usurper. You ken it, as well." He pulled the cursed adoption paper from his sark and opened it, then held it high for all to see. "This document tells of the adoption of Ciaran Robert Ramsay by Dylan Robert Matheson." He turned toward the crowd and shouted to make himself well heard.

"This man who presents himself as your laird is naught more than the son of a dead man named Connor Ramsay. His mother's first husband." He raised high another, newer, piece of paper. "I have been to Edinburgh and obtained a copy of the wedding record, written and signed by an attorney of good repute."

Another murmur made its way through the gathering, but one man—Donnchadh Matheson, who was the blacksmith—spoke up. "You cannae fool me, Calum Og. Ciaran is the image of your father and there's nae doubt who sired him. There never was."

"Ciaran was born in Edinburgh." Knotted muscles stood out on Calum's jaw.

"Aye," said Robin as he stepped forward, directly between the two factions. He took a moment to catch his breath, stooped over and leaning hard on his staff, having hurried to catch up in time. Then, still panting but breathing easier, he straightened and continued, "I was there the night he was born." The murmuring among the crowd fell silent, to hear what Robin would say. Still clutching his staff, he said as loudly as he could though his voice wavered, "I witnessed the birth of Ciaran Ramsay, while his mother was married to Connor Ramsay of Edinburgh. The man standing here was that child."

That brought another outburst from the crowd. Calum crowed, "Aye! Then he is not the son of my father!"

Ciaran struggled to show no sign of what he felt as his heart sank and his throat tightened. His cheeks and ears burned as he stared at Robin, the betrayer he would never have suspected.

But Robin continued, "Nevertheless, he *is* the son of Dylan Dubh, born in late January, nine months after Beltane. He was conceived on that festival night, and the following day the betrothal of Dylan Dubh and Caitrionagh Matheson was announced. Do ye remember it, Donnchadh?"

The blacksmith nodded.

"I recall it, as well." Eóin spoke up, and everyone turned to look at him. "Aye, I was a wee lad, but I remember it. 'Twas before the troubles. And before Ciaran was born."

Robin returned to his narrative. "But when Dylan Dubh was arrested by the *Sasunnaich,* the lass's father married her off to Connor Ramsay. The child was born less than eight months after Cait first met her husband, and he was a big, healthy lad. Even by that it was plain he was nae the son of Cait's husband. Anyone with eyes could see Ciaran had been fathered by none but Dylan Dubh."

Robin gave Calum a disgusted sideways glance. "I'm surprised ye could even entertain the idea he wasnae Dylan's son. He bears a far greater resemblance than yerself can claim."

Robin's tale roared in Ciaran's head. Sired by Dylan, yet born to Connor? The implications were appalling.

Calum said the thing even Ciaran was thinking now. "Then he's my father's bastard, and with nae more right to the lairdship than my sisters."

The reply from Robin was immediate and firm. "Dylan Dubh was married to Ciaran's mother for two years after her husband died. The lad was legitimized."

"This is nae acknowledgment of a blood tie!" Calum waved the paper, an edge of desperation to his voice and tension in his body. Small pieces broke from the edges of the aged document and drifted to the sod at his feet. "In fact, it's exactly the opposite. It makes clear my father did *not* wish to acknowledge publicly a blood tie."

"He dinnae need to. 'Twas plain for all to see in Ciaran." Robin's tone turned to exasperation at Calum's thickheadedness. "*Och*, in all his children there was nae even one to take after Dylan Dubh as Ciaran did. In appearance, in talent, even in thought, they were the same."

Clone. The Colonial word Da had always used was *clone,* and it was supposed to mean they were exactly alike. Especially as Ciaran had grown and become a man, his father had expressed affection and amazement at the similarities between them. Ciaran's throat closed, and he had to swallow hard.

Too much amazement there was, perhaps.

Calum's disadvantage with the clan was now becoming clear to him, and his face began to redden. He said, the desperation in his voice growing to become shrill, "Then why the adoption paper? Why not simply make the truth known?"

The merchant Seumas Glas MacGregor, one whose house stood on the square, spoke up, waving as he did the hook that stood in for the hand he'd lost in the Battle of Glen Shiel. "Your father was an odd sort, and overconcerned with papers. And most likely he hadn't thought there would be a traitorous son such as yourself to go against his wishes, which he'd made plain to all who knew him."

Robin continued, over the objections of Calum, "I say, and I think the entire clan must agree with me, that there is nae doubt who is the true successor of Dylan Dubh. Ciaran is his son, he is the eldest son, and he was, by all that is holy, acknowledged by his father, who was married to his mother for all to see by a proper priest in that very church up the glen. Nae *Sasunnach* legal paper can change those facts, nor cast a shadow on Ciaran's right of accession."

Now there was a murmur of agreement among the clansmen.

Ciaran took the moment in hand, drew Brigid, and addressed

the men in arms against him. "Throw down your weapons now, and I'll spare you for having been misled by this paper."

There was no hesitation. Dùghlas, Gregor, and the other eight relinquished their swords and dirks, looking sheepish. But Calum himself raised his sword instead, and with an angry roar ran at Ciaran.

Ciaran parried and locked hilts. He pushed Calum off him as two dozen weapons were brought to bear by guardsmen and clansmen. Calum found himself surrounded by blade points and farm tools, unable to move an inch lest he impale himself on one of them. Ciaran said, "Drop yer weapon, brother."

Calum complied, and the broadsword thumped onto the sod.

Then Ciaran said to his men, "Take him to the gatehouse."

His brother paled, and though he said nothing further, his eyes beseeched Ciaran as he passed on his way to imprisonment. Ciaran scabbarded his dirk and watched the villagers disperse. His guardsmen picked up the surrendered weapons, then made their way back toward the Tigh. Still Ciaran waited, not wanting to be anywhere near his brother just then.

Sìle, Kirstie, Mary, and Robbie waited with him, but he could see in their eyes they were as shocked at the story as he was. Robin waited, still leaning on his staff.

Ciaran gazed over at Robin. More than anything, he wished he could ask about his mother and Connor Ramsay, but didn't have the courage. What if Robin had embellished the truth? What if Ciaran's resemblance to Dylan Dubh was more a case of resemblance between Dylan and Ramsay? He couldn't bear to hear such a thing. It was best to let the story stand as it was.

Ciaran's brother and sisters came to accompany him home, and Sìle took his hand in hers as he turned toward the castle. There behind him, standing in the middle of the track, was Leah. She'd heard it all, and now he was even more ashamed.

CHAPTER 7

A sterling silver kilt pin, in the shape of a claymore, secured the flap at his side.

That evening, Ciaran evaded the counsel of both Robin and Eóin and ate supper in his bedchamber, then slipped discreetly from the Tigh to be alone. Sunset was still hours away as he climbed the track that led through the wooded hills to the north of the glen. Along the burn that rippled and burbled toward the loch below, he followed the trail to the ancient *broch* that stood in a hollow between two hills.

The gray stone ruins of this unimaginably old tower were avoided by most of the clan because faeries were known to inhabit it. As Ciaran had recently become friendly with the wee folk, there was little fear of it in him anymore. Today he needed time alone to think, and this had long been his father's favorite place for that.

A pang soured Ciaran's stomach as he thought of Dylan Dubh. The center of Ciaran's life had always been his father. Dylan Dubh had raised him to lead the clan, and Ciaran firmly believed his purpose was to carry on after his father's time. Now he feared he wouldn't be able to. Not if his claim to his title could be further challenged.

Here, at the *broch,* there was quiet enough for thinking. An enormous oak tree grew outside the crumbling walls. Its branches reached in through a window and over the broken stone, in a gnarled canopy that shaded much of the inside. Stone steps climbed the curve of the wall, and several chunks of fallen wall lay about the interior.

Ciaran had never been inside before, having been as reluctant as everyone else to encounter faeries and ghosts. He'd heard tell at many a *céilidh* the ground had been stained red by the blood of an ancient Matheson warrior, and he was mildly disappointed to find the grass inside as green as any pasture in the glen. Black fungus grew in wavy lines among the shaggy grass, a common thing in such a shaded place. He sighed and sat on the ground with his back to one of the stone blocks. The warmth left by the waning sun felt good, and he tried to relax and clear his mind.

Idly he poked at the grass, wondering where that story of stained ground had come from, and that was when he saw it. The roots of the grass, and the earth in which it grew, were bright, blood red. He grunted in surprise, and pulled a single blade for a look. Along it the color faded from green to maroon to red, smoothly, as if the color had been drawn from the red ground into the green blade. He sniffed it, and it smelled grassy. He bit the red end of the blade, and the metallic taste of blood filled his mouth. Calmly he spat, and threw the blade away. It was plain the story he'd heard was true. He leaned back his head against the stone.

As he thought through the events of the day, his mind danced around the subject of his brother, unwilling to focus on what he must consider. There was a decision to be made, and Ciaran must force himself to think on the thing he'd dreaded since the day Calum had found that document. If only the lad hadn't come armed! If Calum had presented that paper to the clan when they were gathered in peace, and asked for a fair consideration of his claim, he wouldn't be in the gatehouse awaiting judgment. But now Ciaran needed to decide whether to have his brother put to death.

Some lairds would have had him hanged straight away from the nearest tree. Treason was a serious crime, and the most damaging to the well-being of the people. Allowing such foolishness to go unpunished would foster disruption of clan life whenever anyone saw an opportunity to overthrow the rightful laird with no risk to himself. Ciaran would be a fool to allow Calum to go free to try it again.

But was he obliged to go so far as to kill his brother?

The faerie's voice came from nowhere. "Your da wouldnae have done it."

Ciaran looked around, and found her sitting on the steps just under the overhang of branches. "He wouldnae have done what?"

"Hung Calum."

He snorted and bent his knee to lean an elbow on it, and then his head on his hand. "Of course not. Da was his father." Another pang curdled his soul. He continued, "I'm only his half brother." As he spoke, he wondered whether he was even that.

A movement caught his eye, and he looked toward the gap in the wall that had once been the entry to the *broch*. Leah was there, watching him. She was well bundled for late July. The weather was warm enough there was no need for a coat or cloak, but she held a heavy shawl drawn close about her shoulders, as if she would be cold without it.

With a flick of his fingers he adjusted his kilt to make certain folds of it covered him in spite of his raised knee, and he called out, "Enter with caution, Miss Hadley"—he leaned forward and raised an eyebrow, his brogue thickening as he gestured about at the surrounding *broch*—"for here there be wild Scotsmen and wee folk and all manner of enchantments."

An odd look crossed her face at the word "enchantments," but then she smiled and said, "I wish you would call me Leah."

He sat back and considered that for a moment, then decided he was pleased enough to drop some formality, even if she was a Redcoat's daughter. "Very well, Leah."

She nevertheless took a formal tone as she stepped just inside the *broch* but no farther. "I wish to extend my sympathy for what transpired today. I think what your brother did was unconscionable."

There was no real reply for that, for her sympathy did nothing to alter the situation. He gave a small nod and said, "I thank you." The mystery of why she'd followed him so far and so carefully to tell him this remained one.

She hovered by the gap, standing and appearing uncomfortable, so he gestured to the steps nearby. "Would ye care to brave the faeries in their domain and have a seat?"

Leah went to sit, expertly arranging her hoops to lie grace-fully around her, and Ciaran found himself enjoying the view. There was utter grace in her carriage and obvious pride in her beauty. The pride was most certainly warranted, for she was every bit as beautiful as she seemed to think. Her chestnut hair shone in the waning daylight, a sparkle shone in her eyes.

Once she was settled, she looked around the *broch*. "Do you believe in faeries, then?"

A glance at the spot under the overhanging branches, where Sinann seemed to have disappeared, and he replied, "Aye, I do, with all my heart." He had to smile at the wide look in her eyes. "I also believe in the ghost of the white hound, though I've never seen it. Which is just as well, for 'tis a bad omen and has been known to bring destruction on them as have."

She smiled, and he saw condescension. "How superstitious you are."

For a moment there was an unbearable urge to pull a blade of grass and invite her to chew on it, but he restrained himself lest he then be accused of having made a pagan sacrifice on that spot. He said only, " 'Tis nae more a superstition than believing the world is round, or that seeds planted in the ground will grow." His eyes narrowed, and with full intent to annoy he said, "And no more than believing in the power of the cross or the transubstan-tiation of the host."

She blanched at that, and glanced away for a moment.

He continued, "Do you truly think we're all so backward, then?"

There was a long moment when she said nothing; then she looked at him. "I did at one time. Now I'm not so certain."

This girl was full of surprises. All his life he'd been sneered at by Englishmen for his culture and his beliefs. He'd thought the English were unmovable, and wouldn't expect her to change her opinions any more than he would care to change his opinion of the English.

Then he realized his opinion of her had changed in spite of his certainty regarding the evil of her people. By her compassion she'd shown him she wasn't entirely like all the *Sasunnaich* he'd seen before. Others' opinions of her were changing as well. Fre-quently he'd found Leah in the Great Hall or outside in the fresh air, sewing and talking with Sìle, Kirstie, and Mary. When asked, his sisters had reported Leah to be "unusually bright and able . . . for an Englishwoman." High praise, for the daughters of Dylan Dubh hated the *Sasunnaich* as thoroughly as his sons did.

Rather than snorting in disbelief, he said in a low voice, "Why? What has made ye uncertain?"

"I have come to realize there is actually little difference between your people and mine. We all do our work and we enjoy the company of friends and relatives. We all eat, sleep, and care for the children. We have our good luck charms, though in England I think we might have fewer of them." She paused, took a deep breath, then said, "To be perfectly frank, I've even begun to suspect there might be no particular evil to crossing oneself or saying the rosary."

Ciaran blinked. "You dinnae say? Nae evil to it? You've begun to suspect?" There was some teasing in his voice, edged with the habitual anger of one forced to bear shame for his religion. She was absolving him of an evil he'd never owned, which spoke eloquently of her true thoughts.

She reddened, and fiddled with the front hem of her shawl. "I apologize. No, there is no evil in it. The evil is in thinking it matters so much as to punish those who do it." Then she raised her head, "Or, for that matter, to burn those who choose not to do it."

His immediate urge was to assure her she would go to hell for not doing it, but he bit his tongue. All he said was, "Aye."

"If James Stuart succeeds in overthrowing the king, do you suppose he will begin sending Protestants to prison?"

Ciaran shrugged and blinked. "I cannae imagine he would, for if he did, there would be few left for him to rule." Then he chuckled. "Can you imagine it? All the Protestants in prison, and we Catholics left to do all the work and feed all those prisoners?" Leah giggled, and he went on, "Oh, aye! Everyone would say, 'Bring back King George, and quickly, for 'tis too much work under King James!'" That brought a good round of laughter for the both of them.

When it died down he said softly, almost to himself, "Aye, us lazy, good-for-nothing Catholic Scots . . ."

Her smile faded, but then she said, "I like your smile, Ciaran Dubhach." He cut a sharp glance at her to hear the Gaelic on her lips. She continued, "But I hardly ever see it. You're so serious all the time." There was a warmth in her eyes now, which made him smile though he resisted it. "See? You shouldn't avoid smiling. You brighten the day with it."

"*Och,*" was all he could think of to say.

There was a long silence, but not an uncomfortable one, while Ciaran fiddled with a piece of red-and-green grass in his fingers. It brought him to mind of the story told in these parts of how the ground had turned red. "This ground has a history, ye ken."

"No, I didn't know."

"Once, during the time of the Vikings, there was an ancestor of mine named Fearghas MacMhathain."

"Not Matheson?"

He opened his mouth to reply, then hesitated, unsure whether he wanted to go into tedious detail. But he went ahead and said, "You see, *mac* means *son,* and Matheson is an Anglicization—a corruption—of MacMhathain. It means 'son of the bears,' 'bears' in Gaelic being *mathan*. In addition, the bear symbolizes heroism, so the deeper meaning would be 'son of the heroes.'" He smiled. "We dinnae believe we are actually descended from bears, ye see."

Leah smiled, and he enjoyed the sight. Then he continued, "Fearghas MacMhathain was a brave man, a great hero who died on this very spot." He patted the ground on which he sat. "One day he was left with the responsibility of guarding the glen while the other men were away. Though his brothers all said, 'Fearghas, let us stay with you and help you keep the glen safe,' he replied, 'Nae, my brothers. All will be well. The Vikings are far away from here, and the cattle are too many for the farmers to drive themselves. Go, for you're needed.' But Fearghas was mistaken regarding the whereabouts of the Vikings. That day a band of them took a mind to plunder the glen. A raven—which was the spirit of his grandfather watching over him—came to warn him of their approach, and he met them near this *broch,* down that a way where the glen takes a narrow dogleg." Ciaran gestured off toward the narrow gap in which stood the garrison and the church. "There were a hundred of them, and but one of him, and he never flinched. Never did he give ground. With his sword, he fought them in the glen below."

Leah's eyes were wide with fascination.

Excitement filled Ciaran's voice as he continued, "They were big men, and mean, and strong. But Fearghas destroyed them all, taking a mortal wound as he did so. He ignored it, and continued to fight though his life's blood ran from him." Ciaran couldn't help a glance at the grass under his hand. "To the end, he held off the enemy and fought till the last one of them was dead. And when he'd killed every Viking, and knew he was doomed, rather than let his blood mingle with that of his enemy, he crawled into this *broch*. And here he died on this very spot. He'd saved the entire clan."

"And so you are here today to tell the tale."

He grinned. "Aye. He saved not only his clan, but all his descendants as well. He was a hero and lived up to the name of MacMhathain."

"And are the Mathesons still heroes?" Her teasing tone and sly smile suggested she desired to hear of his own feats, but he couldn't bring himself to it.

Instead, he said, "My father was. He was a great man."

"Your father . . . Dylan Dubh?"

"Aye. They called him *Dilean Dubh nan Chlaidheimh*, meaning 'Black Dylan of the Sword.' His skill with sword and dirk was renowned. It was said he used magic to confound his enemies when he fought, for he was never where he was expected to be when a strike came. He could cripple a man with but a touch."

"You admire him a great deal."

"Aye." Suddenly Ciaran's throat closed, and he was unable to talk. His fear of not being the son of Dylan Dubh loomed so large in his mind he was unable to think of anything else.

Leah came to kneel next to him, and her voice went low. "I miss my mother as well," she said, and her sympathy touched him.

He looked over at her and was now able to say, "It must be terrible for a young woman."

She nodded. "I could tell her things I could tell nobody else, for she always understood. She never scolded me for being weak or selfish."

"As your father does."

She threw him a sharp glance, but then nodded. "Yes. Father is a good man, but is very demanding."

"I've noticed."

That brought a frown, but he added, "I mean, demanding of you. He isnae very gentle with you. Not how my father was with my sisters."

Now Leah nodded. "My mother was the gentle one. She was beautiful, kind, and generous, and she had a fine mind. My mother knew everything, I think. Even more than my father, perhaps." That made Ciaran laugh, but she insisted. "Indeed, I believe she did. She knew so much of the world, and knew Father so well, it seemed she always knew what he would do before even he knew it."

Ciaran smiled as he thought of Da's own power of prophesy. For a moment he was tempted to ask whether Leah's mother had come from the future, but decided his Catholicism and his belief in faeries were enough for her to bear at once. The suggestion of traveling through time would be too much. He wasn't even certain he believed it himself. For a moment he didn't know what to say, and faltered in saying anything. Leah's thoughts seemed far away, and her eyes went misty and unfocused. Ciaran could no longer resist the urge to press his thumb to the cleft of her chin, and he reached out.

Startled, she pulled back. He retrieved his thumb. There was a very long silence, and Ciaran almost dared not breathe. She searched his eyes, and he hers. He tried to think of something to say, but there was nothing.

Finally Leah glanced down and said, "Those checkers on your kilt—"

"Tartan." Relieved she was still talking to him, Ciaran was happy to explain this. "We call it tartan. 'Tis a pattern of weaving, in setts."

"Some of them are very pretty. It amazes me how, no matter how long the cloth is, one can never tell where the pattern begins and ends." She gestured to the kilt he wore, which was a *feileadh mór* fifteen feet long. Some men wore the *feileadh beag*, which was a kilt detached from the plaid. It made for more convenience in wearing, but Ciaran preferred the older style. His father had worn the *feileadh mór* all his life.

He tugged the plaid end of the cloth from his belt, shook it from his shoulder, and held it out before him. " 'Tis easy enough to see where it starts. Here, look. See how the warp threads run so many red, then a few green, then red again, then blue, then red again, and so on." He spread his thumb and finger to indicate the width of this sett. "This is the pattern here. Now see how it reverses. Red, then green, then red, then blue, then red, and so on. It simply keeps reversing and reversing back, for the length of the cloth."

Leah leaned close and put her finger to the wool. Her fingers were long and delicate, the nails oval and slender. He saw the skin of her hands was fine and soft, pale and unlined. Her fine bones stood out on the backs of them, and Ciaran was fascinated by their thinness. Her gentle fingers danced over the cloth, and excitement colored her voice as she said softly, "Yes. I see it. Like a mirror."

He was forced to clear his voice to continue. "Now see how it has exactly the same sett going in the other direction. So, rather than squares, what ye've got is lines that intersect, making some solid colors, some blended colors." His fingers also on the cloth, he took care not to accidentally touch her, lest she think it was on purpose.

"I see." She spread the cloth in her hands, then turned it over. It was, of course, exactly the same on the other side. Gently, she stroked the wool. "It's soft."

"Our sheep are a Cheviot cross my father introduced many years ago, so it's a mite less soft than in some places hereabouts. But soft enough, I suppose."

He looked up, and found her nearness even more unsettling. "We take . . ." His voice faltered, like a young lad's. He coughed and mentally chastised himself for revealing a weakness. "We take a great deal more wool from our sheep than other clans do from theirs. Enough to sell and trade in the cities, and so the sacrifice of some softness isnae so bad." She was still kneeling at his side, and hadn't moved, but now she seemed too close. He found he wanted very much to touch her again. She wore a French perfume, but beneath was the true scent of her, and it filled his head. She smelled like desire. It raced through him, and he was at a loss to know whether she felt it, too.

He had to shake his head to clear it as she tugged at the cloth near his belt and said, "This is all of a piece?"

Deftly he readjusted where she'd pulled it awry. "Aye. I belt the kilt, then arrange the plaid as it suits me." He realized how idiotic he was beginning to sound, and looked at her again. She was gazing at his face, not his kilt, and he thought she must be expecting something. What it might be, he could only hope.

When he leaned toward her ever so slightly, she did not recoil. A smile lifted one corner of his mouth, and he leaned again and not so slightly. Still she held her ground, even tilting her face toward his a bit.

Finally he leaned in to kiss her. Their lips touched lightly, each of them tentative for the chasm of differences between them. Nevertheless, it was sweet to give in to the longing he now realized he'd been denying for weeks. Then, his lips still nearly touching hers, he whispered from the heart in his native language, *"Nighean chaomh."*

She leaned back far enough to see into his eyes, and there was a question in hers. He answered it. "Sweet girl." He kissed her again, opened his mouth slightly, and pressed, tasting her, hoping for her to kiss him in return.

And she did. She laid a hand aside his cheek, and her lips parted.

His heart beat wildly now. He wanted more.

But then she pulled away, and he understood why. She was breathless and flushed, and now her eyes wouldn't meet his. There was shame in her countenance, a flaming redness in her cheeks.

Anger rose in him, bringing his own shame with it, and his face burned. Where there had been joy a moment before, now there was only the ugliness he'd learned from the *Sasunnaich.*

"Och, what a sin it must be to kiss a Catholic Highlander."

Now she looked at him, fire in her eyes. "Stop it."

He propped an elbow on his knee. "Aye. I should nae have started. Go, now. Fly to yer father and tell him how I took advantage of ye." The ache in his loins fed the pain in his heart. "Go, I said!" He waved her away.

Stricken and pale, mouth agape with shock, she climbed to her feet, picked up her skirts, and fled from the tower.

Ciaran sat with his elbows on his knees and his face in his hands, waiting for the ache to subside and wishing he hadn't been such a fool.

L eah was mortified. She fled to the castle—the Tigh—and retreated to her bedchamber, trembling, her fingers slick with perspiration and her cheeks feverish red. Ida inquired after her health, but was easily put off by a story of having hurried too fast up the stairs. The maid went to fetch her a draught of ale.

Leah lay facedown on the bearskin, trembling and wishing she weren't such a coward. She wished she'd had the courage to feel for Ciaran as she would, and tell him so, without heed to what her father would say. She wished for the courage to tell Ciaran he was wrong, even though he was right.

Especially she wished it *because* he was right. Everything about him—his visage, his sheer physical power—made her heart pound and brought the blood to her face, neck, and chest. The strangeness of him was overwhelming. His race and religion were not a small part of what made him exciting. They were not small parts of *him*. He fascinated her. She wanted to know more about him, but had no idea how to go about learning it.

She rolled onto her back and pressed fingertips to her lips. The kiss had been astonishing. It made her know she could become lost in him if she wasn't very careful.

But then, if she was purposefully not careful, she might find herself lost in a most delightful place! Her heart raced, skipping lightly in her chest and pulsing in her throat. She closed her eyes and imagined his face, so dark and serious, his eyes so filled with pain. That pain touched a spot deep in her belly. A heat began there, that radiated to her limbs. Intense longing filled her, a wish that she had not run away from him. She wished she had stayed to see where that kiss might have taken them. Oh, how stupid she was for running away!

For the next two days, whenever she saw Ciaran there was pain in his eyes. He was polite to her, greeting her with a nod and "Miss Hadley," but there was no conversation beyond that. Not that there had been so much before, but now she wished for him to talk. Then she could explain. Now there was no opportunity for it.

Spending her days sewing, she hurried with Sìle to finish the tartan dress, then one morning asked Ida to help her on with it.

The woman frowned. "Ye wish to wear this ugly thing?"

"Never mind your comments, Ida, help me on with it if you please."

"I dinnae please, miss. It's not befitting ye."

Leah's voice was strained, for this was a risky adventure, and she did not care to hear criticism from the maid. "Nevertheless, Ida, I wish to wear it." The morning was late, and Leah was counting on her father to be done with breakfast and away from the Great Hall. Of course, Ciaran might also be finished eating, but there would still be servants about who would most certainly gossip in Gaelic about the captain's daughter wearing tartan. Ciaran would hear of the dress. Perhaps he might even come to see it, and then they could talk.

The maid clucked over the disgrace, but finally did as she was told. Leah was laced into the soft woolen dress over a pale yellow linen blouse. The assembly felt more like a shift than a dress, but was snug enough around the bodice to keep her from bouncing too shamelessly. She smoothed the cloth over her hips, and briefly wondered whether she should follow the local style completely and go barefoot. Ida clucked and muttered to herself.

After a short deliberation, Leah drew on her slippers with the lowest heels before setting out for the Great Hall. If Father should catch her dressed like this it would be bad enough, but without shoes he would be convinced she'd gone completely mad.

Ciaran wasn't in the Great Hall when she arrived. The kitchen maids served her some breakfast, which she ate in a terrible hurry. It was certain to sit on her stomach like a bag of rocks, but she dared not dally, lest her father come. Then she slipped away by a circuitous route through the servants' quarters, up the West Tower, across the western curtain, and into the gatehouse. She'd learned quite a bit about the layout of this castle on her wanderings of recent weeks.

Head down, taking the irregular stone steps carefully in the dimness lit only by arrow loops, she passed a cell containing a single prisoner. Ciaran's brother was at the door, peering at her, his face pressed eagerly to the bars of its small window, his curiosity piqued, and his eyes alert to see who was nearby. A smear of blood under his nose bespoke a struggle, or perhaps a simple beating, since his incarceration several days before. She turned her face from him and hoped he didn't recognize her, but had no luck.

"Miss Hadley!" He tried to reach through the bars to snatch her, but not even his forearm would pass between.

Leah paused at the top of the next flight of steps and looked back.

"Miss Hadley, I've something to tell you!"

She wanted to ignore him and be on her way, but curiosity made her ask, "What is it?"

Calum retrieved his hand, his face pressed hard to the bars. He said in a voice filled with excitement that promised a juicy story, "Come here and I'll tell you."

A small voice inside her beseeched her to continue on down

the stairs, but she ignored it and stepped toward the door. But not too close. As a Hadley, Leah was not stupid enough to come so close to the bars as to allow Calum to grab her. "What is it?"

His wistful smile was near enough the bars for her to see his teeth. "I only wish to touch your hair. Feel its softness. 'Tis terribly lonely in this gatehouse. I havenae been this close to a woman in weeks."

"You've been in there but five days."

"Aye, well, I've also been away." He chuckled, but she was unmoved.

"You said you wished to tell me something."

"That is it. That I find you most fetching." The smile was infectious, but she'd witnessed what he'd done to Ciaran. Trusting him was out of the question.

With a sigh, she turned toward the stairs again to leave.

But he shouted after her, "*Sasunnach* bitch! Ye ken who else finds you a likely cunny? My brother, Ciaran!" Leah couldn't help but pause to listen, and Calum was thus encouraged. "Aye! I've seen him staring at you from across the room, a-hankering and a-whining like a dog after a bitch in heat! Dinnae wander too close to that one, lassie. You'll find him between yer thighs, ye give him half a chance."

A furious blush rushed to Leah's face, and she hurried away from him and down the stairs.

He shouted after, and his voice faded as she went. "All I wanted was to touch your hair!"

At the next floor, well away from anyone who might see, Leah paused in her flight to lean against a cool stone wall to catch her breath and let the flush go from her face. She gazed back the way she'd come, resisting the urge to return and hear more, for her shame came not from hearing Calum's words but from hoping they were true. *Oons, that they might be true!*

Once she'd calmed herself, she went quickly and quietly along her way. No guards from her father's company followed her across the drawbridge, and she smiled to herself as she went on her way. There was a woman in the village who had linen cloth for sale. A seamstress named Iseabail Matheson. Sìle had said Leah would know the house by the thick, prickly gorse at the eastern side of it.

Leah felt a bit silly as she approached the low, earthen cottage covered in flowering vines, but her trepidation was allayed at the look on the seamstress's face. She had no English, but her eyes lit up with approval at sight of Leah in the pale tartan with thin lines of light brown. She held out her hand to draw Leah into her dwelling, speaking the Gaelic slowly in hopes of aiding understanding. But Leah could decipher none of it and knew what was said only by gestures.

Yes, she was there for some cloth. Linen, enough for a man's shirt. An entire shilling? No, she was willing to pay eight pence. She held out the money in her palm, but the woman shook her head. Very well, then, nine pence.

She watched as the seamstress measured out a length of the unbleached linen and folded it into a small package to tie it with a long, narrow scrap. Leah handed over the silver coins, thanked her, and turned to leave.

But the seamstress held her hand and objected in a raised voice and rushed Gaelic. What, then? A small surge of fear made Leah want to simply leave, but she stayed to see what the woman wanted.

Still talking in a rush, the seamstress guided her to a small window where a vine of purple wildflowers grew across the outside of her house. She reached through the window to pluck three of the flowers, and turned to offer them to Leah. For her hair, she indicated by placing them aside Leah's head.

Leah acquiesced and let the woman tuck the flowers into her snood over her ear. She smiled and offered a farthing for the flowers, but it was refused. The seamstress smiled and shook her head a great deal, and Leah was given to understand they were a gift. She smiled, thanked the woman again, and left.

It was on the way back to the Tigh that she encountered Ciaran. Her heart did a flip-flop inside her chest. Sitting atop the stone dike of a sheep enclosure near the drawbridge, chewing the end of a long, thin willow stick dangling from his mouth, he was chatting with three others: his youngest brother, the old man named Robin, and the merchant who wore a hook in place of his hand. They stood casually about, glancing frequently at the sheep in the enclosure. By their gestures she guessed the animals were the subject of conversation.

As she neared, Ciaran glanced at her, then looked again in surprised recognition. His eyes lit with the same pleased look as the seamstress, but with an underlying interest that made Leah's belly go warm and her heart skip. He took the willow stick from his mouth.

"It becomes ye."

She slowed and wandered off the track toward him. The package of linen she pressed against her bosom, for the lack of stays in the bodice made her feel nearly naked. "Thank you. You're quite kind."

"Nae kind at all. In fact, these men here will all assure ye I'm the least kind fellow in the glen in that respect." The young brother and the merchant nodded, the merchant with a huge, toothless grin and a chuckle, but the man with the staff didn't seem to understand what was said and was merely waiting for the Gaelic to resume. The boy spoke, apparently translating Ciaran's comment, and the old man finally chuckled.

"Which respect would that be? Toward women, or only toward English women?"

A shadow crossed Ciaran's eyes, but his voice was still light as he said, "Toward anything I dinnae like." A tiny smile began at the corner of his mouth, and she hoped it would grow.

Though she struggled to suppress it, a smile crept to her own face. She couldn't help it. "Your sincerity is noted. And appreciated."

His eyes glinted, and though he seemed to be trying to look her in the face, his gaze strayed to her bosom and her belly. The shape was natural, not flattened as with stays, and it felt as if he were staring at her naked body. He might as well have been, for all this dress did to control her curves.

He found her face again and said, his voice without edge of any kind, "And so is your sincerity noted."

She nodded, and her heart soared. It would have been a sweet thing to have kissed him right there, but she restrained herself in the presence of the other men and the boy. And to that end, she bid them all adieu and proceeded on her way to the Tigh.

Ciaran watched her go, fascinated by the sway of her hips and the willowy slenderness of her waist. Even without stays, she was like a statue, graceful and pleasing. Enticing. Oh, so very enticing.

Taking a deep breath, he returned to his conversation with

Robbie, Robin, and Seumas, and found them staring at him. Robbie's head was tilted to the side, puzzled, Seumas was struggling not to laugh, and Robin's brow was knitted with doubt.

"Och," Ciaran said, "she's a pleasure for the eye, and dinnae pretend she is not."

Robin added, "And other bits of a man's body as well, I'd say."

There was a glint in Seumas's eye and he said, "It's a good thing, then, the two of ye are so very sincere to each other."

Robbie blinked for a moment, then seemed to get Seumas's meaning. He said, "Does it mean she likes you, then?"

Robin grunted. "Is there a lass in the glen who wouldnae . . . *be sincere* with Ciaran?"

Seumas laughed uproariously at that, but Ciaran shook his head. "It means naught more than that she doesnae hate me. Us. Scots and Catholics."

The group fell silent, and they all watched Leah cross the drawbridge. Robbie said softly, "Well, that's something, at least."

It seemed news of Prince Charles was becoming scarce. The discussions in Hadley's office gave less and less information. But then in August a visitor arrived for the laird, and was received in the Great Hall.

Entering the hall where the young man was waiting, Ciaran saw the stranger was walleyed and taking frequent glances at the Redcoat soldiers standing guard at the entry. He wore a kilt and sark filthy with travel and ragged in the bargain. Ciaran didn't recognize the lad, and his case of nerves gave him away as guilty of something. One glance at the guards said they also had noticed the unusual behavior.

"Ah, friend!" Ciaran called out in English from across the room as he approached. He threw his arms wide, as if welcoming a beloved fellow. It was plain from the confused look on the gillie's face that he spoke no English, but Ciaran continued, "How was your journey? Not too wet, I hope!" He gave a hearty slap on the shoulder and turned the visitor away from the entry. "Have a seat. This chair here will do." He immediately and forcefully guided the lad to sit in his own chair that faced into the fire, then straddled a stool, which he pulled close to the chair.

His voice dropped to a low murmur in Gaelic: "Who are you?"

"There are soldiers here!" It was an accusation, said in equally low Gaelic. The visitor was terrified.

Ciaran blinked at him, then said, "Aye. It's good eyes ye've got. Now tell me who you are and why you've come."

"My name is William. Are you the laird of Ciorram?"

"I am."

There was a sigh of relief. "I come with a letter from Prince Teàrlach."

A charge ran through Ciaran, and it was hard to contain a whoop of joy. Charles Stuart had landed! The crown prince of Scotland had arrived! He said, "Come with me and say nothing."

But when William reached for his sark, Ciaran grabbed his hand and pulled him to his feet. "Aye, William," he switched again to English, " 'tis with great pleasure I'll show you my sheep. They're a rare breed you ken; a skillful cross between the Cheviot and Highland strains." He guided William out the entry, through the bailey, and didn't stop chattering small talk until they were well away from the castle and strolling across the drawbridge.

William reached for the letter again, but Ciaran stopped him. "Wait."

They walked to the sheep enclosure on the other side of the bridge, a low stone dike not far from the village square. Their backs were to the Tigh, and before them was the steep rise of granite mountain. Ciaran returned to Gaelic. "I'm showing off my sheep to you, and we'll simply be standing here for a while. If you happen to have something in your hand and set it on the dike, I would take nae notice of it and neither would anyone else."

William slipped the letter from his sark and set it atop the loose stones. Ciaran laid his hand over it. William said, "You've Redcoats in your castle."

"Their commander is billeted there, and has a guard of two men posted whenever he is on the premises. The main contingent is in a garrison at the other end of the glen. 'Tis naught but one independent company of dragoons, commanded by Captain Roger Hadley. They're bored, untried, and poorly trained. If this information were to find its way to the prince, it would nae be amiss."

William nodded, and Ciaran went into the details he and Sinann had learned in recent months by watching through the tapestry, regarding the numbers of horses, ordnance, and patrol schedules throughout the local countryside. "Taking this all in, are you?" Ciaran asked.

Again William nodded.

"Good." Ciaran then slipped the letter into his own sark and said, "Well, that's enough about my sheep. Let us return to the Great Hall, where you will be well fed, then put to bed in my finest guest room." Never mind there was but one guest room vacant in the entire castle, it was likely to be the finest accommodation within twenty miles. "Then you can be off in the morning."

William nodded, obviously happy to be relieved of his incriminating burden.

Once William was seated in the Great Hall with a bowl of mutton stew and a large bannock before him, Ciaran hurried to his bedchamber to read the letter. On his way, he muttered, "Sinann, are you there?"

"Always." She appeared, fluttering overhead as he made his way down the corridor of the servants' quarters toward the West Tower.

"I want . . ." He looked up at her. "Always? You mean you saw that in the broch . . . with Leah?"

"*Och,* your private life is your own. I've better things to do than look in on your lovemaking."

A soft sound of disgust rasped in the back of his throat. "If only it had been that." He waved away the subject and said, "In any case, I wish you to put a spell of protection on young William out there. I want him to make it safely to the prince." Ciaran reached the end of the corridor and opened the heavy wooden door.

"I can keep him from death by mishap. But I cannae keep him from mere injury, and if another man were to make an effort to kill him, there would be naught for it." The faerie followed him through the door, and he closed it behind her before hurrying up the stairs. "Protecting him entirely from danger would require powers I no longer possess. Were I able to affect more than one body at a time, I would throw protection over every Jacobite from here to Rome, then curse every Redcoat in the kingdom with boils."

That made Ciaran chuckle. "That would be a thing to see."

"Also, you understand I cannae remove a spell once it's done."

He stopped on a landing and tilted his head at her. "Then let the lad go protected for all the rest of his days. Let him be blessed with uncanny good luck."

"Consider it done."

For one brief moment he was glad to have one of the wee folk at hand.

Inside the sanctum of his bedchamber, Ciaran took the letter from his sark and sat in the chair at his table to bend over it. It was a plain letter, small and carefully folded, with a plain seal. He broke the seal, opened the paper, and saw,

Boradel Aug 8, 1745

Being aware of your loyalty, I send my messenger to inform you that I am come into this country. My purpose is to assert the king's right at the head of such of his faithful subjects as have ardor for service and shall be willing to engage in his quarrel. I request therefore your appearance at Glenfinnan on Mon. 19th precisely, when I intend to set up the royal standard. If your presence on that date is impracticable, I expect you should join me thereafter; and you shall always find me ready to reward your zeal and demonstrate the value and friendship I have for you.

Charles P.R.

Ciaran's heart thudded against his ribs. He could barely contain his joy. He whispered to the faerie, "He's truly here. He's landed on the west coast, near Glenfinnan. We must go to meet him."

"Ye cannae."

He turned to face her. "I *must!* 'Tis betrayal of our people if I dinnae take up arms against the oppressor!" He realized his voice was rising, and he glanced toward the door as he returned to a whisper, "Da held the welfare of his people above all other considerations. He taught me my entire life to lead as he would have me. Whether laird, tacksman, or tenant, the greatest life a man can live is one dedicated to the well-being of his people. I must follow Charles. 'Tis what he wanted."

"He wanted nae such thing, as you are well aware, for he told you himself. He kent the rising will fail. Just as he kent the last two would fail."

It made no sense. Ciaran shook his head. "But he fought in both of them. He risked his life for the cause."

"Aye. At first he hoped to find a way to change the history. But after many years of failure, he despaired of changing anything. He came to understand he was a *part* of that history he'd read. Just as you are. Just as he kent you will be at the final battle in the struggle for the Crown."

"He read in the history only that I would be there? Not that I would die?"

She nodded. "Aye. As I recall, 'twas a single sentence in a book. Many men were off foraging before the final battle, and it tells of you going to find them and bring them back."

"Will I even be in the battle, then?"

The faerie crossed her arms and peered at him as if he'd said something unutterably stupid. "Aye, ye will, unless you think you might have it in you to desert."

Ciaran grunted. Good point.

Sinann continued, "But most men did not live through that battle, Dylan Dubh said. 'Twill be a massacre, and the bloody English willnae stop with the soldiers on the field. They'll murder every Highlander they can get their hands on for months afterward. Your da understood the only hope for you will be to stay away from the Jacobites and away from Culloden."

"Culloden?"

"Culloden House on Drummossie Moor, near Inverness. Sixteenth of April, 1746. 'Twas your da's dearest wish you nae be there."

Ciaran frowned, confused now and not eager to hear this. "But if he read I'd be there, and he also said history cannae be changed . . ." The answer to this couldn't be good.

There was a long silence until finally the faerie said, "Aye."

But Ciaran said softly, "If Da wished for me to not go, then I willnae. 'Tis simple enough—if the Mathesons dinnae go, then I willnae die in the battle." There was, after all, such a thing as free will. No written history could force him to do anything. "I'll inform the clan leaders of my decision."

Sinann nodded. "Good lad."

Gathering the clan leaders in the Great Hall to discuss a revolt against the Crown would have been the height of stupidity, given the heavy presence of the English army. To evidence too much activity anywhere in the glen without good explanation was to invite interruption and arrest by the soldiers. So Ciaran slipped the folded letter into his sark and went to find Robin Innis.

The old man was warming himself by the hearth in the Great Hall when Ciaran found him and strode across the stone floor. Standing close to the fire, his head down as if he were also in need of warmth, he muttered in Gaelic, "Go to the still and wait for me." Then he left the room.

He likewise found Eóin, Gregor, Dùghlas, Seumas Glas, Donnchadh, Keith Rómach, and Aodán. They were the ones he would need to support him in his decision to keep out of the fight.

The still was hidden in a cave among the steep cliffs in the forest beyond the peat bog. Barely accessible by foot, never mind on horseback, the area was not patrolled at all by the mounted soldiers from the garrison. To find it, one walked along the track from Glen Ciorram south and upward past the peat bog. Then one left the track where it crossed the small burn that originated in the high southern glen. Taking care not to leave an obvious trail, one followed that stream farther into the forest. In the depths of the trees, where there was little sunlight at any time of year, one found a precipitous track up a granite face to a spot where the rock staggered before erupting again in an impossibly steep cliff. Behind that wide ledge was a cave, in which were hidden the casks from that year's distilling. Before the cave, on the ledge, sat the still and the peat fire on which the laird's germinated barley was malted each year. The men called by Ciaran assembled by that fireplace, though there was no fire today.

Ciaran sat on an outcrop of rock by the cave entrance, and the other eight men settled on the ledge before him, some on a log placed for the purpose and the rest cross-legged on the sod and stone. "I have a letter from the Stuart prince," he announced.

A murmur of excitement rippled through the group. Seumas Glas said, "He's arrived, then."

"Aye. He's landed. Where, I cannae say. He wants us to join him, but I've decided we willnae."

Dùghlas said, "But we must."

Ciaran looked sharply at Dùghlas. He hadn't anticipated an argument. "We willnae, and that is the way it will be."

"You betray the will of yer father. He would have gone to fight, for he hated the *Sasunnaich* with every bit of his soul. He cared for his clan, as apparently you do not."

That cut to Ciaran's very center. His hand balled into a fist at his side. "He would *not* have gone to fight, for he kent . . ." Now he was at a loss as he realized he couldn't tell why he knew they shouldn't go. He finished his sentence in a hurry that hurt his argument. "He kent it would be best not to go." There was a murmur of disagreement and Ciaran said, "You've all heard him say it."

"We heard him keep quiet in public so the *Sasunnaich* would pay him less attention."

"I am his son, and I think I know what he wanted. Furthermore, I'm now laird."

Gregor spoke up. "Now, there's been some disagreement over that, hasn't there? As to whether ye're his son or the rightful laird."

Cold sweat washed over Ciaran. He stood and glared down at Gregor. "Watch what ye say, cousin."

His chin thrust forward, Gregor stood to face Ciaran. "Calum may be in the gatehouse, but he's made it clear he means for us to follow his father's wishes and fight the *Sasunnaich* at every opportunity."

The apprehension turned to cold realization of what Gregor and Dùghlas were up to. He looked to Dùghlas, who busied himself paring his fingernails with his *sgian dubh,* then back at Gregor. "Do not do this. You'll end up in the gatehouse with my brother."

"Brother, indeed," said Dùghlas. "By what I see here, you cannae be any more a brother to Calum than Seumas Glas here, if you persist in denying the wishes of Dylan Dubh."

"The wishes of yourself, you mean."

Eóin spoke up now. "He speaks for more than only himself, Ciaran."

"You, Eóin?" The betrayal was sharp. Ciaran's heart sank.

"Nae me. Never me, Ciaran. I'll stand with you whatever decision you make. But I mean for you to take heed. There's a danger, and not only from the men here. The clan expects you to side with the Stuarts. Aught else would go against all they understood of your father, and all they hold dear as Catholics."

Suddenly Ciaran felt adrift. The power he'd thought he'd inherited was slipping through his fingers. He could feel the support of these men slide from under him as he began to understand the limitations of his title and privilege. Once again he longed for his father's guidance.

Instead he heard the faerie voice above his right shoulder. "Understand, lad, you cannae simply go along with them. It's a tender spot you're in now. You must appear to control, even when you dinnae."

So Ciaran addressed the men before him. "I must think on this. I thank you for your counsel. You'll know my decision soon."

The men seemed to find this acceptable. Several nodded, and there was a shifting of weight.

Ciaran continued, "Go, now. We dare not let the soldiers discover our absence."

One by one the men descended from the ledge and made their way through the forest in different directions, to return to the glen at different times from different places. Ciaran was the last to go, and as he watched them, he sorted his thoughts. The only thing he was certain of now was that, with or without him, his clan would fight on the side of Prince Charles.

CHAPTER 8

Ghillie brogues, dyed black, were buckled to his feet.

Leah stood on the battlement of the north curtain, gazing across the loch. *Loch.* She smiled to herself. Odd, how she was beginning to think in the words she'd thought so strange only two months before. It was at once unsettling and exhilarating. Those words made her think of Ciaran. Saying them out loud was almost like invoking him. *Loch. Tigh. Glen.* When she heard the Gaelic tongue they spoke, she wished she could speak it herself, but the language was too difficult. She couldn't begin to pronounce most of it, and nobody was willing to take the time and teach her. For those who would speak to her at all, it was too easy to simply speak English.

Movement caught her eye, and she turned to observe a man coming down the track from the south. He was walking down a steep trail from the mountains, headed toward the village. She strolled along the wall for a better look, and stopped at a vantage point on the West Tower. Another movement to her right, and she noticed another kilted fellow walking along the southern loch shore, also toward the village. Alarm tickled the back of her neck, and she waited. It wasn't long before yet another man came from the south.

Standing behind the stone crenellation, she continued watching for several minutes. Sure enough, a fourth man came, also along the trail that rose into the mountains to the south. And that man was Ciaran. His carriage gave him away, not to mention the dark head of hair. He was the only Scot in the glen who tied his in a queue. The Ciorram laird had been away from the castle, and more than likely not as alone as he wished to appear. Carrying no guns or bows, it wouldn't have been a hunting party. Especially, a hunting party would not have needed to separate and sneak back into the glen.

Father would be terribly interested to know there had been a meeting of clansmen in the woods. She pressed her face to the stone battlement. He would surely punish the Mathesons for such an illegal assembly. A chill of fear skittered through her, and her stomach lurched. Her eyes squeezed shut, she whispered a prayer for Ciaran's safety, lest someone else have seen them.

At supper she gazed down the long table at him. His countenance was severe, but it always was. It was impossible to know by looking at him what had gone on in the woods that afternoon.

Nevertheless, she continued staring, for she couldn't bear to take her eyes away. She watched him chat with the men to his left and right, leaning heavily on one arm of his large wooden chair and slowly picking food from his plate. Tonight he drank more than he ate, and he listened more than he spoke.

That night Leah lay restless in her bed, unable to sleep. No position seemed comfortable, and she rolled this way and that across the feather mattress. An image of Ciaran was trapped in her drowsy vision, and her heart tripped along at far too brisk a pace. The way he looked, the way he moved, his smile that was so rare and so valued for its rarity.

It was quite late when she gave up trying to sleep, and lay amid the rumpled bedclothes to surrender herself to those thoughts.

Remembering his kiss once more, she placed a finger to her lips. She'd never been kissed like that before. Aside from the languid and wet-lipped attentions of two boys in London, she'd never been kissed at all.

They'd been her same age, and each encounter had been

strictly a matter of curiosity on both sides. The disappointment had been monstrous. She'd felt nothing for either of them, and it was clear they'd felt nothing for her worth the trouble of continuing. After that, she declined all offers of kisses from boys, wet-lipped or not.

It had never been missed. She'd always assumed there would be a husband for her one day and she would either love him or not; it hadn't mattered much to her which. Her anticipation of marriage had always been of a civilized arrangement, a contract in which she would allow physical union in exchange for financial security and social position. That was the way her mother had lived with her father—happily, as she saw it—and that was how she'd expected to live with her husband, whoever he might be. If she were lucky, if he were an honorable man, she might eventually grow to feel affection for him. She'd given up the idea of ever loving a man to whom she was not already married.

But Ciaran . . . the intensity of him had touched her in such private places even she had never before known of them. He had a passion for everything around him, and that by itself was exciting. He seemed to feel things she'd once thought nobody but herself could feel. Now she dwelt on him, asleep in the other tower, and wanted to be near that intensity again. To feel the heat of him and the strength. Perhaps if she were given another chance she could show him how honest she was in her affection for him.

The desire clicked into place in her mind, and in an instant she decided she must do something about it. To lie around, sleepless, her thoughts churning and her body doing nothing, was torture. She leaned up on one elbow to see Ida's dark shape on the low bed across the room. The maid was still, her breathing the steady, heavy rhythm that would not be interrupted till dawn.

Leah slipped from under the covers of her bed and shrugged her nightgown back onto her shoulders. The cold wooden floor and the chill night air raised goose bumps under the diaphanous silk.

Silently, so as not to wake Ida, she went to the wall hook, lifted her cloak with care, and draped it over herself. Then, the hood covering her head, she fled her chamber on silent, bare feet.

Candles in sconces along the way had guttered or been extinguished by the servants, and she felt her way carefully through the darkness, up the spiral stairs, and out onto the battlement. A fat moon lit her path to the next tower as the wind from the loch tossed her hood about. She held the cloak and hood closed with her fists, leaving only enough to see out. Then, through the door into the West Tower, she was plunged into darkness once more. Blessed darkness, to cover her passage to Ciaran. Only one level down, for the laird's bedchamber was at the very top of the tower. At the first alcove, heart pounding in her ears, she listened at the door. There was no sound from inside the room. Though she waited as long as she dared, to be certain he had no visitors, she was afraid to stay there long, lest someone pass by. She lifted the latch on the door and carefully eased it open on silent hinges.

Inside, the fire in the hearth was quite high, though the hour was late, and a candle on the washstand was not nearly half burned. Alarm surged in her, for so much light must mean Ciaran was still awake. She stood, frozen, looking around the room for him. There were stacks of crates and books all around the floor, but no Ciaran.

Then she saw him, lying in the bed and breathing a deep near-snore of sleep. Relief washed over her, and her eyes closed for one thankful moment as she leaned against the edge of the door. Then she closed and latched it behind her and approached the bed. He wore no nightshirt. His chest and arms were bare above the bearskin cover. One smooth-muscled arm lay on his pillow, curled about his head, and his long, thick, black hair lay in tendrils everywhere about. She found herself fascinated by the tuft of straight, dark hair under his arm. She'd never before seen a man quite this privately. A giggle rose, but she swallowed it.

A thrill skittered up inside her. Breathing became difficult, and her chest felt as if wrapped in iron bands. Her heart beat wildly. Father would certainly have her punished were he to learn of this. He'd put a guard on her door at the very least. But her heartbeat was echoed in many places elsewhere in her body, and the surging of her blood made her feel more alive tonight than ever before in her life. Turning back was out of the question.

She examined Ciaran's sleeping face, for he was unutterably beautiful. Peaceful in slumber, the hard lines had softened. His lips were parted slightly, and the urge to kiss them was sweet torture. A finger reached out, wanting to touch, but she hesitated. A warm puff of breath brushed her hand, and she pulled back.

Her fingers found the clasp at her breast, and she lifted the cloak from her shoulders to let it drop softly to the floor behind her. The room was warm, but she shivered nevertheless. Then, with trembling fingers, she lifted her nightgown over her head and let it slip silently to the floor also. Goose bumps rose everywhere. With infinite care, she lifted the edge of the bedclothes and slipped under them onto the bed. Dizzy for the pounding of her heart, she moved close and reached for him.

One hand shot out to grab her wrist, and he twisted it outward. A squeak of pain escaped her as she sat up to follow the pressure. He raised onto one elbow. Blinking as he awakened, he grunted sleepily when he realized who was there.

Terrified, she said nothing. For one endless moment they stared at each other. No smile came. He blinked, struggling to focus. She knew she would die of humiliation if he ordered her from the room. Her breath suspended as she awaited his reaction.

Then the hand grasping her wrist loosened, and slipped down her arm. Lightly, gently, his fingers moved over her skin to her shoulder. Her neck. Then down her breast and across her belly. She quivered at the whisper touch of his fingertips.

Then he leaned over to kiss her. The touch of his lips to hers was more cautious than before, but the heat of his mouth seemed to fill her, warming her through and through. He pressed her shoulder and urged her to lie back. With immense joy she lay beneath him, returning his kiss and letting her own hands discover his bare skin and solid body. Hard muscles undulated under her palm, so strong and unlike her own.

He leaned over her as his mouth pressed hard on hers, and his tongue demanded her lips part. Her tongue met his there, and the strangeness of it overwhelmed her. The rough stubble of his beard rasped against her chin. Swept quite away, she ran her fingers into his abundant hair and pressed herself eagerly to him. More than allowing him to do what he would, she begged him. She needed to know what it was like. What *he* was like. It was as if she couldn't live another moment without knowing. He responded with a strength that surprised her. His breaths broke hard against her cheek, and it felt as if he might devour her.

His mouth left hers and found her neck with his teeth. Then her shoulder. Then her breast, and her back arched with pleasure as he pulled at it. No reservations, no misgivings, she uttered soft, inarticulate sounds at the exquisite wonderment. There was no mind left, only need.

At the whisper of his name, a pleading, he shifted and placed himself between her thighs. Never in her life had she wanted anything as fully as she wanted Ciaran now.

His mouth joined with hers again, he guided himself to her. Her flesh tingled when she felt him there, so hard and so warm. So . . . strange. Only a moment's pause, then a hard shove.

There was a sharp, quick pain, then a dim soreness.

But now Ciaran hesitated, his hips pressed against hers. *"Och,"* he whispered. "Leah . . . ?"

Her arms tight around him, she clung to him and murmured in his ear, "Don't stop. Please, you mustn't stop."

A deep moan emanated from inside his chest, and he began to move. His body tensed, each muscle standing out in relief, unyielding beneath her hand. Her loneliness faded to nothing, replaced by the warmth of him, for she was no longer alone even within her own body. Inside and out, she was touched in places no man had ever ventured. Ciaran's belly moved against hers, and his mouth played with her tender lips. Soon there was nothing in the entire world other than Ciaran's wonderful body and what it was doing to hers.

A long, helpless groan escaped him. Quivers took him. She clung to him as he leaned over her, still for a moment. Then he moved again and pressed himself there for another moment before finding her mouth again for one more kiss, then finally collapsing onto the mattress beside her. His chest heaved, and glistened in the candlelight.

She reached over to lay a hand against his cheek, and he held that hand to his mouth to kiss it. Still panting, he then shifted to his side and gathered her to him. He kissed her forehead as she moved to rest her head on his shoulder, and held her close as they settled down to sleep.

Leah had been reasonably certain she would be able to sleep now, but instead found herself lying awake, listening to her lover breathe, and taking joy in the steady beat of his heart against her face. It would have been a shame to fall asleep and miss even a moment of this night.

T he warmth and brightness of sunlight through the high glass panes brought Ciaran awake with a surge of shame he'd slept so long past dawn. Then a weight on his arm and a numbness in his hand reminded him why he'd needed the sleep, and he opened his eyes to gaze at Leah.

She lay with her head on his outstretched forearm, peacefully asleep, her thick eyelashes against her cheeks, and her chestnut hair in waves about her face. The rippled panes of the windows cast soft streaks of shadow and light on her face that brindled her nose and cheeks. His heart warmed. He reached out to touch a finger to one of those curls. Leah was unlike anyone he'd ever known. All the young women of the glen had grown up with him and were as predictable as the rising sun. Many desired him for his position. Most were related closely enough to trace easily, and all were as familiar as his sisters. Leah was so wildly different, it seemed he could take a lifetime to know her.

The warm feeling faded as he realized he, who hated the *Sasunnaich* and everything about them, now was falling in love with one. For a moment he struggled to deny it. He told himself it couldn't be love. Nothing more than lust for a comely and accommodating woman. She was of the people who would destroy his clan if they were allowed. She was English, and therefore a bigot. She was a Protestant, and therefore anti-Catholic. She was . . .

He shut his eyes and sighed. No, she wasn't. Not in her heart. She'd shown him she wasn't. She was kind, uplifting to his soul, and more genuine in her desire for him than any woman he'd ever known. She'd come to his bed without a hint of coyness, or the slightest promise on his part. She'd made him her first. No woman had ever offered that, let alone given it freely. It touched his heart in a way that surprised him. He leaned over her, reached under the bedclothes, and caressed her bare hip.

Her eyes fluttered open. She stretched and yawned, her lithe body warm beneath his hand. When she saw him she smiled. The morning sun reflected from her eyes, and they glittered as she gazed up at him. What he saw there was the sort of open adoration he'd longed to see in other women but never had. Leah loved him, it was plain, and didn't mind letting him know it.

He touched his lips to hers, then to her forehead. *"Maduinn math."* Her brow furrowed, and he translated, "Good morning."

She kissed him good morning, less gently than he had kissed her, and he found himself wanting her again. But he drew away and murmured, "Yer father willnae be pleased when he hears of this."

Her voice was a whisper. "He would try to kill you. That is why he shan't hear." She laid a hand aside his cheek.

Ciaran searched her eyes for a lie but found none. It was true, Hadley would more than likely kill him if he knew. But first there would be an arrest on one pretext or another, and Ciaran would be shipped off to die mysteriously somewhere far away from Ciorram and Leah. "You ken my life is in your hands."

She smoothed his forehead and brushed the hair away from his eyes. "You've no idea."

That brought him a small, puzzled frown. She continued, slowly stroking his face, "I saw you and your men return from your meeting yesterday. I believe I was the only one who did, but you should know you need to take better care in the future."

His heart stopped for a moment, then he rolled onto his back and held his voice steady. "What meeting?"

She sat up and laid a hand on his chest. "Do not draw away from me. Trust me, Ciaran. If I wished your arrest, you'd be in the garrison this very minute." He opened his mouth to wonder out loud if her intent was blackmail, but she placed a finger over his lips and continued, "I'm telling you this so you will be forewarned. More than anything, I desire your safety."

He gazed at her and hoped she was telling the truth.

When he didn't reply, she settled back onto the mattress, propped her head on her elbow, and said, "Ciaran, teach me how to say 'I love you' in your language."

He blinked, confused now. A smile touched the corner of his mouth as he rose up again on one elbow, and he obliged slowly, "*Tha gaol agam ort.* Literally, 'Is love at me for you.'"

"*Tha gaol agam ort,*" she repeated passably, looking straight into his eyes. The words touched his heart in a way the English never could, for though he was fluent in both languages, his most inner life had always been expressed in Gaelic. "*Tha gaol agam ort,* Ciaran." She kissed him, and he felt it in his soul.

He kissed her in return and pressed her back onto the mattress again. Lips still touching, he murmured to her the greatness of his own love, his voice growing heavy as he realized it himself, "*Tha gaol mór agam ort, Leah. Tha gaol glé mhór agam ort. M'annsachd. Tha thu m'annsachd. . . .*"

Kissing her again and again as he spoke, he shifted his weight and prepared to love her once more.

* * *

L eah brushed a lock of hair away from Ciaran's eyes as he lay on his back, recovering his breath. She delighted in the soreness, feeling where he'd been and wishing he'd never had to leave. She pressed her lips to his shoulder and let them linger there so she could take in the scent of his skin. Her fingertips played idly with the straight black hairs on his chest.

But there was a knock on the door, and she suddenly realized she was the one who needed to leave. The sun was well up, and here she was without a bit of clothing other than a nightgown and cloak. She looked around the room, frantic for a hiding place.

Ciaran placed a calming hand over hers on his chest and sat up. He addressed the door in Gaelic, and ended with a small cough that gave her to know he was pleading illness. The voice on the other side of the door queried, and Ciaran replied with a short command. Then there was silence.

He leaned down to nuzzle Leah's ear and whispered, "Chambermaid. I informed her I would take my breakfast downstairs in spite of the touch of catarrh that has caused me to oversleep." He smiled and gave a couple of faux coughs for effect. Then he looked around the room. "We need some clothes for you. Ye cannae leave this chamber wearing naught but a cloak and nightgown." He pointed with his chin to the pile of her clothing on the floor.

Then he looked over at the table across the room. "Wait." In a sudden burst of action, he leapt from the bed and went to the table. Sitting in the chair, he snatched his black ribbon from the table to tie back his hair.

Leah ogled his naked body, the first living male form she'd ever seen so fully, and admired the smooth muscles and long frame. His utter nonchalance in this state sent a quiver through her, for he appeared capable of strolling through the village like that without the least embarrassment.

Many stacks of ledgers and some crates lay on and around the table, but he shifted one crate to the floor, then reached for a quill from the several in an earthenware receptacle. Taking a trimming knife, he stripped the quill of its inner vane, then slit the end and nicked it to a point. A short hunt through the piles, and he found a stationery box. He laid a clean piece of letter paper on the table, uncorked the ink pot, and set it by the paper.

"Here, write a note." He rose from the table and held the chair for her.

"Me?"

He blinked. "You do write, do ye not?"

"Of course I do." She slipped from the bed and marched across the room as if she cared not a whit for her modesty. But she could feel her awkwardness as her body tried to move inside clothing that wasn't there. She could also feel his gaze as it moved over her. Taking the seat, she picked up the quill and dipped it.

"*Och*," said Ciaran. He squatted on his heels beside the chair, draped an arm across her lap, and gazed up at her. "I dinnae mean to embarrass you. Now you've gone all blotchy and red." He brushed his fingers over her chest, then down across her breast. A smile lit his face, and it was a delight to see. He was so very handsome and his teeth so white, it was a shame he smiled so seldom.

"Yes, then, what is it you wish me to write?"

"Address this to your maid." Leah did so. He continued, "Say, *'Come to me in the bedchamber of the laird's sister Sìle.'*" As Leah wrote it, he leaned in to brush his lips against her breast, and a shiver skittered up her back. Then he said softly, his focus no longer fully on the note, "Now think of something for her to bring to you. A piece of jewelry or a garment you might have forgotten to carry with you to visit Sìle." An idea brightened his face. "Or a prayer book! Aye! Ask her to bring yer prayer book."

Leah did so, then signed the note and blotted it. Carefully she folded it, then handed it to Ciaran.

As he stood and reached to the armoire for a fresh shirt he said, "I'll take this to Sìle, and she will hand it on to a chambermaid, who will take it to your maid. When your maid is away on her errand, I'll slip into your bedchamber and make off with that tartan dress of yours, along with your slippers and linen." His long shirt on, he then took a length of tartan wool and arranged it across the bed with his belt beneath it. Quick fingers put pleats in the wool at the center of the belt.

"Why the Highland dress? Why not one of my ordinary ones?"

A look of disparagement crossed his face. "Steel hoops, corset of whalebone, great streaming lengths of lace, and copious underskirts. Nae overdiscreet for the laird of the castle to be carting about, aye?"

"Then let Sìle—"

"She cannae be told. Nobody can be told. We must be careful, or the news will be spread, and your father will take measures. In any case, you willnae be required to wear the tartan long. 'Tis only so you can make it across the battlement without it being known you spent the night here." He sat atop the pleated wool and lay back, belted the assembly around his waist, then stood. The lower part was now perfectly kilted, and he threw the rest of the wool over his shoulder to tuck it into his belt. Then he sat on the bed once again and donned woolen stockings, shoes, and sheepskin leggings, which he secured with leather straps. Checking the ribbon securing his hair, he tossed that one stubborn lock from his face, then bent to kiss her good-bye.

With yet another shining smile on his face, he glanced back as he made his exit. His eyes were lit up and his skin alive with a ruddy glow. Leah sighed as the door closed behind him.

"Oh, Ciaran, if you believe your sister isn't going to read in your face exactly what happened last night, you're absolutely mad."

C iaran found Sìle in her bedchamber, with Aodán, and the two fell silent when he appeared in the doorway. He'd interrupted an argument, it was certain, for both their faces were dark with anger, and Sìle's eyes were reddened. She wouldn't look at her brother. Sitting on the bed, her head was ducked, and she wasn't looking at Aodán, either. The couple waited for Ciaran to state his business and then move on, but he had no intention of speaking in Aodán's presence, so he waited. His eyes hooded as he stared Aodán down.

It took but a moment for his brother-in-law to understand. Aodán's face flushed red, but he said nothing as he left the room and only threw Sìle a hard glare she never saw.

Ciaran stepped close to his sister and bent to speak. His voice was low, but he didn't whisper, for there was nothing unseemly about what he needed to tell her. "Give this to a chambermaid." He handed over the note from Leah.

She frowned, and peered up at him. "You're delivering notes for her now, like a gillie?"

His eyes opened wide in an attempt at an innocent expression, but even he knew he was a hopelessly incompetent liar. In addition, this was his sister, who knew him better than anyone living. "Do this for me, Sìle."

She went to the door to look out and said, "Aodán, wait for me downstairs."

Aodán's voice was sullen. "I'll nae—"

"Aodán!" Ciaran was in no mood for this.

Sìle waited as her husband retreated down the stairs and allowed them privacy, then closed the door and turned to her brother. "What is it you're wishing me to do for her this time?"

"Surely I dinnae ken what you mean. 'Tis but a harmless missive for her maid."

"Then deliver it yourself to the maid."

"I've asked you to."

"Why?"

His gaze went to the floor. A smile played about his mouth, but he couldn't suppress it. He said, "Because, were I to make the delivery myself, the maid would then tell where she got it, and Leah's maid would tell someone else, possibly her father."

Sìle nodded. It was plain she hadn't needed to be told this. "And her father wouldnae object to her spending time with me, whereas if he learned she was tiptoeing around with you he might have a word or two to say about it."

"Aye." He clasped his hands behind his back, feeling like a penitent child.

"What's in the letter?"

"Naught to concern you."

"You've tumbled her."

The blood fled his face. "Sìle—"

"Dinnae lie, Ciaran Dubhach. Were it aught else, you would tell me."

"Och." His mind flew to invent a story, but nothing came. He finally said, "Aye. The letter is to draw Leah's maid away from her chamber so I might steal in for a dress."

Sìle nodded, understanding. "So she willnae be seen returning from her visit in the same dress she wore yesterday."

"So she willnae be seen wandering about the Tigh in her nightgown."

That brought a laugh. "She came to you undressed? You can't have planned this. . . ."

"Nae."

Sìle burbled with more chortling. "The slut—"

"Sìle!"

"Well, so high and mighty as she is, I can imagine what the likes of Herself would say were I caught in this predicament. Yet I cannae say it ever crossed my mind to go unbidden to a man's bed wearing naught but a nightgown."

"And who's to say she was unbidden?"

"Aye, then it was yourself who suggested she strip before leaving her room."

Ciaran had no reply for that. He pressed his lips together, and his eyes narrowed. "Sìle . . ."

"As I thought. She went on her own."

"There was a cloak."

She giggled some more. "*Och,* I see. That makes it perfectly respectable."

"Aye, as near respectable as yourself and Aodán bent over the kitchen block."

"He's my husband!"

"He wasnae then!"

"So do you intend to marry this *Sasunnach?*" Sìle was no longer laughing. "For if you do, you should understand well what the consequences will be. The clan willnae accept her. It will be a fight, and Calum will do his best to use it against you. You'll be forced to hang him." Her voice had a catch in it now. "Ciaran, you cannae want this woman enough to execute our brother to keep her."

"Calum has made his own bed."

"Ye dinnae need to set it on fire."

"Sìle, 'tis nae your business who I love."

" 'Tis love, then? Truly?"

"Aye." The admission quite took his breath away.

For a long moment she gazed at him, at a loss and searching his face for a clue as to what to tell him. Finally she said, "Very well, then. I'll take the letter. And dinnae carry the dress to her yourself. I'll do it."

Ciaran searched her face for a lie.

"Aye," she said. "I'll do it. I dinnae hold with it, but if you're dead set on carrying on with this woman, I'll nae see you two embarrassed. Though I would counsel better discretion the next time. Meet her away from your chamber, at a decent hour, and fully dressed, aye?"

He nodded. "Aye."

As he scurried down the stairs in the West Tower, headed for the Great Hall, that daft faerie popped into view, blocking his way. At sight of her at the bottom, he stopped between floors in hopes of a measure of privacy, for he knew she would force him to address her.

She rose to meet him. "Are ye daft?" she inquired.

"I'm not. What do you want?"

"You're humping the captain's daughter, ye fool. You ken what will come of it."

"Aye, I'm aware of how bairns are made, ye faerie."

"I'm speaking of repercussions, lad! From both her father and the clan! Now that you're a-going to declare yourself for the prince, you cannae keep seeing her."

"You're the one who said I should court her."

"I dinnae say you should fall in love with her! And you have! I can see it in your face. It's all over you, how ye feel!" He tried to move past her, but she blocked his way. "*Och!* You're exactly like your father!"

That struck a very sore nerve. Ciaran looked away and drew a deep breath to steel himself for this, then looked at her, his eyes narrowed. In a low voice he said, "How am I like him?"

She settled on the steps below and looked up at him, her thin white arms crossed over her chest. "The man loved who he would, stubbornly and without reservation. He fell in love with yer mother without a single thought as to the consequences. And it was the mistake of his life, I'm telling you. He was betrayed by yer mother's uncle for it, and in the end their marriage caused her death. He was daft to fall in love with her."

"*Och,* you and Sìle. No man can choose who he loves. 'Tis fate."

" 'Tis madness!"

"Aye! I'm mad for her. Now stand aside, faerie, or I'll knock ye down." He barreled on through and forced Sinann to move. But she shouted after him, her voice thick with anger.

"Mark me, Ciaran! It will end badly! Ye cannae love the English, for they willnae forsake their treacherous breeding! She will betray you!"

Ciaran ignored her and hurried away, down toward the Great Hall.

That day, Ciaran made known to the clansmen his decision to

join the rising and meet Prince Charles in Glenfinnan. It was after careful consideration, he explained, that he decided the clan's
best chance was to side with the true king, for God surely meant
the Catholic Stuart succession to be restored.

Starting with Eóin, the news was deliberately spread by word
of mouth, for part of that news was a warning against clandestine
meetings. Whisperings in the bailey, in the stable, among the
sheep enclosures, in the houses all down the glen, informed the
men of Ciorram that within the week the laird would take a contingent of men with him. Leaving the glen one by one, they
would melt from beneath the noses of the Redcoats like snow in
the spring.

Ciaran whistled a jig as he made his way across the bailey toward the Great Hall for supper that evening. He hadn't seen Leah
since the morning, and was eager to be in the same room with her
again, even just to gaze at her from across the hall.

The smells from the kitchen were strong as he entered the
huge room. Everyone present stood as he took his place at the
head table near the hearth. Most of the castle residents were already there: Robin, Ciaran's sisters and nieces, and brother Robbie. Only the captain and his daughter had not yet arrived. Also
partaking in supper that night were Eóin, Gregor, Dùghlas, and
Seumas Glas. They all sat when the laird reached his chair. Plates
of meat were brought from the kitchen, big bowls of stewed cab-
bages, and stacks of bannocks. The assembled Mathesons began
to eat. Ciaran stared hard at the door to the North Tower corridor
and began to wonder why Leah wasn't there.

The guards were still at the entry, which meant the captain
was on the premises. Therefore Leah was somewhere in the Tigh.
Ciaran willed the corridor door to open, but it remained closed.

"She's forsaken ye, lad."

Ciaran cut a hard glance at the faerie, then started up a conversation with Eóin, to his right, regarding the number of cattle to
be sold off that fall. Though the front of his mind calculated numbers of animals and the price they would bring if the weather
continued as it had been and the late grazing was lush, the back
of his mind was calculating ways to arrange private time with
Leah. Perhaps they would meet while Ida was on an errand of
some sort? The chamber above Leah's was unused. Perhaps there
would be opportunities . . .

The hall door opened as Ciaran tore off a piece of a bannock, and in came the red-coated captain, followed by his daughter. Ciaran's heart leapt, a smile tugging the corner of his mouth, and his eyes sought hers down the length of the Great Hall.

But she wasn't looking for him. She was subdued, and walked beside her father with her gaze to the floor. Something was very wrong. They approached the head table, and Ciaran sat back in his chair as they came. He tore the bannock again and put a piece in his mouth to chew on it slowly, though he tasted nothing.

"Ciorram," said the captain, "you'll be pleased to learn your unwelcome guests will be leaving soon. My company is needed elsewhere."

In an instant Leah's countenance was explained, and Ciaran realized he was about to be abandoned. It was all he could do to maintain a blank expression and continue chewing his mouthful of bread as Hadley said, "I've decided the Highlands are not the place for an impressionable young lady such as my daughter. With so much unrest hereabouts, I feel it would be prudent to send her to Edinburgh, where she will be looked after by relatives."

Ciaran glanced at Leah again, but her face was impassive, and her gaze would not meet his. She stared in the direction of the hearth behind him. He swallowed and returned his attention to Hadley. In a carefully measured voice he said, "Captain, I have the impression you think little of my ability to protect your daughter."

Leah's eyes shut.

Hadley replied, "On the contrary, Ciorram. I think very highly of your ability; it is your willingness I call into question." Ciaran opened his mouth to protest, but Hadley raised a palm of dismissal and overrode him.

"But it is no matter, for my company has been called away. We leave at dawn tomorrow. I pray the lot of you will refrain from setting upon your neighbors' cattle, at least until we're out of sight."

A surge of anger nearly caused Ciaran to draw Brigid and rise from his chair, but instead he kept his seat and said in as light a voice as he could conjure, "Safe journey to ye."

"I thank you." The captain turned to take his seat for supper.

Ciaran muttered in Gaelic for the benefit of the few nearby, "Dinnae let the door hit yer backside as ye leave." Eóin and

Robin chuckled, but Ciaran watched Leah avoid his gaze as she went to sit with her father for supper, and Ciaran's heart clenched into a tight knot.

Leah was leaving Glen Ciorram, and there was nothing to be done about it.

CHAPTER 9

The tartan waistcoat matched his kilt.

"Father, why must I go?" Leah followed her father up the spiral stairs. Her skirts were too wide for her to walk beside him, and she longed to make eye contact. For the first time, she resented the fashion. "Why can I not stay here under the protection of the laird?" She struggled to keep up with him; it was as if he was trying to make her hurry. She was breathless with both exertion and distress.

"This is not subject to negotiation. You will come with me, and that is all I will say on the subject." He bypassed his own chamber, then stopped at the landing outside hers.

"But Father, if there is trouble from the clans, don't you think it will be safer for me here?" She knew she would be safer here, but how could she convince him of it?

He turned to her, his eyes narrow and an odd, piercing look on his face. "I do not."

"But Father—"

"Leah. There are things you don't understand about the situation here in the Highlands."

"Enlighten me, then."

His weight shifted, and he stood over her as if she were an incompetent private soldier. She cringed. He said, his voice heavy with impatience, "Very well then, daughter. These wonderful people you've become so fond of would love nothing more than to take control of this kingdom and remove our lawful ruler from his throne. They will stop at nothing to achieve their goal. That includes taking you hostage and forcing concessions from me and my men for your return. Furthermore, in such an event I could not guarantee your safety even were I to yield to their wishes. They might very well kill you regardless. I'm sorry to have to be so very blunt to you, but this is a dreadfully serious matter."

"But Ciar—" Leah stopped herself in time, and let her father run over her words in his anger. He interrupted her without realizing she was letting him.

"Therefore you must stay in your chamber and have no contact with any Mathesons until we leave."

She swallowed her protests, for they were futile. Her mind tumbled with what she must do that night. She must see Ciaran.

But then he said, "There will be no argument, and there will be no sneaking from your chamber. I'm posting a guard on your door tonight."

Her eyes went wide. "Father, no!"

Her vehemence seemed to catch his attention, but by now she was too angry to care. His voice rose. "Is there any reason you would need to wander abroad tonight, daughter?"

Her eyes avoided his, and she took deep breaths in her frustration. Helpless tears stung the corners of her eyes, and she held them even wider so they wouldn't spill.

"Is there?"

Now his pointed questioning alarmed her. Her mind flew to find a reply what would keep the discussion away from Ciaran. "No, Father. There is not. I simply don't care for a guard. I don't care much at all for the sorts of men in the king's enlistment."

His voice softened. "Is there a lieutenant you would prefer on guard, then? Jones, perhaps?"

"Kenneth Jones?"

"You spent a great deal of time with him the day you visited the garrison."

She frowned. What could he mean by that? Did he think she'd wandered off with Lieutenant Jones that day? Struggling to know what to say, she bit back the truthful denial that would implicate Ciaran. Finally she said, "No. I simply don't wish anyone at all to guard my door."

That seemed to disappoint him, and her mind boggled. Did he think she had an interest in Jones? One of his men? But then his next words made her understand the question.

"A Matheson, then." It was not a question, but a realization. He had guessed she was seeing someone.

"No, Father—"

"Get inside." He grabbed her by the arm and manhandled her toward the door. "There will be a private here momentarily, and he will have orders to not let you out until morning." She tried to wrest free, but his hand was iron and his sudden rage terrifying. His fingers dug deeply into her arm.

"And if I try to leave, will he shoot me, then?"

"Don't be silly. He will lift you and carry you back to the room and hold the door shut until you've come to your senses." Then he shoved her into the room. Her heel caught on her skirt and she fell, stumbling against the foot of her bed. Tears sprang to her eyes, and this time fell to her cheeks. He'd never hurt her this way before.

He stood in the doorway, seething and red-faced. "If you are not here when he arrives, and I am forced to go in search of you, I will personally kill anyone with whom you are found." The rage in his eyes told her without question he would carry out that threat. "Good night."

"Father!"

But the captain disappeared down the stairs and was gone.

C iaran sat in the chair in his bedchamber, his feet propped on the table and his thoughts in turmoil. There were many ramifications of the captain's announcement, but the one thing roaring through Ciaran's mind was that Leah Hadley would be gone in the morning. Sinann appeared, but he was in no mood for her nonsense, so he reached for a shoe to hurl it at her, and she disappeared. The shoe passed through the space where she'd been and crashed against the mantelpiece. The old wooden bird toy clattered to the floor.

Eóin slipped into the room and closed the door behind him as Ciaran went to restore the toy to the mantel.

"Ciaran." Eóin's tone was thick with meaning.

The laird turned. "Aye. This development makes our situation both better and worse. I wish we had knowledge of their destination." He also now wished he hadn't chased that faerie away, for she might be able to look in on the captain for him. How she had missed hearing about the impending departure was another question he had for her.

Eóin said, "At least we'll have nae difficulties from them when we march from the glen to join Charles."

Ciaran grunted as he turned the toy over and over in his hand. "Perhaps we might, though, Eóin. Do you think it could be a trap? Will they pretend to leave, then wait nearby to see what we will do?" That thought, along with many more, was tumbling in Ciaran's brain. He set the toy on the mantel, then dumped himself into the chair by the table again and draped his arm over the back of it. Not only could it be a trap, but it also could be a trap set by an angry father who had guessed his daughter's whereabouts the night before.

It could even be that Leah had told where she'd been. The sharp sting of betrayal played in and around his more rational thoughts, and it was hard to guess the truth. He needed to talk to her.

But more, he needed to decide what the clansmen were to do. Hesitation would be perceived by Dùghlas and the others as weakness, and the tacksman was one to put such an opportunity to use. Ciaran wished he'd had his brother hanged when the moment was viable. But it was too late to do so without turning the traitor into a martyr to the Jacobite cause.

He said, "If the captain intends a trap, he'll need for us to march straight out of the glen like stiff-necked Englishmen and blunder into it. Therefore, we simply willnae change our plan and willnae be caught marching off to fight. We'll slip from the glen one by one and rendezvous on the way to Glenfinnan, same as if the garrison were still fully manned and watching us. For they may very well be."

Eóin leaned against the bedpost and nodded. "It's a wise laird ye are."

Self-doubt insinuated itself, but Ciaran fought it and grunted as if in assent. Now was not the time for weakness.

That night, he waited patiently for the castle to settle in to sleep. Sitting in the chair, which he'd set beside an open window, he watched the bailey below and listened to the diminishing sounds of footsteps and voices in the tower. He would choose his time carefully, as his father had taught him on cattle raids. Gradually silence took over and flickers of candlelight were extinguished behind unshuttered windows and arrow loops.

Once the castle was in slumber, he slipped from his room, up the stairs, and crossed the battlement to the North Tower. Treading lightly down those stairs, he reached Leah's floor but dodged back when he came in sight of her door. His heart thudded in his ears. A Redcoat sentry had been posted in the alcove.

Ciaran carefully peeked around the curve of the stairs. The soldier was dozing, having propped himself against the alcove wall. Ciaran retreated a few steps, headed back to his bedchamber, but stopped. He couldn't simply leave. It wasn't in him to give up.

He turned around and descended the stairs. But then he hesitated again. *Damn*. Peering around the curve, he watched the sentry and knew it was hopeless. There was no getting past the guard, who carried musket, pistols, and sword. Ciaran could attack, and possibly overcome the guard without much damage to himself, but an uproar would bring others and defeat his purpose. At this moment armed combat would not solve anything.

Up the stairs once more, he went to the chamber in the West Tower where Sìle and Aodán slept, and knocked on the door. There was no answer. Ciaran stepped back to check for light underneath, but there was not a flicker. They must be sleeping. He knocked again, harder. Still no answer, so he pounded.

Finally he heard oaths muttered on the other side of the door, and it was opened a crack. "Very well, whoreson, there'd better be an excellent reason . . ." When he saw Ciaran, Aodán fell silent.

Ciaran said simply, "Get me Sìle."

"Why?"

"I said get her, and if I hear any more guff—"

"Right. Fine. I'll wake her up."

There was a long pause punctuated by muttering before Sìle appeared in her nightgown and drawing her cloak around her shoulders. She blinked sleepily at him. "Ciaran, what's the matter you had to wake us?"

His voice was a barely audible whisper. "I need help."

"Ye need *sleep*. So do I."

"I must talk to Leah before she leaves in the morning, but there's a guard on her door."

"And for good reason, I'm certain." She smiled up at Ciaran, amused by her own joke.

"I dinnae see the humor, for the captain may very well have learnt of last night. I fear for her safety."

"And your own as well."

"Nae, Sìle." He was losing patience with her. "He may do to me what he likes, but I need to know her disposition and that she is well. I cannae do that while she is under guard. That is the reason I need your help." His teeth clenched, and he hissed in a hoarse whisper, "I'd hoped my sister would be so kind."

That silenced her, and her cheeks reddened. "Aye. I suppose there'd be no harm. Wait here a moment." She disappeared into the room, and, after a murmured conversation with her husband, returned. Stopping a moment to adjust the brogues she'd donned, she then followed Ciaran.

In the North Tower, he leaned against the curved wall, to wait for her just beyond sight of Leah's door. Sìle was to convince the guard to release Leah to her custody, then bring her to the empty guest chamber on the floor above. Failing that, she would ask to speak to Leah in her chamber. There she would relay Ciaran's concern, and attempt to learn the truth of the captain's sudden decision and whether he'd guessed the truth about the night before.

Ciaran strained to hear the conversation between Sìle and the guard, but was able to discern none of it. His heart sank as the talk went on far too long and it was plain the guard wouldn't let Leah go. It sank even further when Sìle appeared on the stairs below. He stood and led the way upstairs to the battlement. The night wind tossed his hair and Sìle's hood every which way, and he had to raise his voice to talk.

"What happened?"

She shook her head. "I was unable even to speak to her. She's held incommunicado and isnae allowed to speak even to the guard. I daresay she willnae even be told I was there."

Ciaran blurted his father's favorite Anglo-Saxon vulgarism, then leaned over the battlement to see if one of the arrow loops in Leah's chamber might be visible from there. But he knew they weren't. On the other side they were obscured from view by structures inside the castle curtain. He'd have to shout from the middle of the bailey to catch her attention, and that would accomplish nothing.

"Ciaran, the captain willnae let you see her."

He stood at the battlement, staring out over the black loch under a black sky as the hard reality bound him. Sìle took his hand.

"Perhaps 'tis best for all of us." There was kindness in her voice, and that softened his heart. "If you are able to forget her, the clan and yourself will be better off for it."

For a long moment he couldn't speak. But then, slowly, quietly, he said, "Aye, perhaps."

Sìle stood, silent, gazing at the loch for a long time before turning to return to her bedchamber and her husband.

With heavy heart, Ciaran went to his own bedchamber.

He stripped for bed, depositing his clothes on the floor where he stood, washed in the basin on the stand, ran wet fingers through his hair, then knelt and said his rosary before slipping between his sheets.

But sleep wasn't likely to come soon, and he knew it. He stared at the wood-beamed ceiling, his eyes tracing the ancient and faded decorations along them. Vague shapes of fruit and flowers could be discerned if one looked carefully enough, painted during a time when it had been fashionable, then left to fade and wear away.

His wandering mind wound itself around an image of Leah, exploring, caressing. Loving. Had she betrayed him? He reviewed his memory of supper over and over again, the expression on her face, the attitude of her body, the placement of her hands, the dress she wore. But there was nothing to be learned by the little he'd seen. She'd been as perfectly unreadable as she'd always been while in her father's presence.

Sinann appeared, perched in her favorite spot at a corner of the bed curtain frame.

"Hello, faerie."

"Hello, yourself. Have you calmed some, then?"

"Aye." He felt anything but calm. "Subdued" might have been a better word for it. Beaten. Or, as Da might have said, "trashed." He missed his father with a sudden intensity that made him squeeze his eyes shut and hold his breath for a moment.

"You truly love her?"

He nodded. "She's slipped into my heart like a long, sharp dirk. I dinnae ken how it happened, and now there's naught for it but to suffer, for I cannae have her."

Then he rolled over in bed. "Allow me to sleep now, faerie."

There was a brief silence, but then, "Your father could never

recall my name, either." Ciaran looked back over his shoulder at
the faerie above, and she continued in a soft, wistful voice, "He
was ever addressing me as 'Tinkerbell.' "

"Tink." Ciaran had often heard the word, usually said under
Da's breath. "Why?"

Sinann shrugged. "He never said."

Ciaran grunted and put his face into the pillow again.

"You cannae go to fight with the young prince."

Voice muffled by feathers and linen, Ciaran replied, "I cannae
not go."

"But your father said the rising will be a defeat. The final defeat of the cause. The battle he called Culloden will be the end of
nearly every Jacobite there, and not a few folk who were not part
of the fighting. Your father was adamant ye nae be there, for he
did not wish you to die so young." Ciaran grunted, but Sinann
continued:

"There was another reason he would have kept the clan away
from the rising. Above all else, he desired peace for his people
and wouldnae have them wiped out by a vengeful king and his
cruel hordes."

Ciaran had no reply.

Still, the faerie continued: "And, may I remind ye, now you've
gone and fallen in love with the daughter of a Redcoat. Surely
you must see the benefit of keeping away from the fighting. Stay
here, and you might have a chance at her. She and her father will
surely be back after—"

"No, faerie." Ciaran sat up. "You were right before. I was a
fool to take the woman into my heart. And in the end, even aside
from the clan's insistence we fight, I've decided we must go. As
Da said, I cannae forget who my people are and where my home
is. We must fight for our rights as Scotsmen and Catholics. I re-
vere my father's memory and wish I could do him proud. However, the fact remains I'm nae my father. I've nae the talent to
pretend to kiss the king's white, shiny German ass. Neither will
the clan allow me to stand by and let the *Sasunnaich* treat them
like animals. I cannae continue to bite my tongue when the English army comes to eat at my table and sleep under my roof
when they would as soon shoot me as speak to me, and would arrest me in an instant on the least excuse. I willnae continue to
hide my father's whiskey, of which he was so proud. I willnae

continue to hide my faith. In short, faerie, I willnae continue to live under the rule of King George."

"Then you may very well not continue to live at all."

Ciaran thought about that for a moment, wondering what it would be like to die in battle. To take the wound and feel the pain, and know he would never rise again from the ground. Slowly, he nodded. "Aye."

Then he lay down again and closed his eyes.

At sunrise, Ciaran's exercises in the castle bailey were interrupted by the arrival and loading of the *Sasunnach* baggage train. He stood, silent and with one hand on the bearhead staff he'd been using in his form, as he watched the packhorses being loaded. Men in red coats hurried about the business of their captain, and Ciaran's heart lightened that the English presence was leaving his glen. His people would be in less danger without the young, bored, and bigoted Englishmen always with their noses in everything. He should be glad for the arrival of Prince Charles just for that.

But then a Thoroughbred with a sidesaddle was brought into the bailey, and his heart fell. Now his brogues were rooted to the earth, and his impassive face was quite still as he watched Leah emerge from the Great Hall. She wore a dark riding dress beneath her long, black cloak. Her fingers secured the clasp as she approached her mount. One of the soldiers assisted her onto the horse, and she picked up the reins. Ciaran struggled to retain his utter stillness, achieved only by the discipline of his fight training. Only his eyes moved as he examined her face.

But she was expressionless. Her demeanor betrayed nothing of what she might be feeling, either of elation or grief.

As the captain mounted and gave the order to move, Leah wheeled her horse to comply, and as she turned, her eye caught Ciaran's. For the briefest moment, her head swiveled to keep sight of him, but even so, he couldn't read her. Then she faced forward and urged her mount to follow her father's through the gatehouse.

She was gone.

Ciaran stood for a long moment, staring at the empty castle entry. He whispered, "Faerie, do you ken where she might be going?"

Sinann's voice came from nowhere: "Edinburgh. The company is to be garrisoned there."

"The prince will be glad for that information." With a sigh, the laird tucked his staff up behind his arm and went to organize his contribution to the Jacobite cause.

To Eóin he said as he entered the Great Hall, "Summon Dùghlas, Gregor, Seumas, and Robin. And Robbie . . . summon Robbie as well." Eóin turned to obey, then Ciaran continued, "After you've done that, bring Calum from the gatehouse." Eóin halted. Ciaran stared into the fire in the hearth. "Bring him to me once the others have gathered."

"Are ye mad?" Eóin peered at his stepbrother, frowning.

Ciaran turned to address Eóin firmly. "Do as I said."

Eóin's voice was low, serious. "Ciaran, he's my brother as well as yours, and I'm nae one to trust him for the briefest moment outside his cell."

"I cannae leave him here, for Robbie will be left behind and he's too young and nae strong enough to stand against Calum's supporters. There would be a coup, and I would be declared illegitimate. Or worse."

"Have the traitor executed." Eóin's face was bland and betrayed nothing more than the matter-of-fact reality of the situation. He continued, "You should have hung him from the gatehouse the very day he stood against you."

Ciaran replied, "I cannae, for it would weigh against me in the minds of the clansmen. Also, I am without an heir." For a moment Ciaran thought of Leah and closed his eyes against it before resuming. "Dùghlas and your own dear brother Gregor would then lose no time in assassinating me, leaving Robbie in this seat as their puppet for, again, he's nae strong enough to stand against them.

"Furthermore, if wee Robbie were somehow able to stand against them, he would forthwith likewise die without issue. Dùghlas would then be one of several claimants. He could possibly become laird himself. So I shall avoid helping Dùghlas do away with those who stand between himself and this castle. I'll take Calum with me to the fight, and at the first reason he gives me I shall have him put down and no man will raise a hand against me for it. Or, perhaps, he'll die in battle, and that would be the best for everyone, for we could all safely sing his praises as a great hero, and clan support would go to me rather than Dùghlas. In any case, my traitorous brother willnae stay here."

"And if both yourself and Calum die in battle?"

Nausea turned Ciaran's stomach, but he took a deep breath. "Then God help Robbie, and give him the strength to stand against Dùghlas."

Eóin nodded, understanding, and departed on his errand.

The men gathered in the afternoon, the eight of them constituting an illegal assembly but each of them secure in the knowledge the soldiers were elsewhere. Ciaran sat by the hearth in his large chair, bear-headed staff at his side, Eóin standing behind him, and stared steadily at his half brother, who stood before him with his hands on his hips. It was a long, uncomfortable silence before the laird finally spoke.

"Ye ken how fortunate you are I've spared your life."

Calum nodded. He seemed less cowed than he'd been the day of his imprisonment. He knew he was going to live, and he surely understood why. But Ciaran mustered every bit of power at his command to keep his half brother in his place.

"I will take a contingent of men to fight for Prince Charles, and I cannae have you lounging about in the gatehouse and making of yourself naught but a burden on the clan." They all must know it was Robbie he was protecting, but nobody said so as he continued. "I require you to fight alongside us, and so for your freedom you will take an oath of allegiance. On your immortal soul, swear to me your loyalty."

Calum grinned, a bland, disarming smile, held his palms wide, and said, "But Ciaran, I'm your broth—"

"*Swear it!*" Ciaran knew that smile, had grown up with it, and was not fooled. It was the one their father had used when forced into friendliness with Redcoats. Anger surged to be treated like a *Sasunnach*. "Swear it, or I'll have ye hung for treason."

The grin fled, and anger flashed in Calum's eyes. He glanced at Dùghlas, then to Gregor, then back to his half brother. His weight shifted as he made his decision. Then he slowly lowered himself to one knee before Ciaran.

His head bowed and his hair obscuring his face, he drew a deep breath and said, "I solemnly swear, on my immortal soul, fealty in all things to my laird and brother, Ciaran Robert Matheson of Ciorram. Should I violate this oath, may all my endeavors fail, may I never have a son to follow after me, and when I die may I burn eternally in hell."

His eyes smoldered with hatred as he raised his head.

"Very well, then." Ciaran addressed the gathering, "There will be thirty of us to go with Charles. The rest, including Robbie, will stay here—"

A small, teenage voice broke in. "*Och,* Ciaran—"

"Robert . . ." The laird stood and took the arm of his youngest brother. "You must. You're old enough to fight, but too important to lose. The clan will need you should I die."

"Then let me go, and you stay. Father taught me to fight, same as you."

Amusement tugged at the corner of Ciaran's mouth. "Aye, then." He handed his staff off to Eóin, then stepped back into a casual fight stance and said, his fists at ready, "How about a contest? You best me, and I'll allow you to lead the men in my place. Think you can best me?"

Robbie sighed and looked at the floor, for everyone present knew he was no match for his much older, heavier, and more experienced brother. Ciaran stood down and squeezed Robbie's thin shoulder. "I need ye here, lad. It'll be a tough enough fight for you right here in Glen Ciorram, simply to keep the Mac-Donells away from our kine."

That brought some cheer to Robbie's face and he looked Ciaran in the eye, for he knew the truth of it, and he nodded.

The night before leaving for Glenfinnan, Ciaran again found himself restless. There was no comfort to be found in his bed, though this would be the last time he would sleep in it, possibly forever. He sat up on the edge of the mattress, his head bowed over his knees, and tried to clear his head. Too many thoughts swarmed there. Too many worries about Leah, the clan, the coming fight, Leah, his brothers, Leah . . . Leah . . . Leah. He sighed. There was whiskey in the kitchen downstairs; perhaps he could drink himself to sleep. So he pulled on a sark, buckled his kilt around himself, and stole down the spiral stairs in his bare feet.

But the jug in the kitchen was empty, and to refill it would mean a trip to the casks hidden in the southern woods. A deep, disgusted noise rasped the back of his throat, and he slammed the jug onto the large wooden table.

Returning to bed would be pointless. His mind was too busy to sleep. Working things out was the only way to bring himself any peace. So he picked up a rush light, flint, and striker from the hearth and made his way from the castle.

In the wooded hills immediately to the north he came to the large clearing where the clan held festival gatherings and bonfires in spite of the proscription against them. The pile of ashes at the center was muddy and forlorn with no fire and no gathering around it, distinguishable only by the darkness of the earth. Ciaran picked up some sticks from beneath the nearby trees and knelt at the edge of the dark circle to build his own small fire among the muddy ashes.

With one of the sticks he dug a small, shallow hole, then set his wood in it to light it with the flint and rush light. Before long he had a pleasant little blaze, welcome for its light and heat even on this summer night. Then he stood to remove his clothes and let them drop to the side. Wearing nothing but the crucifix and wedding ring on the chain around his neck, he sat cross-legged by the fire to meditate.

His father had done this from time to time in years past. Da had carefully explained in his teaching that a troubled mind was a distracted mind, and therefore a vulnerable one. Whoever Dylan Dubh truly was to him, Ciaran believed the things he'd taught and so now sought to calm himself.

He took deep breaths of the bracing night air and focused on the flame before him. Emptying his mind, he felt his body relax, muscle by muscle, joint by joint. Breaths came easier. Slower. The world began to seem less overwhelming. He began to enjoy the play of a slight breeze across his skin.

Something small and black near the fire caught his eye, and he absently picked it up. As blank as his thoughts were, and as black as the object was, it took a moment to realize what it was: a human tooth, half decayed at the crown but with three whole roots. It couldn't be one pulled by the blacksmith, for Donnchadh always broke the roots off. And the jaw as well, more often than not. This tooth was the last remnant of a decayed corpse. Ciaran turned it between his fingers, then threw it into the fire to be rid of it and returned to his meditation. Slowly he relaxed. Tension eased, and his senses sharpened. It was a pleasure to feel the world around him, the moonlight on his skin, the night air on his chest.

Someone spoke—nearby, but barely audible and completely unintelligible. Ciaran opened his eyes to see who had spoken so softly to him, but there was nobody. He grunted and shut them again. But the voice came again, louder this time and speaking his name.

A cold shiver raced up his spine. Someone was near. He

looked around, his senses strained to tell who and where it might be. But there was nothing.

Then the fire spoke. "Ciaran."

He scooted away from it, aghast. *Holy moley!* Staring, he waited to hear more, but there was only silence. He began to relax, only slightly alarmed his imagination had run away with him for a moment.

But just as he drew a deep breath of relief he heard, "You stupid Highland get!"

Thoroughly shaken now, Ciaran rose to his knees and crouched by the sentient flame. He wanted to run away, but had never run from anything in his life and couldn't bring himself to it now. He stared, straining to hear, yet fearing the next words.

They came, wavering and barely audible again. "Stupid son of mine."

Ciaran shook his head. This wasn't Da. "No. You're nae my father."

"Nae Dylan Dubh. Absolutely your father."

Trembling took Ciaran. The cool air was no longer exhilarating, but leached warmth from his body until he thought his life might go with it. His fingers dug into the dirt beside his knees. With a throat nearly closed tight with terror, he choked out the words "Connor Ramsay?"

A weak, distant laughter came from the fire. "Then you are a wise child after all."

"No!"

"Aye. Dylan Matheson killed me so he could fuck your mother, but he was too late. You were already born by then. Ciaran Ramsay. Aye, you're Ciaran Ramsay." The laughter now was high, hysterical giggling. "Cannot deny it, lad. You do not belong to him. And you know it in your heart. I can see it there. 'Tis a dread knowledge, but you cannot deny it. You're my son, and no kin to the filthy chamberer who took my life."

"Robin said—"

"He lied! He lied to save his position in the clan! He lied so as to make certain the truth regarding his precious friend would not be revealed! There was no truth in it, but only self-interest!"

That was enough. More than Ciaran could stand. Emitting inarticulate, animal-like noises, he began to shove dirt onto the fire, and it sputtered. The voice continued, assuring him he'd learned the truth at last. He scooped old bonfire ashes onto the fire and put it completely out. Then, grunting with disgust, he scooped more ashes to bury it entirely, lest there be any further smoldering. Finally, he stood to pee on the ashes. With a long, steady stream he soaked them well to banish the ghost.

Then, listening carefully for a long moment, he finally decided the voice was gone. Not even the distant echo of Connor Ramsay's ghost. He considered digging through the ashes and dirt for that tooth, to crush it and scatter it and be rid of it forever, but he couldn't bring himself to touch the thing again. The cold held his bones hard, and he shivered uncontrollably as he pulled his clothes back on. With one last kick of dirt onto the fire, he backed away from it until he was out of the clearing.

His bedchamber was dark when he arrived, but the moment he entered, a candle lit up with a flare of light. It startled him badly and made him leap to the side. There, leaning on the stone wall, he gasped and struggled to regain his sense.

Sinann's voice came, and he squeezed his eyes shut while his racing heart calmed. "Where the devil have you been, that you're all sooty and disheveled?" He glared sideways at her on her perch, and she added, "*Och,* lad, what's troubling you?"

"Shut up, faerie." The trembling wouldn't stop. His mind tumbled with what he'd heard, struggling to push it away, terrified it might be true. That Robin had lied to protect the memory of Dylan Dubh. That a stranger named Connor Ramsay had given him life.

"Ciaran, laddie—"

"I said, shut up!" He'd heard entirely too much already, and didn't care to discuss any of this. Fingers shaking and fumbling, he unbuckled his belt and threw his clothes onto the floor, then flopped onto his bed to stare at the ceiling until the candle guttered. Sometime near dawn he finally slept.

The Matheson contingent left Ciorram the next night. Swiftly and silently, heavily armed men dispersed from the glen one by one, with instructions to form up again in a steep ravine many miles away. Ciaran was the last to leave, with the silver-hilted king's sword in a baldric at his side, Brigid sheathed at his legging, and a wooden targe slung over his back. He carried a water skin, a pistol in his belt, powder horn and primer flask, and in his sporran were some balls for the pistol, a ration bag filled with oatmeal, the brooch talisman, a purse with a few coins, his rosary, and around his neck he wore the chain bearing his father's crucifix and his mother's wedding ring. Quickly, followed by Sinann, he hurried through the gatehouse and toward the drawbridge, where the shadows of trees would cover him from view lest anyone be watching from the surrounding mountains.

Even now, the faerie harried him. "Lad, dinnae go, I'm telling you it was your father's dearest wish ye stay home." The faerie fluttered before him, flying backward as he approached the drawbridge.

"I must." He lowered his chin and pressed on.

"You cannae." She fluttered just close enough to annoy but not close enough for him to get his hands on her.

He stopped walking, and peered up at her. "I despise the English. I would sooner gouge out my eyes than continue to watch the *Sasunnaich* overrun my home. And you cannae tell me Da dinnae hate them as much as I."

"Your father wished you to make peace with the English."

"The rest of the clan thinks otherwise, and they willnae stand still for me to make peace. Furthermore, faerie, I agree with them."

"Will you not make peace even for the sake of the girl?"

Ciaran lowered his head, swallowed the surge of regret over Leah, and made a disparaging noise in the back of his throat. Leah was a weakness he could no longer afford. He looked up again and opened his mouth to reply, but Sinann's eyes were no longer on him. They'd gone wide and were gawking at something behind him. He turned to see.

But she grabbed his face and forced him to turn back. "No! Dinnae look!"

He resisted and tried to turn. "What is—"

But she hauled him back around with astonishing force. "*I said, dinnae look!* Do not turn around, whatever you do!"

"What is—"

"The dog! 'Tis the white hound! He's turning his circles widdershins and settling before the gatehouse." Her hands were trembling against his face, and there was a quaver in her voice. " 'Tis a terrible omen, lad. Dinnae look, and perhaps you willnae bear the bad luck."

It was nearly unbearable to not look, for he'd never seen the white hound, and his curiosity was intense. But he obeyed, for he knew the luck would be disastrous if he saw. He stood still, looking into Sinann's face as he waited. Tears glistened in her eyes. He whispered, "Are you certain the bad luck will pass me by?"

She shook her head, her lips moving silently in what he took to be a warding spell.

Finally she let go of his face and said, " 'Tis gone. The ghost has faded. There's naught to see now."

Ciaran turned, and of course saw nothing by the gatehouse. He crossed himself, and murmured a Hail Mary to ward against the evil.

Then he turned to cross the drawbridge, a sick feeling in the pit of his belly. He made his way to the rendezvous where his men awaited, and from there took them onward to Glenfinnan.

On August 18, at sunset, the band of Mathesons arrived at the head of Loch Shiel, where the tiny village of Glenfinnan lay and a number of clansmen had gathered. Men sat around cook fires, and as the newcomers moved among them on their way to a clear spot by the water, Ciaran heard snatches of conversation speculating about the prince. Some soldiers' wives and ragged camp followers went about the business of preparing food for their men. Children played noisily nearby among the gorse and reeds. A fiddle played somewhere, but for the most part it was not a festive group.

Ciaran claimed a place near the mouth of a small burn, finding plenty of room for his men to build fires, for not many clans had come out for Charles, and the few represented had sent few men. Most who were there belonged to Clanranald. The tiny Matheson contingent was little help in swelling their numbers. Ciaran looked around at the Jacobites lounging around in small clusters among the reeds and gorse, and wondered whether this desperately inadequate army would last even as long as his father had claimed they would. With deep apprehension he wrapped himself in his plaid and lay down near their fire to sleep.

In the morning the men were restive, anticipating the arrival of the young Stuart. The morning was spent in conversation with various of the few men who had come, everyone speculating on whether Charles would make the rendezvous or if he'd been captured already by the English.

Such worries were set aside, though, when a boat was spotted far down the loch and a shout went up. Men gathered near the shore to see, and Ciaran found a vantage point atop a small rise near some trees. A tall, bewigged figure stood in the boat, surrounded by other well-dressed men but noticeable by his scarlet tartan breeches and waistcoat. The boat approached the shore, and as it landed, the young man leapt from it into the water to wade ashore. He wore high black jackboots, so shiny and well cared for the water beaded and ran from them as he gained the dry ground.

As the others from the boat also debarked, Ciaran left his rise and moved through the gathering to greet as laird of his contingent the prince who would lead the army. As he went he cut a glance at Calum, who glowered at him with what could only be envy.

A low murmur of commentary ran among the men on the shore regarding Charles' looks and his bearing. Close up, there was an intensity about the young man that was astonishing. Ciaran found himself in awe. Taking his turn, he bowed to the prince and introduced himself. The intelligent brown eyes looked straight across and into his, and he felt the energy in them all the way to his bones. The prince bestowed a warm smile and echoed him, as if committing the name to memory.

"Ciaran Robert Matheson of Ciorram. I thank you for coming. Your loyalty to my father will be well rewarded." His English was accented with Italian, no surprise since the young man had spent most of his life exiled in Rome. Ciaran was pleased to learn that, unlike both Kings George, Charles was fluent in at least one of the languages native to Britain. It was commonly known King George I had spoken no English at all his entire life, and had resented the idea that he should learn it. The current George spoke the language grudgingly, preferring all things German to anything English, and like his father considered Hanover his true home.

Though the prince must be disappointed to see so few men, his voice was warm and his smile utterly charming. *Bonnie Prince Charlie,* Da had said. He'd certainly been right about that much. The prince had as pleasant a visage as any man Ciaran had ever seen, well built and with a regal and graceful air. His mouth was formed so he appeared to be smiling even at rest, giving him also the appearance of complete confidence. A man could follow easily such a prince.

Charles and his entourage passed, and Ciaran watched them go. But one of the older men, in a fine coat, well-styled wig, and

breeches stopped for a moment, having caught Ciaran's eye. The
man stared, his brow furrowed. Just as Ciaran was about to ask
whether there might be something he could do for the old man,
an even older man called out.

"George!" The older one was bent, gray of skin, and appeared
too frail for this adventure. "Come, little brother."

George's attention broke, and he went on his way. Ciaran
stared after him, wondering what that had been about.

The few hundred men present were charged with excitement,
cheering the prince and chattering to each other. They followed
Charles' entourage toward the head of the loch as a contingent of
MacDonalds debarked from the boats and also followed. There
was much discussion amongst the new arrivals, and Ciaran was
near enough to the prince to learn they'd decided to wait and see
if more men would come before they would raise the flag.

The Jacobites resettled into their camps, ate, and waited. The
afternoon wore on, and the shadows grew long. The hillsides over
Loch Shiel cast black shade on the water. Ciaran began to wonder
if this rising was ever going to begin.

But then a wisp of pipe music arrived from a distance. Ciaran's heart lifted, and he and some others turned to hear. He
would have thought he'd imagined it except for other men who
stood to listen. Then it came again—the faintest skirl, but it was
definitely there now. And it was coming from the direction of the
southern hill. Someone was coming.

All the men by the loch stood now, to see who it was. The wait
was not short, for the nature of pipes was that they should be
heard from a distance. But the sound grew stronger, and now the
lower register was audible.

"Look!" shouted one of the prince's entourage.

A column of Highlanders came over the mountain, descending to the glen. And they came. Hundreds of them. By their ban-
ners they were Lochiel's Camerons, in possession of a handful of
Redcoat prisoners.

Excitement riffled through the men by the loch. The wail of
the pipes grew louder, and the men came onward. Ciaran's heart
lifted at the sight. He couldn't help but smile.

Straight away, the standard of King James VIII was raised
atop a hill above the loch head, and a formal proclamation was
read by Prince Charles in which he claimed for James as his father's regent the throne of England and Scotland. In low voices,

Ciaran and some others translated the statement to Gaelic for those who did not speak English. The red, white, and blue flag was unfurled to blow in the summer breeze, and the men below broke into cheers, throwing their floppy wool bonnets into the air.

Ciaran decided his father must have been wrong. These men would surely take England from King George.

CHAPTER 10

He fumbled with the jet buttons of his waistcoat, then smoothed it against his flat belly.

Ciaran was given the rank of major, though his contingent was small, for each distinct group of clansmen was led by a man of that rank, and a lesser rank would have been an insult to the men he'd brought. There was no merging of small units with larger, for Highland warriors could hardly be expected to fight under authority of someone else's laird. Ciaran shuddered to think of the disaster, were his men forced to merge with the Mac-Donells who were present. Mass desertion would have been the best to be hoped for. Indeed, a lesser rank than major would have been enough of a slight to him to have taken them home.

On the one hand, Ciaran liked the prestige and the pay. But the practical reality was that it made for a great many men giving orders and too few taking them. Confusion and inefficiency were inevitable. Even he could see that, just by his experience leading raids on MacDonnell cattle.

Shortly after the raising of the standard, the Jacobite army began their march to meet the army of King George, their prince walking the route with them. The Mathesons did not walk at the front of the army, so Ciaran rarely caught sight of the prince's inner circle. But Ciaran did learn the name of the man who had been so intrigued by his face the day of the landing. The man had been Lord George Murray, and his older brother the Marquis of Tullibardine, both among the most prominent Jacobites living. Sometimes during the long march Ciaran puzzled over what Lord George could have wanted from him, but was unable to puzzle it out.

At times as the march progressed, there might be a glimpse of Charles at the front, in his scarlet breeches and tartan waistcoat. His confidence was infectious. It was impossible not to be affected by the young man's energy and his utter conviction he and his army would prevail. Even marching behind the more numerous Camerons and MacDonalds, Ciaran could feel it like a heat emanating from the front. The mood was light among the men—all were affected by the leadership of Charles.

Also, Ciaran's heart was bolstered as Highlanders in the livery of the king began to defect to the cause. As they came, they brought word that George's General Cope was marching from Stirling Castle with arms for Highland clans to quell the Jacobites. But they also reported that when he'd arrived at Crieff, Cope had found no loyalty among the Atholl or Glenorchy clans on whom the Crown had relied, and those clans could be counted on to fight for the cause. The Hanoverian army found themselves burdened with weapons and not enough men to wield them.

The Jacobites marched onward, freely using the roads built by the Crown in recent decades to facilitate movement of Redcoat troops. They were high-spirited and eager, most of them young and untried Highland men ready to meet King George's men and prove themselves.

They were halted by the prince at the top of the narrow and steep Pass of Corrieyairack. Scouts reported Cope was approaching them from the south and would have to negotiate a nearly perpendicular route through the pass to reach Fort Augustus, directly to their north. Nowhere could high ground be more advantageous for the Jacobites, for each switchback was a ledge from which they could fire muskets or drop stones onto the trail below. There were seventeen traverses. For the Redcoats that meant seventeen trips across the line of fire, each one closer to the enemy than the last.

Ciaran and his men, as well as the rest of the fifteen hundred or so Jacobites, were of good cheer that day and eagerly awaited the approach of their enemy. They knew Cope could not make it to Fort Augustus without going through that pass, and it was a certainty there would be English blood running freely if they did. Ciaran sat on a rock where there was a good view, and listened to older men tell stories of their own battles.

However, day passed, and it became apparent General Cope had anticipated the trap and was avoiding it. When scouts reported the retreat of Cope's men east toward Inverness, Prince Charles' army mobilized down through the pass and gave chase. For two days they were unable to catch and engage the Redcoats. Frustrated and angry, the prince let his quarry go and turned his army southward.

In Atholl, the army encountered little resistance from the clansmen there. Indeed, there was rejoicing when the Murrays learned their former laird, the marquis of Tullibardine, was with Charles. As the army marched into the town of Blair in the heart of Atholl, folks ran from their houses to greet them and cheer them on. Women waved kerchiefs, and boys leapt into the air with the joy of their prince's arrival. The Hanoverian duke, brother to William and George, had already fled, leaving Blair Castle for the taking. The Jacobite ranks swelled with the Murray clansmen who had denied obeisance to the man who had been their laird according to English law but not in their hearts.

Ciaran watched the procession following the elderly William as he made his way to the castle accompanied by Lord George. What might have happened in Ciorram had he himself defied the wishes of his own clan and kept away from the fight? His father, as well as the writings of Niccolò Machiavelli, had taught him a leader controls only at the forbearance of his people. Dylan Dubh might have been able to steer his people away from the cause, but for Ciaran there had been no hope. With Calum at his heels he could never have accomplished it.

Enthusiasm among the Jacobite soldiers grew with their numbers. After a short stay in a welcoming billet where the food was hot and plentiful and the bed warm, Ciaran continued with his men and his prince on the march south.

On September 5, in Perth, the mass of soldiers and residents witnessed a ceremony at the mercat cross in the center of town at which Charles, as prince regent, once again declared James the king. In the council of clan leaders, Lord George Murray and the duke of Perth were made lieutenant generals. Ciaran realized a command structure of sorts was beginning to form as a natural result of necessity, and thought it a good thing. The Jacobite army was shaping up. They were well received, and the soldiers were once again glad for warm beds and generous provisions.

Quickly the march resumed. Ciaran's pulse surged happily as he realized they were going straight to Edinburgh.

Sinann must have caught him smiling, for she said, "Do you expect you'll find her?"

He glanced sideways at the faerie as he walked with his men. The soldiers, being undisciplined farmers rather than a professional military force, never marched in tight formation, or any formation at all, for that matter. So he was able to fall back and to the side to put some distance between himself and anyone who would overhear his conversation with the wee folk. "I'll certainly try," he muttered.

"And if ye should find her? What then?"

A sigh escaped Ciaran, and he looked over to read her face. The faerie didn't seem in a mood to tease him today, so he said, "I'll seek to learn her mind."

"May I point out to you, laddie, she is a woman. Even more than that, she's an Englishwoman. You might hope to learn her mind, but ye should never count on it."

That brought a tiny smile. "An excellent point, faerie. Then I will seek only to ascertain whether she wishes to see me again, or if she was only sporting that night."

"Do you think she might care for ye?"

The smile died. He thought about that for a long moment, then took a deep breath and said, "I hope so. I've certainly been with enough women who did not. I cannae say as I enjoy that overmuch."

"Would you marry her, then?"

One shoulder shrugged. "Not only is she a *Sasunnach,* but she's the daughter of a Redcoat. I may as well abdicate the laird-ship and hand the clan over to Calum. I couldnae marry her unless we prevail over the Redcoats first."

Sinann fell silent.

Leah thought she should have liked Edinburgh. It wasn't quite so near the ends of the earth as Ciorram, and the surrounding countryside was a bit less severe than those dreadful mountains in the north. The streets were filthy and crowded, but those things one expected in any city. The delights of living where there were many people were always paid for in terms of smells and noise. One grew accustomed eventually.

But even with so many people about, some with acceptable manners and who dressed in a more or less civilized fashion, there was one person missing, and it made the place terrible in her estimation. *Ciaran*. She missed Ciaran desperately. She'd even come to appreciate that dreary castle he lived in, simply because he lived in it. How she wished she could return to it!

Her father had arranged for her to stay with his younger cousin Edwin and Edwin's wife, Martha, in a narrow stone house set amid and against other narrow stone houses. Many of the structures about had been divided to house many families, and the squalor of dirty children and women in the street made going out less than pleasant. The Hadleys' house was set back from the high street, on a close that was shaded by a tall tree and accessed by a steep wynde. It was a very nice house, an expensive place to live in this city crowded onto a hill of solid stone.

Cousin Edwin looked nothing like her father. Whereas Father was fit and well groomed, Edwin sported a huge belly and a spotty face. They bore the same coloring, but the Hadley eyes on Edwin were dull. It was a struggle to believe they were related.

Martha was also a large woman, but with a spark of intelligence lacking in Edwin and a discipline for neatness that kept the servants from letting the household run itself into the ground. Edwin may not have noticed, but the rooms were well organized and immaculate.

Edwin worked for the Crown in a managerial capacity, overseeing the offices of the Edinburgh Custom House. He was an excise official, who determined and collected duty from ships—a daunting and important task in these times of heavy import duty and rampant smuggling, though the job did not pay a handsome wage. He and his wife lived well in spite of their modest means, keeping to themselves and taking less notice of what went on around the corner than they did to what transpired in London. An occasional guest brought news from home, and Edwin Hadley was ever eager to hear it.

The couple had no children, so it was an extremely sedate and somewhat lonely existence in that house. Leah spent her days at sewing and embroidery, attempting discreetly to reproduce the strange, intricate designs she'd seen in the Highlands. Cousin Martha sat with her throughout the day, chattering about friends and acquaintances in London. As the stories and gossip began to repeat, told again and again by her cousin, who never seemed to care how often she related a story, Leah began to realize how far she'd come in accepting her own exile. London and stories of the life there held less interest than she would have thought the months before when she'd first come to Scotland. Now, instead of devouring every morsel of news, she pretended to listen and all the while daydreamed of Ciaran.

Often she prayed for his safety. She pleaded with God to put a quick end to the disturbance in the Highlands and allow her return to Glen Ciorram without delay. Once again she found herself wishing things could return to the way they had been, and felt cheated to have so much taken from her in so short a time.

One day in the sitting room as Edwin read aloud from the *Edinburgh Courant,* he laughed and informed the silent ladies, "They say that Charles Stuart has made a landing somewhere in the Highlands."

Having overheard gossip among the dragoons during the ride south, Leah knew it but said nothing. She also guessed the arrival of Stuart was the reason her father's dragoons had been moved to the garrison at Edinburgh Castle. But she kept her mouth sealed as she had done for the past weeks, and continued her work on the shirt—*sark*—she was sewing.

The cuffs would sport an intertwined pattern of stylized bears embroidered in brown. *Son of the heroes.* She smiled to herself at how Ciaran might receive such a shirt. Though the bodies of the bears were necessarily thin and unlike any living bear, the heads were very bearlike and sported impressive fangs in heavy jaws. As she listened to Edwin disparaging the Jacobites, she wondered if the shirt would ever be worn. Wistful longing settled in her belly.

Edwin went on talking, releasing as he did so the lowest button of his bulging brocade waistcoat. "Apparently Stuart's acquired a band of rogues he's marching about the countryside. By all accounts, none of them even know what they're about. Quite the lazy, undisciplined crew." He shook a crinkle from the newspaper, scratched his belly, and said, "I say, from what I know of Highlanders, it's a wonder he's managed to have them all walking in one direction." He chuckled to himself, not noticing or not caring that nobody shared his amusement. Martha didn't even seem to be listening, though Leah knew she must be.

Leah peered at Edwin, thinking what a fool he was. She'd been in the Highlands and seen the sorts of men living there. It was her opinion King George would do well to avoid a fight with such men as the "lazy, undisciplined" Ciaran Matheson and his "rogue" kinsmen.

Martha said, her voice soft and her tone serious, "I've heard the French are readying to land here in the firth, and that the Young Pretender's forces are ten thousand strong."

Leah shot a glance toward Martha. The woman seemed to know more than her husband did—a possibility, since she, at least, had her ear to the ground and an open mind. At this news, a surge of terror rose in Leah, both for Ciaran and for her father. Her gaze returned to the needlepoint, and she held her breath for a moment so tears wouldn't rise and so nobody would see her fear.

Edwin made a disparaging fart noise with his lips. "Rumors. Martha, you are forever paying too much heed to the servants' nattering. You would do well to ignore them, for they invent things to frighten their masters and mistresses. I'm shocked you would take seriously such a foolish tale."

"You believe it so impossible?" Martha's voice was soft, yet she seemed unmoved by her husband's ridicule.

"Stuart is a Catholic and a foreigner. God would never allow such a thing to happen." There was a long silence while Edwin turned to browse his paper in silence and Martha pulled thread through fabric.

However, before long a smile played about her lips as she said, "Other word I've heard is that Stuart has the support of the Scottish Episcopal Church."

That brought a "harrumph." Edwin's doughy face reddened, and he said, "These Scots and their strange ideas of loyalty. I say they're all mad to throw in their lot with the filthy Highland papists." Then he muttered to himself, "Vile people, Catholics."

Leah cut him a glance and felt her cheeks redden. As much as she believed Catholicism was wrong, she couldn't help wanting to inform Edwin he was wrong about some Catholics. But she couldn't speak against Edwin's dearly held beliefs—not in his own home and not while she was dependent on his generosity.

Instead, she closed her eyes and whispered another prayer for Ciaran.

I n mid-September the forces of King James made camp at Slateford, two miles outside the city walls of Edinburgh. Nearly a month had passed since the raising of the standard, and there had been no sight of a Redcoat to oppose them. Many private soldiers were defecting to the cause, and even the loyal Hanoverian generals continued to evade conflict. George's military leaders seemed reluctant to risk their lives and their men's lives against King James.

Excitement among the Jacobites ran high, and Ciaran joked with his men as they sat around campfires and awaited orders from the prince. Calum was nearby, cleaning his sword, his face lit with his habitual smile. On this campaign, he seemed to have set aside his hatred for his brother, in his greater hatred for the English. Today he sharpened his sword obsessively and made crude jokes about body parts and blood.

Calum was vibrant with pent energy; he was eager to kill. Ciaran found the enthusiasm both unsettling and promising. It was good to have his brother in agreement with him again, but he wasn't entirely certain all that energy would be spent against the *Sasunnaich*.

Neither was Calum the only nervous soldier. Among the gathered clans encamped in the field, men worked off their tension by dancing to bagpipes, or competed at card games as they lounged by their cook fires.

Calum pointed with his chin toward the source of the music. "MacGregors. I was over there earlier, and was astonished to learn the pipers are both sons of Rob Roy."

Ciaran's interest piqued and he glanced toward the MacGregor camp. "Ye dinnae say?"

"Aye. James and Robin MacGregor, they are, and James remembers my father."

A hot flush rose to Ciaran's cheeks, and he threw a sharp glance at Calum. *Calum's father.* But his brother acted as if unaware of the barb. Calum continued, "He had quite a lot to say about Da, for he and Seumas Glas were the finest swordsmen among Rob's men. Aside from Rob himself, of course."

Ciaran remained silent as he peered across the field. Dylan

Dubh had reived cattle with Rob Roy at about the time Ciaran was born. Ciaran knew James MacGregor was in his late forties and old enough to have remembered something of those years. He might be able to tell something of Connor Ramsay and his mother. Perhaps, even, he'd known Ramsay—knew what he'd looked like—and could answer the one question that burned in Ciaran's gut. He could walk over there this very moment, strike up a conversation with MacGregor, and possibly learn the truth.

But instead he turned his gaze to the fire before him and stared deep into it. The truth was worthless to him if it was not what he longed to hear. It would be unbearable to hear Robin had lied. The risk was too high. There was too much at stake. Instead of going to talk to MacGregor, he sighed and listened to Calum relate well-known stories of fights Dylan Dubh had fought while in the employ of Rob Roy thirty years ago.

Then a burst of flame erupted from one of the MacDonald fires, and Ciaran turned to look. Some very young MacDonalds were laughing so uproariously as to be in helpless tears. Then one of them stood, turned his back to the fire, gathered his kilt over his hips, and crouched. Ciaran grinned and poked his brother to watch. Calum in turn caught the attention of the other men, and the Mathesons all fell silent to watch the young MacDonald prepare to light a fart.

Calum, with his easy grin, said as if talking to the MacDonalds but only loud enough for the benefit of the nearby Mathesons, "Take a good close look, lads. Is it blisters ye see, or piles?" That brought snickers and snorts from all around the Matheson fire.

It took several seconds to come, but the wait proved worthwhile. The gas was plentiful and the flame gaudy enough to singe the MacDonald ass. The young man jumped and yelped, sending not only his kinsmen but also the Mathesons and a few nearby Camerons into peals of laughter. Ciaran found himself unable to stop laughing, for it felt good to let go and feel silly for a moment.

But then Leah entered his thoughts again. He'd been unable to think of much else since leaving the Tigh, and the closer they came to Edinburgh, the more she preyed on his mind. He was certain the city would be theirs soon. Then he would find Leah, though he didn't know how. One way or another, he would find her.

Then what? How would he be received? Would she turn him away? Might she even be angry with him for some unknown transgression? Would she only pretend to be happy to see him? Was there hope she might truly be happy to see him? Or would it be best if he didn't look for her at all?

He closed his eyes against that last thought. No, he would look for her. Absolutely, he would look for her and find her. Then he would know the truth of her, at least, and could put his mind at ease. Having decided that, he returned his attention to his men.

Many about the fires took this time of rest as an opportunity to lift their kilts, spread their knees, and pick body lice and other parasites from among private hairs. The wee beasties were then either crushed between thumbnails or tossed directly into the fire. Some men, less fastidious than others, kept their privates covered and merely scratched when the bugs became too lively.

Ciaran, accustomed to traveling in the open, maintained himself in burns along the way nearly as well as he had at home, shaving his beard whenever he could with his *sgian dubh* and scrubbing his neck and hands with cold water. It being late summer and warm enough for it, he had recently stripped for a complete bath. But even regular scrubbing didn't do much about the problem of nits. He often found a bug or two. Or three. Even now, as he sat by the fire listening to Eóin, Calum, and Donnchadh, there was something fleet scurrying up the back of his head. He yanked his ribbon from his hair and dug at his scalp until he found the intruder and picked it out. After squashing the flea between his thumbnails, he restored his ribbon and returned to the conversation.

One of the Camerons hurried to Ciaran's fire and burst into the discussion with, "Lads! 'Tis a delegation from Edinburgh, negotiating their surrender to Prince Charles!"

Ciaran looked where the young man pointed and found a carriage and four standing outside the prince's tent. The men, some residing in tents and the rest on the ground wrapped in their plaids, were all in hopes of a surrender, and in anticipation of beds to sleep in and roofs over their heads. "The hell, you say!"

"Aye. My brother overheard them as they made their request to see Teàrlach. They're wishing to surrender the city."

Calum snorted. "Or they're stalling for time."

"Hoping for the arrival of General Cope? They can wait all they like, but it'll do them nae good. We're in need of a good fight, and the general has so far denied us." The Cameron lad grinned all around at the Mathesons. "And we all ken what happens when a man's needs are denied. He becomes most irritable."

That brought a round of laughter. Ciaran looked over at the prince's tent and hoped the offer of surrender was genuine. His own needs were far more complex than his men imagined and could only be satisfied within the walls of Edinburgh.

But nothing happened until the middle of the night. While the men dozed, Ciaran awoke by his fire to hear excited talk. Someone nearby was telling of an order that had come from the prince for some of the troops to proceed to the city gate. Lochiel's many Camerons were shifting about and pulling their gear together, making preparations for departure, and in an instant Ciaran decided his men should accompany.

He scrambled to his feet, arranged his plaid over his shoulder, and began nudging each Matheson awake with his shoe. Here was a chance for them to be among the first into Edinburgh. He ordered the sleepy men to their feet and to gather with the others, all the men grumbling and stumbling in the dark. His thirty Mathesons went unnoticed among the hundreds of Camerons, sent in a show of force that might weaken the already ambivalent defenses of the city.

At the gate, entry was denied, and that surprised nobody. Lochiel argued, and threatened the city guard. The army stood waiting, ready to move in, but at the back of the detail of soldiers it seemed nothing was happening. Sleepy Mathesons sat on rocks and on the ground, grumbling under their breath, wanting to return to their fires. But Ciaran waited, needing to be inside that gate. Sleep wasn't on his mind. It wasn't even possible.

Then, at the rear, men began to part in a wave as the coach carrying the Edinburgh delegation to the prince returned from the Jacobite camp. Slowly it made its way through the crowd of waiting men and toward the gate. A smile played at the corners of Ciaran's mouth as he and his men sidled from the road. The true intent of this hopeless mission, so oddly timed, was now apparent. He poked the men around him to attention. "Ready yourselves," he told them. Jacobites crowded toward the gate and filled in behind the coach.

As it reached the gate, the authorities inside the walls opened up to allow the delegates entrance. Then, as one, the gathered Jacobites raised a cry and forced their way through in a surge of humanity. Edinburgh was breached.

Ciaran took his men through, hard on the heels of the Camerons. It was a bloodless invasion. No resistance from the residents, and no Redcoats in sight, who apparently were all still in the castle garrison outside the city walls. Only the city militia had been left to guard the gates. Moving through the streets stinking of sewage, up a canyon of high, stone buildings, Ciaran looked around in hopes of glimpsing Leah, but it was dark, the middle of the night, and the faces he saw were nothing more than blurs of light and shadow.

"I cannae see her," he muttered to the faerie.

"Och," said Sinann, "You think she'll be out here searching for you?"

The thought had crossed his mind in the form of a vague, wistful hope. He frowned at the faerie and continued looking. The men made their way up the street, toward the Tolbooth at the very top of the hill on which Edinburgh stood. Some residents cheered, and many soldiers were heartened by it, but none of the invading army was fooled into thinking they were welcomed by all.

His eye out for Leah, Ciaran was taken quite by surprise by a woman running through the streets who threw her arms around his neck and kissed him. Her mouth covered his in slobbery suction, and he had to pry her from himself. She grinned and licked her lips, her eyes wide and her cheeks flushed with excitement.

The Mathesons roared with laughter as they walked onward, though Ciaran didn't see the humor and wiped his mouth with the back of his hand. Calum was bent over, hee-heeing so helplessly he could barely breathe, and Aodán waggled his tongue at the woman in grotesque parody. Ciaran let her go, passing her off to Eóin, who kissed her with a great deal more enthusiasm. Eóin then also passed her off, and thereafter she was happily treated to all the kisses she could want from the Jacobite army.

The Highlanders made an orderly occupation, posting their own guards at the city gates and relieving the local militia of their broken-down, ill-kept weaponry. The Redcoats garrisoned at the castle couldn't reach them now. The city was theirs, and not a shot fired nor a drop of blood spilled.

"Faerie," said Ciaran as he and his men made their way along, looking for an inn at which to request billeting, "how will I find her?"

There was a moment of silence in which Ciaran feared Sinann wouldn't reply at all, but then she said, "If you find she loves you, will ye quit this foolishness, take your men back to Ciorram, and marry her?"

Ciaran snorted. "Dinnae be silly."

"Then I willnae tell you where she is."

"You know where she is?" He stepped to the side of the street, waved his men on, and peered up at her, thinking he might just snatch her out of the air if she gave him any more grief. "You heard it said in the office? Tell me."

"No."

"Faerie—"

"Give up the cause."

"Very well, I'll give up the cause."

Her eyes narrowed. "Swear it."

"Och!" He turned his back on her. "I cannae, and ye know it." Then he turned back toward her. "Tell me, ye wee tease."

She shook her head, and dodged as he took a swipe at her. Then she said, "Give over the cause. Heed yer father's will, so ye willnae die on Culloden Moor."

Glaring now, he no longer cared who witnessed his exchange with the thin air. "Why do you nae love me as dearly as you did my father?" That brought only silence and a long face from the white faerie. She perched on a beam supporting a shop sign, and her wings drooped. He continued, "You would have told Dylan Dubh where to find my mother, were he the one searching."

There was another stretch of silence, then Sinann said softly, "She resides with her father's cousin. Edwin Hadley is his name. 'Twas mentioned while the captain was packing up his office for departure. I'd say the odds are good you might find her, were ye to ask around for Edwin Hadley."

A smile lifted the corner of Ciaran's mouth, and his heart soared. "Aye."

Prince Charles established his headquarters in the Palace of Holyrood at the eastern end of the city. The army all waited while he did so. Whatever else Ciaran might have imagined about waging war, he'd never thought it would involve so much sitting around and waiting. The men who were not immediately placed on guard at the city gates found themselves loitering outside the palace, still with no beds.

Men wrapped in their plaids snored along the ground in rows. Ciaran sat up awake, awaiting news of billets. It was afternoon before a gillie came with a message he was to take himself and his men to the Hogshead Inn. Ciaran woke his men and guided them to the inn, at the other end of the city.

The Hogshead Inn was a tiny tavern on a wynde near the North Loch, which lay at the foot of the steep hill. The Mathesons and a few Stewarts filled it to capacity, with several men to a room. But Ciaran, privileged to occupy an entire room to himself, was able to have a wash, pick off the last of his wee passengers, then crawl into bed. He dropped off to sleep in an instant.

Nevertheless, he was awake, shaved and dressed, at sunset after no more than four hours' sleep. Sinann was nowhere in sight, but he remembered what she'd said about always being about. Muttering under his breath, he bade her to stay in the room while he would pursue his private life; then, without waiting for a reply, he left the room and hurried down the stairs. After ascertaining from the innkeeper the address of Edwin Hadley, he made his way through the crowd in the public room to return to the street.

The Hogshead Inn was overflowing with Jacobite celebrants, both soldiers and local citizenry, singing and carrying on as if it were Beltane. A fiddle played madly as a couple of drunken Stewarts and a few Mathesons danced in the street, staggering hopelessly on the incline slippery with mud and waste thrown from chamber pots the night before. As Ciaran moved away from the uproar, he noticed there were few people on the street who weren't celebrating the takeover. However, he also noticed the streets were not teeming with people.

Though he'd been too young to remember the year he'd lived here as an infant, he'd been to Edinburgh on business in recent years and knew what a congested city it was normally. In spite of the pockets of merrymakers—at the Hogshead Inn and at other places along the wynde—Ciaran could sense the fear in those who made their way quietly to and fro without participating in the celebration. Those who avoided contact with the heavily armed men who wished to change the status quo. Though he himself believed heartily in the cause, he didn't fool himself into thinking the entire city was celebrating the arrival of Charles Stuart.

His pulse picked up, and the prince slipped from his mind as he approached the Hadley residence. He took the talisman from his sporran. Pinned to his coat, it would hide him only when he was standing still. He went to the door, stopped before it, and knew he was now invisible. Listening, he heard nothing inside. The house had originally been a shop of some sort, for next to the door was a window shutter that would fold down to a counter. It was secured with a large, rusty iron padlock. He reached out to try the door itself, and was joyful to find it unlocked. Carefully, he pushed it open, making certain to keep his feet firmly in one spot.

The room inside was empty and dark. Beyond, a candle in a small iron wall sconce lit a short corridor with doors opening from it. At the end of that corridor was a spiral staircase of stone, lit by more candles in sconces. Ciaran slipped inside, appearing for only that brief moment as he moved, then closed the door behind him. Still once again, he blinked out.

Ears perked for every sound, he heard a muffled voice behind one of the doors in the corridor. He crossed the dark room, and saw the door was closed. No footsteps, so he took a chance and moved along the short hallway. A room with an open door was empty. The muffled voice was that of a man, obviously not Leah, but Ciaran couldn't see who that man was talking to. Opening the door to look wasn't a good idea, so he moved on toward the stairs.

Outside the house, Ciaran had noticed the building was four stories tall and assumed it held many families. But once on the inside, he found the entire house was a single residence. In this crowded city, that required quite a bit of money. Rich folks would have many servants. He strained his senses to detect anyone approaching as he ascended the spiral.

The corridor at the second floor was dark. Ciaran stepped into the open doorway and found no light anywhere here. He turned to proceed up the stairs, but froze as he caught the rustle of skirts from above. Quickly, he stepped back into the darkened hall and waited, perfectly still and perfectly invisible. It was Leah approaching. He could smell her perfume. It filled his head, quite replacing his right mind, and his pulse surged.

She held her skirts as she came down the narrow steps. He watched her descend, examined her smooth face in this private moment, her thoughts indiscernible. As she passed, the urge to reach out and touch her was intense. He'd come to see her, and now there was only to speak to her, for he couldn't bear not to, even if she would scream. Before she'd gone more than a few steps beyond the landing, he removed the talisman from his coat and slipped it into his pocket.

"Leah."

A tiny gasp from her, and she jumped. Looking around, she didn't seem to see him in the shadows, so he spoke again.

"It's me." His heart seemed to flutter against his rib cage. It was all in her hands now, and he was in agony to be so vulnerable. A madman wielding a claymore would have been easier to face.

Then she saw him. The candlelight wavered on her face. She stepped toward him as she stared. Time ceased to exist, and it was an eternity they gazed at each other. Neither spoke. She returned up the steps. Ciaran's heart pounded in his ears, and though he searched her eyes, he was at a loss to read them.

Then her face crumpled into tears and she went to him.

"Oh, Ciaran! It's truly you!" she whispered, and threw her arms around his neck. "Thank God you're all right!"

He held her close and nearly laughed aloud with joy. It burbled in his throat as he kissed her, tasted her, holding her body to his. There were tears in her voice as she pressed little kisses to his face. "Oh, Ciaran, I've missed you so! I tried to come to you that night"—her cheek lay against his and she whispered in his ear—"but Father had placed a guard outside my door."

"I know. I couldnae get past the guard, myself." That made her smile, and they kissed again, long, hard, and deep. Ciaran reveled in the feel of her, in the scent of her skin and the press of her tongue against his. For a moment he forgot where they were, and he drew her into the dark corridor to set her against the wall. Her arms still around his neck, he pinned her with his hips, the back of his mind considering tearing the dress from her right there, whalebone and all.

But he came to his senses when she pulled her mouth away and whispered, "This way." She drew him by the hand, into the stairwell and upward.

The top floor of the house was quiet and dimly lit. "Cousin Edwin is quite wealthy, but is nevertheless stingy with the candles," said Leah as she guided Ciaran into the empty room at the top and through to a closed door. A tiny sitting room was beyond that, and she stopped to set a chair under the doorknob behind them. Ciaran kept hold of her hand.

"You were going downstairs. Will they miss you?" His fingers brushed back a strand of hair from her face.

"Yes. They'll note my absence, but they won't come looking for me." She touched her lips to the back of his hand and her voice faltered, distracted. "They'll only complain at breakfast tomorrow that I was being unsociable, and in all likelihood compare me unfavorably to my mother. I'll tell them"—a mischievous light came into her eyes as she removed her snood and let her hair tumble—"I'll tell them I had female trouble."

Ciaran had to chuckle at that, and pressed his lips to hers again, running his fingers into the chestnut cascade. Then, lightly laying his mouth against her cheek, he murmured, "I'm the one with female trouble. I'm out of my head with it." It was dizzying, after a month of not knowing whether to love her or hate her.

Leah pulled him from the room, through to a small bedroom where burned a single candle on a table next to a narrow bed. He closed the door behind as he drew her into his arms again. His blood sang as he devoured her mouth. He reached for the buttons securing her dress, though it would have been far easier to accomplish their goal by simply raising her skirts and his kilt. But mere coupling wasn't enough. He wanted all her skin against all of his. He wanted her breasts in his hands, her arms across his back, and her hips around his. More than anything, he wanted these damned stays gone.

Having accomplished the unbuttoning, he shoved the overdress from her shoulders. Then the hooped petticoat over her hips, and began untying the cloth strips that held closed her linen corset. One knot held stubborn, and he yanked on it in frustration, pulling Leah off-balance. She giggled as she fell against him, and laid a palm against his face to kiss him. A low moan rose from his chest, and he drew his *sgian dubh* to slice through the tie. The corset fell to the floor, leaving Leah in her linen shift. She wriggled from it immediately.

Her clothing on the floor, she stepped out of the mound of linen, silk, and whalebone and drew him toward the bed. Small as it was, it was piled high with a deep feather mattress.

Now it was his turn to drop his clothing on the floor, and he accomplished this simply by unbuckling his belt. His kilt slithered from him, and he drew his linen sark over his head. Brogues slipped from his feet, followed by sheepskin leggings and woolen stockings. She reached for his hand as she fell backward onto the bed, and he followed, to land on top of her. Holding her close, he lost himself in her, covered her mouth with his, and with one hand on her behind pressed her hips to his.

Leah was as breathless as he. She writhed beneath him, sucking on his lower lip. One tug on the ribbon that held his queue, and his hair fell past his shoulders and over her face. He laughed, low and soft, and shook away the dark mass. Neither of them could be more ready, and he entered her without further prelude.

The toil of the past month fled his body before the sweet delirium he drew from Leah's. There was no hesitation in her. No negotiation. She opened herself completely to him, leaving him free to accept and enjoy. Her body met his at every thrust. Soon all he knew, and all he wanted to know, was Leah's flesh. The world was nothing other than the place where they were joined, and it was all he could do to not cry out when the ecstasy grabbed his spine like a big fist and shook him.

Then he lay beside her in the impossibly deep mattress, raining small kisses all over her face and shoulders and hoping there was time to manage another go before he would need to leave.

Once she'd caught her breath, she whispered, "How did you get in?"

He grunted and replied truthfully as he fiddled with one of her curls, "The front door was unlocked." Her body shifted against his, hot and damp with sweat where she touched him.

"Such a bold Jacobite soldier."

He went still and said nothing.

But she continued, her voice serious now, "You're here with the Jacobites. You've joined the Young Pretender."

He lay back against the mattress and stared at the candlelight flickering against the ceiling. "Aye. Does that upset you?" The sweat on him was beginning to cool.

She thought for a moment before replying, "I don't wish you to die, no matter which side you're on."

"I dinnae wish it, either." He turned and pressed his lips to her forehead. A shivering took her, and she shifted to slip under the coverlet and sheet. He burrowed with her to lie with her in his arms, well surrounded by linen and feathers.

There was a long, comfortable silence, and he thought he might doze to the steady sound of her breathing. The warmth of her by his side was a rare treat. Then she said, "You've met him? Stuart?"

Ciaran nodded. "Prince Teàrlach." It annoyed him she wouldn't say "Prince."

"Charlie?"

He grunted. "Nae. Teàrlach. Charles. In the Gaelic it only sounds like Charlie."

"I see." And from the tone of her voice, he thought she did see. A smile touched the corners of his mouth, and he let her entwine her fingers with his, though he wanted to sleep.

"Leave them. Leave the fighting, and return to Ciorram."

He shook his head. "I'm nae coward. I cannac renege on my commitment. I'll be seeing it through, and that is all there is to it."

"And if you die?"

"Then I will die, and it will be God's will." He thought for a moment, then said, "I have it on very good authority there is nae changing what must be." His father had said it, and now he was beginning to believe it.

Some seconds passed. Leah pressed her fingers to her mouth, and a snuffle escaped her. Ciaran rose on one elbow to find her crying.

"Och." He tried to dry her tears with his thumb, and wished there was something to say. But he'd already said all that mattered: he was no coward, and that was the long and the short of it. Leaving the army was unthinkable, and discussing it was pointless.

Instead of explaining, he kissed her. She held tightly to him, as if she could keep him there against his will. For a moment, he thought the ploy might work. Then he pressed his lips to her forehead again and lay back again to sleep.

A few hours later, in the dead of night, they awoke and made love once again. Slowly, carefully, attending to every part of her, he was in no rush for it to end. She cleaved to him, became a part of him and he a part of her. He did all he could to keep her that way, and postponed leaving as long as he could.

The sky was nearly blue when he finally retrieved his clothes from the floor and dressed. Leah drew on a dressing gown to escort him to the front door downstairs. There he left her, but not before kissing her well and gazing long at her face to memorize it, knowing it was quite likely he would never see her again.

CHAPTER 11

His short jacket was black wool. The buttons here were silver, the design echoing the thistles on his belt buckle.

Ciaran returned to the Hogshead Inn and crawled into the narrow straw mattress bed to sleep again. The sun had barely crested the buildings to the east, putting a tiny patch of yellow on the wall above his head, before a knock on the door woke him.

"Ciorram!" came the voice of a gillie. "Sir, there's a message for ye from Holyrood!"

Ciaran rose from the straw mattress, stumbled, groggy and aching, to the door in his sark, blinking as he passed through the thin beam of sunlight, and opened up to receive a small folded paper.

As he closed the door, Sinann remarked, "In a wee bit of pain this morning, are we?"

He grunted and muttered, "I never kent a man could make himself sore doing that."

"You never had a woman like that one."

The corners of his mouth lifted, and his heart warmed. The

image of Leah beneath him stirred him so he thought he might have had it in him to try again in spite of the soreness.

Shaking off the daydream, he took the paper to the window to read it in the scant light. The note was short and to the point:

Form your men at the palace immediately.

Charles, P.R.

He flattened the paper and carefully burned it at the hearth.

Sinann perched at the foot of the small bed. "Yer father stayed here once, long ago."

"My father stayed here many times, while in the city to do business. I've been here before myself."

"I mean, when he came to take your mother away from Connor Ramsay. You were but a wee bairn at the time."

Dylan Matheson killed me so he could fuck your mother, but he was too late. You were already born by then.

Ciaran paused in his dressing, torn between wanting to know the truth and wanting to run away from a truth he might not have the strength to bear. He said, "*Och,* faerie, I havenae time for this. The prince has called us to the palace." He slipped Brigid into the sheath in his legging and went into the hallway. There he began pounding on doors to wake his men.

"All up! Mathesons, all up! Form up, we're moving on! All Mathesons up!" Each door on that floor, and one on the floor above. Soon there were Mathesons pouring into the narrow hallway, grumbling sleepily or grousing about the short time under a roof. Men from other clans were also being called up by their commanders, and there was a steady stream of sleepy, cranky, hungover Jacobite soldiers descending to the street.

Throughout the day the men grumbled over being taken from their comfortable beds and made to wait on the grounds outside the palace. Just inside the arched gatehouse, they crowded together on the lawn beneath grandiose medieval towers topped by graceful lead-clad spires.

The round towers might have reminded Ciaran of the Tigh back home, except for the immense scale, brown color, and sash windows. This place had been built for royalty, while the Tigh had never aspired to house better than local nobility. Holyrood was a vast conglomeration of abbey, apartments, and courtyard gardens. Ciaran wondered what it might be like inside. He'd never set foot in such a grand castle, and neither had his father nor grandfather, as far as he knew.

Nobody among the rank and file was allowed inside the palace, so the soldiers made themselves as comfortable as possible in the space they were given. Fires were lit here and there, in spite of a directive against them, and none of the officers ordered them put out. The air was thick with apprehension, among officers and troops alike. They all knew they must be about to fight, for that was the only thing that could have brought them from their beds this way. Anticipation of danger made them all edgy. It was not a calm crew who awaited orders from the prince.

Night fell, the clansmen slept rolled in their plaids, and it was dawn again before those orders came. The news was that the Redcoats had come by water and landed at Dunbar on the North Sea south of the nearby firth, and were to be met for a fight away from Edinburgh. The Jacobites formed up and marched from the city. Ciaran's Mathesons, being such a small unit, were able to slip into a position near the front of the column. The men were eager to do battle. Ciaran himself was filled with anticipation, and his heart thudded steadily as he led the men to what they all hoped would be their first real test.

It was slow going, for the commanders took care not to meet the Redcoats on ground that would put them at a disadvantage. The next afternoon the Redcoats were sighted as the prince's army made their way along a ridge of hills near Tranent, east of Edinburgh. Below was a place called Preston House. The view from high ground was good, and it was plain to Ciaran that Cope's army intended to stay where they were. There were obstacles on all sides of the Redcoat position: a ditch to the south, the farmhouse to the west, and a marsh to the east, the sea at their backs. Once again, Cope was saving his men rather than inviting battle. The Jacobites paused to eat and rest, and let the sun set entirely.

While the prince met with his high commanders, then rode out to examine the terrain for a way to approach the Redcoats easily, the clansmen waited. Ciaran and his men gathered and lay together for warmth, for there would be no fires this close to the enemy. Plaid drawn around himself, Ciaran only dozed. There would be battle soon, and he would surely kill someone then. In all the cattle raids against the MacDonells, he'd never killed a man. Now he thought hard about what it would be like. He wondered what it had been like for his father.

"Faerie," he whispered.

No answer.

His voice went soft and singsong. "Faerie . . ."

"My name is Sinann." She was close to his ear, and an odd comfort stole over him at her nearness.

"Faerie, were you with my da when he fought?"

"Aye."

"How was it for him then? Was he afraid?"

"As afraid as any sane man would be. But he faced his duty and his fate with as much bravery as I've seen in any man, sane or mad."

"Did he kill many of the *Sasunnaich?*"

"Aye. More than his share, I'd say."

Ciaran wondered if he would do as well. He hoped so. "Will you be there when we fight?"

"Aye. I cannae protect you, but you willnae be alone."

He thought about that for a moment, then said, "Good." But he didn't think he was afraid. Fear was little more than a fluttering in his gut. Difficult to tell from mere excitement. He'd been waiting for this most of his life—a chance to kill Redcoats—and he was glad for it.

Indeed, he wondered if he would enjoy killing Englishmen. How would it feel to cut the throat of a red-coated bastard? He'd slaughtered more than one pig in his life, and imagined it might be similar. When he finally dropped into unconsciousness, sleep was riddled with nightmares of having his throat slit by a very tall, blond dragoon major. In the midst of it he awoke, tense and angry. The fluttering in his gut had been replaced by a knot of hatred. After that, he only lay there awake, dwelling on the *Sasunnaich* and how much he hated them.

It was pitch black, the middle of the night, when the order came to form up again. Rumors rippled in whispers among the men, of a local man who had come to the prince with knowledge of a way through the marsh.

In the dark, the Jacobite column continued on down from the high ground. They were visible against the moonlit horizon, and Ciaran knew their movement from the crest of the hill could not be secret. He only hoped their passage through the marsh would be.

The Mathesons being so few, and the Jacobite formations ha-

bitually so undisciplined, Ciaran's men were swallowed up
among the Stewarts as they formed a single file to enter the track
through the marsh. The sky began to lighten as they walked, the
tiniest bit of sunrise distinguishing as shadows the men before
and behind. Finally emerging from the marsh onto the field, Ciaran saw the shadows of the Redcoats in the distance, some moving around but many asleep in their ranks. During the night the
Redcoats had shifted to face the marsh; nevertheless, they'd been
caught unprepared.

The prince's men began to hurry now, forming up in the dimness lest they be revealed by the dawn. The Mathesons gathered
on Ciaran, and the entire line moved to the north to give room for
the second line still emerging from the marsh. The sky lightened
as the Jacobites raced the sun. Ciaran shifted his targe from his
back to slip it onto his left arm.

An alarm gun down the field among the Redcoats went off,
and a puff of smoke rose from their camp. The sleeping forms
scurried, frantic to ready themselves in the face of the enemy
lines they could now see. Ciaran's heart pounded, and he bent to
draw Brigid with his shield hand. His mouth drew to a flat line.
Those few Jacobites carrying muskets brought them to bear.
Swords up and down their ranks were drawn in a cacophony of
singing metal. Ciaran now brandished the silver king's sword.
Enemy soldiers were still struggling to their feet, hurrying to
draw their lines. The Jacobites were eager to charge, stepping forward like dogs waiting for the order to attack, but their second
line was still half in the marsh.

Ciaran didn't hear the order, or maybe it wasn't given. But
suddenly the first Jacobite line charged, and he went with it. The
Redcoats were still arranging their ranks, many of them yet half
dressed and half asleep, and the mounted dragoons struggling to
find their position. Ciaran led his men, sword raised, uttering a
blood-curdling roar that was lost amid the thousands of other
voices. They closed on the astonished Redcoats and began to
slaughter. Swords, dirks, and farm implements flailed. Blood
flew. The screams of dying men and horses mingled with the
clash of steel on steel. Muskets roared, throwing thick white
smoke over the field, and Redcoats fell, many shot in the back as
they ran away. Ciaran engaged the first Redcoat he encountered
and dispatched him quickly with a slash across the gut, then a

hard hit to the neck. He set a foot to the dying Englishman, shoved him to the ground, and ran on.

One shot came from the Redcoat artillery, then two more, taking a few clansmen, who dropped to Ciaran's right. But there was not a moment's hesitation in the Jacobite ranks. The fight continued to move westward, and that was all Ciaran heard of the cannon. He glimpsed more red uniforms fleeing. Their infantry got off no more than one volley, then turned tail. The clansmen gave chase and slaughtered all they could catch. Every company of dragoons on the field turned their horses and fled, outdistancing their own infantry quickly.

The sight of the enemy in rout enflamed Ciaran with rage and disgust. He ran harder. When he caught up with a running Redcoat, he slashed the coward across the back. Then when the *Sasunnach* turned to defend, Ciaran parried with the targe and took the enemy head nearly off with the sword. With Brigid he stabbed at the dead man's face as he fell. The body jerked and danced weirdly for a moment, but Ciaran was off to chase down another running *Sasunnach*. Again the quarry was slashed across the back, and Ciaran took out his revulsion on the dying body by beheading it with a single stroke, as if wielding an ax.

His stomach turned, not at the butchery, but at the utter weakness of the English. The cowardice displayed by the enemy brought a fury that consumed his soul, anger fed by the lifelong terror these men in red coats had held for him. The sword at his throat was an ever-present memory.

The battle was over in what seemed an instant. The Camerons fired some captured cannons toward the confused enemy, but they hit nothing, for their aim was unskilled, and there was nobody to resist them in any case. The craven Redcoats had fled. Ciaran gave up trying to catch any more and watched as the tardy second line of Jacobites finally took the field, left with nobody to kill but the wounded.

Which they did. Wounded men were murdered, and dead bodies were mutilated by those who had arrived too late for the battle. They all knew it was what the spineless Redcoats deserved. Every Highlander above the age of six knew a man's worth was determined by his bravery, and these they had fought today were cowards worth nothing at all.

Ciaran saw there were no more of the enemy aside from prisoners. He turned in a complete circle to survey the field, then looked down. At his feet lay the body of an English infantryman. The nose had been cut off, and the legs were both severed at the knees. Both pieces of leg lay where they had been, slightly separated from the body.

A small part of him, deep inside where he held a core of himself untouched by the English, knew he should have been appalled. The atrocity should have disgusted him. But he felt neither disgust nor pleasure. Nothing for the desecrated corpse. Nothing beyond a satisfaction there were fewer Redcoats in the world than there had been an hour ago. The men he'd killed today had deserved to die; he felt it even in the center of his soul. He'd known it before the battle, and it had been proven to him by their behavior on the field. Deliberately, Ciaran set his swordtip on the pale belly, exposed by the unbuttoned red coat and shirt, and shoved. It went in easily. *"Gealtaire,"* he said. Coward. There was no lower creature on earth.

There was shouting in the streets. News of a battle. Leah hurried to the sitting room window to hear. Some of the words were snatched away by the wind and the several voices running over each other, but by careful listening she gathered there had been a battle. At Preston House, they said, near Tranent.

Ciaran. Was Ciaran all right?

Father. Tears sprung to her eyes as she realized one of them must have been on the losing side. Either or both could be dead, regardless of the outcome.

Martha entered the room. "Do close the window, Leah. I can't bear to listen to those people—"

"Shhh, Martha. It's news of Father. There's been a battle. Prestonpans."

Martha put her sewing on her chair and hurried to join Leah as the shouting below described a rout. The king's men had fled, and the Jacobites had taken the field and a thousand prisoners while sustaining but fifty casualties themselves.

"Where is Roger, then?" asked Martha.

Leah called to the boy below, "What news of the dragoons from the garrison?"

The boy halted on his way and turned to see his questioner. When he spotted Leah and Martha in the window, he laughed, his dirty face a hideous mask of derision. "Aye, the dragoons live, for they had horses to ride from the field and were the first away. They say General Cope outdistanced his own men, he rode so fast, and was the first to deliver news to his superiors of his own defeat!" The boy thought that was uproariously funny, and slapped his knee with glee.

"So none of the dragoons were killed?"

He shrugged. "A few."

"Officers?"

"Nae. No officers."

Leah squeezed her eyes shut with relief, then said, "And the Jacobites? Who were the casualties?"

"Mostly Camerons, I think. And MacDonalds."

"No Mathesons?"

"The Mathesons arenae with the prince at all, I think."

She knew better, but refrained from asking after Ciorram. The boy obviously knew nothing helpful. "Thank you, boy." She reached through the slit in the side of her skirts, and into the pocket hung beneath, for a silver penny, and tossed it to him. He caught it, smiled, and went shouting on up the street.

Leah closed the window and sat heavily in the chair next to it. Her fingers trembled, and tears stung the corners of her eyes. She pressed her hands to her face and prayed. Father and Ciaran were both probably alive, but she couldn't know for certain. *Oh, please, God, let them both still be alive and whole!*

Martha picked up the sewing from her chair and sat. For a moment she fiddled with the fabric between her fingers, glancing at Leah now and again, then said, "The fellow is a Matheson, then?"

A shock of alarm surged in Leah, and she laid her hands in her lap. She held her voice steady and said, "Who?"

"The Jacobite who worries you so. The man who caused your bed to smell of sweat and male seed so soon after the invasion. I expect he must be a Matheson from Ciorram, otherwise I must believe you were entertaining a stranger so privately."

A sigh escaped Leah as she struggled to know what to say. Finally she said, "He's Matheson *of* Ciorram."

That brought a smile and raised eyebrows. "Indeed? Well, I suppose I should have known it would have been the laird himself."

"Does Edwin know?"

Martha gave her a kind look. "You mean, will your father be

told? No. I've said nothing to Edwin, and neither will the maid. I daresay, when my husband has his nose in the newspaper, he would be oblivious had your Highlander fought his way into the house in full barbarian regalia and swept you off your feet before our very eyes." She went on with her careful stitching, then said casually, "I expect you've taken precautions?"

Leah frowned for a moment, confused, then realized what was meant. "No," she replied, her voice soft and small, "I do not feel caution is warranted."

Martha raised her head to look her in the eye. "And if he cannot return and it becomes apparent you've been . . . incautious?"

The horror of the possibility of Ciaran not returning finally sank in, and grief overwhelmed Leah. She put a hand to her mouth and turned away, struggling for control. Tears squeezed from her eyes, and she held her breath. No sobbing. No crying. Ciaran must be alive. He *must*.

Her cousin came to lay an arm around her shoulders, and somehow that made it worse. A sob escaped, and Leah turned to weep on Martha's shoulder.

It wasn't long before the household had word from Father, whose company had returned to the garrison at Edinburgh Castle. It was but a short note, bordering on terse even for Father, who was not given to effusive communication, but it gave Leah to know he was alive and unharmed. Though the Jacobites held the city, they had never taken the castle, and the presence of the king's forces was still quite visible.

On the first day of October, standing in the Lawnmarket, Leah gazed across to the castle in hopes of catching a glimpse of her father. But it was plain she wouldn't know him if she saw him, for the battlement was too far away. There were sentries watching the Jacobite guard across the rocky expanse separating the castle from the city. The kilted Jacobites stared back.

Leah lingered, a sack filled with purchases from a bakery shop hung on one hand, struggling with the urge to ask the guard about Ciaran. But fear of the rough men kept her away, and she only gazed at them, wishing there might be one among them she could recognize. Young Robbie, perhaps. Or even Eóin, who had seemed a steady fellow.

A woman passing by had a handful of white rose cockades made of silk ribbon, offering them to passersby for a few pence apiece.

"What's this?"

The old woman grinned with a set of otherwise white teeth that had nevertheless gone brown and ragged in between. Her dress was faded and dirty red silk handed down from her betters, but for a shawl she wore a new piece of tartan wool. It seemed everyone in the city was wearing the tartan these days. " 'Tis the badge of the bonnie prince," she said, offering the cockade hopefully. "Are ye in support of the cause, miss?"

Though Leah knew it would go badly for her should the wrong person see, she couldn't keep her hand from reaching out to take the imitation white rose. Then she reached into the pocket under her skirts to pay for it.

"Aye," said the old woman, "it's a wise lass ye are, for King James will prevail." Then with an even wider smile she went on her way.

Leah stared at the cockade for a moment, then returned her attention to the Jacobite guard and noticed an identical cockade pinned to the front of the blue woolen bonnet he wore on his shaggy head.

As she watched, the soldier turned his back on the castle, rucked up his kilt, and presented his full, hairy, white moon to the Redcoats standing guard. A giggle rose, which she hid with her hand and the cockade, as he shook his ass and danced a bit.

A puff of smoke rose from the battery of cannons atop the castle walls, and a moment later a report was heard. The dancing Jacobite dropped his kilt and turned, along with everyone else who heard it. He shouted something in Gaelic with the tone of a curse, and dropped to the ground as the building above him erupted in a shower of stone, wood, and glass. Another report from the castle jolted the witnesses from their shock, and they began to run.

The Jacobite guard then shouted in English for evacuation of the nearby houses. People poured from the buildings as more cannon shot flew from the Half Moon Battery. Leah found herself rooted to the street, for this was impossible to comprehend. Her father was over there. He was one of the Redcoats—an officer. Why was he letting them do this? How could he let them shoot cannons at the city, knowing she was here? A small voice in the back of her mind told her she should run, but there was no accepting this. People were screaming in pain. Bodies were falling from ruined houses. How could her father do this?

Another explosion nearby, and a piece of flying stone struck her forehead. She staggered. Jolted back to reality, she realized she needed to get away from the line of fire and began to hurry back along the Lawnmarket. Pressing the back of her hand to a tickling on her face, it came away red, and she realized she was bleeding. Tears rose, but she swallowed them. Now was not the time.

Men with guns were running toward the disturbance, some in kilts. Each reddish-brown kilt she saw caught her eye in her now habitual search for Ciaran. She searched the faces of men as they passed.

Then someone grabbed her by the arm, and she was spun around. "Leah!"

Her heart leapt. It was Ciaran, wearing a blue cap, the hank of loose hair restrained by it and dangling along the side of his face, and a musket slung over his shoulder with his sword baldric and plaid. She burst into tears and threw her arms around his neck, so relieved to see him alive it didn't matter who saw. Running people jostled them this way and that, and she hung on.

He stepped back, his eyes wide at the blood on her face. "You're hurt."

"It's nothing. Thank God you're all right."

"And you." He kissed her, then dabbed with his finger at the tears, then the blood on her face. "Did it knock you down?"

"No."

He kissed her again, then shouted over the noise of the bombardment and screaming people, "*Och,* Leah, I cannae stay. I've duties. I wanted to come to you after the battle, but the prince has made us responsible for the Redcoat wounded and the other prisoners." He glanced back toward the castle. "And now this. I must say good-bye, and quickly." He gave her one more quick kiss, then stepped away.

She held his arm, and when he turned back, she held up the white cockade for him to see. "Here. Wear this." He ducked his head and allowed her to poke it through the fabric of his bonnet. Then she said, "Ciaran, promise to return."

A puzzled look crossed his face. Dear Ciaran, so plain and straightforward. "But 'tis war. I cannae—"

"Say it. I can't bear to think you might die."

A wistful look came over him, and his eyes glistened the tiniest bit. "Aye. Then I promise we will see each other again. Here."

He reached into the huge leather purse hung at his belt and brought out his rosary. Quickly and discreetly, he folded her hand around the ivory beads and gold-accented cross. "Keep this for me, and return it to me when the fighting is over."

Her brow furrowed.

He said, "I'm nae asking you to pray with it. Only keep it as remembrance."

She shook her head. "That isn't what worries me. It's that I know what this must mean to you."

A smile lifted one side of his mouth. "Then I expect you'll look after it carefully, where it might be destroyed or lost were I to keep it." People running in the street bumped into them as they passed, and he struggled to keep hold of her in the melee. His eyes searched hers, and she hoped he could see the things she didn't know how to say aloud.

A nod, then he kissed her one last time and was off to accomplish the job at hand. She stood in the street and watched him until he was swallowed by the crowd come to aid the injured.

CHAPTER 12

The steel badge pin lay atop his bureau, among some other bits of things, cuff-links, old theatre tickets, a ballpoint pen. He sometimes carried it on days when privacy might be an issue, but today he left it.

The bombardment continued. Leah sat in her cousins' house, listening to the cannon boom in the distance, when Martha returned from visiting friends, bringing fresh gossip. There were rumors, she said, the firing of artillery had been the response to a Jacobite attempt at cutting supplies to the king's soldiers, but Leah never knew what to believe anymore. The French had not landed as Martha had said, and now word was they weren't expected to land at all. And surely the rumor about her father's dragoons running away from battle couldn't be true. Not her father. She flinched at more blasts from the castle.

That evening, when Edwin came home he waited until supper was well under way, then announced they were to close the house and leave Edinburgh.

Martha, cutting her meat into meticulous little pieces, stopped and turned to gape at her husband. "I beg your pardon?"

"We're leaving for Nairn day after tomorrow." It was settled; a fait accompli. No room for negotiation. He chewed a great lump of beef and busied himself trimming gristle from the remainder on his plate.

Leah's cheeks flushed with alarm, but she said nothing and stared at her supper. Then she looked over at the window. Perhaps there would be a glimpse of Ciaran in the street below. Martha continued to gape, then gathered her wits to ask, "And what might be in Nairn?"

"Peace and quiet. A singular lack of Jacobites running around in bare knees and checkered dresses as well, I expect."

And no British army firing at us was Leah's thought, but she kept it to herself. She stared out the window, pretending not to listen, though her entire being strained with the hope Martha would talk Edwin into some sense.

"And what of your job?"

Edwin sucked a shred of meat from between his teeth. "Surely you don't think these Jacobites have paid me a single farthing since they took the city."

Now Leah glanced at him, but quickly and with hooded eyes; then she examined Martha's face. It was plain she knew nothing of the true source of Edwin's wealth, and did not guess the real reason for his wish to relocate. Martha's eyes were wide with horror.

Edwin continued, his tone now cajoling, "There is a business opportunity in Nairn. All will be well; you needn't worry."

Though Martha's eyes narrowed with skepticism, Leah figured this to be the truth. With his position in the excise office evaporated, there was nothing left but to turn proactive in the smuggling trade that all along had supported him in such comfort. Nairn was on Moray Firth, a coastline sheltered enough for easy transport ashore of contraband, but open enough to make patrolling difficult. Leah guessed Edwin intended to turn smuggler, and Martha had not the faintest inkling of it.

But Martha's countenance clouded over, and she took another tack. "Edwin, we cannot go now. We cannot abandon Edinburgh—our home—to those heathens."

"It is because of the heathens we must leave." Edwin rose from the table, went to the hall door, and gestured for the maid, who had been listening. "Now we must pack our trunks."

He addressed the maid when she came, ignoring Martha now. "Make certain it's done by tomorrow evening. The coach will be here early the next morning." The maid nodded, then went to her task.

Martha's voice was plaintive now, for Edwin would not be moved. "Where shall we live?"

"I've taken a house on the square in town."

Leah realized he must have been planning this for longer than the Jacobites had been in Edinburgh.

"Not of peat, I hope." Tears rose in Martha's eyes. She was losing the struggle to stay, and plainly was grief-stricken to be forced to leave.

"Of course not. Don't be silly. It's quite a nice house."

"You've never been to Nairn; how would you know whether there even existed a nice house in that town?"

"I'm told by my agent who arranged the lease." The sudden wideness of his eyes told Leah he'd nearly been caught in a lie.

"It's certain to be small and mean."

Now Edwin's temper was thinning. "Whatever it is, it's where we will be living. That is the end of it."

"How long will we be there?"

He fairly shouted, "Damned if I know, woman! Why don't you ask that fop of a Stuart living in Holyrood? It's because of him we can no longer live here. He and his ragged crew of papist, red-shank cattle thieves. Ask *him* when we might live in our own house again!"

At that, Martha leaned back in her chair, one hand over her face, and dissolved in tears.

Leah took the moment of disarray as an opportunity to leave the table, and hurried up the stairs to her bedroom. Tears tried to come, but she swallowed them. Speed was essential, and weeping would accomplish nothing more than waste precious time.

Quickly she scribbled a letter, folded it, then melted sealing wax onto it. As the wax dribbled, her mind flew to know where to send it. She had no idea where Ciaran might be billeted. *Holyrood*. The prince was in residence at Holyrood Palace. A note sent there would surely find its way to Ciaran. So she carefully wrote on the note, "Ciaran Robert Matheson of Ciorram."

In a feverish hurry, lest Edwin get it into his head to restrict her to the house until they would leave, she pulled her cloak around her, picked up the letter, and slipped away.

The walk to Holyrood was less than a mile, and she arrived there in good time. But at the gate she encountered a coarse, kilted guard of four men who watched her dully as she approached. She addressed one of them, the tallest of them, for he seemed the most interested in paying her any attention.

"I'd like to see that this goes to Ciaran Matheson of Ciorram." She held out the note.

That brought nothing but shrugs, and the men shifted their feet as they glanced at each other. She tried again, repeating herself. Still nothing. Then one of them spoke to the other in Gaelic, and she realized they must not know any English. She said, "Prince Charles."

They all laughed at that, and the tallest one waved her away to illustrate whatever it was he was telling her in Gaelic. The message seemed to be that she should leave because she wasn't going to get to see the prince.

"No, this needs to go to Ciaran Matheson of Ciorram."

There was more laughter, and the tall one continued to wave her away, making a lengthy explanation she couldn't possibly understand.

She held out the note farther, and shook it, hoping the tall one might take it to someone who spoke English. He did look at the name on it, but shook his head and shrugged again. Pointing to his eye, then at the name, he shook his head. It appeared he didn't know how to read. The others, suddenly quiet, had stepped back just far enough not to risk having to admit they didn't read, either.

She sighed, thanked them, and returned the way she'd come. There must be a way to get a letter to Ciaran, but she was running out of time to find it.

On the wynde where Edwin's house stood, nearly to the high street, she went into a shop. The merchant there traveled a bit and might be able to help her—that is, so long as she didn't tell him the letter was for a Jacobite soldier, for she knew him to be a staunch Whig.

"I've a letter that needs to find its way to Glen Ciorram. To the castle there."

The pale, bearded, and potbellied man looked closely at her, then replied, "Can ye not wait for the regular post? Would take naught but a month or two."

"Or three, or more." Leah shook her head. "No, I must be certain of delivery. I can pay for it." She reached for her purse in the pocket under her skirts, hoping the few coins she had would suffice.

The man scratched at a rash on his neck discreetly, as if he thought Leah couldn't see. Then he took the proffered purse and hefted it for weight and jingle. His mouth twisted. "I might know a young man headed that direction. But—"

"That purse is all I have. Everything."

The merchant sighed and started to hand back the purse. Quickly, she took a pearl pin from her snood and placed it in his hand. After a cursory examination, he accepted it, the purse, and the letter. "The castle at Ciorram, you say?" Leah nodded, and he carried the letter to a desk to write on it under Ciaran's name, "The castle at Ciorram."

"Thank you, good man." Relief overwhelmed her, and she smiled.

"My boy leaves for Skye tomorrow. Yer letter will be in Ciorram within the month. Perhaps even less."

"Thank you. Bless you."

He nodded, and she left him with the missive that was her lifeline to Ciaran.

On the third morning of the bombardment, the three Hadleys and only one maid in addition to Ida were on their way in a carriage to Nairn. Edwin stressed his assertion they would be safe from the fight in Edinburgh that was certain to come. For most of the journey, Edwin talked of how safe they would be because of his plan, and how he'd been charged with her safety, therefore it was his bound duty to flee the city.

As they rode, Leah gazed forlornly from the carriage with her hand in her pocket and her fingers entwined in Ciaran's rosary. She couldn't help dwelling on the irony that it was her father's soldiers Edwin was telling them to fear.

After five days of bombardment from the garrison at Edinburgh Castle, Prince Teàrlach relented and lifted the embargo on supplies to the *Sasunnaich*. Once the artillery fire quit, Ciaran was relieved of his alert status, and as soon as he could, donned his talisman and hurried to visit Leah.

But her cousin's house was locked tight, and provided no entry even in daylight.

"Damn."

Unable to get inside and therefore no longer in need of invisibility, Ciaran took the talisman from his sark and returned it to his sporran. A man passing seemed startled when Ciaran appeared, but after a moment of puzzled stare merely shook his head and walked on. Far easier to believe he simply hadn't noticed Ciaran standing there than to think either he'd gone mad or there was magic afoot.

Ciaran paid little attention to the onlooker. Peering up at the windows, Ciaran saw they were heavily curtained. He knocked but received no answer. Then he walked around to the far side of the building and found Leah's bedroom also heavily curtained.

"Damn." Quickly and discreetly, he picked a pebble from the street and tossed it at her window. No response. Then another. Still no response. Not even a servant to chase him away. He looked to Sinann, who then disappeared into the house without being told.

A moment later, she popped back. "She's gone, lad. All of them are. The fires are cold, their clothing missing, and the furnishings covered in linen."

"Where?" Anxiety niggled at him. "Where did she go?" Though he knew she might be safer away from Edinburgh, he nevertheless couldn't feel good she wasn't nearby. God knew where she could have gone.

A small boy standing in the wynde caught his eye, for the lad was staring. Ciaran gestured to him.

"You. Laddie. Can you tell me where the Hadleys have gone?"

Without reply of any kind, the boy turned and fled. Ciaran sighed as he watched him go, then went in search of someone who might help.

There was a shop up the wynde selling miscellaneous goods, so he stepped inside to inquire of the proprietor. The shopkeeper stood near a desk, where he wrote in a ledger book. Mindful of where he was and not knowing the merchant's politics, Ciaran shifted his speech to a more Lowland sort to address him. "Would you happen to know of the Hadleys nearby?"

The fat, bearded, and walleyed Lowlander gave a glance over Ciaran's kilt and straightened, raising his chin and peering at the Highlander as if Ciaran were a servant daring to speak out of turn. It seemed manner of speech was the least of Ciaran's problems in this shop. The merchant said, "I've nae inkling where they might be." It went unsaid that he wouldn't tell if he did know.

Ciaran stared at him, his anger rising at the hate coming from the merchant in waves. It had always been this way in Edinburgh, where people seemed more English than Scottish to Ciaran, but today he had no patience for it. He stared, unblinking and unflinching, into eyes that narrowed and clouded with disgust. Neither man spoke. Ciaran wished to draw Brigid and teach him some manners, but stayed his hand.

Finally the merchant looked away, and turned to examine a stack of flour sacks on a shelf nearby, as if the Highlander suddenly weren't there.

"Thank you for your help." Ciaran stepped through the door into the fresh air, away from the stink of the man's hatred and away from the pain of his own anger. He made his way back to the Hogshead Inn, Sinann fluttering along behind.

"She'll find a way to tell you where she's gone, lad. If she can."

Ciaran glanced up at her but didn't reply, for he wasn't certain he wanted Leah to risk such a thing. He returned to the Hogshead Inn, his mind turning with worry for her.

Several days later, Ciaran received an invitation to a ball at the palace. Because the prince desired the presence of all the clan leaders, Ciaran attended in spite of the rarefied social stratum. Leah wouldn't be there—not the daughter of a Redcoat captain—and it crossed his mind she would have enjoyed such a party far more than he would. It made him wish he could bring her, and he smiled to think of the uproar that would have caused.

He had a new kilt and coat made for the occasion, but knew he had no hope of matching the finery of the more powerful clan leaders. "I've nae business here," he said to Sinann as he passed through the high, columned entry to the palace.

"Of course you have, laddie." She sounded excited to be there, though she could have come at any time and hovered about the prince's head to her heart's content. For all Ciaran knew, she had. He guessed she was more excited for him than for herself, and that amused him. She continued, "Ye're a clan leader. 'Tis yer place to be among royalty."

All Ciaran had in reply to that was *"Och."*

Inside the palace he found himself struggling to recognize men he'd seen on the march every day. Plain cloth had given way to brocade and velvet, loose hair to queues, and queues to elaborate powdered wigs, and even in some cases kilts to breeches. He caught sight of the MacDonell laird in *Sasunnach* getup and very nearly sneered at the pretentious fool. He stopped himself in time, but Sinann said it for him. "Treacherous MacDonells, dinnae ken which side they're on."

Ciaran shrugged and continued on his way to the Great Hall. "Nae, faerie, we're all on the same side now. We must put aside our differences and fight the common foe."

She snorted, then said, "Aye. Then, once the English are purged from the country, you can return to teaching the MacDonells to stay out of Glen Ciorram."

He smiled. "Oh, aye."

Nodding greetings to the other guests, making his way through the chambers and hallways of the palace lit by a wealth of chandeliers and candelabra, he found himself agog at the gilt and silk furnishings all about. Life in the Tigh was pampered and privileged compared to the existences of most in Ciorram, but by this standard he and his family were positively impoverished. Here silk brocade decorated chairs too delicate to hold anyone but a lass of the most fragile build. Enormous paintings, exquisitely executed in rich colors, graced the walls. They depicted haughty men in huge, curly wigs and wearing elaborate armor in burnished shades of silver, bronze, and gold.

In a small chamber along the way, one astonishing mirror graced a far wall, making the room appear twice its size. Ciaran could do naught but stare at the vast, wondrous thing, thinking only of the expense of such a wide stretch of silvered glass. Never mind the frame, in itself a costly piece, as intricately carved and well covered in gilt as the art frames.

He whispered to nobody in particular, "The price of this could feed the entire glen for a year."

Sinann said, "Three years, truth be told."

A sigh escaped him. Then he noticed his own reflection and groaned at the hank of hair that had fallen. A quick swipe smoothed it back, but he knew it would come loose again soon.

Though the men were demonstrating their refinement by dressing like the English, the women Ciaran saw displayed their Jacobite loyalties decked out in all manner of tartan. In silk as well as wool, accented with elaborate lace far too expensive for anyone in the Highlands Ciaran knew, the wives and daughters of the powerful Jacobites of Edinburgh seemed proud of their new checkered finery. Every bosom seemed graced by a white rose cockade.

None of the camp followers who had been attaching themselves to the army since Glenfinnan was among them, and the
women here seemed largely from Edinburgh. Ciaran thought one
very beautiful woman might have let her gaze linger on him a
mite, and allowed himself to be flattered by it. Again he found
himself staring, at the width of skirts and elaborately coiffed
wigs. The women moved slowly and smoothly, so as not to jostle
the cagework at each hip under their frocks. Even Leah's most
ridiculously wide skirt couldn't rival the hoops and frames these
women had installed beneath their dresses. Never a head was
tilted, but impeccable posture was maintained at all times so that
they seemed as barely animated statues. The skirts spread so far
to either side, he wondered how he might stand close enough to
any of the women to talk to one without having to shout.

A dry smile touched his mouth at the thought, for with it came
the realization he most likely wasn't supposed to talk to any of
them. "Way out of my league," was how his father surely would
have put it. Such glittering jewelry, long necks, and white bosoms
he'd never even seen before.

The Great Hall echoed with music, laughter, and talk. The
scent of hot food made Ciaran's mouth water, for during the walk
from Glenfinnan provisions had been mostly cold and usually
oats. Bannocks and *drammach* were filling, but he always liked a
good bit of beef.

The music filling the Great Hall was alien to him and not very
interesting. He'd heard its like before, always here in Edinburgh.
He recognized the violins—and knew they were violins, not fid-
dles. He even recognized the cello and flute, but had never before
seen nor heard the enormous table-looking contraption that stood
amongst them. It was the size and shape of a harp laid flat, and a
man dressed all in white sat on a stool beside it, fingering a row
of black . . . things. Each one he pressed made a pinging note.
Almost like plucking a harp, which he supposed was explained
by the shape. He wondered why the man didn't simply play a
harp and forgo the machine, but had to admit to himself there was
a difference in the sound. This thing had a sprightly, tinkling
quality that was quite unlike a harp, and the notes never lingered.
He watched the musician's fingers for a moment, admiring the
dexterity.

Just as he turned to search out the food, there was a murmur
among the guests. The crowd parted, and made way for the prince

himself, all eyes wide and smiles bright to be so near the conquering Stuart. He commanded the center of attention, cutting a fine, bright figure in white velvet trimmed in gold, breeches fitting like skin, and silk stockings to show off the line of his legs. The star and blue ribbon of the Order of the Garter lay over his chest, bold color against his white coat. Working his way among his guests, he had a charming smile and witty commentary for each man or woman who caught his eye. Laughter and good cheer surrounded Charles, and even Ciaran found himself subject to the infectious smile. He smiled also.

Just then, the woman who had caught his eye earlier did so again. She was very beautiful, and his smile widened. Her response was to thrust her chest against her stays so as to nearly burst from her bodice. Her hair was jet black and tied back under the tiniest of caps trimmed in pearls. From there it cascaded down the back of her long neck in a riot of ringlets, and throughout her coiffeur, like a star-filled night, were dotted pearl stickpins. She pursed her lush red mouth at him. He forced his attention back to the prince, lest he be caught ignoring His Royal Highness.

Charles gestured to one of the musicians, who then handed over his viol. "Alas," said Charles, "my brother is not here to play with us. But I will attempt to muddle along without him." Encouraged by the applause of his admirers, Charles set the instrument under his chin, caught the eye of the man sitting at the harp machine, and the ensemble began to play.

Though the music itself didn't particularly excite Ciaran, he had to admit the prince played well. His bow worked the viol strings with an admirable energy and precision. It seemed Charles' entire being was focused on the performance and for that moment nothing existed beyond himself and the music. The intensity of focus was the sort Ciaran had always striven to achieve when he fought, or practiced his form, and he envied the apparent ease with which the prince managed it.

But then, once the piece was finished to uproarious applause, Charles handed back the viol and he was as quickly on to something else. He wandered away, chatting brightly with the duke of Perth.

Ciaran went in search of refreshments again, and this time found some. Great mounds of meat, vast trays of various round things he couldn't recognize, wine, whiskey, all set among arrangements of fresh cut flowers and elaborate candelabra. Folks around him were eating daintily with plates and forks, and he bit the inside corner of his mouth. He knew how to use a fork, and didn't care for them, but tonight he was in Edinburgh and would eat as the *Sasunnaich*. He picked up a shiny, bright silver fork.

As the evening progressed, Ciaran relaxed and enjoyed himself. Filled with good meat and those little round things he never did quite identify—beyond that they had liver in them—he chatted among the other lairds of his stature. He drank enough to smooth the edges of his apprehension regarding Leah, but he didn't drink Scottish whiskey. Never Scottish whiskey, except that from his own still. So tonight he preferred the French brandy, for he was quite spoiled. Brandy was the only drink offered that not only tasted better than ordinary whiskey, but also was less likely to blind him or even kill him if he should drink too much.

Across the room, standing by the doorway, was that woman he'd seen earlier. Though it would have seemed impossible, her bodice was even lower than it had been. He would swear even from this distance he could see pink areola behind the lace. She was eyeing him again, and now he wanted to learn what she was about. He set down his brandy glass and made his way toward her, wending a route among clusters of other guests.

When he arrived at the other side of the room, he found she'd wandered off. He glanced around, disappointed. But then a voice came from just outside the door. "Are you lost, kind sir?" The voice was soft, low, and French. He took a step toward the door to find a dark silhouette waiting for him in the dim chamber adjoining, and stepped into the room.

Lit only by a single candelabra, the smaller chamber was cool, a relief from the myriad flames and press of warm bodies in the ballroom. He took a deep breath. The dark-haired woman looked up at him with a smile that touched him merrily in his most private places. He'd heard stories about women of the upper classes, particularly of the French upper classes, who were unconstrained by the rigors and disciplines of ordinary life. What she might want with him was a question that excited his imagination and sent the brandy in his head straight to his groin. His head was left quite empty, and felt light.

Glancing around, he said, "Nae in the least." Some upholstered chairs were arranged about a low table, and the candelabra rested on a higher table in the corner. The hearth was large and ornate, the mantel carved with vines and fruits. The dark woman stood in the middle of the floor, and he stepped toward her.

"Tell me your name." Her accent was delicate, her speech soft. Seductive. She reached for his hand. He let her take it. Her face tilted up toward his.

"Ciaran. And what might yours be?"

"You are a Highlander."

"Aye, by the grace of God." A chuckle rose, and it felt good. Her hand was thin, her bones so frail he was afraid he might break one should he squeeze too hard.

Her gaze went to the hem of his kilt. "Is it true what they say about these?" Her bare chest was pinking up, and a quaver came into her voice.

"What is it they say?" Once again he found himself wishing the fashion for hooped petticoats were dead, for he couldn't stand any closer to her without bending her whalebone.

But she didn't seem to mind, and took the step toward him, bending the hoops herself. Now he could feel the warmth of her, and the urge to touch her swelling bosom was maddening. By God, down inside the lace at her bodice, he could see both her nipples. She said, "Is it true you wear no drawers under there?"

"Aye, 'tis true enough." Though the sark under his kilt almost reached his knees, it didn't nearly qualify as drawers. Now he didn't need to ask if it were true what folks said about rich women, for she was showing him how little she cared for sexual convention.

Her free hand brushed the plaid draped across his chest. "You Highland men all seem so strong."

That brought a smile and a nod of agreement, so she continued with a girlish and petulant note of dissatisfaction, "My husband is not nearly as tall as you. And he is quite fat."

"Does your husband nae mind ye asking personal questions of strange men?"

A dry chuckle rose from her, sounding a sour note. "My husband is more than likely in another chamber at this moment with his member buried in the behind of some fellow younger and softer than yourself."

Ciaran shuddered at that image, but it evaporated when she reached for the hem of his kilt. She whispered, "I imagine a strong man such as yourself would have better things to do with his member." Her face tilted toward his again.

"Oh, aye. Far better things." He kissed her and allowed her to reach under the kilt. His head swam with the brandy and desire, and his enthusiasm for this freedom enjoyed by the upper classes rose as her hand closed around him. He would be quite happy to accommodate this poor, neglected woman for one night. Perhaps, even, only for the hour.

She continued as she squeezed him and made stars dance in his vision, her voice growing heavy and breathy, "I've never had a Highlander before. If it is true you wear no drawers, perhaps, then, you fuck differently from civilized men?"

Suddenly Ciaran's head cleared. This woman thought he was an animal, different from "civilized men." His face and neck warmed as anger rose to replace desire. He reached for her hand to disengage it, and squeezed until she cringed. "Aye, 'tis true. 'Tis a wild, uncouth, unmannered pack of dogs we are."

He laid his mouth over hers and pressed the back of her head to kiss her with all the vicious power at his command. A whimper of fear escaped through her nose, and he thrust his tongue into her mouth as hard and as far as he could. Mouth open wide, thrusting deep, he then suddenly let her go and stepped back, leaving her agape and astonished.

In a low, infuriated voice, he said, "However, bitch though you are, I've better things to do with my member tonight. I'm certain there must be a lonely sheep somewhere close by." Then he returned to the Great Hall.

The heat of the party and the stares of people who saw his face made him duck and hurry away toward the exit. Sinann wasn't helping.

"That was singularly idiotic."

"Shut up, faerie."

" 'Tis fortunate for you the woman and her husband mean naught to your superiors, or there may have been consequences of your indiscretion."

"I said, put a cork in it." Wending his way among the crowd, he made his exit through the various chambers to the outside air. He gulped the cool fall breeze to clear his head before setting out through the gatehouse and on up toward the high street.

"Ye would have done well to have simply given her a good banging then handed her back to her husband."

"I was a fool to have gone into that room."

"*Och,* there is that. But once in there, it was unwise to leave the lass frustrated."

"She thought I was an animal." He stopped and turned to look back at the palace. "A wild Highlander who lives the way I do because I dinnae ken any better. She's nae more consideration of me than a rutting boar in the forest or a horse put to stud." He looked up at Sinann hovering overhead. "Faerie, she's one of them as thinks my people are nae people."

Slowly she lowered until she stood on the track beside him. "Aye, Ciaran Dubhach. She is, and will continue to be."

With a deep sigh, he turned and went on up the hill. She followed on foot. After a long silence, she said, "Correct me if I'm mistaken, but I had been under the impression ye loved Leah."

"Shut up, faerie. I'll nae be making this mistake ever again."

Sinann giggled, then obliged him with silence.

CHAPTER 13

Gold wristwatch, gold wedding ring, small gold crucifix hung from a gold chain and resting amid the lace.

In early November, the Jacobites left Edinburgh to make their way toward England. Though winter was nearly upon them, it seemed the prince had his heart set on invading London at the earliest opportunity. It was a reluctant group that followed Charles, but they followed him nevertheless.

During the march south there was a great deal of time to think. Ciaran dwelt long on Leah, recalling her sweet face, the comfort of her body and her company, the peace he had felt when holding her. There was no thought of what would happen after the rising. His chances of dying in battle were high, especially if what Da had said was true. Even were he to survive, Leah's father and his own clan would prevent them marrying. There was no point in looking to the future.

But though he had no hope of a future with her, he at least had the past, holding dear in his memory the sound of her voice, the scent of her skin, the warmth and joy of her flesh entwined with his.

As the army passed through Scotland, the Jacobite forces

grew. The more men there were, the more casually the army as a whole marched, for leadership was by social rank rather than military merit, and discipline was lax. Surrounded now by large numbers of men from the more powerful Jacobite clans, Ciaran observed spontaneous comings and goings, desertion by those who were homesick, and the careless target practice of men still learning to use the muskets captured at Prestonpans.

Ciaran himself needed to take an occasional moment to fire off a ball or two and get the feel of the weapon he'd picked up on that battlefield. He found its report was louder than that of his pistol, but the kick was easier to control. Aim was better. The smoke from the powder nearly choked him, though, close as it was to his face. His father had despised firearms and distrusted powder, preferring to take his chances with edged weapons or even to go unarmed, but Ciaran loved the power of this. To put an enemy down at so great a distance was a good thing. It didn't bother him much that the bayonet was broken.

In his own ranks, keeping discipline was a relatively simple matter. The Mathesons, under the direct eye of their laird, weren't so free as the more numerous Camerons, Murrays, Stewarts, and MacDonalds, and therefore appeared better disciplined. However, listening to the talk among his men, Ciaran knew the truth.

"I did not leave my home to save the *Sasunnaich* from their king." Donnchadh was outspoken, but kept his voice low as he walked. "Our bonnic great prince is taking us where we dinnae need to go."

Ciaran tended to agree, but told Donnchadh to keep it to himself. "I'm dead certain bonnie Prince Teàrlach has reasons for us going."

"He's a fool," said Aodán.

"Shut yer gob," said Ciaran.

" 'Tis naught but the truth."

Ciaran's voice rose and he fell back to walk nearer to Aodán. "The truth of it being questionable in any case, 'tis also neither here nor there. You'll keep it to yourself or you'll fight me over it. And this time I'll kill you. Do ye wish that?"

Aodán fell silent. Ciaran heard a snicker and glanced over at Calum, but received only a bland smile. Nothing further was said on the subject of whether they should go to England. They simply went, making an excellent pace Ciaran figured to be almost thirty miles each day. Hard, rocky hills soon gave way to rolling landscape and astonishingly wide pastures. Ciaran had never seen so much sky in his life.

A week out from Edinburgh, while his men settled down for a night's sleep, Ciaran remained awake by the fire, idly gnawing on a piece of hardtack that was part of his ration that day. The overcast sky was encroaching on the land, the mist and fog creeping here and there among the heath, deadening sound to a soft muffle. His coat and kilt were damp with it, and somehow he felt colder than if it had been snow. As he watched his men roll themselves into their plaids, he thought of how few they were. His contingent would barely make a good-sized hunting party back home. Hardly enough for the prince to care whether they fought or not.

Yearning for home crept into his thoughts like the mist on the moor. It would be so easy to simply take his men and walk away. Nobody among the command would know, and if they did, few would care. He looked around at his men and wondered what they would say if he took them home.

Then he imagined the reception they would receive once they arrived, and realized it didn't matter how he or the men felt. In Ciorram there would be only the baleful stares of kinsmen who counted on them to uphold the honor of the clan. Kinsmen who their entire lives had experienced the oppression of the Redcoats these men had been sent to oust from the country. He sighed. There was no turning back.

He looked up at the approach of Lieutenant General Lord George Murray, accompanied by two aides. Ciaran went to meet them before they could come close enough to require his men to stand in Lord George's presence.

"Good evening, my lord."

The group clustered around him, looking the laird of Ciorram up and down as if he were applying to them for employment. Murray addressed him.

"How many do you command?"

"Thirty, my lord."

"Who is your best artilleryman?"

Ciaran stifled the urge to laugh, and mildly replied, "Having received none of the pieces captured at Prestonpans, I confess my men and I are all of the same completely unskilled level of expertise."

A sour look crossed the old man's face, and he grunted. "Not even yourself? You've never aimed a cannon before?" He had a crisp, efficient way about him. Though his voice had the dry rasp of fall leaves, it was nevertheless strong and commanding.

"Naught heavier than this here pistol, and my musket." He laid his hand on the butt of the flintlock pistol in his belt and nodded toward the musket among his accoutrements by the fire. "Much to our disgrace, my men wouldnae know what to do with an artillery piece were it to reach up and bite them on the arse."

That brought a hearty laugh, even from the otherwise silent entourage in their fine coats and boots, and Murray nodded his thanks for the information. He opened his mouth to speak, but then hesitated. There was a pause as he peered into Ciaran's face for a moment. Then he blinked and frowned, and adjusted the plaid draped across his heavy coat.

"Something else I can help ye with, my lord?" Ciaran hoped not, but held his patience.

"What is your name?" Murray shifted his weight, then said, "You seem familiar."

Ciaran should seem familiar, being among the clan leaders privy to council meetings. But he said only, "Ciaran Robert Matheson of Ciorram, my lord."

Murray grunted and his eyebrows raised, surprised. "Laird of Ciorram? Iain Mór's son? I would never have known it by looking at you."

The edges of Ciaran's soul darkened, and he replied though it felt like a lie, "My father was Dylan Robert Matheson of Ciorram, my lord. Also known variously as Mac a'Chlaidheimh or Dylan Dubh nan Chlaidheimh." Murray's eyes narrowed with concentration of memory, and Ciaran provided the missing information to explain the succession. "Iain Mór was my maternal grandfather. Dylan Dubh was his cousin."

Still, that didn't clear Murray's frown. Beetled eyebrows knotted over his nose, and his mouth pursed. He pressed, "Nevertheless, I'm certain I recognize your face somehow."

"My father fought for King James thirty years ago."

Then the light flickered in Murray's eyes. "Aye! Yes, indeed! I remember now. In Glen Shiel. I was attempting to convince my brother to disband the army after that ignominious defeat, but he would have none of it. I argued desperately, and yet failed to move him. But then your father came from the ranks and was able to make William see sense." A dry smile touched his mouth. "I certainly never could, for I am, and always will be, the hopelessly callow younger brother, you see. But your father stood up to him, and convinced him that to persist in the fight was no more valiant than suicide."

This sounded so familiar, knowing Dylan Dubh, Ciaran could only nod as the spirit of his father seemed present for a moment. His voice caught as he said, "Aye. That's my da."

The smile faded. "I'm grieved to learn he's passed on."

"Aye, my lord, just this past spring, God rest him."

"Alas. Though I'm certain he's left Ciorram in capable hands, I would have liked to have thanked him for saving all our lives that night." A gesture to the Jacobite camp at large, "So we could fight another day, aye?"

Ciaran agreed with a nod and, "Aye, my lord."

Murray then looked away to another camp where he would continue searching for artillerymen, and said, "Well, then—"

"Begging your pardon, my lord, but you truly wanted to run away from the fight?"

Murray turned back to him and frowned. "Nonsense. It would never have been a fight at all. It would have been a massacre. Our men were exhausted and demoralized. Asking them to face the English mortar again would have been akin to placing them all before a firing squad. Your father and I were among the few who understood it."

"I see."

With that, Murray bid Ciaran adieu and went on his way, leaving the laird of Ciorram feeling as if his guts had just been stirred with a large spoon.

"Ciaran—"

The laird turned to find Eóin standing behind him, "Eóin, maintain the order. I'll return shortly."

"Aye." Ciaran's second seemed curious about what was going on, but held his tongue and refrained from asking.

Ciaran strode quickly to a burn meandering through the heath nearby, his hands deep in his coat pockets and his neck turtled into its collar. The streambed was deep, leaving an overhang of sod that quite hid him from the Matheson encampment when he dropped to the water's edge. "Faerie," he said as he sat himself on a smooth, rounded rock, "where are you?"

There was a long moment. Then he said, "If you dinnae show

yourself, I'll shoot the prince and then where will Da's precious history be?"

"You willnae shoot the prince, for you havenae got it in you. And that is why the history will be what he kent it to be." Sinann popped into sight, perched on the overhang to Ciaran's left. "And my name is Sinann, if you please."

"I need to talk."

"Of course you do, or otherwise why did you call?"

"Do I truly look like my . . . do I look like Dylan Dubh?"

An exclamation of utter surprise burst from the faerie, and she laughed. Long and hard she laughed, leaving Ciaran with his head down and his face burning with shame. In a moment he was likely to pick up a rock from the streambed and throw it at her.

But as soon as she could catch a breath, she cried, "Of course you do! You've seen yourself in a glass often enough to ken it!"

He squirmed in his seat. "Aye. But if I'm his son, then why—"

"He wanted folks to stop calling you Ciaran Ramsay, is all. He wanted you to grow up never knowing any name but Matheson."

"But it's possible . . . if Connor Ramsay resembled him—"

A snort of fresh laughter blew through Sinann's nose. "Only as an ass resembles a saddle horse. Lad, you must realize Connor Ramsay was as fair and languid a man as ever set foot on the earth." Ciaran's heart began to lift, and the faerie continued.

"Furthermore, laddie, I'm here to tell you he never laid a hand on your mother. Not at any time, until . . . until the day she died."

Ciaran couldn't believe what he was hearing, and shifted excitedly on the rock. "The hell, you say."

"Aye. For your father's sake, when he lost your mother to Ramsay, I crafted a talisman of strength regarding her. I kent she would want to resist her husband in the marriage bed, so I tied a red string with seven knots for her. From the day she left Ciorram to the time your father came to claim her, she never allowed Ramsay to come near her."

Heart lifting, he said, "You're certain of this?"

The faerie's eyes went wide. "*Och,* are you doubting my power, lad? For if you are, I'll change you into a toad to demonstrate." She lifted her arms as a threat, and he raised his palms in surrender.

"No. I believe you."

"Also, there is that I was present the night you were conceived."

He frowned. "I thought you never looked in on that sort of thing."

"Well, they woke me, did they not? In the broch, it was, at Beltane, and I was perched in the tree and there they were down below it, a-going at it like . . . well, like a man and woman in love." She leaned toward him, and her voice went low. "That is who your parents were. Never doubt it, lad. Your mother was the love of his life, and you were always his proof of it. You werenae merely his son, you were his *favorite* son."

It took a minute or so to absorb the faerie's words. "You wouldnae lie to me?"

"I wouldnae lie to one as meant so much to Dylan Dubh, who was a great man and deserving of my fealty. Ciaran, you and your sister were everything to him."

Ciaran's throat closed, and his eyes stung. The doubt of the past several months lifted, and the relief of it took his breath away. He suddenly felt whole again. He whispered, "Aye, Tinkerbell. I thank you."

A wide grin lit up her face. "Tinkerbell, ye say!"

"Aye, Tinkerbell. Tink."

She giggled, a high, musical sound. "Ye called me Tink!" Another giggle. "*Och,* he called me *Tink!*"

As Ciaran returned to his men he chuckled to himself that she was so easily pleased.

The following day, the Jacobite army crossed into England. For the first time in his life, and he hoped the last, Ciaran departed Scotland.

Soon the prince's army besieged Carlisle, in the north of England, and for a week lay outside the town walls, battering them with their captured artillery and threatening to burn the place down. It had been reported the king's General Wade was marching toward them from Newcastle, but that was soon determined to be a false alarm, and the siege continued unabated. The local militia surrendered the town soon after, and now the prince's soldiers were billeted in the houses and inns of Carlisle, warm for the first time since the weather had begun to turn. Their numbers had grown since Prestonpans, and so men were crowded in on each other, often sleeping on floors, wrapped in their plaids, as they had been on the heath.

Ciaran, for his rank, had a small room to himself on the top floor of a tavern in which the pitched roof prevented him from standing straight anywhere but the very center. Cannon boomed in the distance as the castle garrison held out against Jacobite artillery.

It wouldn't for long, though, Ciaran was certain of it. He stood at the gabled window glazed with small, swirled panes of glass, which he opened to see out, and idly watched puffs of smoke rise from the battlement. It was plain the people of Carlisle would give up soon, for nobody on either side believed Wade would come.

It seemed even the English were beginning to comprehend the reluctance of George's men to fight. The surrendered militia men Ciaran had seen in the town had seemed awfully ambivalent about the entire conflict, an attitude he found incomprehensible. He couldn't imagine not wanting to defend one's home, but the townspeople didn't appear to care much whether the Jacobites were there or not. Though the countryside was not leaping to arms against George, as Charles had hoped, neither were they sticking their necks out to defend their king. Once again Ciaran found himself disgusted with English ambivalence and ennui.

The small fire in his hearth burned merrily, and the warmth settled nicely into Ciaran's bones. The march had been long and hard, for the prince had pushed them many miles each day, and now the chance to rest was welcome. Ciaran felt detached from the distant smoke, and it seemed to have little importance. He almost hoped the castle garrison would hold out for a week or two, if only to delay his own departure south with the prince. Maybe a month. Yes, he could do with a month of sitting by this fire, resting while listening to cannon thunder in the distance.

But London was where Charles was headed. If they could conquer London quickly, there was a chance the French king would send support. If they could master London, they might hold the entire country, and even the Scots most hardened against invading England knew it. The men were eager to go there, to fight that decisive battle, for they all believed success could be had.

Nevertheless, for the moment Ciaran was content to be warm. In the back of his mind lurked the possibility his father had been right, that they would turn back at Derby before gaining the capital, and it was a terrible thought. The longer the march was delayed, the longer it would take to find out whether the prophesy would be true.

After closing the window, he stripped to the skin and sat on the floor before the fire to begin the ritual to rid himself of parasites. No matter how often he picked himself clean, new intruders annoyed, biting and scurrying here and there beneath his clothing. It was the crawling he hated most. The itch of a reddened flea bite was nothing compared to the revulsion he had for a wee beastie making its way across his skin. Most of the men didn't bother with removing them, for there were always more to come, and it seemed a useless effort. But as a child Ciaran had never been allowed to let such things go, and now he was as incapable of suffering a flea to live as he was of pissing down his leg. As he worked methodically, starting with his feet and quickly running his hands over his legs before going after the invaders of his privates, he said in a murmur, "Tinkerbell, are ye there?"

"Aye. Always." Sinann appeared, perched at the foot of his bunk.

"Have ye been looking in on the Tigh?" He found a louse among his private hairs and flicked it into the fire, then continued the search.

"Aye."

"And nothing?"

"Nae, there's something."

He turned to face her, and leaned against the wall to listen. But something crawled across his balls, and he hurried to find it. "What, then?" He found the bug, and it joined its fellow in the fire. Then he leaned back again to search further.

"News of Leah."

Ciaran looked up and set his hands on the floor at his sides. "What of her? Is she well? How is there news of her at the Tigh?" This couldn't be good. Nothing out of the ordinary was ever good news.

"A letter she sent to you, which young Robbie received in the office only yesterday and translated aloud to Robin Innis because she makes reference to having seen you in Edinburgh after the battle. I'm afraid the cat is out of the bag for the two of you."

Alarm rose. He pulled in his feet to sit cross-legged and upright. "What did the letter say?"

The faerie chuckled. "If you think she wrote in detail of carryings-on, you should be ashamed. Nae, the letter was for naught but to send word to you of her whereabouts. She wrote shortly before she and her father's cousins left Edinburgh for Nairn. Most of the city is in fear of the Redcoats. Even those who dinnae support the prince have nae faith in being distinguished from those who do."

"Who is she staying with in Nairn?"

Sinann shrugged her tiny shoulders. "The letter dinnae say. Perhaps she did not ken who."

"Did it say why she sent it to the Tigh?"

" 'Tis plain enough, to my mind. She sent it there because she couldnae be known to contact one among the Jacobites. Daughter of a Redcoat that she is, it wouldnae have made its way to you in any case. To be sure, she took risk enough in sending a letter north at all. If you are to find her after the disturbance, she needs for you to ken where she's gone."

Warmth seeped into Ciaran's heart. "She risked her father's anger to be certain of seeing me again."

"She loves ye, lad. Were you to leave the Jacobites to their own resources, you could join her in Nairn and nae die on Drummossie Moor."

Ciaran snorted. "I cannae desert the prince and the cause. Dùghlas and Calum would brand me a coward, and the rest of the clan as well, and I wouldnae care to go in any case. We're near enough to London for us to imagine George's craven army cannae stop us. We are many, and we are eager to fight."

"Many of your army have deserted."

Anger flashed in him. He leaned toward her and shook a finger at her. "And, by God, none of them Mathesons. None will be Mathesons. Let the Cameron gillies or the cowardly MacDonells run back home, but the few I brought are still with us. Besides, Tinkerbell, you cannae be certain I would die. You've said even Da never foretold whether I would live or die."

"Aye, he said the only mention of you was that the day of the battle you had gone in search of men who were foraging."

"And he wasnae certain I ever returned." But then he frowned, and leaned back against the wall again, one elbow on his raised knee. He thrust his fingers into his hair and stared at the floor. It made no sense to him he would ever turn his back on a fight. Could he? Did he have it in him to run? Might his nerve one day break? A niggling doubt fluttered in his gut, but he fought it down. No, he was not a coward. He would never run from a coming battle. Da's history must be mistaken. But what part of it?

The faerie continued, "I've told you, it willnae matter. Very few will live, he said. Those who survive the battle will be captured and most executed. The rest will be imprisoned. Further, the countryside will be ravaged in the search for Jacobites, and many will die who had not fought. In more than thirty years yer father was never wrong about such things. Heed him, lad. Make for yourself a destiny that includes the woman you love. Decide for yourself the path you'll take. Do it now, and it willnae be desertion."

For a moment there was an overwhelming urge to throw over the cause and go to Leah. So sweet it would be, to tie his future to hers. But when he thought of how he would live the rest of his life, bearing the reputation of a coward and ashamed of himself, he knew he couldn't do it. Even in obedience to his father. It was asking too much.

"But it would be desertion. I cannae."

"Ye must."

"No, Tinkerbell. I must do the thing I've set out to do."

"And die."

"If that is my fate."

"Och!" She shook her head and her face flushed. "Fate!"

Both his hands balled into fists. "You said it yerself. I do what I will because I've naught else in me. If there's the smallest chance of taking London and saving the country from George, who by all accounts thinks of himself as German and would rather be in Hanover in any case, then I must take it."

"Even if—"

"Aye, even then. Naught happens until it happens. I cannae live my life according to what my father read in a book centuries after the fact."

"But Leah. Do you nae love her?"

Ciaran nodded. "Aye. I do. And I wish to return to her. But not at the cost of my pride and position."

"Yer father gave up everything for your mother."

That took him aback. He blinked. Both knees raised, he rested his arms on them. "My father was laird. What did he sacrifice?"

"His home in the future. His friends. His"—a frown clouded her brow as she struggled to recall—"his television, he said, which could tell stories inside a box, like a puppet show but with real people and things. He also spoke of his 'frigerator, where food could be stored and kept sometimes for weeks. He lived in a time when men could—*will*—fly in machines like birds and ride in carriages many times faster than the fleetest horse. When houses will be heated by lightning and food kept frozen in large trunks until needed. He even said"—Sinann leaned close and lowered her voice, though nobody but Ciaran could hear—"there will be a man to set foot on the moon! An *Armstrong!*"

That made Ciaran laugh. "The moon, you say! Now you've said too much! The moon indeed!" Chuckling, he went back to checking himself for lice. "A man on the moon!"

Sinann leaned back and said, "Aye. 'Tis ridiculous. A faerie tale."

That quieted Ciaran's laughter, and he glanced sideways at the faerie. That wooden toy came to mind—the one shaped like a strange bird. His father had carved it for him long ago, and Ciaran had always thought it a poorly rendered swallow. Could it have been a flying machine instead?

Finally he said, "Of course it makes sense the man to fly to the moon would be a Scot." He eyed Sinann some more, then said, "Aye, he gave up many wondrous things. But where he was from . . . was he the laird there, and was he responsible for the well-being of hundreds of people? Did he fail his clan to be with my mother?"

The faerie sighed and her wings drooped. "Nae."

Ciaran nodded. "I thought not." He pulled at the black ribbon and shook his hair loose over his shoulders to run his fingers over his scalp. "Neither will I fail my clan."

The castle garrison surrendered the next day, and a Jacobite garrison was installed there in its place. The prince and his army stayed in Carlisle for another week to rest before moving on, and a few days later arrived in Manchester. There King James was declared at the Market Cross, and several hundred volunteers joined the cause that day. Spirits were high, and the mood of Ciaran's men was of elation. They believed themselves unstoppable. Even Ciaran began to hold out hope for the cause.

However, as the army continued southward, through Stockport, Macclesfield, and Leek, there seemed more lip service among the English Jacobites than real support for Charles. Many drank to James' health in the presence of the prince's men, and crowds came out to cheer them on, but few wanted to join his army. More and more it became plain that Charles needed the decisive victory in London to sway the country. So far since entering England, they'd not seen the face of one Redcoat, and it seemed their goal was just within their grasp.

As the key battle approached, Ciaran worked off tension by

returning to his workouts each evening when encamped. Though he'd been raised to fanaticism about his physical discipline, he'd had little opportunity to practice his form of late. Since leaving Glen Ciorram he'd been able to perform his exercises only a handful of times, so he took a moment while camped in Leek to stretch muscles cramped by the march and hone unarmed fighting skills dulled by the army's emphasis on armed combat. At sunset, while his men encamped in a pasture outside a manor house, he found a level spot, bowed to an imaginary opponent, and began his formal exercise.

It brought comfort to his soul, and his blood sang with release. Practicing a habit of the days when his father had been alive put him in touch with who he was. What he was for. He focused on the task at hand, all other concerns falling to the wayside, and it brought a measure of peace to his troubled mind. His heart beat strong and steady. Breath filled his chest. Colors brightened and sounds sharpened. He found himself glad to be alive.

Near the end of the form, he turned and was quite surprised to find Prince Teàrlach there, staring at him. A small cluster of attendants stood off to the side, awaiting the prince's bidding. Ciaran stopped his exercise and stood at attention. "Your Royal Highness."

Charles waved at him to continue. "Don't stop. Do continue, Ciorram."

Ciaran was taken aback that the prince remembered his name, but managed to regain his focus and return to his place in the form. With the eyes of the prince on him, he finished a mite less gracefully than he might have. The tips of his ears burned at what his father would have said about such sloppy concentration. He finished, bowed again to his imaginary opponent, and turned to the prince.

Charles applauded, and his perpetual smile became a genuine one. "Bravo, Ciorram! What a fine performance! And without music. Do you do other dances as well?"

"Aye, Your Highness, but that wasnae dance. 'Twas training for unarmed combat."

The prince's eyes went wide. "Fighting? Indeed? In what way? You must show me." The enthusiasm in his voice brought a bit of smile to the corner of Ciaran's mouth. He'd felt that way as a boy, wanting to know everything his father knew and right *now*. He stepped toward the prince.

"Then try to hit me."

A bright grin lit Charles' face. "Be careful what you ask for."

"Hit me. As hard as you can."

Charles, still grinning, hauled off and took a swing at Ciaran. Well announced, it was easily deflected with a simple movement of one arm. Ciaran remained standing where he'd been, not disturbed in the least.

Astonished, Charles took another swing, and Ciaran redirected it. Another swing followed by another with the left, and Ciaran easily rendered both harmless.

"My God!" The prince stared at his fists as if they were to blame for his inability to land a punch. "Teach me this trick. I must learn how to do this."

" 'Tis nae trick. Neither is it simple to learn."

"Teach me. Now."

Ciaran resisted the urge to sigh. He nodded, then said, "Very well, then, Highness. First you must stand with your feet like so." He demonstrated the most basic stance, the one his father had always taught first. "At shoulder width apart, toes facing forward, knees slightly bent."

Charles shook his head. "No, Ciorram. I want to learn what you did with your hands."

Ciaran stood hipshot, his patience thinning. "With all respect, Your Highness, I did what I did with my entire body. The hands were but a small part of it."

Charles gazed at him for a moment, thoughtful, then said, "All of the body?"

"Aye. 'Tis a discipline my father learned in America, and taught to me when I was a wee lad. Mastery of the art takes years of training." The prince's eyes went hard with denial, so Ciaran added, "But I can teach you quickly to balance yourself so an opponent cannae knock you over so easily."

That seemed to satisfy His Royal Highness, who said, "Then show me." He copied the stance Ciaran had tried to show him, and had it in an instant. "Like so?"

"Aye, Highness. Good. Now see if you shift your weight from side to side you dinnae overbalance. I cannae shove you so you stagger." He demonstrated, and Charles grinned and laughed like a boy. For the next several hours by torchlight Ciaran taught him the bare basics of martial art, and Charles was a quick and eager student—so eager, in fact, that he wouldn't quit until Ciaran was exhausted and struggling to stay awake.

As Ciaran rolled himself into his plaid by his fire, he muttered to Sinann, "We'll get to London on that lad's enthusiasm alone, for a certainty."

There was a soft giggle in the darkness.

On December 4 the Jacobite army marched into Derby nearly five thousand strong, expecting to encounter soon the Hanoverian forces led by King George's son the duke of Cumberland. They were less than a hundred miles from London.

The following day, Ciaran looked around him at the eager soldiers in town, having their weapons sharpened in anticipation of using them, and whispered to Sinann, "Are you certain Da said we'd turn back here?"

The faerie seemed puzzled as well. "Aye. He said you'd never make it past Derby."

"Did he say why?"

She shrugged. "No. He never kent why."

"Perhaps he was mistaken?" Hope rose. Would that his father had been mistaken about it all.

But the faerie shook her head. "He was certain of it. Though he did not recall everything, what he kent he was sure of."

A gillie in the service of Lord George came running, breathing hard with the excitement of his task. "Sir, 'tis a meeting of the council. All the clan leaders are requested at Exeter House." Then he ran off to spread the word.

Ciaran was certain this would be nothing more than a routine dissemination of the battle plan for their anticipated encounter with Cumberland. Cut and dried. He headed for Exeter House at a slow mosey.

But when he entered the hall, raised voices told him there was something very wrong. Though not all the clan leaders had yet arrived, an informal discussion had already begun. None of the chairs was in use. The men crowded and shuffled, confused and agitated. Lord George Murray had the floor, and it seemed he was demanding they make a retreat to Scotland.

Surprise made Ciaran stop cold. His jaw quite dropped, and at Sinann's suggestion he closed his mouth.

Murray was saying, "Drummond's reinforcements will give us a better chance against Cumberland. Nearly three thousand await us in Scotland."

Ciaran whispered to Sinann, "Three thousand? The French have sent men, but they're in Scotland?"

"It would appear, lad."

Murray continued, "If we make our stand there, we won't be required to risk our army here in England."

Cameron of Lochiel said, "We willnae be required to risk our army *for* England."

That brought some murmurs of agreement.

Charles, sitting in a large chair near a pole from which his father's standard hung, raised his voice as his face flushed with rage. "We must march south, cross the Trent—"

A voice among the crowd said, "If you advance to London, you'll be in Newgate jail within a fortnight."

"The men are ready to fight *now*." The young prince thumped the table before him with a fist. "We are almost to London. Victory is nearly ours. Cumberland and Wade have been traipsing around in search of us for weeks, and their men are unused to fighting under winter conditions. We have an army filled with Highlanders who think nothing of sleeping in the open and shaking off the frost from their beards before going to a fight."

Murray countered, "But our numbers are smaller than theirs. We haven't the support you promised, from the countryside or the French, and there are no reports of any better support in London."

Charles shouted, "The people will rise up and follow us!"

"With all respect, Highness, I must disagree," said Murray. "Our intelligence tells us George has gathered men in Finchley. Cumberland is nearly upon us, and to take London we'd be required to fight not only his more numerous army, but also those gathered closer to London against our arrival. Our chances are far better if we consolidate our forces in the north."

On the meeting went, the tide apparently very much against the prince. A few clan leaders spoke up in support of proceeding to London, but the arguments were weak and went ignored by the more strident and more powerful lairds. Ciaran had absolutely nothing to say on the matter, for what he would say could not be believed. He knew for a certainty the army would turn back, and there was nothing any of them could do about it. Charles remained obstinate, and by noon nothing had been decided. The meeting was then adjourned until the evening.

Ciaran never attended the evening meeting, for he knew what the outcome would be. He stayed with his men in a tavern, drinking ale and listening to their talk of marching into London after finally giving Cumberland what-for. They filled the close and stuffy public room with laughter and hope, but Ciaran couldn't partake. What lay before them was not nearly what they expected. A sourness grew in the pit of his stomach as he drank. He tried to think of nothing, for thinking at all would lead him to dwell on what his fate would be next spring at the final battle near Inverness.

The following morning as usual, they rose well before dawn to begin the day's march toward London. The cold December day would be dark and frosty. The many thousands of soldiers, camp followers, and servants followed their leaders through the unfamiliar countryside with weapons, supplies, and baggage, ready to face the enemy they'd come for. They all were eager, waiting to hear Cumberland had been sighted.

But as the sky lightened, men became confused, for the sun was rising on their right rather than their left. As they looked around them and realized what had happened, that they were headed away from London instead of toward it, anger rose with the sun. Surprised grumbling turned to shouts of rage and accusations of betrayal. Ciaran refrained from complaint and urged his men to do the same, for he knew it had been unavoidable. Fate had stepped in, and that was that.

For the first time, he suspected he might really die next April on Culloden Moor.

CHAPTER 14

Fringed fly plaid to match the kilt and waistcoat. Tossed over his shoulder, it dangled past his knees. He had to scratch the back of his leg where it tickled, then adjusted the fall of fringe.

The retreat, by itself, turned the spirit among the soldiers from anticipation of victory to conviction of defeat. Cumberland's army could never have done a more thorough job of demoralizing the prince's men. The days of retreat through England were more difficult than had been the advance, for not only were the men's hearts not in it, but the weather was growing far harsher now in winter than it had been coming into England in late fall. The scant English support there had once been for the cause now evaporated, and the Jacobites found themselves fugitives instead of conquerors, with intelligence reports coming in that both Cumberland and Wade were in hot pursuit. It was in shamed silence the men walked.

Near Cheadle, as they approached the Scottish border, Sinann popped into view, wide-eyed. "Come, quick! *Och,* lad, they've taken Aodán!"

Alarm surged in Ciaran. He looked around for Aodán but of course didn't find him, then moved away from the cluster of his men as they walked and whispered, "Who's taken him?" He glanced around at his contingent. Wandering off to forage or to dally with a local girl was common, and it was only now he realized he hadn't seen Aodán since the night before.

"The townsfolk! He was off in the woods with a camp follower and went missing! I looked everywhere for him, and only now found him in Cheadle! 'Twas a trap! You must rescue him, for they mean to hang him and in a hurry!"

Ciaran turned to his men. "Who has seen Aodán?"

Nobody replied, and many stared at the ground, avoiding eye contact, and continued to walk. Only Calum would look at him, with their father's false smile.

Ciaran's voice betrayed his impatience. "Aye, he's off banging a public woman. Who last saw him, and when?"

"Yesterday," said Calum. "He borrowed a horse from the Atholl Brigade and was headed to town up ahead with the girl." He nodded in that direction. "Said she could offer a more comfortable spot to entertain than on the ground." He shrugged, and his meaningless smile widened. "You needn't worry about him. He'll be catching up with us by morning."

"And you let him go?"

Still smiling, Calum said, "I'm nae his commander, am I?"

For a moment Ciaran wished to punch his brother out onto the ground, but instead he went to their baggage train and began pulling bundles from one of the horses. He threw them to various of his men. "Take these. Carry them yourselves till I return." There was a general murmur of dissent, but he answered it with, "Dinnae whinge at me! Ye dinnae ken the danger Aodán is in!" The men fell silent. Eóin took the packsaddle from the horse, and Ciaran mounted.

He drew his pistol to prime it. As he tapped powder from the flask, he said, "Eóin, take the men. I'll be back as quickly as I can."

"And if you go missing more than a day?"

"Dinnae come after me. Calum will be here, and he'll take the men if I cannae return."

Eóin nodded and threw a sideways glance at Calum. Then Ciaran reached into his sporran for the talisman and kicked his mount to a gallop.

Cheadle wasn't far, for the column was just passing that town.

At a discreet distance Ciaran stopped to tie the horse to a tree, then approached with care, for his manner of dress made him stand out in these parts. But with the talisman pinned to him, pausing every so often and keeping to the shadows, he was able to get to the town square without attracting any attention.

But as he hurried along behind a high dike that took him to the edge of that square, the sight that met his eyes stopped him cold, for he was far too late to save Aodán. Hung by the neck from a gibbet off the side of a public stable, the kilted body of Ciaran's brother-in-law twisted lazily from side to side. Urine dribbled from his brogues and formed a puddle on the ground beneath. A man on a ladder leaned against the gibbet and was in the process of cutting him down. Small clusters of people loitered about, even more ghoulish than those who had watched the execution and moved on, for these people had nothing better to do than watch the execution denouement of body disposal.

As Ciaran watched, unmoving and quite invisible, a man shouted from across the square, "John! Let me buy that body from you!" Ciaran swallowed an objection as he looked to see a man who appeared more well off than the average man this far from a large city. He wore a plain coat and breeches, but they were nearly new and decorated with carved buttons.

The hangman appeared none too prosperous in his ragged coat and stained breeches, and a gleam of avarice lit his eyes. It took little convincing for him to agree to relinquish the body. "How much ye willing to give for it?"

"Four shillings."

"Five, and he's yourn."

"Four and six."

"Done." John finished cutting the rope, and Aodán's body flopped to the ground like a sack of grain. Ciaran flinched.

The buyer then said, utterly businesslike, "For another thruppence, man, would you flay him for me?"

John turned with a puzzled look. "What ye want him skinned for?"

"I desire the hide, to make breeches."

"Ye wish a man's skin for leather?" Even the low fellow whose job it was to hang people was puzzled by this, and his face darkened with distaste.

The buyer made a disparaging noise with his lips. "That's no man, it's a Highland Scot. And a Jacobite in the bargain. More than likely I'll be required to douse the breeches in vinegar more than once to get out the smell."

Ciaran swallowed hard as his bile rose and his vision reddened. From behind the dike, he slowly leveled his pistol, taking aim at the buyer, but Sinann gently pushed the muzzle aside.

"Aodán is dead. I dinnae wish you to join him."

So, horrified, Ciaran watched as the hangman laid Aodán out on the wagon originally intended to take away his body for burial. With a short knife he cut the belt and ripped the kilt and sark away to dump them on the ground. Then, working like a man who was accustomed to butchering sheep, he made slits around Aodán's neck, his wrists, and his ankles, a long one from his neck to his groin, along the undersides of his arms, around his privates, and down each of his legs. Then, slipping his thick fingers under the edges of the cuts he'd made, he pulled, and sliced with the knife, until the skin was away at all the edges.

The blood was bright, even in the overcast day. The hangman flopped Aodán's body over, then cut around the crack of the buttocks, leaving as much usable skin as possible, before setting the knife aside. Ciaran's stomach lurched and sweat stood out on him. He couldn't bear to watch, but neither could he look away.

Then the hangman began to yank the hide from Aodán's back. Horrid tearing sounds came as skin separated from musculature, the sound deepening as the piece of loose skin became larger and larger. Blood ran in rivulets, and dripped from the wagon onto the ground as the hangman continued to rip. A dog came to lap at the puddle that formed. Occasionally the hangman was required to reach for the knife again to loosen a particularly stubborn spot. Before long, Aodán's skin was entirely free of his bloodied body. It flopped about, limp and unwieldy, and the hangman had a struggle to fold in the arms and legs, then roll the dripping thing into a bright red bundle.

Money changed hands, and the buyer took his bloody prize with a twisted smile on his face. There was a fevered gleam in his eye that made plain who was truly the inhuman creature in this place.

Ciaran turned away, dizzied by the spectacle. His stomach lurched again, and he took great gulps of breath to control it. The ground seemed to swell beneath him, then slanted sideways. One hand reached for the stone wall beside him to stay upright. Then his stomach finally won control. He vomited prodigiously onto the ground, then stood over it, retching, unable to stop and wishing he could purge the memory of what he'd just seen.

When he wiped his lower lip with the back of his hand and looked up, he found Sinann hovering, her eyes closed, her legs folded beneath her, and her hands waving slowly in the air. She spoke a few words in a language that sounded a bit like Gaelic but wasn't. Then she opened her eyes and there were tears in them.

Ciaran spat into the puddle at his feet and said, "What did you do?"

Her face flushed red and her eyes snapping with anger, she said, "That skin will never make leather, no matter how the tanner tries. Whatever paltry power I have left, I can assure that for poor Aodán. No Englishman will be wearing his hide for clothing."

Again Ciaran spat, then slipped his pistol into his belt. "Come on, Tinkerbell, I've got to tell my men I couldnae save him." He returned to his men.

In Clifton, just short of the border, a hard-riding messenger approached the Mathesons and asked for Ciorram.

"Here, lad," said Ciaran, dreading what news might be brought now.

"Lord George Murray requests you and your men for a rearguard action. You're to separate from the main force, meet him on the road, and accompany his brigade."

Ciaran nodded, and the boy rode away. There was a muttering from among his men. "We're a-going to die in England, we are."

"Never mind your mouth, Donnchadh. If we die here, it will be so we dinnae all die here and others can see Scotland again." Ciaran waved his men off toward the road down which Cumberland's men would come. Soon they joined the much larger Atholl contingent, and found themselves swallowed up by them. The Mathesons kept together in a cluster, but were surrounded by Murrays.

Lord George chose a spot on the road flanked by high hedges, and deployed the men along it where they would be hidden by the foliage and a shallow ditch. There they lay in wait for the rapidly approaching duke of Cumberland.

All that day they sat and lay on the ground while the bulk of the prince's army continued the retreat northward. The boredom was stultifying and anticipation nearly unbearable.

Donnchadh muttered, " 'Tis useless."

"I told you to shut up."

Seumas Og said, "How many do you think there are?"

"We don't expect to defeat them."

"*Och,* aye," said Donnchadh, "or we would have done so at Derby. What we're doing here is throwing ourselves on Cumberland's sword so Charles can make his escape."

" 'Tis an honorable thing."

" 'Tis suicide."

Calum spoke up. "Your laird has told you to shut your stupid gob, Donnchadh. It is my opinion you ought to obey."

Ciaran threw him a sharp glance, but found no sarcasm in his demeanor. His brother was peering intently southward, where the enemy would approach. Ciaran said to Donnchadh, "If we can delay the Redcoats long enough for the main army to escape to Scotland, where there are reinforcements, we might save them all from dying. We might save the cause. Fighting for the cause is what we came for. If it means dying in England, then so be it."

Donnchadh didn't reply, and instead looked to the dryness of his powder.

While they waited, sitting in loosely drawn-up lines alongside the road, Ciaran watched his brother, whose habitual smile now had a hard edge. It was certain Calum must have been hardest hit by Aodán's death, having been good friends with him all his life, but was putting on the most casual appearance of them all. It seemed nothing could daunt his energy, and now he was cracking wise with the other men, making jokes about their situation. The humor was sharp. Angry. But even Ciaran—who had no desire to laugh at anything anymore—could see it was keeping the men's spirits alive.

He murmured under his breath to the faerie as if he were praying. "Do you wonder if perhaps Calum would not have been the better leader?"

There was silence, but then she said, "Are you thinking, perhaps, of abdicating the lairdship to your brother?"

Ciaran bit his lip, then said, "You wish me to avoid Culloden."

" 'Tis nae what your father wanted, to see the clan go to Calum."

"Tinkerbell, do ye think—"

"Nae for a second, lad." She uttered a disparaging sound. "You are the one meant to lead the Mathesons, and do not wonder about it. You were born to it, and were trained your entire life for it. 'Tis what you were meant for."

"But look—"

"I said, lad, dinnae think it. If you would see a man who will never fulfill his destiny, look at Prince Teàrlach. You've seen how he has withdrawn to his tent to sulk and nurse his anger, and nae longer shows himself on the march. You've seen how he has ceased listening to the clan leaders. He's given over the leadership of this enterprise to the various of his generals. The bonnie prince has given up.

"You, however, will never give up on your people. You lead your men as you were taught, with their best interests in mind at all times, and will continue to do so until all of them or yourself are dead. You're a man who will fulfill his destiny."

"Which is to die."

"All men die, Ciaran."

"Do you think Da was right? That I'll die on Drummossie Moor?"

There was a long silence, then the faerie replied, "I cannae guess. The only way to be certain is if you keep entirely away."

Ciaran said nothing further.

Night had fallen by the time the lookout came with news the Redcoats were approaching. The Atholl Brigade and Ciaran's men readied themselves, hidden behind the hedge along the road. Tension rose as the minutes ticked away. Ciaran's pulse surged, though he was certain he wouldn't die tonight. Dying was one thing, but there had been nobody to say he wouldn't be wounded before Culloden.

A while later, they heard the approach of marching boots along the road. The lines of Jacobites shifted and crouched, and readied their arms. As the moon appeared from behind some clouds, the dismounted dragoons became visible, their red coats gray in the night, their muskets at the ready and glinting. They were hurrying, likely to catch up with the prince and engage him. Ciaran waited, his heart thudding in his chest, more glad for a chance to kill Redcoats than afraid for his own safety. The Jacobites waited for Cumberland's men to march into their grasp.

Then the shouted order came to attack. The Jacobites crashed through the hedge. The barrier of winter-bare branches was as nothing in the fury of the charge. Bursting through to the road,

Ciaran aimed his musket at the nearest Redcoat. He fired, then ran through the cloud of powder smoke to find his target buckling. He drew his pistol to fire again at another man. Then he returned the spent pistol to his belt before sticking his broken bayonet through the throat of the first he'd wounded. In, slash to the side, move on. No movement, thought, or emotion was wasted. It was as efficient as a slaughter of cattle.

Quickly, he slung the musket over his shoulder and drew his sword. Musket balls zinged through the air, and one tugged at the sleeve of his sark. The surge of alarm it gave was heady, and he roared as he ran at a Redcoat who presented his bayonet. Stopping short of his charge he dodged the thrust, and Ciaran was then able to close and hack the dragoon's throat nearly in two.

But another dragoon attacked in his place, and Ciaran found himself parrying a quick sword. The numbers were daunting. It soon became obvious the small contingent of Jacobites would be overwhelmed if they did not retreat. As they withdrew, more dragoons worried their flanks. Men fell from the fire, and those still standing hurried onward.

Ciaran found himself running, and hating himself for it. He hadn't killed enough Redcoats. Not enough English were dead. He wanted to exact revenge, but was forced to flee instead. The Murrays and Mathesons ran until they were free of the pursuit and Cumberland didn't care to chase anymore that night. But though the goal had been accomplished, and the king's men would now be unable to intercept the prince's army before they reached the border, Ciaran felt the burning shame creep up his neck. He'd run before the enemy.

The contingent rejoined the Jacobite army and continued the march, unsupported by disappointed Scots throughout the Lowlands. On Christmas Day they entered Glasgow and found themselves singularly unwelcome. After more than four months on this campaign, their clothes and shoes were worn to tatters, and there was nothing to replace them. Public confidence in the cause had dwindled so much during the march from Derby, the prince's men spent half the morning marching up one street and down the next, then back around, to give the impression of greater numbers. Ciaran searched the faces of those bothering to watch the parade and figured nobody was fooled. So much for the value of reinforcements.

The Mathesons were billeted in a tavern by a graveyard, the

lot of them crammed into three rooms. Ciaran was privileged with the bed in one of the rooms, but that was as far as his status took him anymore. No supplies came to them. Pay had been sporadic, and food was scarce. The men spent the day after Christmas dozing, Ciaran bone-tired and on the verge of a cold, waiting for orders. Eight other men with him sat and lay about the room, drinking from a cask of ale, passing a quaiche back and forth, and Ciaran was glad for it. The ale dulled the pain of his fever as well as his disappointment in the prince.

Seumas Og sat on the chamber pot in the corner, suffering from diarrhea and making the others groan with the smell of it.

"Och," said Donnchadh, "can you open the window, Alasdair? I believe your brother has eaten something he would better have left alone."

Alasdair shoved on the casement and managed to open it some. "There was a dog lying dead in the street yesterday, about a week gone, I'd say. Did it taste good then, Seumas Og?"

Ciaran groaned as his already touchy stomach lurched. "Shut up, Alasdair. Let him do his business, then set it on the ledge outside."

Poor Seumas Og was purpling at the face with the cramps in his gut.

Donnchadh muttered, "I'm hungry enough to eat a rotting dog myself."

Calum rose from the floor and left the room. Ciaran watched him go.

Eóin, who also watched Calum go, waited till he was well out of earshot, then said softly, "Calum isnae so sanguine about Aodán's death as he would have us believe."

"We've all taken it hard. 'Twas an ugly thing happened to him." Ciaran squeezed his eyes shut to block the memory of poor Aodán's bloody and skinless body. It was treason for which he'd been hung and flayed, and they all knew it would be their own fate if they failed in this cause.

Seumas Og finished straining, replaced the lid on the chamber pot as he sighed with the relief of it, and handed it to Alasdair to be set on the ledge outside the window.

Eóin continued to Ciaran, "I only wondered whether you'd noticed."

"Aye. I have. He's my brother, after all." Ciaran turned over in his bed and wondered how much of the ache in his joints was from the cold room and how much from fever. There had been no peats for the fire since dawn, and what little heat there was came from close bodies in the small room.

Calum returned with a jug of whiskey, reclaimed his spot on the floor, took a swig, then passed it to Ciaran. "Here, for your cold."

Ciaran rose on one elbow, sniffed the jug, and jerked back at the harsh whiff. "*Och,* how can ye stand to drink whiskey that is-nae ours?"

" 'Tis what was to be had. Drink it. It will either kill you or help your cold. Either way, the pain will ease."

Ciaran grunted, then shrugged and took a drink. It was like fire going down, and heated his gut like a torch lighting a bonfire. He gasped, then said, " 'Tis witch's piss!"

The men laughed, and Ciaran took another drink, for it did help the pain in his bones. Then he passed the jug on to Eóin. Ciaran lay back on the bunk and let the whiskey seep into his flesh.

Donnchadh said, "The prince is sulking, they say."

"He isnae," said Seumas Og. "He's tipping the velvet to a young cunny these days."

Gregor's attention perked. "The prince has a woman friend?"

Ciaran said, "Nae. She's a woman, and she's his friend, but he isnae banging her."

"Is, too," Seumas Og insisted.

"Is not. He's talking her into raising money to pay us. And feed us."

Seumas Og crossed his arms and raised his chin. "I dinnae believe it. It isnae as if he's got an interest in us anymore."

"Shut up," said Eóin. "You sound like a jilted lover."

"I only—"

"I said, shut up!" Eóin was half up from the floor, ready to pounce on Seumas Og, who cringed in the corner and shut up.

Ciaran glared at the both of them but said nothing. Eóin settled back into his spot on the floor, and deathly silence fell over the group. The anger on Eóin's face was palpable, but Ciaran felt none of it. He wanted none of it. Anymore, he didn't even want to go home because he knew he couldn't. He knew he was fated to live this through and die with the cause. The jug came around again, and he drank the vile witch's piss until he felt nothing, not even the pain of his illness.

Lying on his bed, he tried to think of Leah but couldn't. She had nothing to do with this. She was one of the nice things—the pretty things—that had been a part of his life back when there had been hope. Her beauty, her warmth, her love for him were all things that had become surreal. The things that were real were cold, hunger, lice, and knowing the future was hollow.

The room spun with too much alcohol on an empty stomach. Leah. He had to regain Leah. Needed to feel her presence. Wanted to remember her touch. He was losing her.

Then he remembered the white cockade on his bonnet, and reached into his coat pocket for it. He pulled the artificial flower from the blue wool, then stuffed the hat back into his pocket. The white ribbon was now gray and dirty, nothing like the shining white badge it had once been. One bit of petal had come undone, and so one side was a limp loop of ribbon. But it had been given to him by Leah. Dear Leah. Dear, sweet, beautiful Leah. In an alcoholic haze he put the bit of ribbon to his nose as if it were a real flower, but he wasn't trying to smell a rose. He wished to catch the scent of his *annsachd*. And for one delusional moment, he thought it was there.

The next day his low-grade fever broke, replaced by a sopping sweat and a raging hangover, and he spent the remaining time in Glasgow with a deep, hacking cough. After a week, when Ciaran was nearly recovered, the Jacobite army moved north.

Two weeks into January, icy rain soaked Ciaran to the skin, dripping from his bonnet and from the folds of his threadbare kilt. His targe was gone, having been stepped on by a horse and broken to splinters a week before. Nearly a month had passed since crossing back into Scotland. Though the reinforcements had swelled the Jacobite numbers to about eight thousand, local support was nevertheless dwindling. Supplies were dangerously low, the men were hungry, and morale was no better than it had been during the retreat from England. Now Ciaran and his men were lined up, more or less as part of the Atholl Brigades, on the crest of Falkirk Muir, looking across at lines of Redcoats.

He felt dead inside. Nothing left but hard determination to see the fight through to the end with as much honor as was at his command. No thought remaining but to kill the enemy. His musket was in his hands, primed and ready, as was the pistol in his belt. He stared across at the mounted dragoons, waiting for the moment when the shooting would begin. His heart was as cold as the January rain, pounding hard in his chest, but with nothing more than anticipation of exertion. He knew he wouldn't die today, for his father had foretold it.

A great shout went up from the dragoons, and they charged. The Highlanders waited calmly until the Redcoats were within range, then raised their muskets and loosed a hail of fire. Through the copious white smoke, quickly thinned by the heavy rain, Ciaran watched holes open up in the Redcoat lines, then slung his musket and drew his pistol to fire again. Jacobites charged as the dragoons turned to flee, and chased them back to scatter their own infantry lines.

Ciaran ran with the charge as the Jacobite lines attacked the confused dragoons. He slipped his pistol into his belt to draw his sword, but the quarters among the horses were too close, and Brigid in his left hand was of more use. The rain beat on them all, washing the enemy blood from his hands even as it flowed over them. His sword clanged with a dragoon's, who then was dispatched by another Highlander. Ciaran hamstrung a horse with a great whack of his sword to a rear leg, then slammed Brigid into the heart of its rider when it fell. He moved on, and soon it was apparent the entirety of George's forces was in disarray. Few stood up to the assault. After only a few minutes, Ciaran found himself standing among the fallen dragoons, watching through the rain the shadows of those in retreat.

Finally he felt something, and it was disgust. There was some fighting off to his left, but it seemed distant and dreamlike. He couldn't see much through the rain. Now he looked around to find most of his men still standing. Eóin was there. Calum. Gregor. Others.

"Who's missing?" He shouted over the falling rain.

Eóin replied with heavy voice, "I saw Alasdair MacGregor die. Other than that, I dinnae ken."

This flank of Jacobites was still advancing, so Ciaran waved his men on through the rain. They slogged through mud and over slippery rocks, carrying the weight of their sodden wool kilts and coats, chilled to the bone but feeling it not at all. There were some MacKenzies and MacDonalds ahead, advancing behind the fleeing Redcoats, and the Atholl Brigades were following. They passed abandoned artillery pieces mired on the slope, the horses saved but the cannon abandoned.

Soon they came upon the Redcoat camp, deserted. Finally a spark of joy lit a small corner of Ciaran's heart as he realized not

only had they won the battle, but they'd also captured supplies.
So quickly had the *Sasunnaich* fled, they'd taken nothing with
them. Hungry Jacobites swarmed over the cluster of tents, and
shouts of pleasure announced discoveries of food and ammuni-
tion. In one tent the Matheson men crowded around as Ciaran
broke open a crate and began handing out strings of powder car-
tridges. Then he took a shiny new bayonet and replaced the broken one he'd been carrying since Prestonpans.

As he secured it to the muzzle of his musket, a faint glow of
hope warmed him. He wasn't entirely certain what he hoped for
anymore, but the victory and the supplies made him think perhaps all was not lost.

Soaked and dripping, he and his men settled into the otherwise dry tent. Other crates they found contained hardtack and
wine. The men fell upon the dried meat, but Ciaran found himself
more interested in the wine than the food. He opened a bottle, sat
on the camp cot belonging to the tent's previous occupant, and
took a long drink. It felt good going down, and warmed his belly
in a way the hardtack could never have done. Other bottles were
opened and passed among the men.

"Long live King James," he said, raising his bottle high.

"Aye!" echoed the men, "to the health of King James!" They
all drank deeply, and Ciaran more deeply than any. His empty
stomach sent the wine quickly through his body. Soon he hardly
noticed his freezing, soaked clothing.

"Lad," said Sinann by his ear.

"Go away."

"There's something you need to learn."

Ciaran glanced over at her for her to continue, and she did.

"Your father never told you about your grandfather. Nae Iain
Mór, but his own father, Kenneth." A shake of Ciaran's head, and
Sinann continued, "Are you aware your father hated his father?"

"A man cannae hate his father." The whisper was low, as in
prayer.

"Yer grandfather was a drunk, Ciaran. He spent his days so
deep in the drink he was no father at all. He was mean to all who
loved him, until they hated him. He drank to kill the pain of living. I thought ye might want to know that. And think hard on it."

The men were still drinking to James' health. Over and over
they upended bottles. Ciaran looked at his own bottle and felt the
warmth in him. He whispered, " 'Tis is a comfort."

"Too much a comfort. With it you could spend all your final days with no knowledge of your life. You could be exactly like the one man your father hated most."

That struck Ciaran. He stared at the bottle some more, wishing to drink himself to sleep, but now found he couldn't. "Here," he said, and passed the bottle off to Eóin. Then he reached for a piece of hardtack and began to gnaw on it.

Later he did sleep, curled up on the cot with his dirk in his hand and sword and musket at his side, and a belly full of English beef.

The following morning, bolstered by food, sleep, and victory, the prince's men woke to a day that held promise. When the order came to fall in for the march to Inverness, an odd sensation skittered up Ciaran's back. Drummossie Moor, known to his father as Culloden Moor, lay between Inverness and Nairn.

CHAPTER 15

He pinned on a plain, round brooch to secure the plaid to the shoulder of his jacket.

The house in Nairn was small, though it was also the largest dwelling in the village, and shabby in the bargain. It stood on the square, next to the town's only tavern and across from the church. In that rented house Leah passed the winter with Edwin and Martha, far from the struggles for the larger cities and towns, and far from the Jacobite sieges of Fort William and Stirling and Blair Castles. The news was that Edinburgh had been taken again by the king's forces, and Leah wished to return there, to the comfortable house where the beds were feather rather than straw, and the cold night did not seep through cracks in the door and window frames. But Edwin said he deemed it best to stay out of harm's way throughout the conflict. The bombardment had frightened the pants off him, so they would stay in Nairn until the troubles were over, no matter how small, ugly, and smelly the rooms might be.

Spring approached, but kept its distance in this northern country. The only sign of it yet was a scent of earth and sea in the air that had been frozen and odorless only days before.

At first, for weeks Leah had been under the scrutiny of
Martha. There was no privacy in this tiny house, and the vigil
was relaxed immediately when it became apparent Leah was
not breeding a new Matheson. As relieved as Martha was, the
disappointment had been crushing for Leah. She spent days
curled in her bed, grieving for Ciaran and for her hope, feeling
it bleed from her. She gripped his rosary in her fingers, the
smooth ivory beads hard between her knuckles, and prayed for
his safety.

Reports of the Jacobite retreat from Derby reached Edwin,
who crowed the news, his voice booming in the close, rickety
rooms. Gleefully, he continued to report of this skirmish or that
hanging, and day by day Leah became more fearful Ciaran may
not have survived. Even were he still alive, the ultimate failure of
the cause would mean his execution or outlawry. To save his life
he would be forced to leave the country. She would never see him
again, and now there would be nothing at all left of him for her.

Leah lived her life every day in dread of bad news, torn by the
knowledge that the worst would be to not hear at all.

So her heart leapt with terror and hope the day she heard
shouting and gunfire nearby. To the window at once, she threw
aside the curtain to look out. In the midst of drifting white clouds
of powder smoke there were men across the square. Kilted men.
Her gaze went from one to the next in search of a long, black
queue, hoping against hope one of them might be Ciaran.

They were running. Dirks and swords out they fled, and soon
she could see the soldiers in pursuit up the road. A guard of
king's men ran after, bristling with bayonets. One luckless Highlander fell behind, and was skewered for it. Leah gasped as she
watched him fall, screaming, to the road. He still screamed,
writhing in the mud, as the king's men continued away in their
pursuit and the wounded man's fellows ran on.

Leah turned from the window and reached for her cloak by the
door.

"You're not going out there." Edwin stood in the door to the
adjoining room.

"That man needs help."

"He'll get it from someone other than yourself, if you wish to
not be arrested for giving aid to the enemy."

"If nobody sees—"

His voice went high with panic. "Are you mad? There are British army soldiers everywhere. They'd be certain to see—"

"He's *dying!* He's in pain, and I can't bear to sit here and do nothing."

"That is exactly what you'll do, girl! Now, sit down!" Edwin pointed. "In that chair, there!"

Leah stared at the floor, wishing for courage to simply don her cloak and go to the poor man outside. But she hadn't any courage, and so she sat. Appalled, she covered her ears to banish the horrible sounds of the dying Jacobite, pleading desperately in Gaelic and English for help that wasn't coming. She sat by the fire and wept quietly as the cries dwindled. Finally they went silent. Leah trembled and prayed, selfishly but fervently, thanking God it hadn't been Ciaran.

Sometime later, Martha returned from the market and settled into a chair in the sitting room with a book. Leah took little note of her presence as she remained huddled on the footstool near the hearth, trying to not cry anymore. Martha stared for a moment, as if wanting to ask what was wrong, but then glanced toward the window. At that moment the townsfolk were carrying away the dead body outside. She kept quiet and focused on her book.

Soon Martha's head lifted from her book. "Listen," she said.

Leah looked stupidly over at her. "What?"

"Listen."

Her head turned toward the windows, Leah strained to hear. Drums. A marching cadence. Her heart in her throat, she picked up her skirts, hurried to the window, and pushed aside the curtain. "O God, let it be him." Alive, and among a strong contingent.

Martha returned her attention to her book and said with an edge to her voice, "Indeed. Your father's men have been assigned to the duke of Cumberland. They are on the march, so I expect it would be him."

Her lips pressed together, Leah knew Martha hadn't really thought she'd meant Father. The comment had been a rebuke. Even more, Leah's heart sank when the approaching men entered the square and she saw they were Redcoats. She had wanted them to be Jacobites, and now found herself in confusion at her disappointment, for her father could very well be among these soldiers. She should be glad to see them, but she wasn't. Guilt singed her soul.

"They're here to save us from those who would harm us." Martha's voice still had that edge of condemnation.

Leah glanced toward the stairs to be certain Edwin was not eavesdropping, then whispered, "They're here to kill someone I care for."

Martha looked up. "And you care nothing for your father?"

Leah turned away from the window. "Of course I do. I don't want him to die, either. But I can't help thinking that if they would all just leave it alone and go home, we could all live in peace, and Ciaran"—her voice failed for a moment and she had to clear her throat—"Ciaran would live. Everyone would live, and nobody would have to hate anymore."

Lines of strain appeared on Martha's face, and she shook her head woefully. "You live in a dream world, Leah. There will always be war, for what else would men do with themselves? Killing each other seems to be all they ever care about." She also glanced toward the stair, lest Edwin hear and come to volunteer his perspective of the issue.

Leah pushed aside the curtain at the window again, to observe the men passing by. The infantry marched in rigid drill order, their uniforms well tended and their weapons shiny and whole.

Then came dragoons. Row after row of men on horseback, red uniforms like a river of blood. Her father was there, riding at the head of his company, and her heart leapt. His face was hard, his eyes expressionless. What he was thinking, she couldn't imagine. She'd never seen him like this. Though she'd seen him in command of his company, leading men and making decisions, she'd never before witnessed him at the most serious work of his job. She'd never seen him ride into battle. It made her shiver.

She continued to watch him, until he rode past and out of sight. "Where are they going, do you think?" she asked Martha. The curtain fell back into place, and she leaned her forehead against the wooden window frame.

Having resumed her reading, Martha said absently, "Inverness, no doubt. Stuart has based himself there, and they've been harrying the countryside for months. The army must rout them out."

Leah blinked, and peered hard at Martha. "The Jacobites are in Inverness?"

Martha looked up. "You knew it."

Leah's chest and face warmed as anger rose. "I knew there

were sieges. In Stirling and other places. I had no idea Stuart was in Inverness. Why were you hiding that fact from me?"

Martha's face reddened. "Come, Leah. We hid nothing."

"You did. You were afraid I'd go to him."

Finally Martha closed the book, folded her hands in her lap, and looked straight into Leah's eyes. "Nothing could be further from the truth. Nevertheless, I'm now beginning to wonder if it wouldn't have been best to keep it from you. You've been pining about this place as if your entire life depended on seeing that wild man again. Your father would be mortified were he to learn of it." She returned to her book with one last comment: "Besides, your Highlander is more than likely dead by now."

A sudden calm came over Leah as she stared at Martha. All at once nothing mattered but her need to see Ciaran. What Martha, Edwin, or even her father might say on the matter was of no consequence. Her first thought was to declare her intent, then storm from the room and run to Inverness, but the anger hardened as she realized it would get her nowhere. Her father and his men were now between her and the prince's base of operations.

Instead, she took a deep breath, arranged her face in a bland, wistful smile, and said, "I suppose that's true. I cared for him very much, but there's no denying he cannot still be alive."

A great sigh escaped Martha, and she nodded. "Yes. Sad to say, but Jacobite casualties have been high. There's a very good chance he hasn't survived." Then she smiled up at Leah and said cheerily, "So you must look at the bright side. Your father has come to Nairn and will surely visit you while he's here."

Incredibly, the thought of seeing her father did perk up Leah's spirits. "You think he'll visit?"

"He must. He knows you're here, and tomorrow is Cumberland's birthday. Surely the duke won't have them march tomorrow."

A smile crept to Leah's face. "Surely not." Father was nearby, and a visit would be terribly nice. It had been so long since she'd seen him, her heart fluttered at the thought. Just as she had done as a little girl when Mother had announced impending visits. He'd always brought her something, and though she knew he wouldn't have the chance this time, it would nevertheless be good to see his face again and talk to him.

All the next day Leah waited. She sewed, read from a book, and sewed some more, every so often looking out the window in hopes of seeing a red officer's uniform in the square. But the day passed, and in the evening the sun set without so much as a glimpse of her father. Gradually her heart sank. Cumberland must have gone on to Inverness. Now she was decided she must go as well. She must find Ciaran before the British army did.

It was April 15, birthday of the Duke of Cumberland, and the day before the battle Dylan Dubh had said would end this war and possibly Ciaran's life. Ciaran's belly was a tight knot with the hunger, well beyond a mere growling stomach. There had been nothing to eat since yesterday but a single onion for each of them, and those had been a wondrous find. Pay had stopped two weeks before. The prince's men were required to go far to forage the depleted countryside. Even now most of Ciaran's own men were not near, but were away in search of food.

The gathered force awaited the approach of Cumberland's army. By all accounts, reported by men retreating from Nairn, the Redcoat numbers were high. They were well fed and well equipped. Ciaran now fully understood what was to happen on Drummossie Moor, and why. But there was nothing he could do about it. There had never been any way for him to prevent this. He sat on a stone and laid his musket across his knees, his head down.

Sinann's voice came. "Would ye care for bread and cheese, lad?"

Ciaran looked up and sighed. "I would care for the entire army to have it."

"I cannae. I havenae the power to feed them all."

A wry smile touched his mouth. "Nae fishes and loaves from the faerie, aye?"

Her voice was low and sulky. "I do what I can, and dinnae talk of what I cannot. Do ye wish the cheese, or nae?"

He looked around at his men, only two-thirds of whom were there. Calum, Seumas Og MacGregor, Eóin, Gregor, Donnchadh, and thirteen others were still with him, but Aodán Hewitt and Alasdair MacGregor were dead, and nine had gone off to forage. Ciaran almost hoped they'd deserted, for he didn't wish to see any more of his kinsmen die than was necessary. He said, "Can ye give me a sack of onions?"

"But laddie—"

"They'll believe onions. Were I to produce a cheese, they would think I had been holding out on them. Give me a great sack of onions and they'll believe it is today's ration from the prince."

The faerie sighed. "Aye." A wave of her hand, and a rough sack, lumpy with onions, appeared at his feet. He took it and rose to distribute the food to his men.

At nightfall, orders came from the prince through Lord George Murray's chain of command they were to march toward the Redcoat camp at Nairn. It being the duke's birthday, Murray was counting on surprising the enemy after a night of heavy celebration. The Jacobite forces formed up as best they could, given their depleted numbers and poor condition, and began the trek. Ciaran's Mathesons marched with the Atholl Brigade, having been more or less assimilated by the much larger group, and were in the vanguard of the assault.

Cloud cover hid even the sliver of waning moon, and they marched through pitch darkness. The first column outdistanced the rest of the army so badly they often had to stop and wait for the rest to catch up. Nevertheless, though the terrain was soggy and rough, wanting to suck Ciaran's worn brogues from his feet, the Atholl Brigade approached Nairn well ahead of Perth and the prince. They stopped to wait, most men falling exhausted to the ground, in their ranks.

Ciaran took this moment to kneel. His heart pounded in his chest, and the tips of his fingers tingled with numbness from the cold, exhaustion, and hunger. His arms and legs felt heavy, unwilling to move. Leaning hard on his musket, he whispered, "Dear God, give me the strength to do what I must. Allow me the courage of my father, to not shirk my duty." Gradually, as he whispered under his breath, his body calmed. "Help me to die with honor tomorrow . . ." He looked up, and saw the sky was becoming light. Cold sweat broke out to make him shiver, and he closed his eyes as he continued, ". . . today." A wave of self-pity tried to overtake him, but he fought it back until it was gone. "Please watch over my family, that they might be safe in the days and years to come. Especially, keep safe your daughter Leah, for she is my heart and my life, and she hasnae any real home nor family to speak of. Keep her in your bosom and let her know I love her as You do." He crossed himself, "*In nomine Patri, et Filii, et Spiritus Sancti, amen.*"

Strength seeped back into his limbs. His pulse was slowing,

and he was now able to stand. Men ahead were shuffling and grumbling, nudging with their brogues those who had collapsed to the ground to sleep. They were not nearly close enough to Nairn yet to make it there before full daybreak. There would be no surprise attack that night, and as expected the order came to return to Inverness, lest they be discovered here at daylight. With heart reconciled to dying, Ciaran turned with his men for the re-treat to the battleground.

Hours later, the prince's hungry, exhausted army found them-selves once again on Drummossie Moor, near Culloden House. A light rain was coming down. Word came, spreading through the ranks like wildfire, that Cumberland was on the march toward them. They would be forced to make a stand.

"Tinkerbell, let me have the bread and cheese." Damn what the men will think; he would feed them, and it would more than likely be the last thing he could do for them.

Without a word, or even an appearance, Sinann produced two good-sized cheeses by Ciaran's feet and a sack filled with ban-nocks. He picked up the cheeses, put one under an arm and broke the other, then turned to the others.

"Here. Eat." He parceled out chunks of the food as equitably as possible, and none of the eighteen men remaining under his command made the least murmur. They ate, then wrapped them-selves in their plaids to curl up in wet grass and rest. Ciaran fell into a deep, utterly exhausted sleep.

An Atholl colonel, one of Lord George's aides, approached, and addressed Ciaran. "Are these all your men, Ciorram?"

Ciaran raised his head and said sleepily, "All as are left." He struggled to his feet out of respect for rank, but wished to return to the soggy ground and unconsciousness.

"Where are the others?"

"Off foraging, for the most part."

"Go retrieve them, then. We'll need them today."

It took a moment for Ciaran to decide whether to even reply to that. Then he said, "Aye. Straight away, sir."

Busily, the aide went along his way, and Ciaran watched him go. When the man was out of sight, the laird of Ciorram pulled his plaid around himself once more and lay back down on the ground. He'd be damned if he was going to force anyone to return to this battle and be murdered.

No sooner had he closed his eyes, it seemed, than the army

was roused by shouted orders to form ranks. Wearily, Ciaran and
his remaining Mathesons climbed to their feet in the cold rain
and wind. They found their position, a single line directly behind
the Atholl Brigade at the right of the battle lines forming. As they
waited in their ranks, the rain gave way to drizzle, and patches of
sunlight emerged, but the cold wind persisted. Men pulled their
wet plaids around themselves, more to keep their powder dry
than for any comfort, and they waited.

A red line appeared on the rolling horizon, across the broad,
muddy field. Ciaran found himself breathing more deeply, his
blood surging with the familiar hatred as he watched the *Sasunn-
naich* form their lines. Pain and exhaustion drained, replaced by
thudding heart and grim determination. He stared across the way,
eager now to charge and get this over with.

Cannon reported, and Ciaran jumped, startled in spite of himself. Other artillery replied with a dull thud in the distance. To the
left, he could see Highlanders falling and others adjusting to fill
the ranks as their own artillery proceeded to harry the Redcoats.
Visibility was poor. All Ciaran could tell was that men on the
front line were falling. The numbers were appalling.

"Grapeshot!" someone shouted, his voice cracking with terror. "The bastards are using grapeshot!" Lord George was also
shouting something, but Ciaran couldn't hear what it was. Lines
continued to shift, filling in holes, but none broke.

Finally the order was given to charge, and the pipes relayed it
to the men. With a roar, the Mathesons ran with the Murrays.
Musket shot flew among them, cutting the ranks of the Atholl
Brigades to pieces. The lines before Ciaran opened. At sight of
the Redcoats he fired his musket, then slung it to draw his sword
as men to his right flew apart in hails of blood.

To his left, he had a glimpse of Calum, sword raised, running
with full intent. At that moment his brother's head burst apart,
splattering like an uncooked pudding. Swallowing his shock,
Ciaran erupted in a roar, looked to the front, and kept running,
leaping over fallen soldiers. Shot pelted Atholl's men, hitting
many in the back so they fell forward. Ciaran glanced to the right,
and found they'd been flanked. An enclosure had hidden a number of Redcoats, who now fired from behind the stone dike. The
sway of men at the Jacobite center pushed him toward that fire.

Ciaran resisted the crush and pulled his pistol with his left to
shoot toward the flanking fire, but never knew whether he hit any-

thing. He returned the pistol to his belt. Sword raised once more, he charged into the approaching Redcoat lines. Survival mattered less now than did taking the damned *Sasunnaich* with him. Hate drove him forward. He stumbled over the bodies of those who had fallen before him, but kept running toward the enemy.

Closed on the Redcoat line, just as he hauled back to strike, a searing pain ripped into his chest and he screamed. The next second, nothing.

CHAPTER 16

The sgian dubh tucked into the top of his right stocking was ancient, an heirloom of deer horn and steel. The blade was delicate, having survived much use and many sharpenings.

Leah awoke before dawn, certain to find her cousins still asleep. Edwin's snores reverberated in the upstairs room. Now was her chance. She crept from her bed and opened the trunk in which she kept her linens. At the bottom was the tartan dress she'd brought from Ciorram. Quickly she put it on over her shift and blouse, then drew on her wool cloak and pulled the hood up over her snood.

In utter silence she crept from her room and down the stairs to the square. Head down and in a purposeful hurry, she set out along the road to Inverness.

The distance, she quickly learned, was much farther than she'd walked in her life. Frequently she was forced to find a place to sit and rest, and by the time the sun rose, her feet were aching. More and more slowly she walked as the pain grew. A storm came up, sending sheets of rain, and the wind blew her skirts and cloak out before her. A small voice in the back of her mind implored her to give up this quest for a man she couldn't be certain was even alive, but she took deep breaths and pictured Ciaran in her imagination. Surely he waited for her at the end of the road. She couldn't contemplate anything else. She kept on.

The weather abated some, confining itself to a light drizzle, and as the sun came out, she realized it was quite high. Noon, at least. She began to pass clusters of pack animals and women at work, and wondered if she had come upon Cumberland's camp. The assemblage was quite familiar. She'd seen many a baggage train since Father's return from the Continent, and had seen the sorts of women who followed an army on the march. Moving on, she soon left behind the motley assemblage.

Then she came over a slight rise, and what she saw stopped her heart. Immediately before her, the British army was formed into battle lines, their backs a broad expanse of red that spread to her left and right. There were bagpipes somewhere. They wailed in the distance, the sound eerie as it drifted in the wind amid the rain. Men nearby shouted orders to each other, readying for a deadly fight. Their voices were tense. Dire. Fell. They seemed hardly human in their preparation for killing, and possibly dying.

Her heart leapt and began thudding recklessly in her chest. She wanted to shout for them to stop, that nothing was worth what they were about to do, but though her mouth opened, no sound would come out. Glancing wildly around at the soldiers near her, she then ducked to the left. There were some trees down by a river in that direction, which might afford some protection.

Before she could get far, there was an explosion in the midst of the ranks. Smoke rose. More explosions followed. Shouting broke out, and the tempo of the pipes quickened. Leah broke into a run, ducking. Spent musket balls began to fall around her, dropping like hail, and she hurried faster to be out of the way when the shooters could be closer and more deadly.

She thought she might never reach those trees. Lurching and stumbling, she crossed the rough, soggy ground, flinching at each explosion so near. Finally she reached the shelter and threw herself onto the ground behind a great oak.

Tears of panic tried to come, but she wouldn't let them. Father had always spoken with such contempt of soldiers who showed their fear; she could never allow herself to be like that. She swallowed her terror, and under her breath prayed for Ciaran's life. Pleading with God to let him not be in this battle, she clutched the ivory and gold rosary in the pocket under her skirts for whatever power it might possess.

A cannonball crashed through the trees and sent chunks of pale green wood flying. Leah screamed and cringed. The firing was soon joined by the clash of steel against steel. Men shouted. Some screamed. Horses shrieked. It went on, and on, and on.

It seemed like days. By the time the cannon had stopped firing and the swords were silenced, Leah was nearly too exhausted to move. Musket fire dwindled to an occasional report in the distance, now replaced by the strident screams of wounded men who knew they were about to die and who no longer cared who witnessed their terror. When she thought it might be safe, she rose from her hiding place and emerged on wobbly legs to survey the field.

The wind had carried away the smoke, leaving only the occasional wisp of a freshly discharged musket in the distance. Leah approached a dike at the edge of the battlefield, and as she came near, the smell of blood was so thick it choked her. Warm and metallic, meaty, it made her gag so she coughed.

Other spectators were running onto the field with none of the hesitation she felt. Women in search of husbands and sons, and also looters who hurried to tear valuables from dead bodies, both Jacobite and Hanoverian. Riderless horses wandered, some wounded and limping. Dead animals lay here and there, huge mounds among the piles of broken and bloody men. The sharp smell of gunpowder wafted across the field to her and stung her nose.

Copious tears came. They wet her cheeks and dripped from her chin as she gazed upon the carnage. The screams and moans of the wounded rose everywhere, dwindling only as red-coated soldiers walked among the bodies and thrust their bayonets into those they found still alive.

Leah pulled the hood of her cloak over her head and made her way around the enclosure. On the field, blood stood in pools. Faces of dead Highlanders were stark white splashed with black mud and fresh blood. Bodies lay upon bodies, nearly like cordwood in some places. She picked her way among them, searching for Ciaran's face and praying she wouldn't find it.

So many! Moving across the field, she wondered if she would find him even if he was there. Two women near the center of the mass of bodies were hauling a dead man from the ground to put him into a cart. She was forced to fight the urge to run over there to make certain it wasn't Ciaran they were taking away.

As she watched, those women were approached by one of the king's men. Without exchange of any kind, he ran one of them through with his bayonet. The other woman screamed and turned to run, but the soldier gave chase and within three steps stabbed her as well. She collapsed, screaming until he stuck her through the throat as casually as if he were stamping out a beetle in a garden.

Leah ducked, trembling with terror, and saw the tartan of her dress peeking from below the hem of her cloak. Quickly, she trampled the ends of the cloth into the mud and blood, covering the woven squares lest she be taken for a Jacobite lass.

As she did so, she realized she was becoming one in her heart.

Knees barely able to hold her up now, she continued the horrific task of ascertaining Ciaran was not on the field.

Then, just ahead of her, a sword moved in the mud.

Of course, she was seeing things, for there was nobody near it. But it moved again. She stopped walking and watched it. The sword obliged her with another lunge across the soft ground. Her skin tingled, and she felt light-headed, as if about to swoon. The sword was covered with mud, but she could see it was a very old silver weapon with a swept hilt, rather than the steel baskets so common on this field. She stepped toward it, and it jerked away from her. Again she stepped forward, and it retreated before her.

"What is this?"

There was no reply, and she wondered why she'd expected one. But she continued to follow the sword a few more feet, where it stopped. Then it leapt into the air and came down to embed its point in the ground near a cluster of dead men.

"What? What am I to see?" She looked around, but saw nothing that made sense.

"Och," came a small voice. "He was right about you from the start. You havenae a brain in your head."

Every hair on Leah's body stood up, and she took a step backward as a small, pale woman dressed in white gossamer appeared before her, one hand resting on the hilt of the sword. Pointed ears poking through her short, feathery locks and white wings gave away her race. But though she was obviously not human, her eyes were red with weeping, and her face stained with tears.

"You're a faerie."

"And you're a *Sasunnach* idiot. Hurry and pull him from there before he dies, ye sumph!"

"He . . ." She blinked, confused.

"Ciaran! Get him!" The faerie pointed. "Under there. He yet breathes, but nae for long if you dinnae quit your gawping."

Leah's heart leapt, and she hurried to shove aside the body of a dead Highlander. Beneath, she spotted the familiar rusty red of Ciaran's kilt and a shirt that had once been white but was now as red as a dragoon's coat.

"O God! Ciaran!" She lifted his head from the muck in which it lay, and found it bleeding as badly as his chest. A whimper escaped her and tears came anew, but she swallowed them as she saw he was breathing. Slowly and not deeply, but his chest was still moving, and his color was not quite the same gray as the bodies among which he lay. "Oh, Ciaran!"

Looking up, she saw the Redcoat assassins were closer than before. Finally she was galvanized into action, for it was up to her now to make certain they would not murder Ciaran.

Quickly she unbuckled his belt and pulled the tartan kilt from him.

"The dirk!" said the faerie. "Use his dirk!"

There was a knife in a scabbard lashed to a sheepskin around his shin. She took it and cut the bindings of those leggings, then the thongs that tied his deerskin shoes to his feet. They and the tartan stockings came away, and she tossed them as far as she could. Then with the knife she slit his shirt up the front and along the sleeves, and pulled it from under him. A small knife was strapped to his upper arm. She cut its binding and quickly slipped the tiny weapon into her bodice. With that gone, Ciaran was completely naked and without the least thing to indicate his affiliation in the battle.

For a moment she gawked at the enormous red hole in his chest, still seeping blood, directly over his heart. It was inconceivable he could still be alive with a wound like that.

Then she looked up and gasped to find her father riding toward her, his sword in hand and a hard look on his face. It was an evil glare, his mouth set in a twisted way that sent a shiver of terror and revulsion through her. Unable to see her face beneath the cloak hood, he must think she was a Scot. For a moment she struggled with the urge to reveal herself, knowing he could still

murder Ciaran. Indeed, she realized he would be more likely to
kill Ciaran were he to learn she'd come to the battleground in
search of him. But she couldn't let that happen, no matter what
Father might do to her, and she dropped to her knees over Ciaran,
careful to hide his face.

"Och!" She cried in a Scottish accent she pulled from her
memories of Glen Ciorram. *"Och, m'annsachd! M'annsachd!
Tha gaol agam ort! Tha gaol agam ort! Och, m'annsachd!"* Continuing to weep and murmur the only Gaelic words she knew, she
listened for the progress of the dragoon horse. It paused nearby
for a long moment that seemed an eternity. There was a *zing* of
metal on metal as Father's saber was pulled from its sheath. Leah
began to weep, truly horrified at what he must be intending. But
then the horse moved away. She waited, still with her arms pro-
tectively around Ciaran, until Father was far enough away for her
to feel safe in moving.

"Hurry! You'll need a horse if you dinnae wish to carry him
away yourself!"

The faerie's voice hauled her thoughts back to the immediate
need, and she looked around for a horse. One wandered not far
away, whole and not limping. She walked over to it casually,
calmly, and took the reins. It followed her obediently to where
Ciaran lay.

Leah was taller than most women, but was neither large nor
particularly strong. Ciaran, on the other hand, was a very tall and
solidly built man. Though he'd become appallingly thin since the
last she'd seen him, it was all she could do to pull him from the
mud. Nevertheless, as she did so, he suddenly seemed weight-
less. Magically, as if he were an empty sack, she lifted him onto
the horse, and the flying faerie guided his leg over the saddle. Together they situated him, slumped over the saddle and his head
dangling aside the horse's neck. He appeared dead. Leah took the
reins again.

"Dinnae leave the sporran! Nor the sword and dirk!"

Hurrying, she took the belt with the sporran tied to it and
lifted her outer skirt to buckle it beneath. Then she stuck the dirk
into the belt and lowered her skirt over it all.

The sword went into its scabbard, and she doffed her cloak to
hang the baldric beneath it. The cloak barely covered the sword,
leaving only the tip of it exposed at the hem. Then she took the
reins of the horse and drew it away.

"Nae! Take him straight down the road! Dinnae skirt the field like a fugitive!" The faerie settled onto the horse behind the saddle.

The faerie was right. The soldiers were killing anyone they thought might be even a Jacobite sympathizer. To appear to be fleeing would raise a red flag for them. She turned and made her way to the road that cut through the bloody battlefield, headed for Nairn, in the opposite direction of the Jacobites in Inverness.

Just as she reached the road, though, a soldier approached them, brandishing his bayoneted musket.

"Halt there, you!" Leah said it before the soldier came too close, for it was not nearly certain he would say anything in the way of questioning before dispatching her like the other women. Remembering Ciaran's words about manipulating one's speech, she affected the most refined, upper-class London accent she could reproduce. Cumberland himself, who was the king's son, could not have sounded more royal. "What are you doing?"

The Redcoat was taken aback and lowered his musket, blinking. "Ah, miss . . ."

She maintained the offensive. "How dare you come at me with that . . . weapon. I assure you, when my father hears of this you will pay for your effrontery. And here, I am merely trying to recover the remains of my poor, dead fiancé." Tears came easily, and the soldier turned bright red with shame. She felt some vindication as she twisted the knife. "I've lost my own true love. My heart is broken. He gave his all for the king, and you assault me as if it meant nothing." She broke down, crying, and took the soldier's moment of extreme confusion to proceed on her way, weeping for all she was worth.

The faerie said dryly, "Allow me to make my apologies for my earlier remarks, Miss Hadley. Shakespeare himself wouldnae have produced a more masterful fiction."

Leah only glanced up at her to catch the gleam in her eye, then focused her energy on the long journey to Nairn.

CHAPTER 17

A small sporran of black rabbit fur, attached to a steel chain, was strung through the loops in the kilt and hung about his waist. A targe design decorated the front, and its cantle was silver-plated.

Somewhere along the way, the faerie disappeared. Leah wished she'd stayed. The galvanizing immediacy of the battlefield was draining away, leaving her trembling and ill. She'd not eaten since the day before. It was all she could do to keep putting one foot in front of another all the way back to Nairn.

It was well after nightfall when she finally reached the little town. But she couldn't go straight in, not with a naked Highlander draped over a stolen cavalry horse. There was a nearly collapsed peat house not far from the road, and she made for it, hoping for a bit of shelter. Though its roof tree was down at one end, the thatching was more or less intact. Vines overgrowing its entirety made it difficult enough to find. She'd nearly overlooked it herself. From a distance, particularly in moonlight, it almost appeared to be a small, low hill.

Outside a gaping hole in the earthen wall that had once been a window, she pulled Ciaran from the horse, and collapsed to her knees under him. Tears of frustration stung the corners of her eyes as she struggled to her feet again and hooked her arms under his. The blood on him had dried now, sticky in some spots. It was like carrying a butchered carcass. Quickly, lest she be seen, she dragged him into the pitch-dark hollow under the thatching and laid him on the dirt floor inside. Then she went back outside and slapped the horse on its rump to make it run away. Not that she feared the consequences of being caught with a stolen horse—she had a Jacobite fugitive on her hands, after all—but the animal would make them conspicuous. It would be best to do without it.

Inside the decrepit house she felt her way around in the dark with trembling hands to find Ciaran again. She unbuckled the belt under her skirt and laid dirk, sporran, and sword on the floor beside him. Then she removed her underskirt and laid it over him. He hadn't moved or made a sound all the way from Inverness, but he was still breathing. So long as Ciaran was breathing, she knew she could accept nearly anything.

Hastily, she felt in the dark again to find his head, laid her mouth aside his ear, and murmured, "I'll return, my love. Stay alive for me. Please don't die. *Tha gaol agam ort,* Ciaran."

With that, she hurried from the house. Her throat closed, and tears stung her eyes. Her exhausted legs could barely hold her up, and her knees trembled as she walked. The terror of possibly being caught sapped her strength, but she carried on. Ciaran needed her.

There were things she would have to find for him: food, water, bandages, candles, blankets, clothes. She returned to Cousin Edwin's rented house as quickly as she could, her mind tumbling with what she would say to Edwin and Martha. They were certain to confine her to her room the instant they saw her in this bloodied and bedraggled condition. Her mind tumbled to know what she would do then. Slip away? But what if she were followed?

As she reached the place, a cart trundled past, containing a number of wounded soldiers. An idea came to her, and her heart lifted. Then she paused for a moment to rid herself of elation.

She burst into the house, in tears. "Oh, Martha! Edwin, it was horrible!"

Only Martha was there, sitting near the hearth with eyes swollen from crying and a handkerchief twisted and misshapen in her fingers. She looked up and leapt to her feet. "Leah! Where have you been?" In an instant her arms were around Leah, helping her into the nearest chair.

"It was *horrible!*" Leah sat, and burst into genuine tears when she saw she'd marked Martha with a smear of Ciaran's blood. "I went to find Father, and there was a battle! Right there before my eyes!" The memory of that terror choked her. Her hands shook, and she rocked in the chair with her grief.

"Dear Leah! It was foolish—"

"I saw Father. He's alive and whole. But they've brought wounded here. I must take bandages to them. And food and water. Blankets. Martha, I cannot rest until I've done something to help." *Ciaran might die. Alone.*

"Edwin is out looking for you. We were worried sick."

Cold fear washed over Leah. She didn't want anyone looking for her.

Martha hurried to gather the things for Leah, clucking over the terrible fright they'd had over her going missing. "We were in a terror over what we would tell your father."

Of course they were, Father's opinion being the important thing to them. Leah grabbed three candles from a candelabra, and the flint and striker from the drawer beneath it, and hid them in her pocket. Martha handed Leah the bandages and a package of meat and bread she'd wrapped in a linen cloth, and they hurried outside.

On the square, Leah said quickly, "Here, wait! What if Edwin returns and finds you gone as well? It's best you stay here and wait for him." Martha looked doubtful, so Leah added, "They're setting up a hospital over there in the church." She pointed to the spired church across the way, where the cart for the wounded now stood, having been emptied of its cargo. "I'll take these there."

Martha nodded, handed over the blankets and water jug she carried, and returned to the house. Leah took a few steps toward the church, where other townspeople were gathering to help the poor Redcoat soldiers, then ducked behind the tavern and hurried away toward the broken peat house.

Feeling the weight of the food she carried, she realized she should eat to keep from making herself ill. But when she ate a piece of bread from Martha's package, it sat on her stomach like lead. Nevertheless, she forced herself to finish the entire piece as she continued toward the hiding place.

Ciaran was still breathing when she once again slipped through the entrance and found him in the darkness. She felt of his bloodied chest and it rose, slowly but steadily, beneath her hand.

"Thank God." As quickly as she could strike a flame, she lit one of the candles and set it in the dirt floor nearby. Then she laid the blanket over Ciaran and drew it to his waist. His face was ashen. His breathing was shallow.

Leah reached out to touch the ragged hole in his chest, and for the first time noticed there was a silver chain around his neck that disappeared into the wound.

She picked up the chain and pulled. Ciaran moaned, and his eyelids fluttered, but he remained unconscious. She tugged again, but the end of the chain wouldn't come out. Her fingers probed the edges of the bloody hole, but she could determine nothing by it. Finally, she decided whatever was in there needed to come out, and being gentle wasn't going to accomplish that. Though it made Ciaran moan again with the pain, she gave the chain a good, steady pull.

Out from the flesh aside Ciaran's breastbone emerged a shredded wooden cross and a bent gold ring.

"Oh, my," she whispered. The ball that had struck his chest had been deflected by these things hanging around his neck on the chain. The angle of ricochet had been enough to protect his heart, but the ball had nevertheless burrowed in behind the muscles of his chest. She felt of him, hoping to find where the ball had exited, and found another wound above his right elbow. Swelling on the right side of his chest told her the ball had gone along inside the flesh of his chest and upper arm before leaving him. A likely route, if his sword arm were raised at the moment he'd been shot.

The entrance wound was bleeding again. She took a piece of the linen she'd brought for bandages and pressed it to his chest, making him groan again. There was a lump under the skin. Something was still inside the wound, and she looked at the wooden cross still attached to the silver chain.

Most of it was still there, but the lower part of the upright was frayed and too short. The tiny silver feet of the bent corpus dangled in space. Now it was Leah's turn to groan as she prodded the edges of the wound again.

Quickly, decisively, she poked a finger into the hole and felt the end of the broken piece of cross. Ciaran groaned and writhed, but without hesitation she pinched the wood between the tips of her thumb and finger and pulled it out.

Ciaran cried out with pain, and bellowed something in Gaelic.

"Shhh," she said into his ear. God forbid anyone nearby had heard the Highland language. "It's all right. The thing is out now." She wiped the blood from her fingers onto the blanket.

His eyelids fluttered, and this time opened. Again he spoke in Gaelic, less loudly now.

"Speak English, my love. They'll hear you and come if you speak Gaelic."

He shut his eyes and made a disgusted sound in the back of his throat. "English. I've gone to hell." Then he looked at her, his eyes dulled with pain, "You're dead as well, then?"

She smiled. "Neither of us is dead. We both are alive."

"Alive . . ." His voice was weak, drifting. "I cannae . . ." He blinked in the semidarkness, making shallow gasps. "How . . . nae . . . my head . . ." Then his eyes shut, and a long groan escaped him. "Calum . . ." He burst into tears and began talking deliriously in Gaelic again.

"Shhh, Ciaran." She leaned down to press her lips to his forehead. He calmed at her touch, and blinked up at her. "You've been wounded. You must rest." The tips of her fingers dabbed tears from the side of his face. He blinked some more and looked to his right, at his arm.

His fingers twitched. "I cannae raise my arm." Confused, his voice was panicky and cracked with grief.

"Don't try yet. You'll only make it bleed more." She lifted his head and raised the water jug to his lips. He sucked greedily on it.

Then he let go and lay back, gasping. The pain of each breath showed on his face. Leah wet a piece of the linen and began cleaning the blood and dirt from his face. His eyes drooped halfway closed for a moment, his breathing steadied, then he looked up at her.

"Where am I?"

"Nairn. If they find you, they'll kill you. So they mustn't find you. You'll stay here until you're better, then we must find a way to France."

It took a moment for him to absorb her words. Then he said, " 'We'?"

She stopped wiping his skin and looked into his eyes. "Yes,

both of us. I'd rather live in exile with you than live in Britain without you."

"Nae exile. Never. I'll be staying here, even to die."

Leah continued cleaning him. "You're delirious. We'll talk of this later."

The water seemed to revive him, and before long he was able to devour the cold beef she'd brought. Once his other wounds were clean, she turned his head to see where the blood in his hair had come from and was shocked to find his head had been shot as well. A long, narrow wound traversed the side of his skull, and the top half of his right ear had been shot off. As she poked at the swelling on his scalp, he began to heave as if to vomit.

Quickly, she reached around and pressed the wet linen to the side of his face. "Hold it down, my love. Hold it in."

"I cannae breathe." His gut jerked and his breaths were fast and shallow.

She continued to stroke his face with the cool cloth until he settled and was no longer in danger of losing the food and water she'd given him. His eyes closed, and she let him rest.

Once he was asleep, she tucked the blanket around him and blew out the candle to return to town. As much as she hated to leave him, Edwin and Martha would come looking for her if she stayed much longer.

Every day she came to him, making various excuses to Father's cousins for her absence and bringing with her whatever food she could filch or buy. She also smuggled into the broken house more blankets; a small pillow for his poor, sore head; and a thin straw mattress for him to lie on, which she rolled up and carried to him in an old oat sack. In a far, dark corner of the broken house she found a low, wooden footstool, which she sat upon while attending him. With needle and thread she'd brought from Martha, she sewed closed the three wounds in spite of Ciaran's protests the items should be boiled first. There was no fire, for smoke would bring the Redcoats, so boiling was impossible.

Two days after the battle, Leah was returning to town in the rainy afternoon after nursing Ciaran. As she entered the square and was about to slip through the front door of her cousins' house, she was stunned to see a red-coated soldier dragging a man from the church across the way. Naked but for a shredded shirt, he was covered with blood, both old and fresh, from a wound in his thigh that had reopened from this rough treatment.

The thin, defenseless soldier wailed pitiably his innocence, that he'd been mercilessly pressed into the service of Charles Stuart. He slipped in the mud as he was dragged to the center of the town square, his leg streaming with red blood running pink in the light rain. Old blood and mud blackened him, and he wept for his life. His long hair stuck to his face, and he wiped it away with trembling fingers. In quaking voice he spoke of his wife and children, begging abjectly, his eyes wide with terror, to be allowed to live.

But the English soldier was unmoved. He pulled his pistol from his holster, pressed it against the back of the prisoner's skull, and fired.

Leah flinched as the top of the man's head flew off in a rain of gore, hair, and bone, and he flopped to the ground. The soldier restored his gun to its holster and returned to the church, leaving the Jacobite lying in the rain and mud. One leg and some fingers jerked and spasmed before the body lay completely still.

Cold overcame Leah. Trembling took her, and suddenly the world turned inside out. There was no thinking; she could barely find her way inside the house. Then she spent the night seeing that moment in her mind over and over, the doomed man weeping no more as his brains splattered to the wind.

The following day, fever came to Ciaran. He burned with it, groaned and tossed in his sleep, for three days nearly straight through, while Leah cooled him with wet cloths. She woke him to give him water, but he had no stomach for the food she brought. With linen rags and skin after skin of water, she wet him and washed him, cooling every part of him and cleaning the souring blood still clinging to his ears and hair.

On the third day, the fever broke. A film of sweat covered him, and he was finally able to take some oats mixed with water. He seemed nearly dead, but the fact that he could eat was so encouraging that Leah ignored his thinness and pallor. Ciaran would live, she was certain, and that meant all would be well. For another two days he alternated between eating and sleeping, gaining strength.

Eventually, one day while he swallowed bits of the oatmeal paste he called *"drammach,"* he began to notice his surroundings, coming out of the confusion he'd lived in since the battle.

•

"Where are we?"

"It's a deserted house." She looked around also. "More of a lean-to now, actually."

"Nae. I mean, *where* are we? Inverness? I recollect naught but an angel telling me she loved me. I was dead certain I was on my way to heaven."

"Not heaven, but only Nairn." She put another glob of the *drammach* between his lips, and he swallowed.

" 'Tis Scotland. Close enough. I've been to England, and you can have it." He was silent while she fed him some more, then touched his chest near the wound and said, "How is it I am yet alive?"

"See the cross around your neck?" The cross, still on the chain, lay on his pillow, and she picked it up to show him. "It kept the ball from going straight into your heart."

With his good hand he took it and examined the broken cross and bent ring. "My father wore this. 'Tis my mother's wedding ring."

"Hmm," she replied, "it's fortunate you wore it also."

He seemed to think about that for a bit; then he looked around. "How did I come to be here?"

"I brought you. Ah . . . *we* brought you."

He looked into her face for a moment, seeming to consider her words, then said, "Aye. Ye've met Tinkerbell, then."

"Tinkerbell, you say?" She smiled. "What an extraordinary name. She neglected to introduce herself, but I imagine that must have been she. I suppose now I know why you believe in faeries so strongly."

He grunted, then took another bite of food. "You went to the battle to watch your father fight?"

A tiny gurgle escaped her. Her throat closed as she recalled her father's face that day and what he'd nearly done. She needed to clear her throat to say, "No. I was on my way to Inverness to find you, and I came upon the battle. Once the firing had stopped, your Tinkerbell guided me to where you lay."

There was another long silence as he seemed to drift off, thinking of something else. Then he said softly, "Calum is dead. Eóin . . . Gregor."

"The army is still killing. They've shot everyone in Nairn they thought might be sympathetic to the cause. I'm told Prince Charlie has escaped, and it's a hot pursuit through the Highlands. Cousin Edwin is following it with far too much relish, I think."

A long sigh escaped him, and he closed his eyes. "I cannae care about the cause any longer. I've other worries."

"Such as escaping to France."

"Nae. Such as returning to my clan."

"The army will catch you and hang you."

"I cannae leave my people. My father and clan tradition have charged me with their care."

"But there is your brother. He can lead them."

Ciaran shook his head. "Da taught *me*. And Robbie is far too young. I must return, or shirk my duty to them. Whether Robbie can carry on in my place isnae the important thing. Leading my people is what I was born to. I must not run away. I cannae. My life, away from my people—away from my home—would be worth naught."

"Oh, Ciaran . . ." Leah sighed as she proffered the last of the *drammach*.

"Nae." Ciaran opened his mouth for the oats, then took her hand and held it as he swallowed. He licked the bit of oat mush left on her fingers, then her thumb, then kissed the palm. *"M'annsachd,"* he murmured.

"What does it mean?" Though she thought she might guess.

"It means 'my most dearly beloved.' "

She knelt by the mattress to press a gentle kiss to his lips. He gave a small moan and parted them, so she pressed more and touched his mouth with her tongue. Welcoming it, he also reached around behind her to fumble one-handed with the buttons at her back.

A smile foiled her kiss, and she murmured against his mouth, "Such ambition."

"Take it off."

"I wouldn't wish to hurt you."

A light sound of disparagement rasped the back of his throat. "Dinnae lay your head on my chest then. Nor grab me by the ears in your throes."

A giggle rose. It felt wondrous to laugh, as if it had been years since she'd done so. "Are you certain you're strong enough?"

A tiny, wry smile touched his mouth. "I'm nae strong enough to resist the wanting."

She turned to allow him to help her with her buttons, then

stood to step out of her overdress and blouse. Her stockings and shoes were quickly peeled off, and she knelt by him again before lifting her shift over her head.

His eyes danced as he watched her. When she leaned over to kiss him, he reached out with his good left hand to touch the very private skin of her breasts. It was with reverence he stroked her, and he said softly, "Nearly dying has a way of making a man appreciate keenly the things of this life." Then he lifted his blanket for her to join him beneath it.

Afraid of hurting him, she only knelt over him on all fours and kissed his mouth. She could tell it still pained him to breathe, for his breaths were shallow but many. He pressed the back of her head for a stronger kiss, tasting her and half raising his head to meet her. His longing was obvious. Intense. She straddled him, and found him eager.

"Aye," he whispered with a laugh in his voice, "I'm as whole as I need to be."

As she settled onto him, his eyelids drooped. His hips tilted, but much movement would be impossible for him yet, so she gently moved her own hips.

It fascinated her to watch his face like this. Eyes closed, he was suffused with a joy he never seemed to feel at other moments. Serious Ciaran was gone, and when he opened his eyes to look at her she saw deep in them his utter adoration of her.

Breaths came hard for him, and now a crease of pain appeared between his eyebrows. She slowed.

"Dinnae stop. *Och,* please dinnae stop." He pressed his good hand to the small of her back, and she quickened her pace. "*Och,* Leah . . . Leah, *m'annsachd . . .*" Then his hand touched her face and stroked her cheek. She kept on, and his eyes closed once more. His mouth opened, but no words came. Breath came in quick, hard, shallow gasps, then a long, low moan. More moans followed as his hips twitched beneath her and he was surely now feeling the cost of his exertion. Sweat beaded on his face.

Her hips settled onto him one last time. "Have I hurt you?"

He gasped, "Sweet pain. Wonderful, lovely pain." He reached up to draw her down for another kiss. " 'Tis good to be alive." She slid from him and onto his good side to lie next to him, then propped her head on one elbow and idly stroked his belly as she watched him drowse.

"We must marry," he whispered.

"I'm told that by Scottish law we might be considered already married." She indicated the broken house above their heads. "The term, I believe, is 'having a bidey-in.' "

He smiled, a bright, unaccustomed grin. "Aye, they call it that. But, alas, part of the requirement for it is that there be not only habit, but repute. Folks must ken what we're up to."

"Shall I go now and call out to the townspeople of Nairn, then?" That brought a laugh that ended in a groan of pain and a touch of fingertips to his chest. "I could leave this place, even as I am, and proceed up the High Street naked as the Lady Godiva, declaring myself for you so all the people of the town will know."

He continued to chuckle though it hurt, and said, "Nae. No 'bidey-in.' Nae handfasting, either. 'Twill be in a church with a priest, for it wouldnae be a proper thing for a laird to be married in a furtive and irregular manner for the sake of expedience only." His good hand found her hand resting on his belly and squeezed it. "I mean for ye to be my wife, before God and the world, so that no man, nor even ourselves, can put it asunder."

She smiled and kissed him, and wondered if he was truly as naive as he sounded.

A frustrated voice came from the field outside. "I'm telling ye, there's someone in there!"

Another voice shushed the first, but Ciaran had already thrown off his blankets and was reaching for his sporran. Leah grabbed his dirk and sword, for though she was unskilled with them, she at least was able enough to lift her arm.

Ciaran fumbled in his sporran and produced a small brooch he then hung by its pin on the chain around his neck. "Come," he whispered, and struggled to his feet to draw her away from the mattress.

"What . . . ?"

"Trust me. Come."

She went, and stood with him against the wall opposite the opening, directly in the patch of sunlight from outside. His knees started to buckle. She caught him and slipped under his left arm to help support him. "Are you mad? They'll—"

"Shhh." He placed his mouth directly against her ear. "Trust me."

"Ciar—"

"Trust me. Dinnae make a sound, and dinnae move a muscle, nae matter what you see or hear." He put his good arm around her and held her close. She stood still as he asked, naked and shivering in spite of the heat of his body against hers, terrified and absolutely certain of being seen.

Shadows appeared at the opening of the peat wall, and a Redcoat entered, bayonet first. He thrust the long, slender blade into the shadows near the opening, then stood to look around. Another figure entered behind him, a small, thin man Leah did not recognize. "See, she's here. Her candle is still lit, and there are her clothes." His voice was triumphant, and carried with it an expectation of reward.

The soldier said nothing, but continued to peer into corners. With his bayonet he poked at the thatching that slanted to the floor. "I see nobody." He looked straight at Leah, and she was certain he could see into her eyes, but there was no sign he saw her at all. He poked at the straw mattress on the floor, but it was far too thin to conceal a person. Then he picked up a blanket to sniff it.

"Ah. I see we've interrupted a whore and her customer." He held out the evidence for the little man to smell, but was declined, so he dropped the blanket onto the mattress. "They must have heard us coming, and fled." He nudged the dress with the toe of his boot and added, "A sight to delight the eyes with her clothes left behind, I'll wager."

"I saw nac man enter the place."

With a sigh, the soldier shrugged and said, "He was here, I assure you, and he was enjoying himself to the fullest." One more glance around, and he declared, "She'll most likely seek another place to take her customers, now that we've found her out." He then passed the little man and made his way from the house.

The Scot looked around as if certain the soldier had merely overlooked the woman guilty of secreting a fugitive, but after a thorough search of the shadows even he had to utter a grudging grunt and make his way from the house.

Ciaran collapsed to his knees, then crawled to the mattress before falling entirely onto it, gasping. Leah went to hold his head gently on her lap, and lifted the brooch from the chain around his neck. It was a badge of some sort. A hand wielding a sword.

"They couldn't see us."

"Nae."

"Is this magic?"

"Aye."

"It makes one invisible?"

"Only if you stand still. 'Tis the symbol of our clan. My da said it's like our clan because it protects only if you stay in one place. Move, and you forfeit the protection."

She thought for a moment, then said, "We need to leave this place. We need to get ourselves to Ciorram."

"Aye. And quickly."

CHAPTER 18

It was with great reverence bordering on awe he donned the large silver-hilted dirk, in a scabbard hung on his belt. The weapon had been in his family for centuries. He gazed for a moment at it, his mind wandering among the stories he'd heard of its history.

Ciaran hated the breeches. Leah had brought a pair she'd obtained in town. He'd pulled them on for lack of anything else to wear, and he hated them. They were doeskin and therefore stiff, and they squeezed his man parts mercilessly. There were *seams* digging into his crotch, annoying in the extreme, even with linen drawers to soften them. Also, when he moved, they rode up into places he would rather not have to suffer wads of leather. He pulled at the seat of them, but there was no relief. There was only so much give.

"Never fear," said Leah, "they'll tighten up once you've gained back your weight."

He peered at her. "Dinnae make fun." But her humbled expression told him she hadn't been joking. The breeches really were supposed to be tighter. A long, truly disgusted noise rasped the back of his throat.

Then she handed him a sark, and it looked new. He held it out to the blue light of dawn coming through the hideaway entrance, and saw it was embroidered on cuffs and placket with bears intertwined in a Celtic pattern. "This is an excellent sark. Where did you find it?"

"I sewed it for you."

Surprised, he looked into her face in expectation of a joke, but she seemed quite sincere. "You made this? This is your stitching?"

She nodded.

He also nodded. "As I said, 'tis an excellent sark. And the bears will bring us luck." She helped him pull it over his head and tuck it into the breeches, but it bloused out from them terribly.

There was no waistcoat, but Leah had managed to find a long woolen coat, and a black tricorn hat that felt stiff and unwieldy on his head. "I look like a fucking *Sasunnach*."

"That is the very idea. Indeed, if they so much as see your torn ear they will wonder how you received the wound and will ask questions." She carefully arranged his hair over the ear and began to braid it in back.

"Och!" He shook his head and stepped away. "I'll nae braid it."

"Because you're a Highlander. And that's exactly why you should let me braid it."

"Nae. I'll tie it in a queue, and that is enough." He pointed an admonishing finger at her until she nodded, then turned around to let her tie it for him. That one stubborn lock was still too short to reach, so it hung down aside his face. He hooked it over his left ear, but she reached over to unhook it and said, "Show neither ear. Better you should appear slovenly than wounded or hiding something."

"Very well. Let us go, then."

"Wait." She reached under her skirt to her pocket, and pulled out a long string of ivory beads. His rosary. When he saw it, a warmth swelled in his belly.

"You kept it."

"Of course I did."

He took it and let the string drape about his fingers. "I missed the feel of the beads in my hands. But I told myself it was all right, for you had them safe."

She folded them into his hand and kissed it.

He dropped the rosary into his sark, then picked up the knapsack that held his sporran, Brigid, a water skin, and some food.

Leah carried the sword as before, slung from a belt beneath her skirts. It had taken nearly a week to gather the clothing and equipment necessary for travel, all the while taking extreme care to avoid discovery. She wore a maid's dress she'd pretended to buy for Ida then hid away for herself. Nobody would be looking for her as a wandering servant. According to their story, she and Ciaran were manservant and maid, married to each other and in search of positions near each other.

The sun had not quite risen when they emerged from their hiding place and took to the road that led north. Even so, the light was a strain on his unaccustomed eyes, and he squinted for several minutes.

The response of Ciaran's wounds to movement was immediate, and by the time the sun was fully up, he struggled for breath. Pain thudded across his chest and into his right arm all the way to his fingers. He was yet unable to move that arm, and was even uncertain whether he would ever recover use of it. As for his head, the swelling of his scalp had gone down; nevertheless, the wound over his ear throbbed badly enough to make him worry he had resumed bleeding. Blood running down his neck would surely attract attention.

As they walked, the sun rose on a Scotland Ciaran hardly recognized. Some houses they passed had been burnt to the ground, leaving piles of ashes that stank of things other than peat and wood. Few people were about, and nobody wore tartan. There were no kilts anywhere, other than on some bodies hanging from a tree near the road. The flesh was rotting from them, picked apart by ravens, and the tartan wool was torn and black with dried blood, dangling to the ground. One of the corpses was that of a woman.

They came upon the battlefield. By then Drummossic Moor had been cleared of the dead, and the disturbed earth of fresh graves dotted the area. Ciaran's heart clenched as he gazed across the rolling landscape. Calum was there, somewhere, under the earth. The king's men had accomplished the thing he had been unable to do himself, and now he fully realized why it had been impossible for him. Calum had been his brother. As much trouble as the lad had caused, they were nevertheless brothers, and nothing could ever have changed that.

Calum had proven himself as his father's son. Had faced the enemy of his people with as much bravery as Ciaran had seen in any man. There had been no flinching in the charge. He'd endured starvation and exhaustion; then when there was nothing left to give, he had given his life for the cause.

Ciaran then thought of himself, still alive, and an astonishing pang of jealousy came over him. Calum's struggle was ended, and he was a hero. There was nothing more at stake for him. But he himself had been left on the earth, faced with further danger from the *Sasunnaich*. Ciaran drew a deep, piercing breath, shook his head to rid himself of the awful thought, then lowered his head and gazed at the ground as they passed through.

The sun was high as they approached Inverness. White lines had formed around Leah's mouth and dark circles beneath her eyes. Ciaran thought it might be time to call a halt for rest. Perhaps there would be a room in Inverness they could hire for the night at a rate they could afford. With what little cash they carried, it wouldn't be a good room, or even a decent one, but any shelter tonight would be a blessing, for the spring was yet chilly.

They sat under a tree at the side of the road, finding comfortable seats among its gnarled roots, to eat some of the bread they'd brought. Leah's face was drawn with exhaustion, but there had been no complaints from her. She stared at the ground before her as she chewed slowly, her chin down and her eyes half closed. Her hands lay in her lap, the one occasionally lifting the bread for her to take a bite, then gently returning to her lap.

As he gazed at her, both silent as they ate, he thought about how very wrong he'd been about her when they'd first met. Now he wanted to find out what else there was to learn about her. He hoped there would be enough time for it, and that hope brought strength. The future loomed large and indefinite, and he would have to face it now that he'd survived.

Though his chest and right arm throbbed horribly, the swelling had gone and he tried to flex his elbow now. But the arm was stiff. It was all he could do to bend it even slightly, and the effort was agonizing. Bolts of pain shot through to his spine. He was panting after only a minute.

"Rest, my love." Leah laid a hand on his shoulder.

"Nae." He shook his head. " 'Tis my sword hand. I'm useless in defense without it. I must regain control of it."

"And if you cannot?"

"I will. A fortnight ago I couldnae move it at all, and now I can bend it a bit. I will have it back, and my skill with the sword as well. Soon." He flexed the elbow some more, struggling against the pain, and she watched him.

The sound of hoofbeats and the creak of a cart reached them, coming from the direction of Inverness. Too late to grab the talisman, Ciaran shoved Leah down to hide as best they could in the grass behind the tree, utterly still. The cart was preceded by two Redcoats who seemed bored into a stupor and not alert to their surroundings. A garron was harnessed to it, and it carried crates that appeared quite heavy. The wheels rumbled over stones and creaked dangerously beneath the weight. Ciaran and Leah waited as the cart passed them and rounded the bend toward Nairn. Then Ciaran sat up, staring after it.

"I think 'tis time to move along." He made to rise, but again there were sounds from the road, this time a detail of soldiers marching. Ciaran and Leah lay flat on the ground again, completely still until the Redcoats had passed. Gradually the step and crunch of their boots faded into the distance.

Now Ciaran sighed, pointed with his chin away from the road, and said, "I think 'tis time to move along into the hills."

"How will we know where we're going if we leave the road?"

He didn't reply, but only said *"Och."* She was a good woman, but she needed to learn to trust him. Then he stood and helped her to her feet. He gestured to the knapsack hung on his shoulder and said, "Reach into my sporran and take the talisman. Dinnae pin it to the outside of your clothing, for I may need to find you when you cannae move. But slip it inside yer bodice so it's handy."

She complied, then took his hand and followed him west, across a field toward the cover of hills and trees.

They halted for the night in a thicket he chose for being well off the beaten track and somewhat fortified by outcrops of granite on two sides. They ate more of their cold provisions, then settled in to sleep in a hollow scooped from dead leaves. Leah lay with her head on his good shoulder, and he drew his coat around them both. He cursed the loss of his kilted plaid, which had once provided more than five square yards of wool against the cold of night.

Damned *Sasunnaich*.

L eah kept telling herself that as long as Ciaran was alive and as long as she was with him, all would be well. She knew Ed-

win and Martha must be beside themselves with concern, but
only because they feared her father's reaction when he would
learn she'd gone missing. For the time being, she walked beside
Ciaran and trusted him to take them where they needed to go. To
Ciorram.

The mountains were steep and harsh. She had no idea how
many miles they traversed in a day, but believed they couldn't be
many. Poor Ciaran was still healing, and the pain he bore was revealed in the crease at the center of his brow.

Since leaving the beaten track, they traveled by night, and by
day slept where they could hide themselves. They lived on
cheeses and oat bread, of which there seemed an unending sup-
ply in Ciaran's knapsack. In that way she knew the faerie was still
about. When it rained they kept on, walking among the dripping
trees and losing no time.

The devastation wreaked by Cumberland's men was everywhere, and in the darkness took on an even more horrific aspect.
Burned houses, people, and animals made themselves known by
their stink. Clearings in which dead men hung from trees loomed
in the night, waiting for an incautious traveler to come too close.
If the moon was out they saw these things; dead children sometimes lay alongside their parents, ghastly pale in the silvery light.
All had been shot or stabbed. Many were mutilated. The few living people Leah and Ciaran did encounter they avoided, for they
didn't dare trust anyone who was still alive and not in prison.

But one morning at sunrise they came upon more smoking
houses and everything changed.

They'd smelled the destruction from afar, and as they neared,
though they'd been walking all night, Ciaran picked up the pace.
"MacKenzies," he said. " 'Tis the MacKenzies. My mother's
cousins." Leah was certain they should avoid the sight, but wasn't
at all certain she could talk Ciaran into following another track.
She'd come to know him that well, at least. The sun was golden in
the east when they descended into a tiny glen where some ruined
houses lay, smoldering along a winding burn. A shaggy white
pony lay dead in the middle of the track, nearly beheaded, and
covered with flies. They stepped around it.

It was in the center of the glen they saw it. The earth spun for
Leah. Panic filled her and she gasped at the sight, unable to ex-
hale. She had to turn away, but Ciaran looked. She watched him
stare hard, his face as white as when she'd found him on the bat-

tlefield. "William. Alasdair." He began to gasp, heaving for breath, the air wheezing in and out of him. Turning, he seemed to be looking for someone to kill. Or an escape from his own unbearable rage. Then he turned back to stare again.

"Ciaran, don't look."

But he wouldn't turn away. "No, look," he said. "See what they have done to us." Slowly, she turned back around and looked also. Fifteen or so bodies, lying along the trail. Women on one side, and men on the other. Very orderly. Very military. In fact, the men were lined up in a row. They'd been stripped and bayoneted, some through the face, and each one held his own severed private parts in his hands. Flies swarmed over the blood, and that was all that moved.

But it was the women who made Ciaran stare. They were not naked, and not so neatly laid out. One had been shot while trying to run away, and lay sprawled facedown near some trees. Others lay facedown or crumpled in a heap along the track, all with their skirts lifted or torn off, and all bayoneted. Another lay on her back with her legs spread, her knees bent and frozen in that horrible position. Her face was gone, having been shot at close range by a musket or pistol. Ciaran trembled. When Leah tried to take his hand, it was shaking, and he pulled it away.

"You knew these people."

He nodded, and declined to elaborate beyond that they were cousins to his mother.

Not a thing moved in that glen, aside from a wisp of smoke still rising from one of the destroyed houses. All the animals were gone, either stolen or slaughtered and left to rot. No children were in sight. God only knew what had happened to them.

Leah's throat closed, and as she looked away again, tears squeezed from her eyes. Her father's army had done this. The king he defended condoned it. Her skin crawled, and she wished to flee it. She no longer thought it a good thing to be English.

"Come," said Ciaran. He took her hand and guided her toward the trees. "This way."

"Where are we going?"

" 'Tis a place the folks here once used for clandestine meetings. Long ago, it was ceremonies the priests frowned upon, and these days 'tis for political meetings that are none of His Majesty's business."

"Where are the children, Ciaran? I saw no children."

The fire of anger rose brighter in his eyes. His jaw clenched until knots of muscle stood out. "Taken, perhaps. To imprison them. Sell them to be transported to the colonies."

"Infants?"

"We havenae looked in the burn." He glanced back the way they'd come. "The truly wee ones would be there. Or in the ashes of the houses."

Leah clapped a hand over her mouth as her bile rose, and tears stung her eyes. She lurched to a halt and bent nearly double, struggling to contain her revulsion. Ciaran waited for her to recover herself; then they moved on.

They climbed a steep trail that wended its way among wooded hills thick with Scotch pines, and came out on a large clearing at the top of one hill. Ciaran held out his arm to stop her, then examined the ground. Excitement filled his voice. "They're here. There's someone here, and it's nae soldiers."

"How can you tell?"

"Redcoats dinnae wear brogues, and they have heels on their fine, sturdy boots." He pointed to the heelless tracks in the dirt. "These were made since the ground was last wet, which was—"

An arrow swished past his face.

"Shit!" He ducked on reflex, though the arrow had missed widely, then straightened and turned in the direction from which it had come. "Alasdair! Alasdair Iain William Thomas MacKenzie! Show your face, Ailig Crùbach, 'tis me! And you're a lousy molly with a bow, like I've told you since ye were a lad!"

"Ciaran." There was a crashing through the trees, and a man came limping from them. "Ciaran Dubhach! Oh, God, 'tis yourself!" He came on, limping horribly with a clubfoot. He was followed by some others: an old man, two young boys, and a young woman. Alasdair handed off his bow to one of the boys, then threw his arms around Ciaran. "*Och,* Ciaran, they've killed us! They've taken everyone hereabouts! 'Twas horrible! They came two days ago."

"I saw, Ailig."

Alasdair was sobbing now, and the rest of them were weeping as well. "We ran, Ciaran. We ran and hid as best we could. Though they searched, they couldnae find us. But they killed the rest. We heard the screams. The wailing of the women and the screams of the dying bairns. My father, Ciaran. They killed Father and William. I couldnae stop them, Ciaran, I could do naught to stop them!" Ciaran held onto him and let him cry.

When Ciaran was freed from the hug, he turned to the young woman who was also weeping and hugged her as well. "Elizabeth," he murmured, then turned to Leah. "Elizabeth, here is my wife, Leah."

Leah barely felt the hug from Elizabeth, stunned as she was to be called "wife." It was a struggle to hide her surprise.

Then Ciaran named the others. His cousin, Alasdair, William's sons, Robert and Seumas, who were nine and ten years old. And the old man, a cousin to Alasdair's father, nodded but stood where he was, for it was apparent walking was painful for him. "Iain," said Ciaran.

"Come," said Alasdair. "This is too open. Come where there's shelter."

He guided them into the woods, downward into a hollow among three hills, to a place that at first appeared to be a thicket.

"You must stay with us," he said as they approached, "for 'tis too dangerous abroad in the countryside." Bracken and gorse stood all around beneath a stand of birch, too thick to see through. But when Alasdair ducked under the gnarled branch of a pine, he disappeared into the thicket without so much as a jostled leaf. The others followed.

"We cannae stay," said Ciaran. "We must return to Ciorram."

Leah, following, found herself inside a half-buried enclosure of wood, peat, and holly branches, in which birch trees grew here and there like pillars. Paths wended among living undergrowth, where small spaces had been cleared here and there for storage and sleeping quarters. Then they came to a larger space, a clearing where a small fire burned in the center. The ceiling was too low for the men to walk upright, but Leah could stand if she ducked her head only slightly. The peat fire was beneath a thin spot in the cover where the smoke dissipated among the branches of the birch near it. There was a strong scent of blood here.

"You must stay for a time, then. We need you."

Not far from the fire, a woman lay under a bloodied blanket, her skin stark white even in this dim light. She seemed stuporous, and ignored the tiny bundle that lay still beside her.

Alasdair explained, "Caitlin was stabbed. Her bairn came last night, and seems unhurt, but he's weak. Her own bleeding has stopped, but a fever is setting in. She'll likely die if we travel with her."

Iain said, "She'll likely die in any case."

Alasdair's shoulders hunched. He replied with deep impatience and frustration, "Dinnae say it again, Iain! We'll nae leave her!" Obviously an ongoing argument.

"We must get away!"

"No! We must stay with her!"

"They'll find us and kill us!"

"We must stay!"

Ciaran interrupted. "Have you food for yourselves?"

Alasdair replied, still glaring at Iain, "Some. We hunt the woods, gather animals scattered by the soldiers. But we've nae found one to provide milk for the bairn. If Caitlin dies, he'll nae be far behind."

Leah looked over at the sick woman, already gray and still as death.

"Oats?"

Alasdair shook his head. "They burned the crop and took the stores."

"Is there nae place for you to go?"

"We dare not move from here. We're defenseless and slow, and Caitlin cannae take the travel." He tapped his clubfoot with the end of his bow. "There's naught to do but wait here until they tire of hunting us."

Iain said, "We can leave."

"No!" Alasdair raised his hand to the old man, who flinched and finally sat down on a rock to retire from the argument.

Ciaran sat by the fire. "They'll never tire until they've killed us all."

"Aye. So we need someone lighter on his feet and better with the bow than myself."

There was a silence as Ciaran looked at the bow. Then, slowly, he took it and stood to draw back the string. The pain showed at the corners of his mouth and in his eyes, but the pull was smooth and even, and his right arm didn't tremble. Relaxing the draw, he sighed and said, "Very well, then. I can be of help. We'll stay a spell, but must move on soon."

Alasdair nodded, and all the MacKenzies seemed relieved to have an able hunter with them.

Once they'd all eaten and Ciaran had gathered pine boughs for a bed, he and Leah settled in to sleep in a small pocket of the hideout just large enough for the two of them, where a birch and some gorse provided a small measure of privacy. Ciaran's sword and dirk were tucked under the bedding off to the side. Leah settled in next to him, as always on his good side.

He looked up, rubbed his eyes, and muttered under his breath so the others couldn't hear, "Why did ye nae tell me?"

"I beg your pardon?"

Then he looked at her. "Not you." Then to the air again, "Tinkerbell, why did ye go all this time and nae say it?" Tears were standing in his eyes now. "Tink!"

But apparently the faerie did not provide a satisfactory answer, for he uttered what sounded like a curse in Gaelic. For a while, Leah lay next to him and listened to him breathe. Such a wonderful sound, Ciaran breathing. She whispered, "What did the faerie not tell you?"

There was a long, tense silence. She waited for a reply, and eventually decided there would be none.

But then Ciaran said in a low, still voice, "I witnessed my mother's death. The memory was lost, and only returned to me when I saw those women."

Leah squeezed her eyes shut and wished she'd left it alone, but he continued, "I never kent it until today. I never remembered what I saw until I chanced to see that woman lying like that, with her legs like that, as my mother had been when she was murdered." He stopped talking for a moment and drew several deep breaths before continuing in a thickened murmur. "Sìle and I were hiding, I think. He didn't see us. He came into the house, and did that to my mother. But I remember coming out of hiding and he was gone. Someone"—he paused for a moment, thinking—"it was Sarah, I believe. Sarah came and took us away. But I remember . . . I . . ." his voice wavered now and was barely audible. "I looked. While she was taking us from the house, I looked. I saw my mother . . . like that. Lying on the table with her legs like that, and her skirts pulled up, and blood running from the table." He was choking now, unable to speak, struggling to overcome the tears.

"Oh, Ciaran . . ." Leah stroked his hand, which lay on his belly.

Through clenched teeth he said, "I wish . . . I dinnae remember. I . . . wish I could send the thought . . . away."

Leah kissed his hand. "So much death. Far too many people have been killed."

"The *Sasunnaich* would kill us all. They will never stop until the land is emptied of Scots."

There was no reply for that. With all she'd seen in the past week, it certainly seemed true.

Ciaran raised up on one elbow to find her mouth with his. With more intensity than she'd ever seen even in Ciaran, he kissed her, probed her, sucked her. There seemed a special need in him now, a tension she also felt herself. His weak hand fiddled with the buttons of his breeches, and she helped him open them. Not to remove them, but only to free the necessary parts of him. He lifted her skirts and separated her knees with his. Quick and to the point. She held him close as he moved, and sensed in him more the intent to complete the act than to enjoy it, less to celebrate life than to create it. She knew what he must be feeling, for she felt it as well.

It took only a minute or so. Afterward he lay beside her, her face pressed against his arm on which it lay. She began to weep.

A soft grunt came from deep inside his chest, and he whispered, "Shhh. They havenae finished us off yet."

Sniffling, she continued to press her face against his arm and said nothing. She wasn't quite ready to tell him she suspected herself to have been with child since before leaving Nairn.

CHAPTER 19

*His wife called from the corridor. "Are you ready yet, Iain?"
Startled to attention, he replied in the affirmative and took a deep
breath.*

Ciaran's cousins accepted Leah as his wife, and though they
surely knew she was English, they at least didn't know she
was the daughter of an army captain. Leah was glad for that, for
the MacKenzies made it plain they suffered her *Sasunnach* presence only for her relationship with Ciaran. There was no telling
how they would be if they knew the truth about her father.

Caitlin clung to life, though fever raged in her. A nursing ewe
was found, and so the baby was saved by her milk, but the sense
of relief was tentative as they all awaited Caitlin's death or recovery. Sometimes she could be heard speaking in her delirium, addressing a man Leah was told had been her husband. The baby's
father had died in the prince's service at Falkirk.

Leah found concentrating on work, caring for Caitlin, and
keeping herself and Ciaran clean and everyone fed made the rest
of the world feel just distant enough to seem not real. Ciaran and
the boys buried the corpses in the murdered village, but after that
none of them returned there. Evenings around the fire were spent

talking in low voices, and though they all spoke only Gaelic, and though Ciaran declined to translate—or perhaps because he wouldn't translate—Leah knew they must be talking of the massacre. The tears and the anger overwhelmed them all, as if no amount of expression could ever ease the pain.

Leah was unable to contemplate the horror of what had been done to them. If she found herself thinking about those poor people, murdered and left to the animals, she would shake her head and think about something else. To dwell too much on what had happened would take her too close to thoughts of who had done it. It was too awful to bear.

During these days, Ciaran picked up his sword—the silver one he said had been a gift to his family from King James I and VI. Outside the thicket, Leah found him with it in his left hand, making circles with the tip. Then without a word he headed in the direction of the large clearing atop the hill.

Leah followed. "What are you going to do?"

"I cannae be without the sword any longer, and my right arm is nae strong enough or limber enough yet to control it. I must learn to fight with the left hand." He lifted his right arm to demonstrate the range of motion he'd achieved recently, and could bend his elbow far enough to touch his left shoulder. "I cannae lift the arm higher than my shoulder, and I've nae speed to speak of. I would be dead in a fight. With my left I might have a chance."

"You'd be too slow with your left."

He stood in the middle of the clearing and made wider circles with the sword. Single windmills followed by a flexing of his grip, his face a mask of concentration, getting the feel of the weapon. "My father could fight equally well with each hand. For him, there was almost nae difference. When I was a lad, he made me practice with the left. It was nae good for me, and I resisted, but I remember what he taught me. 'Switch-hitter,' he called himself. If you ken how to fight with the left, a bit of slowness might be made up for by confounding your opponent's expectations."

He stepped back into an *en garde* position and tried some movements. Even Leah could see he was hopelessly slow, but he stood straight, twirled the sword from the hilt, and tried again.

While Ciaran honed his skills as a left-handed swordsman, it seemed to be all he thought about. From the moment he awoke in the morning till he fell into deep sleep with his arms around her at night, his focus was on training his off side and exercising the damaged arm, stretching it, strengthening it, and making it do what he wanted as he scoured the countryside for wild game and domestic strays.

Often, before the summer sunsets, he went to the clearing to practice left-handed with the sword. Sometimes he tried his right, but was not pleased with his progress there. She could see the white lines of pain around his mouth if he worked too long with his weak arm. In addition, he practiced the unarmed combat, dancing prettily in the clearing. His health improved, and though he gained little weight there was better color in his skin, and movement of his right side was becoming freer, more fluid.

Leah spent her days helping with chores and learning to cook with nothing in the way of utensils. Elizabeth was quiet though industrious, having taken charge of the baby. As Caitlin's condition worsened, that arrangement began to develop into an informal adoption, and soon Elizabeth was behaving as if the child were hers. Ciaran explained Elizabeth had lost her father in the massacre, but she held out hope for a miracle that would bring her husband home from the rising. Taking the baby as her own seemed to bolster that hope, so nobody objected on Caitlin's behalf.

Roasting a rabbit one day over the small fire, Leah found herself staring at the infant boy, named Donnchadh after his father. The sight of Elizabeth with the baby in her arms filled Leah with longing and anticipation so intense it was dizzying. Her belly fluttered each time she thought of being a mother herself, and daily she prayed for the safety of her own child. The concern in Elizabeth's eyes gave her to know the terrible weight of responsibility for that tiny life, a responsibility Leah already felt.

She struggled not to think of the children burned by the Redcoats, but the images came. Try as she would, she couldn't keep from her mind the horrible things she'd seen and heard of. Sometimes, when alone, she found herself trembling, unable to stop. The world seemed surreal, as if nothing could ever be right again, for nothing had ever been real to begin with. Her pride in her father was now a fiction she saw in its bright, theatrical colors that had always been false.

Finally one day, on her way back from the stream with a bucket of water, the weight of the grief overcame her. Her confusion and loss, knowing that loss was inconsequential in the midst of the horrors she'd seen visited on others, finally knocked the legs from under her and she crumpled. She knelt on the track, hugging herself and sobbing for her lost innocence, longing for the security of knowing all would be set right. She wept, and kept on weeping, as her soul darkened and she feared there would never be light again.

A few moments later, Ciaran burst through the underbrush at a run, coming from his traps with a stray chicken. She hurried to dry her eyes. But he saw her, and stood staring, chicken wings flapping as the bird dangled by its feet.

He muttered to himself, "You said she needed me." One sharp glance at nothing, and Leah knew the faerie was present. Then he let the chicken flutter to the ground and came to squat on his heels before her. The bird ran a few feet, then promptly forgot its distress and began pecking at the ground. Ciaran tilted his head down to see into Leah's eyes, but she turned away.

Finally he spoke. "You wish to return to your father."

Another sob shook her, and she looked sharply at him. "No. I couldn't bear to see him ever again."

Ciaran didn't seem to have a reaction to that, but then reached out to touch her hair near her face. "I think I ken what is wrong, then. I could not imagine feeling that way about my father, and it must be a hard thing for you." There was true understanding in his eyes.

She said, "Those people. The men hanging from trees everywhere. All the murdered people. Murdered *children*. How could this happen?"

Ciaran shrugged, as if the answer were obvious. "They dinnae think we are people." There was a long pause, then he said softly in a low voice, "Leah, *m'annsachd,* you never thought we were people. Not until you came to know us."

Slowly, she shook her head. Her eyes grew wide at the accusation.

"Aye," he said. "Think hard on it."

Concentrating, she thought back over her first days at the Tigh. How fascinated she'd been by the "wild Highlander." As if Ciaran had been some sort of ape that had learned to walk upright. Hand over her mouth, she shook her head, still denying what she couldn't anymore.

He continued, "If we're nae people, we're easier to hate. Easier to dispossess and transport. Easier to kill."

Tears spilled over her cheeks and her hand. Sobbing once more, she said, "O my God."

He knelt by her and drew her into his arms as she continued to sob. "Oh, Ciaran . . . oh . . . I'm so sorry."

"Do ye love me?" he murmured into her ear.

"Yes."

"Then there's naught to be sorry for. Ye dinnae hang those men, nor use those women and shoot them, nor did you mutilate those bodies. So long as you love me, you cannae hate my people."

Leah continued sobbing onto Ciaran's shoulder, and he held her while she wept on and on until she could cry no more.

Caitlin's fever passed, but her condition never seemed to improve. She wasn't able to raise her head, and showed no interest in her baby. Her color remained gray, and she wasted away on her pallet. It was thought she preferred to die, and the MacKenzies were at a loss as to how to change her mind.

As Caitlin slowly dwindled, a small peace of resignation came to the tiny group, and even Iain stopped talking about leaving Caitlin. Though they still took care in not being seen from a distance, they no longer jumped at every sound in the woods. Life proceeded. Leah never heard any of the MacKenzies except Alasdair speak English, though she suspected the adults knew at least a little. She didn't much blame them for their silence around her. Unable to communicate with anyone in English, Leah began the struggle to learn Gaelic. Happily, she found the MacKenzies were pleased with her effort and eager to help her learn. It didn't take long for her to master enough of the language to make the work around the fire go more smoothly.

Summer was quite high, and bathing in the burn down in the glen was pleasant if not entirely convenient. Leah bathed more often than she'd been accustomed to in England, taking to Ciaran's habit. In winter that would surely change, but for now the weather was fair and the water a pleasure.

The shade under the trees was dark and dappled near the deep part of the burn at the head of the glen. Moss covered the rocks at the bank, and the bottom was carpeted with reeds flattened by the current. Leah removed her clothes and sat on a grassy overhang on the bank with her feet in the water, and took a deep breath of the warm summer air. The Scottish winter in Nairn had been so cold and so long, she'd wondered if there would never be nice weather again. But here it was, sprinkling golden patches among the whispering trees. She slipped into the water, and goose bumps rose.

Once she'd acclimated to its temperature, she reached for her linens to scrub them in the stream. She hoped there would be a chance to obtain new clothing soon, for her servant's dress had been old to begin with and now was wearing horribly thin in spots.

Then, having laid her underclothes over a limb, she returned to the water to wash. Kneeling to immerse herself, she stroked her belly, and her mind wandered. She wondered how long it would be before it would swell and become round and full. She couldn't tell Ciaran until then, for it would be foolish to announce a child this early no matter how healthy she might feel. They were too easily lost, retrieved by their Maker before they even truly there. But her heart quickened, and she indulged herself in the hope for a healthy baby and a safe delivery in seven months or so. It would be a Matheson and a Highlander, a clansman like its father, and she was glad for that.

A footstep up the track caught her attention, and she turned to greet Ciaran or one of the MacKenzies. But a flash of red in the sunlight beyond the trees nearly made her gasp. She swallowed it. Quickly and smoothly, she knelt in the water until only her eyes and nose were above the surface. Watching the Redcoat come, her heart sank as she realized he couldn't help but encounter the clothing she'd draped over the tree branch. She surfaced enough for her mouth to clear the water, and whispered, "Help me, Tinkerbell." Then she began to drift with the current, down the stream to gain as much distance between herself and the soldier as possible.

But the shallows were not far, burbling over the bed of smooth rocks. She found herself climbing over them as the soldier behind her exclaimed, "Oh-ho!" He'd found her clothes.

There was great crashing in the woods near the burn now. Leah hurried to get away, but it didn't take much for the Redcoat to spot her, knee-deep in the water. "Ha!" Chortling with great glee, he waded in after her.

Fighting the urge to hopeless flight, she turned to face him instead. She stood straight, chin up, as if she were fully clothed, and summoned her most imperious royal voice. "Soldier, it would behoove you to have respect in the presence of the daughter of Captain Roger Hadley."

That gave him pause for nothing more than another great guffaw. He came on, shouting, "Were I to give a damn about His Majesty's army anymore, that might be a concern."

Leah turned to run, but the rocks were slippery, and her unshod progress was far slower than his. With great heaves of splashing, he chased her down and grabbed her about the waist. She screamed. He held her against his belly with one arm as he tugged at the front of his breeches, apparently meaning to take her right there, standing up. She shrieked, crying for Ciaran. Kicking the soldier's shins and writhing, she whacked him on the side of his head with her elbow the way she'd seen Ciaran do in his exercises. But the deserter only laughed and held her all the more steady. A wail erupted from her as she felt his bare skin press her from behind, probing for a way in. One hand grabbed her by the throat, and he muttered she should cooperate lest he choke her.

Underbrush cracked and rustled behind them. There was no voice, but Leah knew it must be Ciaran. The Redcoat let go of her, and she dropped to her knees in the water. There was a *zing* of swords and scabbards, steel clanged behind her, and she looked up to see Ciaran locked hilt-to-hilt, left-handed, with the Redcoat. The soldier, heavier than he, pushed him off, scrambled up the bank of the stream, then took the seconds he'd gained to refasten the top button at the front of his breeches. Now, with the high ground, he smiled at Ciaran in the knee-deep water.

"Go, then," said the Englishman. "Take her. I didn't want her in any case. She rather stank."

Leah hurried to the opposite bank and scrambled onto it, relieved the soldier was going to let them go. But Ciaran's mouth widened in a smile as cold as any Leah had ever seen on him or anyone else.

"*Och,* ye dinnae understand," he said simply. "I mean to kill ye." With that, he whirled his sword like a windmill and in a single motion whipped it around to catch the Redcoat at the side of his knee.

A roar of pain, and the English sword came straight down toward Ciaran's head. But the high ground was suddenly a disadvantage, and there was a distance to cover. Ciaran dropped to one knee in the water, and as he did so drew Brigid from his legging scabbard to parry. Further assault with the sword forced the Redcoat to back away in another clang of metal. Ciaran seized the moment to hurry downstream some steps, then leap onto a stone, and from there to the bank.

Now he was level with the Redcoat, and with two good legs. The soldier hopped on one, face white with pain and fear. Ciaran closed and attacked without hesitation. There was a flurry of clanging steel, and suddenly the Redcoat was on his knees, bleeding from his opposite thigh. He swung hard and fast, but Ciaran coolly sidestepped the English saber and circled.

The Redcoat struggled to present his front, but both his legs were gone from under him. He cried, "Yield! I yield! Mercy, I beg you!"

Ciaran appeared unmoved. Leah shivered at the look in his eyes. There was no mercy there. She could see in them the murders he'd witnessed, the pain he'd suffered, and knew there would be no stopping him destroying this *Sasunnach*.

The Redcoat deserter appeared to see it also, and a quaver of terror rose in his voice as Ciaran's sword whirled lazily in circles at his side and he continued to pace like a stalking cat. "Please! Spare me! Let me go, and I'll be no bother to either of you! I swear to you I'll not reveal you to the unit of dragoons in Cannich."

Then Ciaran's eyes changed, and Leah knew why. They'd come through Cannich shortly before arriving here. Those Redcoats were very close. This was news. Very bad news, and even worse for the deserter, for it meant Ciaran couldn't bring himself to let the man go even had he been inclined.

Which he decidedly was not. In a flash of steel and silver he attacked, parried the riposte with the dirk, then with the sword calmly slashed the Redcoat's throat. The doomed man slumped to the ground. For a minute or so he writhed, gurgling and spraying blood; then he lay still.

Ciaran stared at the body and called out, his voice solid stone. "Are ye whole?"

It took a moment for Leah to realize he was talking to her. Then she said, "Yes. I'm unhurt. Completely unhurt."

He relaxed with profound relief, but all he said was, "Then dress." Without ceremony of any kind, he dragged the body by the collar of its red coat into a thicket and arranged the bracken and reeds around it for disguise. Then he turned and crossed the burn. "Quickly. If yer linens are wet, there's naught for it but to be wet. We must light out for Ciorram before they discover him."

"He's a deserter. He said so."

"They'll be looking for him. Only less intently than if he were missing from a patrol. Hurry, Leah. We must go."

*D*amn. Ciaran had hoped to avoid discovery by the English long enough to regain full use of his right arm. He'd wished to be whole on his return to Ciorram. But there wasn't time. Cumberland's devils would be looking for their deserter, and if they found him, they would be swarming over this place in greater numbers than Ciaran cared to face anymore. He found Alasdair MacKenzie, on his way to the shelter with an armful of deadfall wood.

"Alasdair, I've bad news." Ciaran gestured to Leah she should go into the shelter and begin preparation to leave. He continued to Alasdair, "There is a Redcoat company nearby. We all must leave."

Poor Alasdair was stunned. They all knew Caitlin would die of any attempt to travel. His voice was dull, devoid of hope as he said, "How did you learn of this?"

"I've just killed a deserter. They'll want him back, though only God would ken why."

"Ye *killed* . . . !" Alasdair's eyes went wide, and he sighed with impatience. "Why? Why did you have to kill a Redcoat, for God's—"

"He laid hands on my wife, Ailig."

Understanding lit Alasdair's eyes. He sighed. "Aye. Very well, then. We must flee. But where?"

"Come with us. We can make it to Ciorram, I'm certain. From there it will be but a short way to Killilan. Perhaps there will yet be some MacKenzies there."

Alasdair nodded, his face pale and gray. "I hate to leave my land, Ciaran."

"Aye. I understand. But the land belongs to King George now, and he doesnae want us cluttering it. We cannae make a stand in this place. Not by ourselves. We must make a retreat. Live to fight another day."

His cousin nodded again, then went inside the shelter to tell the others.

* * *

Quickly Alasdair and Ciaran put together a litter for Caitlin, but the journey was hard, and she died on the first day away from the hideout. Saddened but not surprised, they buried her and moved on. Even without the litter to carry, they covered very few miles in a day, for Alasdair's foot, the old man's health, and the baby all held them back. Leah was glad for it, for nausea often overcame her, and whenever they stopped for the sake of one of the MacKenzies, she found a secluded place to vomit or a brook in which to wash her face. They all knew she was ill, but she never told them the reason for her weakness, and let Ciaran believe the fight had upset her.

Her slippers, not meant for this sort of use, were ripping apart at the seams and began flopping from her heels. Eventually they became such a chore to keep on her feet, she took them off and threw them away down a ravine. Ciaran said nothing, but gave her a thoughtful look as she picked her way along the track amid the stones and such. But she also said nothing and continued to walk barefoot. Her feet would toughen. She could bear it.

The need to flee in a hurry was well understood, and that made the route they took seem strange. Leah was an Englishwoman, but she was also her father's daughter, and her sense of direction was keen. Particularly after these weeks walking through the trackless mountains of Scotland, she could tell they were traveling in a series of half circles and roundabout routes. As weak as many of the MacKenzies were, this made no sense to her. Further, it made no sense that none of the MacKenzies seemed to notice.

While circling a wide hill that should have been low enough to hike over, she leaned close to whisper privately, "My love, why are we going this way?"

He stopped walking and stared at her for a moment, but she only stopped and waited for a reply. It was a long wait, for he let the MacKenzies pass them entirely and out of earshot before speaking. Finally he said, "Are ye arguing with me now?"

Leah had a sudden mental image of Ciaran's sister with her teeth knocked out. Most men, including her father, were inclined to resort to hitting if they thought an argument had gone on too long. She had no idea where Ciaran's threshold might be with his own wife, and was certain he didn't know, either.

"Not at all," she replied. "I only wish to know." His brow furrowed, and she added, "In order to know what to expect and what will be expected of me."

He grunted, and his brow cleared. His glance covered the surrounding area. "We may be pursued." He continued walking, and she followed. "Even were the dead Redcoat nae discovered, our trail might be picked up by His Majesty's minions and followed. 'Tis vital we evade, though we're nae certain whether they're near or exactly where they might be if they are. So we travel out of our way to make our trail across solid rock, we keep away from the crests of hills so as to avoid being seen on the horizon even in moonlight, we keep to the trees when we can, and do not sleep in or near large clearings that may be used for that purpose by our enemy."

After a short distance, she spoke again. "You seem to know a great deal about evading pursuers."

Again he stopped to look at her, and his eyes darkened.

Firmly, she added, "I'm glad for it."

His eyes softened once more. "Aye." They continued walking. " 'Tis a useful skill in these parts, where enemies are numerous and deadly."

After a long silence, she said, "You learned it stealing cattle."

"Of course I did. I learned from my father, who reived cattle with Rob Roy, who was known for it."

"Would you ever do that again?"

A dry laugh erupted from him. "Rather than let my clan starve? Aye. Without the least hesitation. Have you an objection to that?"

Captain Roger Hadley's daughter would once have had a strong moral objection to any sort of theft. But Ciaran Matheson's common-law wife had of late witnessed many harsh realities and knew exactly where the line was between survival and death. She said, "No. It's good to know my husband will never let me starve."

He kept walking, but his mouth curled into a smile. His hand reached for hers.

It was the dead of night when the cluster of refugees approached Ciorram after several days of travel. Ciaran led them over the bald granite mountain behind the garrison, a route that completely bypassed the entrance to the glen. They came to the valley floor without ever having seen a British soldier from the garrison. Leah wondered if her father knew how little control he had over the comings and goings of these people he supposedly governed.

Ciaran was eager to be home, the excitement rising in his voice as he spoke of seeing his family and friends again.

But as they walked along the track toward the Tigh in the darkness, Ciaran fell silent. Something was wrong. Leah realized it, too. There were no animals here. No dogs barking. No shadows in the pastures, and no crop in the fields. A smell of burnt things hung in the air. Alasdair began to mutter in Gaelic, his voice quavering with apprehension. Elizabeth began to weep. Ciaran touched his palm to the ground at his feet, then smelled of it.

"Mo Dia," he said. "They've burnt the place. 'Tis naught but ash here. Ailis Hewitt's house should be there." He pointed, but in the moonlight there was only black ground. "Donnchadh's house and his outbuilding in that direction. We should be able to see the edge of the village from here. There's naught."

Leah took Ciaran's hand. "Come. We must flee."

But he wouldn't move. He held her hand tightly and drew her with him the other way. "Nae. I must find the survivors."

She held back and stopped him. "There won't be any."

"There must be." The desperation in his voice came to her through the darkness. "Robbie must have taken them somewhere, and I can guess where." He pulled on her hand again, and this time she and the MacKenzies followed.

It was a long walk in the darkness, and Leah had no idea where they were going. Ciaran was impatient at the slowness of his charges, but held back with them. Up an incredibly narrow ravine scattered with small trees and huge rocks, then out onto another valley. Grassy hills rose closely on either side, distinguishable from the sky as it lightened toward dawn. The fields here were burnt as well. The ash that rose as they walked through it choked her and made her eyes water.

"It hasnae been long since this happened. Since the last rain, only. Perhaps they've nae scattered yet." The hope that rose in his voice filled her as well.

At the far end of the little glen, they followed a track that led downward through a thick forest, following a stream that burbled nearby. Dawn was upon them, and soon they could see the stream as well as hear it, gray in the earliest light. They left the track to follow the water downward still. Cliffs rose on either side. Leah was completely lost, trusting only in Ciaran knowing where he was going. .

His steps slowed, then he stopped in the deep shadows and whispered something in Gaelic. They listened, but there was no reply. He took a few more steps and repeated himself.

From astonishingly close by came a whispered word. Ciaran turned toward the voice. "Seumas Glas! 'Tis Ciaran."

"*Och!* Ciaran Dubhach!" The elderly merchant came from a thicket of bracken and threw his one whole arm around Ciaran. When he saw the MacKenzies, he greeted Alasdair and the others warmly. A stream of Gaelic poured from Seumas that Leah found unintelligible in spite of what she'd learned, for his lack of teeth garbled it all beyond comprehension. But the relief in his voice made clear the faith he had in his laird that all would now be well. Leah's heart was touched with pride.

"In English," said Ciaran to Seumas. "Leah is here."

There was an incomprehensible pause as Seumas registered her presence, and his eyes narrowed at her. Then his gaze went to Ciaran's breeches and back to Leah. He said to Ciaran as if ignoring her, but more than likely translating what he'd just said, "Thank God ye're here." His voice took on an edge. "Hadley and his company of devils have returned."

"How many of us are left?" Ciaran and Seumas led the men up the hill, and Leah followed with Elizabeth and the boys.

"We lost one infant: my own new grandson, Alasdair's wee boy."

Ciaran nodded and sighed, and tears of grief stung Leah's eyes. It could have been much worse, however. Unlike many villages throughout the Highlands, the people of Ciorram were at least still alive.

Seumas continued, "Eóin and Donnchadh made their way here after the last battle. Both are wounded, but living."

"Eóin . . ." The relief in Ciaran's voice was deep. "Alive. Eóin is alive. Where are they?" He peered ahead in the dim light to find them.

"In the caves. The women and children, in any case. What men are left have placed themselves outside, for there is little room under shelter. It has been nearly two weeks since the Redcoats came. What food we are able to glean from the countryside without their knowledge hasnae been nearly enough to keep body and soul together for long. Ailis Hewitt is failing, and poor Dùghlas isnae far behind."

"Have you any news of the others who went with me?"

Seumas Glas stopped walking and looked the way they'd come, at the MacKenzies. "There are no more coming?" He seemed stricken and said softly, "Seumas Og?"

Now Ciaran's voice tensed. "I've nae seen Seumas Og since the last battle. I was wounded there, and I'm told the entire army has dispersed. Alasdair, Aodán, and Calum are all dead for a certainty, but I dinnae ken the fates of the others. There were some deserters, and I've encountered none of the remaining men since the last battle."

There was silence as they all realized the rest of the Matheson contingent was more than likely dead, captured, or fugitives. Nearly every man of fighting age in Ciorram had been lost. Tears welled in Seumas' eyes, and he lowered his head to hide them.

Ciaran turned to continue walking and said, "The men remaining will—"

"Dùghlas was shot, but he lives—for now, at any rate. The rest of us are either too old, too young, or nae whole enough to give the *Sasunnaich* much to dread." He raised the hook at the end of his arm to illustrate his point. Then his voice lowered until Leah almost couldn't discern his words, though she strained to hear, "And Ciaran, ye must listen but hold yer anger." Ciaran glanced back at Leah, but he and Seumas kept walking. Seumas continued, in Gaelic.

Ciaran listened for a moment, then stopped dead in his tracks. He interrupted in a voice so low and shocked he could barely get a single word from his throat: *"Cùis-éigin?"*

Elizabeth turned away, her face gone pale. Leah knew this word well, for it had been uttered repeatedly during their time with the MacKenzies. It meant "rape."

Ciaran flushed with rage. "Sìle . . ." Seumas nodded. Ciaran said, "Her daughters saw? Her wee *daughters?*" His throat worked as if he were choking. He stared, aghast, at Seumas, then turned as if looking for something or someone to hit. He turned again, then again, unable to find any course of action that would do some good. A muttering under his breath, in Gaelic, she recognized as vile cursing at the *"Sasunnaich."*

Leah flushed, mortified. This time it had been her father's own company to commit these barbaric acts. Her stomach turned, but she kept very still.

Ciaran turned to Seumas Glas and asked, *"Kirstie's Mary?"*

The merchant nodded slowly.

Ciaran turned again, noticed Leah as if he'd forgotten she was there, and an odd look crossed his face. "Your father and his men . . ." But his voice failed. He shook his head. Tears rose in his eyes, but he said nothing further. He only pressed his lips together and turned to continue on his way. Seumas gave her a hard look, then followed. Leah brought up the rear behind the MacKenzies without a word. Her heart lay heavy in her chest, and she struggled to swallow her tears.

They climbed between some rocks along a steep slope, and soon came upon some men and young teenage boys who awoke from among the boulders and bracken as Ciaran approached. They rose, and as they realized who accompanied Seumas, they exclaimed their joy and gathered around to slap Ciaran's back and shake his hand. Ciaran spoke only Gaelic now. Everyone talked at once, the discussion stumbling over itself. The blacksmith was there, with a bloodied bandage over one eye, and Ciaran's good friend Eóin walked with a limp.

Young Robbie was among them, and to Leah he appeared matured in a way that made him seem almost an old man. His eyes and cheeks were sunken, and his clothing hung on him like drapery. He had no smile for Ciaran, but only a brief embrace and hushed words. Neither were there tears, but a fiery rage that suffused him. Robbie was no longer the earnest boy of before, but an angry man.

They proceeded up the hill, and came to a level spot where a tree-covered slope on one side descended to the stream below and a steep granite cliff rose at the other. From a recess in the cliff, women began to emerge at the sound of the men talking, bleary-eyed with sleep and frowning with curiosity about the racket in the clearing. Leah realized the recess was a cave reaching well into the mountain.

Sìle saw her brother and let out a cry. She picked up her skirts to make her way through the crowd to Ciaran, and threw her arms around him, in tears. He held her and kissed her cheek. Kirstie and Mary came to embrace him also, and the four stood for a long time, comforting each other in their grief.

Other women were talking now, asking after the men who had

not been seen since the battle, and when the answers came, each one dissolved into tears at the final loss of hope.

Leah stood back from the scene, involved but not a part of it. Her heart broke for the grieving women. She wished to comfort them, but knew her presence was not welcome. She was a *Sasunnach,* and everything English was despised here. There was no argument for that, for the soldiers had done terrible, unconscionable, irreparable damage. And her father had led them to it.

She did not think this would be a good time to announce to the clan she was carrying a child that, if male, would be their laird's successor.

O nce the newcomers had been fed and given room to sleep, Ciaran sat with Robin, Seumas Glas, and Robbie near the fire at the center of the clearing, talking in low voices of their situation. Staring into the fire, Robbie was talking fast, and his cheeks were flushed with the anger, his head hunched into his shoulders, as he related to Ciaran how he, Dùghlas, Seumas, and Robin had orchestrated the escape of the clan into the hills in small groups and clusters while the village was destroyed. Over and over again he begged forgiveness from his older brother for not fighting the dragoons, and Ciaran forgave him as many times.

Alasdair MacKenzie approached and sat on his heels next to Ciaran. "We cannae stay here, Ciaran Dubhach." Alasdair was to the point, and Ciaran knew he was right. It wasn't safe for his small cluster of kinsmen. It wasn't safe for anyone.

"Where will you go?"

"On to Killilan."

"And if there remains nobody for you?"

All the air seemed to leave Alasdair. "Then we must go to a city. Glasgow, perhaps. Perhaps to the coast. The kelp is bringing in money there. It could keep us alive, so long as we're of use to the Whigs."

Ciaran nodded. "Aye. 'Tis better to be alive and in Scotland. Better than death or transportation to America."

"Both the same, to my mind. In any case, that is our plan. We'll be moving on at daybreak tomorrow."

Again Ciaran nodded, and Alasdair bade them all good night, then retired to sleep among his kinsmen. With heavy heart, Ciaran considered the truth of Alasdair's words, for his father had often said that transportation to America was hardly better than death, and too often was merely a short postponement of it.

Old Robin interrupted his thoughts. Softly, he began relating what had happened to their people after their flight to this mountain. The lack of food, the weeping of the women and children, the longing for homes and belongings that were now ashes. It was all Ciaran could do to keep still. All his life he'd despised the English, and now he wanted to kill soldiers more than he wanted to live himself. His fingernails dug into his palms as he was told of the burning of the young oat crop. Tears of rage stung his eyes, and he stared hard at the ground to keep them from spilling as he heard tell of the grief of his people.

Robin fell silent as Sile approached and knelt beside her brother. "Ciaran." Her blue eyes brought back the memory of their mother, and his heart clenched till he could hardly breathe. She looked deep into his eyes, and he felt it in his anguished soul. Her voice was low, barely audible. "Will you kill Hadley?"

He looked around at the other men, but each was staring at the fire before him. To his sister he said, "I want to."

"Do it. Kill him."

A palm aside her cheek, he sighed and said, "*Mo banacharaid,* more than anything I want every Redcoat north of the Borderlands to die."

"No, Ciaran. Hadley. You must kill *Hadley.*" A tremor took her voice, and her eyes went wide.

"Hadley?" Understanding struck. "*Och.*" The captain himself had committed at least one of the rapes.

"He must die. Whatever you do, Hadley must die." Tears flooded her eyes and spilled onto her cheeks. "You must kill him, Ciaran."

He squeezed her shoulder. "Aye. I understand."

Having put her message across, she now hurried back to the fire where the women sat, near the cave entrance.

Ciaran turned to the men of his council and said, "Where is the *Sasunnach* captain? Are the soldiers yet garrisoned here?"

Robin replied, "The dragoons are in the garrison, but Hadley has once again installed himself in the Tigh."

That caught Ciaran's attention, and excitement rose as ideas came to him. "Has he a close guard, at all?"

Robin looked to Seumas, and they both shrugged. Robin said, "We've nae been so close recently as to ken his habits. In fact, we've scrupulously avoided the Redcoats, as ye might well understand."

Seumas said, "What is there to do now, Ciaran? Ye cannae stay here, for the land is forfeit. The clan willnae stay without you, for they regard the Redcoats with too much terror and will-nae accept a new landlord. Shall we make our way to the colonies? We'll follow you wherever ye go, Ciaran."

Ciaran shook his head. "Nae. 'Tis nae for us." He glanced at Sinann, who sat in a tree on the slope, and said, " 'Tis not our destiny. Were we to leave our homeland, then what did my father live for?"

Robin grunted and nodded, and Seumas Glas couldn't deny the truth of those words. But he said, "What then, sir?"

Ciaran's heart was heavy, for he knew even his father would not approve of what he was about to do, and the clan even less. Though his people would all live, and in Scotland, it would also mean the demise of the Ciorram Mathesons as such. He said quietly, "Tonight I will talk to Hadley. I will seek terms for surrender. If I dinnae return by dawn tomorrow, everyone must go to kinsmen elsewhere. Go to anyone who will take you in and give you work. You all must live as best ye can, even if I fail. Dinnae allow yourselves to be transported."

Sinann scowled at him. " 'Twill be your death, for certain. You'll leave Robbie to lead the clan, and you ken it was nae your father's wish. He wanted you for his successor, and for the clan to continue in Glen Ciorram."

Ciaran ignored her.

In response to the plan, Seumas Glas and Robin both nodded, but Ciaran couldn't meet their gazes, for he knew he would not return from his talk with Hadley. He knew there would be no talking at all with Hadley.

Sinann followed him to the spot near the mouth of the cave where Leah had curled up to sleep. "Are ye mad?" She fluttered around him like a moth at a flame.

He shook his head.

Sarcasm colored her voice. "You think Hadley will simply hand the land back over to you and say, 'Sorry for the misunderstanding, young fellow'?"

Again, Ciaran shook his head.

"Then for what are you returning to the Tigh?"

He turned a narrow gaze on her for a moment, then brushed

aside a spray of bracken to lie under it next to Leah. She was heavily asleep, but woke just enough to settle in beside him with her head on his shoulder and one arm across his belly. He fidgeted some to find a comfortable lie, still annoyed at the breeches, then sighed and kissed Leah's hair. His heart ached that this would be the last time he would touch her, and that she would be left without him after tomorrow, but there was nothing for it. The land was forfeit, and so was his life, so he was going to kill Hadley, and as many other Redcoats as he could take before they would kill him.

CHAPTER 20

Finally he held in his hands the sword of his ancestors. The ancient silver-hilted broadsword, presented to the laird of Ciorram by King James I and VI, had been handed down from one laird to the next for exactly four hundred years. Hung in its scabbard from a rich baldric of supple leather, it settled over his shoulder as if it belonged there and nowhere else.

It was sunset when Ciaran donned the silver king's sword, hung for a left-handed draw, and his father's dirk Leah had carried from Nairn. His heart was deadened now, feeling nothing but hatred. Even the grief was gone, leaving a gut that seemed made of stone. His pulse thudded with a heavy, steady beat.

No longer wearing his accustomed kilt and leggings, he hung Brigid on a belt at his waist, then slung the sword on its baldric over his shoulder. He looked down at the breeches and muttered in colonial English as his father had in the past, "Candyass." He longed for a kilt and hated he was about to die in breeches.

Then he turned to Leah, but was unable to meet her gaze as he said, "Wish me luck." He said it only for the sake of form. All the luck in the world wouldn't save him tonight.

She smiled, but her voice revealed her worry. "Luck to you, my love. Are you certain you wish me to stay? Wouldn't it be better for me to come with you? He's my father, and I daresay I might have some sway—"

"Nae. Ye'll stay here, and nae argument about it."

"But—"

"I said, *no*." He had no patience for this. "Is that clear enough English for you? You're to stay here, and go with Robbie in the event I dinnae return. He'll care—"

"Surely my father—"

"*Leah*. Do as I say. 'Tis of utmost importance you heed me in this. If you've never in your life obeyed a command, do this one." The shocked look in her eyes finally touched him, and something stirred in his soul other than hatred. His voice softened. "Please, Leah." Then he kissed her and said, "If ye love me."

There was a long pause as she looked into his face and tried to see into his eyes, but he wouldn't let her. He busied them as he brushed a wisp of hair from her face, straightened her snood, and tugged her cloak more snugly around her shoulders.

She said, "If *you* love *me*."

He finally looked into her eyes and was shaken by the terror he saw there. Laying one hand aside her cheek, he pressed his face against the other cheek and murmured into her ear, "I love ye with all my heart and soul. So long as you live, understand that." Then he kissed her again one last time, touched his thumb to the cleft in her chin, then turned to make his way down the track toward the Tigh.

Leah watched him go, and needed to hug herself for the chill that ran through her. She couldn't explain the tears that welled. There should be hope, but she felt only fear. Her father was a hard man, but a fair one, and so Ciaran must have every chance of arriving at acceptable surrender terms. But somehow the air stank of something besides hope. There had been none in Ciaran. A tear spilled as she returned to the fire.

"Follow him." The voice came from nowhere, and she recognized it. A glance around confirmed nobody human had spoken.

She sat by the fire at the mouth of the cave where the women sat, pressed her clasped hands to her forehead, and whispered as if praying, "What will he do?"

"I dinnae ken, but you cannae let him go alone. You must follow him."

"And what will *I* do then?"

There was a tiny faerie sigh. "*I dinnae ken*. But with you there
he will have the advantage of a clearer mind at hand. So quit your
arguing, and hie yourself to see what he truly intends with your
father."

Leah looked up, and found the faerie hovering overhead.
"Aye," Leah whispered, and stood to mutter to the other women
something about finding a place to relieve herself, then went in
the direction Ciaran had gone.

The walk was long. Back through the high glen Ciaran went,
and down the ravine, then across Glen Ciorram under cover
of darkness to the churchyard and into the woods behind it. The
track through these woods was barely discernible, for it was
rarely used, and it wound and twisted through some low hills before it emerged on the spot where the faerie tower stood. On reflex he looked around for Sinann and wondered whether she'd
followed. He hoped not. He was not proud of what he was about
to do.

Past the *broch* another, more visible track took him down
along a wide burn that rushed over rapids amid the oaks and
bracken. Trees rustled in the breeze overhead, and his exhausted
mind, too filled with apprehension, imagined it to be a harsh
whispering of disapproval. He hurried through the forest, fleeing
the tree spirits. He was nearing the glen again, but before the
track came into the open he veered from it and let himself down
a short rockface. A shallow cave lay between two broad expanses
of granite, and at the back of that cave was a heavy oaken door.
He pulled hard on it, and yanked several times to achieve an
opening large enough to let him through.

But when he tried to pull it shut, the thing wouldn't budge. At
first he tried to be discreet at it, but as the door proved reluctant
he hauled harder on it. There was no moving it again no matter
how he cursed it. Impatient to complete his mission, he left the
door and went on his way. The secret of the passageway would be
meaningless after tonight, in any case.

Down stone steps he went, down and down, feeling his way
with his fingertips against the damp stone wall. It was extremely

cold down here, and even he shivered in the dampness at the bottom. His shoes were soaked by shallow puddles, icy cold this far underground. Though he'd never been through this passage, he knew where it came out, for his father had shown him. Up the other side, the steps slanted and slippery, the route tortuous, he finally paused behind the oaken exit door.

Barely breathing, he listened for sounds inside the office he'd turned over to Hadley a year ago. There was nothing. It was very late in the evening, so Hadley might be in his bedchamber. He whispered, "Tinkerbell, can you tell me whether the office is empty?"

There was no reply.

He grunted in disgust and drew Brigid, then shoved on the door just enough to squeeze into the room. Quickly, he entered with his dirk at the ready, for he didn't know what he might encounter.

But it was dark, lit only by the moon at the arrow loops, and the hearth had the damp, sour smell of a fire that had been dead for days. He moved quickly across the room and lifted the latch on the door to the corridor.

There was no light there, either. If Hadley was in the castle, he wasn't making much use of it. Ciaran had expected the place to be lousy with Redcoats, and possibly even visitors from clans loyal to George, but there was only darkness and silence. Having known these passages all his life, it was simple enough to find his way around by feel and memory. He ducked up the dark stairwell.

One candle burned in the bedchamber Hadley had occupied, so it was apparent he was still in residence. A red uniform lay across the bed, and various items of linen and leather adorned the floor, but there was nobody in the room. No servant, and no captain. Ciaran moved on.

All the other chambers in this tower were dark and empty. Quickly and silently, he descended to the first floor again and slipped into the corridor that led to the Great Hall. Here there were candles in the sconces along the wall. Ciaran's pulse picked up, for he must be approaching an occupant of some sort. More than likely the captain. He held Brigid at his side, ready.

The door into the Great Hall opened on silent hinges, and he stepped inside.

Only two of the trestle tables were in use, standing end-to-end near Ciaran. The hearth opposite was high with a wood fire, and before it sat Captain Hadley. Lounging in the laird's chair with a glass of wine in one hand, he faced away from Ciaran and toward the hearth.

Dark rage rose at sight of the *Sasunnach* in his father's chair. *His* chair. Before *his* hearth. With utmost care, he stole across the room, keeping to the shadows and behind Hadley. There was no guard inside, now that the castle was empty of Mathesons, but dim sounds of work were discernible from the kitchen beyond the hearth. More than likely, along with the kitchen and chamber servants, Hadley had brought a guard to post at the gate. The captain's personal arms—his sword and pistol—hung in scabbard and holster on pegs inside the entryway. Ciaran smiled with the cold knowledge the captain was unarmed.

Quickly, silently, Ciaran ran the last few yards to attack.

"Father!" There was a hurrying of bare footsteps, and a click of gun hammer.

Hadley looked up, leapt from the chair, and dodged Brigid by not more than a hair. Ciaran spun, stunned, to find Leah in the middle of the room near the tables, her father's pistol in her hands but its muzzle drooping toward the floor. The horrible realization of betrayal gripped him. His heart sank to his cold, wet shoes. He was wide-eyed and voiceless, and he could only whisper, "Leah, you've killed me."

Meanwhile, her father rushed to the entry and drew his saber from its scabbard. "What is going on here? What are you doing here, Leah? I demand an answer!" His face was flushed with rage as he faced off against Ciaran, his back to Leah.

Ignoring her father, Leah said, "Ciaran, don't do it. Please!"

Hadley muttered, "I'd hoped you'd died on Drummossie Moor, you traitorous whelp!"

Without reply to either of them, Ciaran shifted Brigid to his right hand and drew his sword. Talk was pointless. He was here to accomplish a task, and nothing else mattered.

But Leah shouted, "Father, I beg you not to hurt him!"

Her father also gave no reply to that, but stepped toward Ciaran with a look in his eye that said he also intended to kill. Ciaran readied for an attack, maintaining the relaxed stance his father had taught him and eyeing his opponent for weaknesses. Hadley was angry, and Ciaran felt himself go calm, for he knew he could exploit that anger. He began to shift his position, circling Hadley in hopes of using the wall of the entry to his advantage.

Then Leah called out again, "Stop it! Stop this fight!"

There was a click of latch from the kitchen door. Leah raised the pistol to point it across the room and shouted, "You! Halt or I'll shoot you!" She trained the weapon on whoever had just entered. Immediately there was another sound of the latch on the kitchen door as the servant retreated. Confusion stirred Ciaran's heart as he realized Leah had more than likely just saved his life.

But then she lowered her weapon and shouted, her voice cracking with tears, "Father, you cannot kill him!" Her words had no effect on Hadley. His expression remained murderous. Then she said, "You must let him live! I'm carrying his child!"

The tip of Ciaran's sword lowered to the floor. The astonishing news caused the room to tilt for him, and his soul skewed in several different directions at once. He gawked at her. "Leah?"

But Hadley spun on her. His sword was raised, and his voice carried an offended edge of betrayal. "You!" His breaths became heavy panting as rage consumed him. "Whore!" He ran at her.

Ciaran ran also, and swords clashed just above Leah's head. He shoved Hadley off to the side with his shoulder, and followed with a broad attack that was easily parried. Again he attacked hard, trying to get Hadley away from Leah. The captain was forced back, but recovered and made a series of reprisals. The broadsword clanged against the saber, and echoes rang throughout the huge hall.

"Leah, get away from here!" shouted Ciaran. He wanted her gone. He wished she would run away and return to the kinsmen hiding in the cave. Then he could carry out his objective and know she was safe.

"No! Both of you, stop!" Her voice was gummy with tears, and desperation made her shrill.

Ciaran kept on, knowing if he let down his defense Hadley would kill them both. He swung hard and fast, forcing the *Sasunnach* toward the far corner, keeping himself between Leah and her father. Leah screamed and wept, jarring Ciaran's nerves and dividing his attention.

The old soldier had a couple of tricks. He feinted, and Ciaran fell for it, but recovered in time to dodge the true attack. That gave Hadley a chance to flee the corner and move onto the open floor.

"Leah! Get away!" Ciaran's voice was hoarse as panic rose. But she was already running to get behind him, leaving her father by the tables. Hadley stepped onto a stool and then onto a table.

Ciaran kicked the stool aside and parried the attacks about his head. Hadley's attacks tended to Ciaran's well-protected left, revealing his inexperience fighting a left-handed swordsman.

"Father! No! Stop!"

Hadley didn't seem to hear. He parried an attack to his thigh, and on riposte caught the side of Ciaran's nose with the tip of his saber.

Hot pain shot through Ciaran's face, but he ignored it and the blood running over his lip. He took a step aside, and raised his foot to the edge of the table. With one quick shove, he knocked the boards and trestle sideways. Hadley tottered and tried to leap to the floor, but Ciaran hit the boards again, and the captain fell.

Desperate, Hadley scrambled to regain his feet, but he was too slow. Ciaran kicked him as he'd kicked the table, and the captain fell backward over a trestle. In a flash, Ciaran slashed his sword arm. The saber dropped to the floor with the clatter of metal on stone. With Brigid, Ciaran came in for the kill at Hadley's gut, aiming upward for his heart.

Leah screamed.

To Ciaran's own surprise, his hand was stayed. He laid his sword across Hadley's throat and shouted, "Leah, get away from here!" He was about to kill her father, and in cold blood. Not murder, but execution.

"No, Ciaran! You can't kill him!"

"I cannae *not* kill him!" He looked into Hadley's eyes, and the abject terror turned his stomach. His weight shifted to shove the dirk, but her pleading stopped him once again.

"I beg you!"

"I said, get the bloody hell away! Leave me to this!"

"He's my father!"

His teeth gritted with rage. *"He raped my sister!"*

There was a choked silence, then she said, "No. Father, no, tell him. Tell him you didn't do it."

"Go ahead." Ciaran pressed Brigid harder. "Deny it. Deny it, then die with a lie on your soul, for I'll be killing ye regardless."

Hadley blinked and squirmed under Ciaran, but made no attempt to deny the accusation.

"Father," Leah's voice was small and plaintive, "please say it's untrue." But her father only pressed his lips shut and closed his eyes in readiness to die.

Leah dissolved in sobs. "O God . . ."

Ciaran urged her again, "Get away, Leah! Get as far away from here as you can! Save yourself and . . . and the baby." He shook off a swarm of emotions. Focusing on his rage, he told himself it was time to die and there was nothing for it but to see it through. His voice was choked as he said, "There's naught for you here. 'Tis done, now leave."

"I won't."

"Leah!"

"Do not kill him! Spare him, and there can be peace!"

"No! There cannae!"

"Father, tell him!" Her voice was choked with tears as she sobbed, pleading with her father. "Father, for my sake. Tell him there can be peace."

But Hadley remained silent and stared up at Ciaran. His nostrils flared as he gasped, and fear glittered in his eyes, but he said nothing.

Ciaran's hand on Brigid began to tremble with the effort of staying the final thrust. More than anything he wanted to feel the warm blood rush over his fingers and know this monster was dead.

Leah stepped closer, and Ciaran turned his face away. She said, "Ciaran, you cannot do this. Not in cold blood. He's my father. For God's sake, Ciaran, where does this stop? When King George has destroyed every clansman in Scotland? Will my father's death solve anything? Will *your* death?"

His lips pressed together, Ciaran tried not to listen. He wanted to hate. He'd hated Redcoats all his life. It was impossible to imagine a world where the English were not the enemy.

She continued, "You said we English don't think of you as people. Ciaran, are you seeing my father as a man? Do you see him as a loving parent and husband? Do you see him as a man of honor doing his duty to his king?" Her voice darkened. "Can you see him as a flawed human being who has made a terrible, terrible mistake?"

More trembling came, for in that brief instant he glimpsed in himself the sort of bigotry he'd despised in the English. But he said, "He deserves to die."

Her reply took him aback. "Indeed, he does." Ciaran looked up at her and she continued, tears streaming down her face. "But do you deserve to die also? Do I deserve to lose not only my father but also the father of my child? My *husband?* Does the clan deserve to lose their beloved laird? Must the killing continue, or might it stop here?"

Ciaran's left arm ached as horribly as his right. He needed to end this. But her words had reached him. He no longer wanted the blood for its own sake.

"Please, Ciaran. For me. And for your people."

Slowly, forcing his body to comply, he rose from atop Hadley and stepped back, his sword and dirk at his sides. The captain recovered himself and stood. His eyes went to the sword on the floor at his feet, but Leah grabbed it by the hilt and flung it across the room, where it clattered and clanged to rest by the wall.

"Father, you cannot arrest him. Aside from yourself, there is nobody to call him traitor, and if he deserves to hang for his crime, it's no more than what you deserve for . . . for what you did. The clan has paid for his folly, and more. Promise me you'll declare Ciaran innocent of treason. For God's sake, Father, give us both hope. Give us all hope. Give your grandchild a future."

There was a long silence as flames of rage danced in Hadley's eyes. He glared at Ciaran, who returned the furious gaze with his own and gripped his weapons in readiness for another fight. Finally Hadley said, "You wish to marry him, then? And remain here with him?"

"Dearly. You brought me here against my will, but you won't remove me. I refuse to leave, no matter what happens here."

He threw her a sharp glance, then seemed to deflate. Thinking for a long, painful moment, he appeared to struggle to speak. "Then I'll do what I can to settle the issues between Ciorram and the Crown." A hard look at Ciaran, and he opened his mouth to say something further, but then he turned away and said nothing.

Ciaran scabbarded his weapons, and Leah went to him. He folded her into his arms, stunned at what had just transpired. A wide, unknowable future opened up before him, and once again it held hope.

CHAPTER 21

"A braw morning and a braw new beginning, aye, laddie?"
The voice came from nowhere, but Iain smiled. "Hello, Tinker-
bell. Having your jollies watching me dress, as usual?"

There was no priest, but there was a minister—the chaplain
from the garrison—and the wedding took place inside the
Catholic church. No handfasting, no bidey-in, no common law.
Ciaran married Leah before God and the world, so no man might
put it asunder. There was also a gold ring, for Donnchadh the
blacksmith had straightened the ring Ciaran's father had given
his mother more than thirty years before. It was a mite large on
Leah, but not so much as to be in danger of falling off.

Ciaran and Leah stood before the altar on a bright July morning, the sun cascading over them from the rose window in deep
colors that bespoke reverence and grandeur. Dark smells of old
wood and stone permeated by centuries of incense and beeswax
enveloped them. There were still no chairs in the sanctuary, but
nearly the entire village was packed onto the open floor to witness. It made Ciaran wonder what it had been like to attend Mass
here in his father's day, to hear the prayers and receive the bless-
ings. The lack of a priest weighed heavily on his soul.

The bride's father attended the brief ceremony in civilian attire, appearing as uncomfortable in this papist sanctum as the Mathesons were ill at ease in the presence of the man who had ravaged their homes, their property, and their women. But nothing untoward was said. Very little, indeed, was said out loud.

Keeping the ceremony simple and within the bounds of the chaplain's ability, Ciaran and Leah exchanged vows quickly, kissed, and then it was over. The celebrants filed from the building, bagpipes at full skirl, to make their way to the Tigh for an afternoon and evening of drinking and dancing. There was precious little food in the glen, but the whiskey had gone undiscovered and untouched by the dragoons. There would be plenty to drink. Ciaran hung back with his wife for a moment, and watched them go.

The recovery of the village was only two days along, but already there could be seen signs of it in the distance. Some of the homes had been reconstructed, but not nearly enough yet to house everyone. Folks lived in British army tents here and there, and some of them remained in the cave in the woods or camped in the castle bailey. Given the burned fields and the few remaining livestock, there would be little to eat this winter. Many would die. Dùghlas was already gone, and Ailis wasn't expected to remain past fall. Nearly all the able-bodied men had died in the rising, and the young boys would have to carry the Mathesons into the next generation. The struggle ahead would be a hard one.

"We're alive," said Leah. She stepped so close to him he was forced to let her under his arm. He held her about the waist and turned to read her eyes.

"We."

"Of course, we. We have survived. I believe we will continue to do so, but if we don't, we will face the end together. The people of the glen are alive, together, and living in their homeland. We're still alive."

Ciaran grunted, then guided her toward the graveyard for a visit to his parents. Standing over the trio of white marble stones, he realized there was something to be said for knowing exactly which spot of ground held his father and mother. He fell silent at the intense wish they could have been alive to see this day.

Then he thought of Sìle, who had not been able to bring herself to attend the wedding. Kirstie and Mary had come, but not without complaint. His voice was subdued. "My sisters might wish we were not alive. Particularly Sìle."

Leah sighed. "Oh, give her some time. She'll eventually—"

"Nae, she willnae. And I willnae ask her to. What was done to them cannae be undone. All my sisters will hate your father and his men all the rest of their days, and I will allow them their behavior toward him. Never will I ask them to tolerate his presence, and never will they be forced to speak to him. I must allow them that, to keep the peace with them regarding the marriage."

"And what of my father? He's not particularly sanguine about it, either."

Disgust curdled his gut, and he glanced at the garrison across the way as he growled under his breath, "Ask me if I give a damn what yer father—"

"Ciorram . . ."

"Shhh. Here he comes." Her hand found his, and she stepped from under his arm to face the captain. Ciaran noticed she stepped a bit behind him and said nothing by way of greeting.

He turned to face the Redcoat as an adversary. It was appalling he'd come to the wedding, but for now Ciaran held his tongue on the subject. Hadley approached formally, as if in diplomatic negotiation. Other Mathesons near the church halted to observe and listen in.

Captain Hadley stood, erect and dignified, a note held gingerly in his hand.

"Ciorram, I expect you'll take good care of my daughter."

"Better care than—" Leah dug her knuckles into his back ribs, hard, and he struggled to control his tongue. Finally he said, "Aye. She'll be safe as any other Matheson in the glen."

Hadley blanched, and caused Ciaran to wonder for a moment if the *Sasunnach* might have a conscience after all. Then Hadley held out the note and said, "Here, then. For the sake of Leah's future. An introduction to a friend, who is in a position to help you license your whiskey production."

Ciaran's jaw nearly dropped, but he held it. "The still will be legal?"

The captain's chin raised. "Well, then, that's up to you. I can't force anyone to give you the right to distill spirits, but this will give you an opportunity to make your case and some influence to sway the decision." He paused, as if debating whether to admit anything further, then said, "I have reason to believe he would be predisposed in your favor at this time." Then he nodded, affirming the truth of his statement as well as making it plain this was all he would say aloud on the matter.

Leah squeezed Ciaran's hand and pressed her face to his shoulder. Even Ciaran felt his heart lighten, in a way that felt alien to him. His father had always insisted the still would be the future of the glen. As a legitimate distillery, he could distribute the whiskey beyond the Highlands and demand a higher price. With the quality of whiskey waiting to be sold, that price could be quite high indeed. Cattle could be bought in the Lowlands, new seed obtained, and the fields replanted. Husbanded with care, this year's whiskey could be the thing to save them all from starvation.

"Captain," he said, "I happily accept your letter. But know this"—he braced himself for more knuckles in his back, but they never came—"this is the least you can offer. We accept it as recompense due to us, and we want you to know you and your English soldiers and your English laws will never be welcome here. Ever."

Then he put his arm around his bride and they walked together to the Tigh, where they would celebrate the future.

EPILOGUE

" *Och!* " cried Sinann, "shall I demonstrate again for you how easily I could see you naked if I wished?" She raised her hand, ready to snap her fingers. Iain raised both his palms in surrender.

"No, ye wee brat. Once was entirely enough, thank you."

She giggled, then flew to follow him as he left the bedchamber and made his way down the stone spiral staircase of the North Tower. His mind was on the coming ceremony, and he barely listened to the faerie hovering about. He held the sword scabbard so it wouldn't bang the steps behind him.

"Iain, I've come to remind you that Scotland should be nobody's fiefdom."

He grunted. This was a subject dear to Sinann, and the only way to get her to shut up was to let her talk herself out. She wished him to take a more active role in Scottish nationalization. She felt his political influence, such as it was, could help force complete independence from England. She wouldn't be happy, it seemed, unless he would begin calling for armed insurrection against the Crown. A silly notion, to be sure, and certainly not the quickest or most effective way to independence. *Och,* she would have to be patient, was all. Lucky faerie, she would more than likely live to see the results of his efforts, which for him was not at all assured.

He sighed as he exited the Great Hall and went down the walk to the driveway where awaited his wife and his car.

Kate informed him the others were already on their way to the church, and they would be late if they did not hurry.

"Are the wee folk causing trouble again?"

He only rolled his eyes toward Sinann, though the faerie was invisible to all but himself, and gave Kate a quick peck of greeting on the lips. Then he went around to get in behind the wheel of the Jaguar. With a skill born of practice, as he sat he slipped the scabbard between the seats so the tip rested on the seat behind.

Our Lady of the Lake Catholic Church stood at the far end of the glen, fewer than ten minutes away, tucked against a wooded hill and just up from a football field where an informal rugby game was taking place. Iain was forced to park on the road, for the small gravel church lot was filled with wedding guests. He grumbled as he locked the car, "One would think the parents of the groom would be reserved space to park."

Kate muttered in Gaelic, an edge to her voice, "One would think the father of the groom would be on time."

He said only, *"Och,"* ignoring two females now as he crooked his arm to escort his wife up the steps to the church.

Inside was warm and close, the chairs filled with wedding celebrants. Two chairs near the front had been left empty, and he and his wife sat. At least the ushers had left them a place to sit, so he was mollified.

The ceremony was long, but each moment weighted with significance. Young Dilean Robert was only twenty-two, just back from university, but today he seemed to grow and mature before Iain's eyes. Sun shone brightly through the rose window above the altar, bathing the scene in warm, rich color. Dilean stood straight and tall, proud in his kilt as the prayers and exhortations of the priest transformed him into a husband and his girlfriend into a wife. Sinann, thankfully, was silent throughout the proceedings, for which Iain was grateful.

He felt himself transform as well, as the possibility of grandchildren became expectation rather than risk. The thought of another generation coming along made him smile, for he now saw the future unfold before him as well as the history behind. A warm feeling stole over him. He now saw clearly his place in the continuity.

After the benediction, guests filed slowly out to the church yard, cheerfully chatting and milling about, looking for an opportunity to greet the newlyweds. Brightly colored dresses in tartan and solid scattered among suits and formal kilts, and even one fanciful kilt that brushed the heels of its wearer's trail boots. Iain stood to the side to watch his son, red-cheeked and smiling bright, his too-long hair tossed by the breeze. Then he wandered off a bit to enjoy the fresh air and have a glance at the scattering of stones about the graveyard.

The names were familiar to him, not only because he'd read them many times before but also because the stories had been taught to him of his ancestors. Tales of valor and sacrifice, of terror, love, and loyalty, of a ghost dog, bloodied ground, seal folk, faeries, and uncanny skill with a sword. Whether all those things had actually happened or not, he knew them to be true just the same. They were part of his history and his identity—part of his soul.

Across the way was a rather large stone building, standing between the post office and a fish and chips take-away shop. The decrepit stone walls declared its age—this was no replica—but the sign out front was fewer than fifty years old. That sign couldn't be seen from the church; however, Iain knew it from memory: *Queen Anne Garrison Museum—Open Saturday through Thursday, 10:00 A.M. to 5:00 P.M. Admission, £3. Children and seniors, £1.*

He gazed about at his home and his people, sighed as a smile curled his mouth, and his heart was warmed with joy for this day.

The acclaimed romantic fantasy series by

J. ARDIAN LEE

Dylan is an ordinary modern guy until extraordinary forces transport him to medieval Scotland—where he finds the bitterness of betrayal and the sweetness of true love.

SON OF THE SWORD   0-441-01050-4
OUTLAW SWORD   0-441-00935-2
SWORD OF KING JAMES   0-441-01185-3

"A veritable *Braveheart* buffet."
—*Kliatt*

"The making of a legend."
—Jennifer Roberson

Available wherever books are sold or at
www.penguin.com